SUMMER
OF THE THREE
PAGODAS

By the same author

Tears of the Dragon

SUMMER
OF THE THREE
PAGODAS

JEAN
MORAN

HEAD
of ZEUS

First published in the UK in 2020 by Head of Zeus Ltd

9 7 5 3 1 2 4 6 8

A catalogue record for this book is available from
the British Library.

ISBN (HB): 9781788542586
ISBN (ANZTPB): 9781838934453
ISBN (E): 9781788542579

Typeset by Silicon Chips

Printed and bound in Great Britain by
CPI Group (UK) Ltd, Croydon CR0 4YY

Head of Zeus Ltd
First Floor East
5–8 Hardwick Street
London EC1R 4RG

WWW.HEADOFZEUS.COM

To my daughter and my granddaughters.
May they never have to experience anything like this

Chapter 1

Hong Kong, 1950

Wind and heavy rain swooped under ill-fitting doors, through cracks in crumbling walls and funnelled up narrow alleys. Waves in the harbour piled up into mountains and sent huddled sampans crashing and rolling into each other. Larger vessels fared little better, freighters and oil tankers from all over the world lolled like listless whales whilst inside their cavernous bellies their crews hunkered down until the typhoon – the dragon wind – had breathed its last.

On the battered land, ramshackle dwellings took flight on the furious updraught. Clothes and baskets, umbrellas, leaves and branches became air-borne missiles, some more dangerous than others. Cooking pots and tin cans rolled along streets, clanging like bells.

Fragments of humanity who hadn't been blown away with their makeshift dwellings crowded the reception area and narrow corridors of Victoria House; some injured and all of them hungry.

Life went on as it always would and the typhoon would pass – as it always did.

In the midst of the deluge babies were being born with uncommon regularity; already today Dr Rowena Rossiter had delivered three, one of them born outside on the steps of Victoria House in fluid and afterbirth that was quickly swept away by the pouring rain.

Immediately following the birth and being told she had a daughter, the mother struggled to her feet. Someone held an umbrella over Rowena's head as she tidied up the child and wrapped it in a scrap of blanket that they kept for such eventualities. The mother was quick on her feet. The moment she became aware of the girl child, she escaped their clutches as speedily as the wind, disappearing into the filthy night.

A porter was sent to give chase, but his task was a difficult one. Soaked by rain and blinded by darkness, the odds were against him. By the time he came back the baby had been given its first post-birth feed and was bedded down in a metal crib that was only just a little bigger than a bucket. Well lined with clean blankets, the solid sides kept out the worst of the draughts.

When the porter shook his head droplets of rain trickled from his hair and eyebrows. 'I'm sorry, Dr Rossiter, but she ran very quickly.'

Resigned to what had happened and from experience knowing there was nothing she could do about it, Rowena thanked him for his efforts. 'I'm sure you did your best.'

His head remained bowed with apology. Rowena knew he had no real need to be apologetic. Similar things had happened before. Women already burdened with a large family and no means of feeding another mouth – especially a girl – made considered choices. The baby could have been left outside a church or convent – worse still, thrown onto a refuse dump or into the sea – smothered beforehand, sometimes. This baby had been lucky enough to be left with people who would ensure she was looked after.

The windows of the old building ran with rivers of condensation. The rain continued to lash against the trembling panes as though trying to break through. The windows were draughty, the metal frames becoming rustier with the passing of time.

The storm was subsiding, as was the number of people seeking medical attention. In a brief moment of respite, she slumped into the chair behind her desk, closed her eyes and slipped off her shoes.

The night became quieter with the advent of midnight. She was glad of it. A peaceful moment. There were so few and when they came were to be relished.

Hong Kong was crowded and getting even more so. The tide of refugees from mainland China had grown; so had the incidence of babies being born. It was, she thought, as though humanity was attempting to make up for the millions of war dead. Her only regret was that she herself had not conceived. She had the man and there was no doubting the passion between her and Connor O'Connor. They'd been through a lot together, not least imprisonment during the war, she in Hong Kong and he, ultimately, in Japan, taken there as slave labour. To some extent they'd found the sunny uplands Churchill had promised in the midst of war. There was only one thing they'd so far not achieved and wished for. They deserved the absolute happiness of a child and had promised themselves that they would marry once she'd conceived. She smiled. It certainly wasn't for the want of trying.

Her musings faded when Sister Barbara Kelly poked her head around the screen that served as the door to her office, flashing a dimpled smile.

'Cup of tea?'

'I would love one.'

'Ginger biscuit?'

'I would love one of those too.'

Ignoring the raging storm battering at the windows and making the linen screen wobble, they sat on either side of Rowena's battered desk, dipping biscuits into the tea, discussing patients, the way of the world, the many babies being born. They also discussed those abandoned on the doorsteps of churches, police stations and army barracks. Worst of all were those small bodies found floating in the harbour, bouncing like mangled coconuts between the sampans and junks.

The conversation naturally turned to the latest abandoned newborn.

'The mother ran like a greyhound. I wonder whether she would have run away if the baby had been a boy.'

Rowena shrugged. 'Less likely. But I do feel for her. No way of limiting family size and condemned for giving birth to a girl child.'

'Who knows? She might have a few daughters already and no boys. People do keep trying for what they really want. Sad though.'

Rowena sighed and held her hand to her brow. 'Sad indeed. Sometimes I feel totally helpless.'

Barbara shook her head, the corners of her lips downturned. 'It's a very sad state of affairs, but there, what can we do? And so many reasons; women with too many mouths to feed. Single women, their reputations ruined if it becomes common knowledge that they're pregnant – even if they've been raped. Then there are those who miscarry a malformed child...' She shrugged. 'That's the way it is. There really is nothing we can do about it.'

Rowena frowned at her teacup and shook her head. 'At this moment, not much, but who knows what the future holds. Science is continually unlocking more and more of Mother Nature's secrets. Things will change. Perhaps not in our lifetime...'

Barbara regarded the thoughtful look in Rowena's eyes but found it difficult to read. In a bid to drag her back from her thoughts and get her talking again, she mentioned the details of an abortionist who had been arrested by the Hong Kong police, but released when nobody would come forward to condemn the person concerned.

Rowena sighed and unclasped her hands on which she'd been resting her chin.

'That abortionist was responsible for the deaths of at least three women.'

'Whoever does that kind of thing is a criminal. Abortion will always be illegal and that's the way it should stay. That's what I think anyway. Get married first and all will be well – and if not be careful. It's the only advice we can give,' said Barbara, eyeing the last ginger biscuit which had obligingly broken into two halves. She reached out and took the largest piece.

Rowena had known Barbara for only a short time. She found her bouncy and fun, but at times a little dogmatic, even a bit self-righteous. 'It might not always be that way and I for one will be glad when a woman can approach her sexuality on the same level as a man; without fear and able to enjoy lovemaking without worrying about an unwanted pregnancy. Men certainly don't.'

Barbara winced at the stalwart manner in which Rowena stated her case.

Finally she found her voice. 'I can't really see things changing that much. I mean, abortion will never be legalised and...'

Barbara had the kind of complexion that always looked as though she'd just finished washing it with scented soap and water. It always looked healthy and outdoor fresh and was naturally pink. Even so, Rowena perceived a deeper pinkness seeping over her peaches and cream complexion and knew she was thinking about available forms of contraception which at present were mainly the man's prerogative. Most women thought that way; leave it up to the man. It was enough to be an object of a man's desire, to be wanted, to be possessed.

Rowena had her own views and they were becoming more entrenched along with her growing inclination to question the status quo. At one time she would have bitten her tongue before declaring her corner. Not now.

She leaned forward, hands clasped in front of her, eyes shining with fervour, so much so that Barbara retreated into the back of her chair.

'I firmly believe things *have* to change and believe they will. Not yet, perhaps, but great freedoms were won for mankind in the first half of this century and there's another half to go. The first step for women was gaining the right to vote. It was the first tentative step, but, Barbara, there are more domestic freedoms needed to be won for women.

Things will change, Barbara. Somebody will develop a better contraceptive than a rubber johnny and quite frankly I'm all for it.'

Barbara winced at Rowena's mention of rubber sheaths but then pulled herself together and made her own statement.

'They work if you're careful.'

Rowena leapt onto what was almost a confession of personal experience. 'I take it you're speaking from first-hand knowledge.'

For a moment it looked as though Barbara was disinclined to say more. A forthright toss of her head and she made her confession.

'Of course I am. Touch wood I've never known one to fail. God forbid I ever have to consider something more drastic.' She shivered. 'I wouldn't have an abortion. At least I don't think I would.' She shook her head. 'And I don't like Dutch caps. It's too… well… planned, the having to shove it in beforehand. But definitely no to an abortion, back street or otherwise. I would never do it.'

'You might. It depends on the resultant fallout – loss of respectable reputation and your career in ruins. Hospitals dislike employing unmarried mothers – not because they're incapable of doing their job, but purely as a moral statement. Fallen women need not apply here!'

She was on fire with all this. For the most part she controlled all these buried beliefs, but there were times when they poured out – like now.

Barbara, respectful as ever because Rowena was a doctor – even though only a female one – and she was only a nurse, shook her head. 'With all due respect, Dr Rossiter, I can't see abortion ever being made legal.'

'I think you're wrong. It will come; when, I don't know, but mark my words, it will be legalised – and in our lifetime.'

Barbara looked very shocked.

'And you agree with it?'

'Absolutely. A woman should be able to choose whether she wants children or not. Better contraception is the first step. Prevention is better than cure – in this case abortion. But even that will come. At some point in the future it will become legal.'

Barbara looked thoughtful as she clutched at her cup. 'You sound as though you're in favour of it.'

'To some extent, yes. Especially in rape cases or where the mother's health is endangered – though I wouldn't condemn anyone out of hand. Everyone has a reason and deserves to be listened to. Things happen. Anyway, it's only the poor who don't get abortions – we both know that. If you've got enough money, anything is possible.'

'Yes. I have heard that. As you say, anything is possible for the right money.'

Rowena sipped at the last of her tea. Barbara had slipped into silence and seemed to be holding her breath. Somehow Rowena guessed what was coming.

'Would you carry out the procedure?'

Rowena found herself being more forthright than she'd meant to be. 'Yes. In certain circumstances. Rape leading to social stigma. Or if the child was deformed, though ultimately it's the mother's decision.'

'What about the father? Do you think he should have a say?'

Rowena winced. The question was unwelcome. Without her being aware, Barbara had resurrected old images with alarming clarity. Wickedly laughing faces flashed into her mind, Christmas decorations dancing overhead, and the abuses of a number of Japanese soldiers, one of whom had fathered her daughter.

'Not necessarily. It depends. As I said, ultimately it's a mother's decision. It's her body. Anyway, that's enough of that subject.' She stretched her arms above her head and tried to pretend that she wasn't tired out and that this unnerving conversation had never happened. 'Let's talk about what you're going to wear this evening and where you're going.'

Barbara flushed slightly and her eyes sparkled. 'How did you know I had a date tonight?'

Folding her hands on top of her head, Rowena looked at her and smiled. 'You hum romantic ballads when you've got a date – even when administering a bedpan. And you usually tell me you're undecided what to wear.'

Barbara beamed. 'Not tonight. I know exactly what I'm going to wear. I had a tailor just off Shantung Street make me a blue silk dress. The feel of it... wonderful!'

'And who is the lucky man?'

Barbara, whose romantic notions kept a spring in her step and a very full social diary, tapped her chin with one finger. 'I can't tell you. Not yet anyway, but he's a real gentleman. He's taking me to the Shanghai Midnight Club. It's very exclusive. Drinks, dinner and some dancing. But nothing else,' she said, smirking as she got to her feet. 'Especially following this conversation.'

Rowena smiled and her eyebrows arched almost as far as her hairline. 'Unless he's a true boy scout?'

'What?'

Rowena grinned. 'Well prepared!'

The wind sent something crashing outside.

On looking out they saw the tin roof of an outhouse had been ripped off and sent cavorting into the old dovecote. The shadowy branches of a naked cherry tree waved like spindly arms. An item of escaped laundry, a long tunic, had wrapped itself around the trunk of the tree, twigs looking like hands protruding from the voluminous sleeves.

'Goodness,' said Barbara. 'Look at that. It looks like just like a Chinaman – or the ghost of one at least. Don't you think so?'

Rowena did not respond as she too stared into the darkness. The shadow had startled her and for a moment it had truly felt as though somebody had walked over her grave.

The typhoon didn't subside until late at night though the water in the harbour still surged, sending vessels bobbing up and down, their lights twinkling like grounded stars.

Rowena poured herself a stiff drink. Her head ached, her arms were tired and she was glad that Barbara was the one going out tonight and not her.

She reopened a notification she'd received from the Trustees of Victoria House. Her contract was coming to an end.

'...Under the circumstances...'

The circumstances were that they wanted to wrest control from her. The prospect of being dismissed hurt. Victoria House had been hers from the start. It seemed she had now reached the end.

Connor rang to say that no ferries would be running from Kowloon to Hong Kong until the storm had blown itself out.

Rowena adopted an air of exasperation that she did not feel. 'It's after midnight.'

'I still thought I'd say goodnight. I trust Dawn is sleeping through all this?'

'A weekend home from school and a typhoon descends on us. I'd promised to take her swimming. I don't think we'll be making it this weekend. Still, it's nice to have her home if only for a short while.

Rowena smiled into the mouthpiece as she closed the door to her daughter's bedroom behind her. The first thing she'd done since coming up here to her penthouse on the top floor was to look in on her daughter. Luli, her maid and all-purpose servant, had put Dawn to bed. Tomorrow she would do the job. Tonight a kiss on the forehead of the sleeping child had sufficed.

'I'm off duty tomorrow night but was planning to soak in the bath and do my hair. I'm free the night after that.'

'Think of me when you're lying naked in that bath. Pretend you're soaking in a tropical sea.'

'Your imagination is working overtime. I'll think about sending you a postcard and already know what I'll write on it.'

'It wouldn't be "wish you were here", would it?'

'How did you guess?'

The great thing about Connor was that he didn't try and convince her to change her mind. He knew how tired she could get, how great the responsibility.

Their goodnights were whispered and heartfelt.

A light supper, another drink, one more glance at the panorama of Hong Kong harbour and she was ready for bed. Not for an instant did she envy Barbara out there enjoying herself with the new man in her life.

Strange, she thought, that Barbara had told her so little about this man. Usually the buxom nurse was more than willing to share the details of her latest beau, but not today. A sneaking suspicion entered her mind. There was one reason above all others for Barbara not to be forthcoming with details. Whoever the man was, he was married.

Days later and the people of Hong Kong dusted themselves off, rebuilt their battered homes, cleared the debris from the streets and repaired the broken hulls of sampans that were businesses as well as being homes. The weather had improved, though it didn't mean another typhoon wouldn't follow the previous one. The air was fresh and the water that had seeped beneath the entrance doors had been swept away. Life went on and in Victoria House another baby had been born.

The newborn lying tightly against his mother's chest had the glossiest black hair she had ever seen, especially considering he had only been born just over an hour ago. Already the woman was trying to rise from her bed and join the rest of her family, though through pride rather than having any thought of abandoning the child. It helped that it was a boy. As yet the small family, recently arrived from mainland China, had no permanent residence but had been allowed to build a shambolic hovel of corrugated iron and flimsy pieces of wood in the garden of Victoria House.

Satisfied that mother and baby had come through the ordeal of childbirth with flying colours, she made her way back to what passed as her office. The linen screen gave little privacy and the wooden swivel chair wasn't the most comfortable, but she needed to close her eyes, take a breather, and force herself to look forward to having some time off.

The moment of respite was short-lived. Barbara's cheery face appeared from behind the screen. So far she'd said very little about her recent date except to say when asked that she'd had a great time. The furtive look in her eyes said that something else had happened, but whatever it was she was keeping it to herself.

'There's a man here to see you.'

'By the look on your face, he's worth seeing. Do you know what he wants?'

'He said it's personal. I can send him away if you want.'

Rowena looked up at her, surprised by the sudden edginess in Barbara's voice. 'On the contrary. I'm intrigued. Send him in.'

Young and wholesome-looking, the corporal saluted sharply. 'Corporal Samuel Cohen, Dr Rossiter. Colonel Warrington's compliments—'

'Wait.' Rowena held up her hand to stop him going any further.

She looked past him to where Barbara's shadow fell onto the linen screen.

'That will be all, Sister Kelly.'

She frowned. Never before had she known her to eavesdrop.

The shadow dissolved. She and her unexpected visitor

were as alone as they were ever likely to be bearing in mind the fragile division between her office space and the corridor beyond.

She folded her hands in her lap and eyed the young man with undisguised curiosity. 'Right. Tell me what this is all about, Corporal.'

The young man saluted again, his body held stiffly, his eyes looking straight ahead as though he was standing in front of an officer – or was merely on official business, she said to herself.

'Colonel Warrington's compliments, he asked if you could join him in his office at fifteen hundred hours, ma'am.'

'Doctor.'

'Doctor.'

'At three o'clock this afternoon.'

'That's right, Dr Rossiter. At fifteen hundred hours.'

She fingered her diary, picked up a pen then struck a thoughtful pose.

'Who is Colonel Warrington?'

The young man blinked. 'Well, he's Colonel Warrington. US Army Intelligence attached to the United Nations peacekeeping mission.'

'Intelligence and peace. Odd bedfellows.'

The young man looked confused. 'I'm sorry, ma'am…?'

'Never mind. An uncalled for quip. Can you tell me what this is about?'

He saluted again and stood so stiffly to attention she thought him in danger of breaking in two. 'I'm sorry. The colonel did not impart to me any further details. He just asked me to approach and schedule you into his diary.'

Her eyebrows arched quizzically. 'Did he now? Well I

think I need more information than that. I have a very busy schedule.'

Corporal Cohen's straight ahead stare fell to her face. He was definitely unnerved. 'He did say it was a matter of national security.'

'In what way?'

'I couldn't possibly comment, Dr Rossiter.'

'You mean you don't know.'

She knew she was right when his cheeks turned pink.

'Ma'am…'

'Anything else?'

'He did say it might be to your advantage.'

She raised her eyes. He flinched in response and seemed to have trouble meeting her direct look. One thing she knew above all else was that she no intention of presenting herself at this colonel's office without knowing who he was.

'Would you wait outside please?'

He looked as though he was about to refuse, but then thought better of it, saluted and did as requested.

'And stop saluting,' she called out after him. 'You're giving me a headache.'

Her first inclination was to phone Connor. Running a bar where military and colonial administrators and others gathered meant he was privy to much information.

She got as far as picking up the phone but changed her mind. Corporal Cohen had specifically stated the man was a member of the US army attached to the United Nations. She interpreted that as meaning that he'd been brought in to help sift true refugees from Communist insurgents suspected of being planted in Hong Kong to stoke up civil unrest. She might just as well hear it from the horse's mouth, so to speak. She spoke to Roger Quigley, a senior UN administrator who sometimes sat in on refugee centre committee meetings.

Her strategy proved successful. A few questions over the telephone and she had confirmation.

'You've just about got it right that he's with some branch of the US army attached to the United Nations. Don't ask me exactly what he does, but I fancy he's more army than UN. Any particular reason for asking?'

'He's asked to meet me. I presume it's in my field.'

'My guess is that it's to do with the refugee part of your field not the medical side.'

She smiled to herself. 'He wouldn't be needing my medical advice anyway; not unless he's in need of an obstetrician.'

She was curious. Now what would the United Nations want with me? she asked herself as she replaced the phone in its cradle. Whatever it was, she couldn't help being intrigued. She found Corporal Cohen and duly informed him that she would meet with his colonel that afternoon.

She was directed to a two-storey brick building that had survived the war and was now spruced up and stuffed with UN and American personnel.

Corporal Cohen appeared and took her to an office on the ground floor at the far end of what seemed a never-ending corridor. He rapped on the door before affirmative permission was received from within, opened the door and stood to attention as she crossed the threshold.

Colonel Warrington had the whitest teeth and pale blue eyes that at first seemed to fill his face before she became used to his forthright stare. His hair was sandy and thinning, which was probably the reason he kept sliding his hand over it, flattening it against his skull as if to help it stick there. All the same, he had presence.

'I knew you would come.'

His manner was brusque. No welcome or thank you and he didn't offer to shake her hand. He waved at the chair on the other side of his desk.

'I was in two minds whether to come.'

He carried on with what he was doing. 'You couldn't help yourself. You're a woman. You were curious.'

She stiffened. If there was one thing she really hated it was being prejudged.

'So, what is this about?'

'A mission.'

'Corporal Cohen suggested it was a matter of national security.'

'International security. That's what I prefer to call it.'

'What's it got to do with me?'

'Everything. We've all got a duty to maintain the peace after fighting a war.'

'I'm not a soldier.'

'I hear you're a damned good doctor.'

'I was unaware that my fame was so widespread.'

He shot a quick glance at the file in front of him, before redirecting it to her.

'Wasted here. You're experienced. Been through tough times. Know what it's like in war. No place for pussies.'

A prickle of fear induced by bad memories turned her blood to ice.

The colonel's head bowed once more over the file,

flicking backwards and forwards through its contents. He said nothing. The clacking of typewriters outside in the general office overrode the whirring of the overhead fan, the buzzing of a fly beating its wings against the window. With one incisive glance she'd seen the make-up of the general office, clerks in the pay of the US and the UN, pimply-faced youths half hidden behind piles of paperwork spilling from filing trays.

At last he spoke.

'We need a doctor at a hospital near Seoul in Korea. An obstetrician would fit the bill.'

'Excuse me, but I'm not available...'

His eyes shot up from studying the file.

'That's not quite true. Things are changing in Hong Kong. It's rumoured that your present contract is coming to an end.'

So that was it. He'd been speaking to the trustees currently in charge of Victoria House. It was from them that she received her funding. Her blood that had been frozen now boiled.

'Nothing has been decided.'

'I'm given to understand otherwise.'

'I'll wait for them to tell me. Until then, I'm not available.'

She half rose from the chair.

'Now wait. No need to take offence.' His look was intense, almost as though he was trying to glue her to the chair just by looking at her. 'I may be jumping the gun, but you're here so might just as well hear me out. Would you like coffee?'

Although she was still bristling with anger, she did realise that he was trying to make amends, even though it was only now he made the promise of coffee, which was bound to be American and very good.

She nodded.

'Coffee,' he shouted at the door, so loudly that he made her jump. A shadow passed across the reeded glass of the door just seconds before it opened and the corporal appeared with a tray holding two cups, sugar and cream.

Without being asked, the corporal poured, asked if she wanted cream and sugar. She said yes to both.

It was as good as she'd expected and perhaps the reason why she reined in her initial dislike of this man. Coffee as a calming influence; it was a new one on her.

'What sort of appointment is this?'

'A promotion. It's a new hospital attached to some kind of convent. All those nuns. It makes sense to use a woman doctor. They asked for a woman. I for one thought it a tough call. Until Dr Grelane mentioned you.'

Her eyes blinked rapidly. Dr Simeon Grelane, a French physician in the pay of the United Nations. Well that wasn't much of a surprise. He wanted her out of the way, leaving him in complete control of Victoria House, the refugee hospital she'd set up of her own volition. Her own home was the penthouse at the top of the building. She wondered when these two had met. She certainly had no knowledge of them meeting, but who could know for sure in the melting pot that was post-war Hong Kong.

'Colonel, I'm very flattered that you've considered me for this post, but I do have a life here in Hong Kong – and a daughter.'

'Hmm.' He reached forward and reopened the buff-coloured file in front of him, flicking papers through his fingers before closing it again. She could well imagine what the papers in the file might say. Memories best forgotten erupted in her mind like long dormant volcanoes.

'You were imprisoned by the Japanese.'

'Yes. I was.'

He looked at her over the top of his steepled fingers in a way that made her fold her arms across her front so that her breasts were squeezed together and less noticeable.

In the blink of an eye, his gaze darted to her face.

'You must hate them. For what they did.'

She kept her cool, gritted her teeth. 'It was back in the war and there's nothing I can do to change anything. Anyway, I was also at Hiroshima in the aftermath of the war and saw what was done to them.'

'They had it coming. And you were kept prisoner by this guy, Pheloung. I'm surprised you're still living in the Orient.'

'Circumstances.'

'Your daughter?'

'What about my daughter?'

'You didn't go back to England.'

'No.'

'Any particular reason?'

'I thought she'd be better here.'

She winced when he leaned forward, making her feel like a bug beneath the lens of a microscope.

His look was direct and too probing. 'You mean she might not be accepted back home. Isn't that right?'

This was a subject she had gone over in her mind on numerous occasions. At first she had yearned to go home, to catch up with her brother, see the nephew and niece she'd never met. The truth was there just below the surface. The colonel was winkling it out, had surmised how she'd suspected Dawn would be treated. Despite friendly wartime occupation by the soldiers of many countries, there could still be hostility towards anyone who was different. Britain wouldn't have changed that much. The offspring of an enemy, her little girl, would be bullied for something she had no control over, for simply being of mixed blood. Enemy blood.

'I thought about it and decided it wouldn't be a picnic.'

'Only to be expected. This won't be a picnic either. You'll be roughing it. That's why it has to be a woman doctor who's experienced war. A male doctor wouldn't do. The nuns wouldn't like that. It has to be a female doctor who knows what it's like to go without the ribbons and bows.'

'Please don't patronise me. I am not at all like the little woman you've left at home.'

He held his hands up as though in surrender.

'I'm saying it as it is. It wouldn't suit a woman who paints her nails or slaps on the lipstick.'

It hinted at insult. 'I think I should point out that I do occasionally paint my nails and apply lipstick.'

'I'm sure you do, Doctor.'

'Do I have time to think this over?'

'Of course you do. Ever been there?'

'Korea? No. Have you?'

His jaw tensed as though he suddenly found himself chewing on iron filings.

'Yes. I served there as a military attaché for a while. Korea would be a fine country if it wasn't for the Koreans.'

She fancied he'd been about to laugh at his own joke. It came out as though his voice was cracked and the laughter begrudging.

Not appearing to notice her disdainful expression, the colonel continued.

'Seoul is a fine city. Peaceful too. We, meaning the United Nations, want it to stay that way. We don't want more ruined cities like Hiroshima and Nagasaki. No more piles of rubble.'

His statement brought the past vividly to life in her mind; piles of rubble and people suffering the aftermath of the atomic explosions. Back at the end of the war she'd served with the Red Cross close to where the atomic bombs had destroyed thousands of lives. The likes of Colonel Warrington tended to refer to Hiroshima and Nagasaki in terms of the destruction of cities. She would always refer to the subject in terms of the lives lost at the time of the bombing and the horrors that followed: those who had not been close to the blast but suffered radiation sickness and condemned to a slow, lingering death.

'You would be doing us a favour. Doing the Koreans a favour too.'

She shook her head. 'I have a daughter to think of.'

'That shouldn't be a problem. I understand she's in boarding school.'

'Yes.' He'd done his research, but to what end?

'You're saying it could be an impediment that would prevent you going.'

'Yes.'

'How about you take her with you?'

'I'm not saying I would go.'

'The compound and the convent are well protected. The money's good.'

'I'm not worried about money.'

'Is there nothing that could persuade you to leave Hong Kong?'

'Not at this moment in time. Anyway, the nuns might be of an order that doesn't allow children inside its hallowed precincts.'

'One more female in a convent? Can't see it's a problem.'

She couldn't believe how irrepressible he was, determined to persuade her to take up the posting. If he was trying to prove himself patriotic, he was doing a good job.

'I'm not inclined to go. Anyway, I understand the situation there is a little unstable.'

He shrugged. 'Some. Not that we're expecting anything to happen. The North Koreans know better than to defy the United Nations.'

He sounded pompously sure about this.

'There are other issues...' she began. 'I set up Victoria House when there was little else, and even though things are changing—'

The colonel cut in. 'Just to clarify my earlier comments regarding the trustees, there's been talk. They're a strait-laced lot and you're unmarried.' He said it sharply, accusingly. 'I'm surprised they've let you stay on.'

'I set up Victoria House without their help,' she said, bristling with indignation and not giving him the satisfaction of blushing.

'But they're in charge now. Even if they let you stay on, they could give you a hard time seeing as you've got a kid and no husband.'

'How dare you!'

'I'm paid to dare, but quite frankly your sexual morals are of no importance to me. First priority is to get the job done. Being married or single is of no consequence.'

'I might suddenly get married. Would it bar me from going?'

He grimaced.

'Not necessarily, unless you decided to start a family on your honeymoon.'

Again, that forced laugh that didn't quite make it to his lips and made her shiver.

She shook her head. 'I really don't think—'

'I don't need an answer pronto. Think about it.' His tone was dismissive. His pale blue eyes swept over her file to many others. Their interview was over.

She left, unaware of him watching the door as it closed behind her.

Once she'd gone his eyes snapped open, looking at the door, his mouth a thin straight line. He was determined to get her there and if he couldn't persuade her through normal channels, then he'd have to use alternative methods and dubious contacts. Subterfuge was a skill learned over years of worldly turmoil, getting the job done for his country and mankind in general. But not this time. This time he had his own agenda. This time it was for him.

He picked up the phone and dialled a number in downtown Hong Kong.

'I need a statement from you in writing.'

'Oh, do you now!'

'Don't play with me, Sister.'

'Why?'

'I want it in writing.'

'I told you. Isn't that enough?'

'No. I want it in writing.'

'It'll cost you.'

She laughed in a way that made him want to slap her, or at least pin her to the bed and do what he usually did to her.

'No it won't. A one-way ticket to America. That's it.'

'And a job there?'

'That too.'

'Any other fringe benefits?'

'I'm married.'

'But not happily. She doesn't give you what I give you. I give you everything.'

'A statement. I want a statement from you. Not for me to use straight away, but just in case.'

'I'll get it to you.'

He thought about her firm breasts and the fact that she never refused him anything. Anything!

'No. I'm coming to you.'

Chapter 2

The old man's white beard trailed like a wisp of smoke from his chin. His features were as smooth as a piece of jade moulded by many years of variable weather. It was assumed by those who saw but did not know him that his unflinching gaze saw only shadows of the world he'd once seen so clearly.

Every day he sat in the doorway of the house opposite Connor's Bar smoking a long thin pipe that looked as though it might once have been a sinewy rib and thus naturally shaped for its present use.

At night a woman they assumed to be his daughter, a black-haired woman with a flat face, emerged from the gloom inside the house to fetch him in for his evening meal, heaving him up from his chair as she might a sack of rice.

No matter the weather, he did not remain inside for long. As darkness fell the tobacco in the bowl of his pipe waxed and waned like a firefly permanently perched in the same place, the same position. They could see him from inside the bar.

'He's there all night. Nothing else to do, I suppose. Poor old guy; mind you, his daughter takes good care of him. Brings his meals out, fills his pipe with tobacco...'

'Have they lived there long?'

'A few months.'

Rowena took a sip of her drink, her thoughts her own and far from the scene across the way. The notice from the trustees had been expected. She could cope. Being summoned to Colonel Warrington's office had been something of a surprise.

So far, she had kept the meeting to herself, but Connor's sidelong looks were unsettling. He knew something was troubling her, her speech was clipped, her manner taut, the message that she was loath to share her thoughts abundantly clear. But he wouldn't press. He would stay patient until she was ready to confide in him.

She could almost feel his curiosity, seeping out through his clothes just like the warmth of his body. At present he was standing next to her, pretending to be absorbed in tuning his beloved violin, his eyes darting between her and the old guy across the road.

'Do you think he's watching us?' he asked in a light, non-confrontational tone.

'He's blind.'

'Are you sure?'

'Are you sure he's not?'

Connor grinned. 'Not being a medical man, I haven't given him a full eye test, but he looks blind to me.'

'I suppose he does.'

She fingered her glass, tapping the rim in time with her unspoken thoughts. Her hair had fallen forward, her bent head hiding her downcast eyes.

Connor could barely take his eyes off her, wanted her just as much now as he had done the moment she'd entered his bar back in 1941.

He reckoned he knew every inch of her better than anyone, both what was on the surface as well as the more intimate zones. Today he was settling for what everyone else could see, though reckoned he appreciated it far more than they ever could.

Tendrils of fine dark hair lay slightly damp on the nape of her neck, tempting him to reach across and stroke each tress in turn. He held back as he always did when he sensed her retreating into herself.

'A penny for your thoughts, me darling.'

She smiled. He'd purposely put on a deeper Irish brogue than normal.

'They'll cost you more than that.'

His eyebrows arched. 'Will they now!'

She pressed her empty glass against his chest. 'Another Singapore Sling.'

'Your wish is my command.' He took the glass from her, passing it to the part-time barman he'd recently hired.

'How was Dawn?'

'She was well.'

'Enjoying school?'

'Queen Alexandra's was a good choice.'

'But missing her mother?'

Rowena took a sip of her drink pulling in her lips behind it.

'She's fine.'

Dawn was Rowena's daughter and one of twins, fathered by a Japanese whose name she did not know in circumstances she preferred not to remember. The war had been over for some years. What had happened could not be reversed and despite everything, Rowena had learned to love her daughter, though God knows she didn't always show it. The pressures of her work with refugees meant she had little family time, so even though Dawn was only seven years old, Rowena had opted for a school where she could board five days of the week and have her home at weekends.

After passing her the fresh drink, Connor reached for his fiddle. 'You need cheering up. And don't tell me there's nothing wrong. You've got a face like a rhubarb crumble.'

'What?' For the first time this evening, her voice gurgled with laughter.

He winked suggestively. 'Don't worry. I like a good rhubarb crumble meself. The custard takes away the sourness of the rhubarb and makes it taste sweeter.'

She flipped his shoulder in mock condemnation when in fact she knew there was serious sincerity in the saucy comparison.

Connor's wily hands enticed an energetic jig that had her tapping her feet despite herself.

'Whiskey in the Jar'.

She hummed along. Neither of them seemed to have the strength or inclination to sing tonight.

Once the notes had died away and the night deepened,

the bar got busier, regular drinkers mixing with regular gamblers sidling quietly towards the door that led to the room where chairs crowded around roulette and poker. The door to the ad hoc casino was firmly closed once they'd entered.

His eyes were on her. He hadn't asked how her day was and unless he did she would keep the details to herself. The details of Colonel Warrington's offer could wait to be aired another day.

'Are you staying tonight?'

She shook her head.

'I've an early start in the morning. A late one too, no doubt.'

'Me darling, you work too hard,' he said, passing his arm around her shoulder before his fingers found her neck, massaging and fingering the soft fronds of hair that he'd wanted to stroke earlier.

'I like my job.'

'I know you do. You're a veritable Florence Nightingale. And the flood of refugees goes on. Like a tide they are. Have you seen the walled city? The buildings are getting higher and higher – skyscraper hovels.'

'Yes. I have. The war's long been over, but the repercussions are still with us, God knows for how many years.'

'The tide won't be stemmed. Anyway, it doesn't mean you have to wear yourself out trying to make things right.'

'But I do,' she responded, her eyes flashing. 'I do. I think of all those who died before my eyes and at times – I know it sounds crazy – but I can't help feeling guilty that I'm still alive. I survived against all the odds. And now I have to make amends. I thought you of all people understood that.'

There was pleading in her eyes and despite it being an inappropriate moment he was stirred with a sudden longing to take her to bed, and it wasn't entirely due to a need to reaffirm that he was still alive.

Connor's face clouded over. 'I understand that. Harry died and I lived.'

Harry had been his best friend. Even after all this time he still thought of him, how he'd died, how much they'd loved one another – not in the physical sense though Harry would have welcomed that. Not as lovers, but brothers. *We happy few, we band of brothers...*

She looked up at him. '"We happy few, we band of brothers." Shakespeare certainly got that one right.'

He blinked. At first he'd put the way she could read what he was thinking down to pure coincidence. Now he understood it was because the two of them were almost melded together, no longer two people but one – joined at the hip – whatever that might mean. His mother would have known.

'I've got time off at the end of the week – my first weekend in ages.'

'Just the two of us then.'

'Three actually. Dawn will be home.'

'Family outings then.'

'You were hoping it was just going to be the two of us.'

'Oh, come on. We'll only bore each other, longstanding as we are. The child keeps us young. Gives us something to talk about.'

'We've always got something to talk about.'

'This is true.'

It was indeed, but no matter the light-hearted banter

between them, there was something she wasn't saying and it irked him. It wasn't like her to hold back, not this woman who so easily read his thoughts, almost word for word at times.

As she gathered up her things, preparing to leave him – at least for the night – he got out his accounts book, running his finger down a column of figures he should have checked weeks ago. Accounts were not his strong point though he could be quite creative when he wanted to be.

The night air was crisp with the smell of things sizzling in soy and oil, crisp leaves curling in a pool of spiced heat.

They were close enough to breathe each other's breath and he was about to kiss her but suddenly looked up and down the alley.

'You do realise I have nosy neighbours, waiting for us to kiss and squeeze the life out of each other.'

She laughed and shook her head.

'When has that ever stopped you? Us,' she added, correcting herself.

She saw the twinkle in his eyes replaced by a more searching look. There was humour but also concern.

She opted to match his humour.

'We're not going to make love in the street. At least not right now.'

'Being a bit of a show-off, I'm disappointed.'

'You'll have to stay that way.'

He was compensated with a peck on the cheek, then a more lingering kiss on his mouth.

The smell of tobacco smoke came from across the road. A yellow flame flashed into existence, the pipe being relit. The smoke increased in volume and pungency.

'We are being watched,' he said, his chin almost resting on her head, his eyes catching the small happenings across the road.

'Then you'd better make it look obvious than I'm going home.' She chucked him under the chin. 'We don't want to ruin your reputation, do we, darling.'

He laughed, put his arm around her and opened the car door.

'Goodnight.'

One more kiss. Her hands were on the wheel. She switched on the engine.

'A big improvement on that old starting handle you had with the other car.'

'I loved that other car. Though not the starting handle.'

Accompanied by a puff of exhaust smoke she was off.

Without even a backward glance, he thought dismally. That was before she raised her hand in a static wave. Then she was gone.

Back in the bar he played a sad song because that's how he was feeling. '*Plaisir d'amour*'.

A sad song about the pains of love, but any music gave him pleasure. His mood faded along with the music and soon he was feeling his old self again.

'I'm going upstairs,' he said to Yang who smiled cheerfully at first. The smile faded when he saw the look on Connor's face.

'Dr RoRo upset you?'

Connor frowned. 'Not really. She just didn't seem her normal self.'

'Ah!' exclaimed Yang. 'Women are not normal like men are normal. Their mood is either up in the sky or deep in the water, upsetting the balance that is within all men but not in women.'

'So, as a man of the world, what do you suggest I do about it, Yang?'

Yang shook his head soulfully.

'There is nothing you can do. Women have been that way since the day they fell from heaven.'

She was in time to catch the last ferry. The dark water was peppered with lights from swinging lanterns on fishing boats and sampans. The latter were bundled together forming a causeway from the furthest out to those nudging the land.

As far as she could see, Hong Kong had not changed very much since the first time she'd set foot here just before the outbreak of war. She'd entertained the option to go home, but seeing as the war seemed confined to Europe, she'd stayed put. It had proved to be her downfall.

How many times, she wondered, have I used this ferry?

Memories burst into her mind. Foremost amongst them was the night she'd met Connor on what had been planned as a fun night in Kowloon.

Back then in 1941 she had driven aboard in a car lent to her by an admirer who had gone on to leave it to her in his will. Unwilling to continue using its cantankerous starting handle, she had long since got rid of it and bought a new one. Much easier to drive, not that she was thinking about cars as the ferry headed towards the blinking and ever increasing light of Hong Kong Island.

You should have told him about your meeting with the colonel, so why didn't you?

The answer came like a page that suddenly turns in a book and reveals the interior thought that points to an instinctive feeling about somebody's motive. Colonel Warrington was not a charming man. His abrupt speech, his curt manner declared a man of black and white views. There were no grey areas, no leeway given for making the wrong decision or wrong move. In effect, he had his own set of rules and something, something she couldn't quite work out, was behind this trip to Korea.

'Never mind,' she whispered as she watched luminescence stream along the side of the ferry. 'You've no intention of going, so it really doesn't matter.'

In fact, she thought, something pretty drastic would have to happen to change your mind. Your home is in Hong Kong with Dawn and with Connor and something pretty big would have to happen to change that.

Chapter 3

Noon the next day was hot and humid which was only to be expected. What happened next was not expected.

Connor heard the grinding gears of a Land Rover before the brakes were put on and knew even before he ventured out that the Hong Kong police were in the neighbourhood. Land Rovers were robust vehicles and as a consequence their engines were built to last and not to be silent. The Hong Kong police had a whole fleet of them and could be heard coming long before they actually appeared.

Brandon McCloud, a look of disdain on his rugged face, raised his hand in Connor's direction and when Connor crossed the street, filled him in on his reason for this morning visit.

'A woman came screaming into my office to say that the djinns had come in the middle of the night and killed her father. I asked her for a description of these djinns and had she seen them in the act of killing her father, but you know how it is.'

'Djinns are shifting, shapeless things that disguise themselves as anything they want to be.'

'Correct. Having nothing much else to do, I've come to investigate. The doctor's with me.'

He indicated a gruff-looking fellow with an overshot lower lip and a freckled skull. 'I'll pop over before I leave in the hope that you've wangled some decent coffee from your American friend.'

'That particular friend has flown back to California.'

'Now that's a shame. Still, no doubt you'll find another.'

'That I will. In the meantime you'll have to settle for Camp Coffee and like it, Brandon. Or tea.'

Brandon shook his head. 'Coffee, Connor. Even that disgusting Camp and chicory stuff might help settle my head.'

Connor smiled knowingly as the police inspector, smartly turned out in khaki shorts, a swagger stick tucked beneath his arm, made his way to the house opposite. Brandon was more than a police acquaintance, he was a regular customer. He'd downed at least six double whiskies the night before. He'd also had a good hand at poker playing some Chinese gambler in the back room.

Connor suddenly became aware of Yang's presence at his shoulder. From the very start, when he'd still been an enlisted man and bought the bar from Yang, the former opium dealer had managed the place, and continued to do so when Connor was incarcerated in a Japanese prisoner-of-war camp.

Although a former criminal, he was totally devoted to Connor who had helped him out of a tight situation by purchasing the bar. Back then it had been an opium den – like a bar but selling the heavily addictive drug rather than imported bottles of Newcastle Brown, Gordon's gin or Johnnie Walker whisky.

'Seen any djinns around here, Yang?'

Yang shook his head. 'No, Mr Connor.'

'Not last night?'

Yang shook his head again. 'No. Not last night.'

'Would you recognise one if you saw one?'

Yang laughed. 'I do not believe in djinns though my uncle Broken Chin told me he saw one.'

'Is that your uncle's real name?'

'Not the name he was born with, but one he acquired. Like a nickname. It suits him. He fell down and dented his chin when he saw the djinn and ran away.'

'You mean he was drunk?'

'We never accused him of that. He is old. It would be most impolite.'

'The old man over there. Did you know him?'

'Nan Po. The house belongs to his daughter. She did not want him there but he moved in anyway.'

'Was there any particular reason he wanted to move in?'

Yang shrugged. 'I don't know. One day he was not there and then he was.'

It was a lame explanation and there could be any number of reasons. For a start the old man didn't seem very mobile and the Chinese take care of their elderly. It would be unusual if the daughter had refused to allow him to move in.

Brandon was scowling when he came to claim his coffee.

'Come on now, Brandon. That's a sour look you've got there. My coffee's not that bad.'

Brandon took a sip, winced then raised his eyes. 'The mud from the Clyde tastes better than this.'

'Made any progress?'

Brandon jerked his head in a so-so fashion.

'According to the doctor, the old man's neck was broken. He's not sure how. He could have fallen and hit his neck on the parapet, or it could have been a death blow.'

'Which do you think?'

Brandon shrugged. 'Your guess is as good as mine. This is Kowloon and I've got enough to do without investigating something that might or might not have been an accident.'

'Or might or might not have been a murder.'

'Let's not speculate just yet, but all the same I might begin asking a few questions of the locals around here.'

'Before you ask me, I didn't see djinns or anybody else hanging around last night. You were here. Did you see anyone?'

'Now let me think. I left just before twelve…'

'You left after one, Brandon.'

Brandon's face froze but swiftly relaxed once he'd conceded that he couldn't possibly have exited Connor's Bar without being seen. He took another sip of coffee which in turn led to another wince.

'Did you know him well?'

'Not at all. I didn't even know his name until Yang told me, only that he was blind and used to sit out there from morning to night.'

'He wasn't blind.'

'Are you sure?'

'His name was Nan Po and we know he was connected with the opium trade or had been when he was younger. But he certainly wasn't blind.'

This came as something of a surprise to Connor.

'Yang told me the daughter hadn't wanted him to move in.'

'Yang knew him?'

'No. He just repeated what the daughter told him. I think he's been getting the benefit of her widowed state.'

'Good for Yang. Lucky bugger. Wish I could find one.'

'You're a married man.'

'I quite like dining out now and again as an alternative to home cooking.'

'Is that what you call it.'

Brandon took another sip of the bitter-tasting coffee. Camp Coffee had been a mainstay of colonial Britons for years. For some reason chicory had been added to enhance its taste by somebody who was not a regular coffee drinker.

Connor dropped two sugar cubes into the dark brown liquid.

'It might help.'

'Kill or cure,' grunted Brandon, took a sip then raised his eyes in a meaningful and very serious manner. 'His daughter told me he just liked watching people.'

The two men's looks collided as they both reached the same conclusion.

'He was a lookout,' muttered Connor.

'More specifically, a planted lookout to watch whatever was going on around here. You know and I know that some of your clientele are far from being well respected upright citizens – with a few notable exceptions, of course.'

'Of course,' said Connor. 'Including your good self.'

'I doubt that I was the subject of his scrutiny. It wouldn't be the first time that one gang boss was looking to take control of new territory. Or bump off an official that's not playing the game. We have been clamping down heavy on bribery of late. Gambling too.'

Connor nodded stoically and reached into his shirt pocket. 'Your winnings from last night.'

'Oh, thank you very much. Right, I'd better be off.'

Connor proceeded to escort him to the door noting that despite his comments, the coffee cup was empty. 'I'll keep my eyes peeled for anything suspicious.'

'I would very much appreciate that.' Brandon rubbed at the small of his back and stretched. 'Oh, and give my regards to Dr Rossiter. A fine woman, though I'm at a loss as to why she bothers with the likes of you.'

'Shared experiences.'

'And a beautiful woman. Shame she deals mainly with childbirth or I'd ask her to give me a thorough examination.'

'Wouldn't do you any good.'

'It wouldn't?'

'I'm pretty good with a scalpel, especially around the ribs – or scrotum.'

'Point taken.'

Brandon McCloud climbed back into the Land Rover where the bald-headed doctor was nodding over his Gladstone bag, jerking into wakefulness when the engine rumbled into life.

Connor frowned at the retreating vehicle. Brandon and he were not exactly close friends, not in the way that he and Harry had been close friends. However, late at night or early in the morning, they did chew the fat over a bottle of whisky or two.

After Brandon had left, he let his gaze shift to the house on the other side of the alley from his bar. There was no sign of life. The windows were like black plates, the door firmly shut. A crow hopped along the upper parapet, perching on the uplifted corner of the red tiled roof and cawing to the sky.

The man that had dwelt therein was no more, but what about the daughter? More importantly, who had paid the old man to be a lookout? Who was he watching and why his sudden demise?

There were possible answers, of course. This was Kowloon and the old man had once been involved in the opium trade. Perhaps he still had been right up until his death. Such a background made it easy to believe that his death had not been an accident.

Perhaps whatever he'd learned had fallen into the hands of the opposing interest, or he'd upped his price for the job, or gone over to the other side, or merely outlived his usefulness and had to be silenced. Or he might have been killed for nothing. Life was cheap in Kowloon.

Chapter 4

The phone rang just as Rowena was coming to the end of her shift.

She sighed, considered not answering it, but then relented just in case it was Connor.

To her surprise it turned out to be Colonel Warrington.

'Doctor. I'm compiling the list for UN Korea. I've added your name to it.'

No hello. No introduction. And such presumption!

'I suggest you take it off again.'

'I'm convinced you're the right person for the job. I'm a good judge of men. And women. I need your confirmation.' His words were delivered like machine gun bullets – rat-a-tat-tat – without a pause for breath.

'I'm telling you I'm not going. Is that confirmation enough?'

The line fell silent. She sensed her brusque manner had matched his and momentarily halted retaliation. She thought she could almost hear him thinking, metal cogs in a clockwork mind.

She was about to slam down the receiver when he spoke again.

'I apologise. I should not have presumed. Anyway, talking on the phone isn't a great idea. Perhaps we can meet up and talk more about it face to face. How about coffee tomorrow morning?'

'I'm on duty.'

'Dinner tomorrow night?'

'I've a prior engagement.'

'Well. Perhaps you could suggest a time convenient to you. Give me a ring.'

With that the line went dead. He'd meant to have the last word and he'd succeeded. Next time…

Even at this hour the noise and smell of despair still permeated the narrow corridor that served as a waiting room and wafted around the canvas screen designating her consulting area.

She glanced at her watch. She wanted to go home.

'All yours,' she said, barely giving her relief time to place his bag on the desk.

'An eventful day?' he asked.

'More so than usual.'

'Do you want to run through the details?'

She shook her head and rubbed at her neck. She nodded at the paperwork threatening to topple from the in-tray.

'Everything you need is there.'

Sad-looking people drew in their legs and huddled closer together as she picked her way through those waiting to see the doctor – newcomers from the mainland. Children with hollow cheeks and scared eyes clung to parents. Women sat with bowed heads. Men, their faces lined and weary, hands hanging limp from their knees, glanced listlessly up at her then looked away.

Not all the refugees were peasants. Some of them looked as though they might be professionals; teachers, doctors, sons of landed gentry fleeing the Communist regime. Others of greater age – some still wearing their hair in a cue, a long plait at the back, their skulls shaved – she guessed were farmers, the illiterate who could not come to terms with what was going on, confused by the conflict, bereft of land their families had farmed for centuries.

One war was over for some but not for others.

More people were gathered in the entrance hall, a wider expanse where stairs and a lift served the upper floors, including her flat.

In the past the sight of that lift and its iron grille had sent a shiver down her spine. Not until it had climbed halfway to her flat did she confront the past and feel a sudden surge of triumph. The whole of Victoria House had once belonged to Kim Pheloung, the most beautiful – and most lethal – man she'd ever met.

Thanks to her efforts Victoria House was no longer the heart of a criminal empire, but had been put to good use. Everything that had been his was now in the hands of a board of UN appointed trustees and used for the good of people he would have considered unworthy of his attention, peasants who to him were no more than sheep, created only to be fleeced and controlled.

A metallic screeching followed by a dull thud announced the arrival of the lift. Holding her medical bag in her left hand, she used her right to tug the outer iron grille open, and then the inner one. It was halfway across when a familiar voice called out to her. She turned back towards the main doors at the far end of the foyer.

'Doctor. You must come.'

Luli's black hair was as glossy as polished coal. Her expression was tense.

Rowena frowned. The Han girl had originally been employed as Dawn's nurse and was now a kind of factotum maid, cook and housekeeper, doing anything that her beloved Dr Rossiter required, though not today.

'I thought you were having a few days off to visit relatives.'

Luli's pale face looked paler than usual, her black eyes wide with alarm.

'A baby is being born. You are needed.'

Rowena frowned. She was tired and the last thing she wanted was to spend most of the night bringing a baby into the world.

'Get a midwife.'

'It is not possible.'

'Why isn't it possible?'

'The lady should not be here,' Luli blurted.

Rowena's frown deepened but she understood Luli's meaning. If a local midwife suspected the mother to be an illegal refugee then her price for attending the birth would double.

She sighed. 'Where is this baby being born?'

'In the old city.'

'Kowloon?'

'Yes. She very soon have baby. You must come.'

'Luli, I've had a very long day. I'm tired.' Again she suggested finding a doctor or midwife close by.

Luli shook her head emphatically. 'She has no money. She

a friend. She needs you.' Luli paused, her mouth open as though she was searching for the right words. 'She knows you are the best.'

So she was a friend of Luli, a very good friend judging by the pleading look in Luli's eyes. From Hong Kong to Kowloon wasn't that far, but to her weary mind a few miles seemed like a hundred.

'Pleeease?'

Luli had a moon-shaped face and larger eyes than normal for a Chinese. When she adopted her most appealing expression her eyes seemed to fill her face. Rowena was beaten. She found her impossible to refuse.

Rowena sighed. 'Such is the lot of an obstetrician.'

Although obstetrics remained her field of expertise during her years of incarceration, she'd adapted to whatever branch of medicine was required. During the war she had done her best for her fellow prisoners despite a severe lack of medicine. Nowadays she was one of many Red Cross personnel administering to the pathetic tide of people pouring over the border from mainland China, refugees uprooted from their daily lives and dependent on the charity of the wealthy West of which Hong Kong was a shining outpost.

'I take it this is a relative of yours?'

Luli nodded avidly and yet seemed apprehensive. 'A very old friend.'

'Which?'

'Please you come now?'

'To this friend who might be a relative?'

Luli's pretended she didn't hear and was already heading for the door.

Slamming the lift grille shut Rowena resigned herself to the fact that she might not get back until dawn.

Luli got into the passenger seat, staring straight ahead as though she was wishing the car could fly.

Rowena wished the same though she also wished the night would fly too – better still that Luli had not managed to persuade her. Back in her flat she would be sitting there listening to music whilst sipping a drink and sniffing the aroma of this evening's supper.

She left the car behind, taking traditional transport to the ancient walled city. The walled city had changed from being an outpost of old China and anything of value left unattended might not be there when you got back.

The night was drawing in and the water was black and smelling of fish stew and rotten eggs when they took the ferry across to Kowloon. Rickshaw drivers hovered and hassled around the passengers as they alighted. Luli chose one to take them through the maze of alleys and ultimately to one of the half-hidden entrances of Kowloon Walled City. Luli barked an address. For a moment Rowena wasn't sure he was going to take them and thought she knew why. The old city was a rickety structure where crime lived alongside the destitute and dispossessed with nowhere else to go. Ill lit and stinking, it was a warren of unseen evils, bad enough in daytime but far more unpredictable at night.

Luli barked the address again and the rickshaw driver set off at a dogtrot.

They wound their way through the rebuilding that was going on all around, tall buildings rising from the rubble of the previous decade.

People were thicker than flies, going about their business

and shouting their wares, their grievances and their opinions in various dialects, though mainly in Cantonese.

The neon lights of the city were brighter and more brazen than in pre- and wartime years, advertising everything from cigarettes to the latest wireless sets, Bovril to Cherry Blossom shoe polish and genuine American chewing gum. Many flashed on and off as if that alone would establish a need in the minds of the many beholders.

A taste of things to come, thought Rowena as the rickshaw rattled on through the newer buildings and finally entered an area where traditional houses frowned across narrow alleys.

Ahead of them loomed the old walled city where the box-like towers built higgledy-piggledy one on top of the other dissected the sky. No longer was it a place of few buildings and even fewer people. Ramshackle home had been built on top of ramshackle home, the leaning structures beginning to bear resemblance to a particularly unwieldy house of cards.

Coming to an abrupt stop, the rickshaw driver set down his shafts at one of the narrow entrances to the city indicating that this was as far as he was prepared to go. Nobody entered the walled city unless they lived there or, like Rowena, was willing to do what she could. The rickshaw driver obviously preferred to keep as far away from it as possible.

Rowena paid him then turned to Luli. 'Are you sure this is the right entrance?'

Luli assured her that it was then signalled for her to follow. 'Come. This way.'

It was as though the darkness had deepened. Gloom descended the moment they entered.

Rowena held her breath and concentrated on where she was placing her feet. Picking her way carefully over slime-covered stones gave her little opportunity to look above her. When she did she marvelled how the surrounding structures actually stayed upright. It was as though a child had attempted to build a tower of misshapen building blocks. The buildings to either side of them seemed close to toppling inwards, the strip of star-studded sky above their heads far narrower than the ground beneath their feet. The strip became swiftly obscured by the growing height of the buildings.

Luli continued to urge her onwards along passageways dripping with water, stinking of human waste and at times barely the width of a human body.

'This way. This way. We must hurry.'

Rowena sensed an unqualified urgency in Luli's voice that made her apprehensive and think perhaps that there was more to this visit than attending a difficult birth. And why had Luli come herself? she wondered. Usually she would have sent a messenger, a street urchin for preference, with swift legs and small enough to weave in and out of the crowds.

Stumbling along the twisting corridors, turning left here and right there, Rowena determined to keep up some speed, terrified in case she lost sight of Luli and couldn't find her way out of this never-ending labyrinth.

Suddenly Luli disappeared into a dark recess and Rowena truly thought she'd lost her – until her moon-shaped face reappeared, a sphere of pallor shining through the gloom.

'Here.' She waved her arm, beckoning her to follow.

The clinging stench of decay was all around them, mixed with the smell of cooked rice, chicken and fish.

There was a door in the recess hanging lopsided on broken hinges. Luli pushed it open.

It took just a few minutes for her eyes to adjust between the gloom behind them and the only slightly brighter interior which was narrow and consisted of just one room. There was a bed in the corner, a candle burning in a brass holder and a paper lantern above the bed that was shielding a flickering flame.

'That,' whispered Rowena, 'is a fire hazard.'

Her attention turned to Luli who was standing at the side of the bed looking guilty. She whispered something to the woman lying on the bed in the last throes of labour.

Despite the dim lighting she recognised the fine features and porcelain complexion of the woman who'd helped her escape from Kim Pheloung. Even so, she couldn't quite believe that this was her.

'Koto? Is it really Koto?'

The woman's face, flushed with perspiration, looked up through narrow eyes, both hands laid across her pulsating stomach.

Rowena looked at Luli accusingly. 'You should have told me it was Koto.'

'I thought you might refuse.'

'How could I?'

She owed this woman her freedom. Koto had been foolish enough to love Kim Pheloung and had aided Rowena's escape from his clutches purely because she regarded her as competition for Kim's affection. What she'd failed to understand was that Kim preferred to own people rather than love them.

Events of the past were water under the bridge that sometimes threatened to drown her if she dwelled on them for too long. She must live in the moment and for now that meant concentrating on Koto's contractions.

She addressed Luli. 'Ask her how often the pains are coming.'

Luli did as asked.

'Every half an hour at first but much closer together now. She says it is nearly time.'

'Tell her I'm the doctor and I will tell her when it is time. On second thoughts, don't bother.'

First she opened her bag, then, with Luli's help, raised Koto's shift until it was beyond the swelling of her belly and resting on her chest.

There was barely enough time to listen to the baby's heartbeat. Koto had timed the birth well, almost too well. It was well engaged and forcing its way down the birth canal.

'How long have you been in labour?' She looked at Koto, but her question was aimed at Luli who translated both the question and the answer.

'One day and one-half day.'

It was just as she'd thought. The waters must have broken some hours ago. The baby was about to make its entrance, Koto's belly pulsating as the foetus lengthened, body and legs flat out behind the head that her muscles were forcing into the outside world.

'Slow down. Luli, tell her to slow down and not to push. If she does, she'll tear.'

Again Luli translated and Koto gritted her teeth, her eyes squeezed shut as she fought the urge to push.

A gush of bloodied water came out followed by the crown of the skull. Once the head was out, the crumpled face like a pink plum in the mellow light, Rowena got hold of the baby's shoulders and turned them so that the child was laid on its side and could more easily slip through the perineum between the mother's legs.

The biggest part, the head, was out. The shoulders came after and then the rest of the body, slithering out in a rush of pink liquid.

Once the cord was cut, Luli wrapped the baby in a white sheet, her eyes glowing with pleasure as she looked down into the child's crumpled face.

'She looks like a squashed plum,' she said cheerfully, as though such a thing was somehow beautiful.

'A girl? I never noticed.'

Koto held out her arms and said something which Luli then translated.

'She asks how much she must pay you.'

Rowena shook her head. 'Nothing. I owe her for helping me escape from Shanghai.'

A thought suddenly struck her.

'Does she know how Kim died?'

A look of shocked amazement came to Koto's face in response to the question, her answer given swiftly and softly, as if afraid the very walls were listening to what she was saying.

In turn Luli's face drained of colour and she visibly swallowed what seemed to be fear before responding.

'Kim is not dead. She fled from him because he wanted her to destroy baby or give it away. He said he had no need for more children. He had enough to follow on behind him.'

It was as though an icy shroud had fallen over her. 'Kim is the father of this child?'

Luli nodded. 'Yes.'

Rowena froze. This was such a shock. She'd really believed that he was dead.

Swallowing her shock, she found her voice. 'Why here? Why did she come here, Luli?'

'She knew I was here. Knew I would help.' An innocent smile brightened her broad face. 'And she knew you were here and would help.'

'She knew I was here? How did she know I was here?'

Luli shrugged. 'Somebody told her.'

Two questions surfaced that chilled her to the bone. 'Ask her who told her where I was – and where you were.'

She asked.

Koto looked a little sheepish, as though she'd suddenly realised something wasn't quite right.

'One of the other women.'

'But how would they know?'

'Somebody told them.'

She grabbed the Chinese girl's shoulders and shook her. 'But who, Luli, who?'

Luli's jaw trembled.

Terrifying thoughts crowded her mind, not least that she was holding Luli's arms too tightly, the girl wincing with pain. She let her go. 'I'm sorry. I didn't hurt you, did I?'

Luli rubbed at her arms but still looked frightened.

So many people seemed to know she was here, some people she herself did not know. And Koto was here and Kim was the father of her child. That in itself was the most shocking news of all.

Panic grabbed her as she surveyed the tiny room that had no window and only the narrowest of doors. A range of cooking pots were cluttered around a small wood burning stove. A mouse poked its head out of a hole, smelt danger and disappeared.

That's how I feel, she thought. Like a mouse being watched by a cat. Yet she couldn't see the cat, but Kim Pheloung was a clever man. He'd always had eyes and ears everywhere and it wasn't likely that anything had changed.

Reassuringly the room was too small for anyone watching to hide in. Nobody was watching her. Not here.

The reassurances rang hollow. What about outside? Had he sent somebody to follow her onto the ferry or entering the walled city?

Her survival instinct urged flight. The sooner she caught the ferry back to Hong Kong Island the better. She would be safe there; at least that's what she told herself.

Stethoscope and other instruments were gathered up and swiftly dropped into her bag. She left the bandages in case Koto needed them to help staunch the postnatal blood flow which could last for some time. The baby was suckling, its pink lips fixed tightly to Koto's nipple. She noted the birthmark on the side of the face – heart shaped and so prettily perched on the baby's pink cheek that it made her smile.

She addressed Luli. 'I have to go. Are you staying?'

Luli nodded. 'If you allow me to stay. If you do not need me?'

'I can manage until you get back. She's very stable and should be up on her feet in no time.'

It was absolutely true that Koto would recover quickly. Unlike European women spending two weeks or more in bed after giving birth, Chinese women were back up on their feet within hours, ready to work the paddy fields or do whatever other business their family was involved in.

As for Luli, well, she hadn't been around much of late, disappearing for days at a time. The excuse was always that she had met up with friends or relatives that needed her help. Not that her services were needed quite so much nowadays. Dawn was older and at boarding school, and Rowena enjoyed nights alone or with Connor, either in the cosy flat above his bar, or in her flat at the top of Victoria House.

Heart racing, she stuck her head out of the door, wincing as the acrid smell of human waste and cooked food assaulted her nostrils.

She looked up and down the passageway. To her right were shadows. To her left were shadows. Each way she looked there was blackness except in those places where a single hanging electric bulb on fizzing wire threw a small pool of light over the slippery stones. Shadowy figures appeared then disappeared. Her blood ran cold.

Which direction?

She hung there, one hand clinging onto the doorpost. Fear made her knees feel weak, her body leaden and it wasn't merely due to being here in the walled city. The news that Kim was still alive was devastating. For five years she had thought him dead and had lived her life without fear of him reappearing. Hearing the news had thrown her back to that frightening time. The Japanese had been bad enough, but Kim, beautiful but mad, had attempted to destroy her both body and soul. His mind had been warped, but despite that he'd been irresistible to anyone who came under his spell.

Desperate to get away, she considered the labyrinth of passages, up and down stairs, dark places, fetid pools of dirty water. It was obvious that without Luli's guidance she could so easily get lost. Before she had chance to re-enter the room she'd just left and ask for assistance, Luli was there behind her.

'I will show you the way out of here. You will get lost by yourself.'

As she followed Luli back along the uneven floors of the narrow passageways, sometimes ascending, sometimes descending, a worrying question arose in her mind. Only once they were outside the city did she finally overcome her dry mouth and ask Luli another pertinent question.

'Luli, how come you know your way so well inside the walled city?'

'Friends.'

It struck her that the response had come too quickly.

'I didn't know you had friends in the walled city.'

'Yes.'

Avoiding any more questions Luli ran out into the night, calling a rickshaw and sharply shouting instructions.

Keen to put as much distance as possible between this place and its memories, she threw herself into the rickshaw.

'To Connor's Bar. Do you know it?'

Without answering, the rickshaw set off, bumping over

the uneven ground, splashing into puddles, driving through hordes of feral dogs and cats, their smell and yowling hanging like shards of glass in the air.

The rickshaw hurtled past the glare of neon lights, the street vendors and the sweaty sailors holding a beer bottle with one hand and a prostitute with the other.

Her fearful gaze strayed beyond them to broad-faced figures in black tunics or suits, some of them sporting a a plaited cue, the hair black and glossy. In the past a man had no choice but to adhere to this style. These men obeyed no such law but wore it by choice, almost like a badge advertising what they now were, henchmen of brothels, gambling and opium dens, keeping a lookout for any sign of a visit from the Hong Kong police.

Her eyes searched for any sign that she was of interest to them. It seemed not. Watchful eyes met hers for only the briefest of moments. One lingered a little longer than the others. Did he know her? Did he work for Kim? Her heart pounded, until thankfully he turned his back and disappeared into the shadow of a gambling club doorway.

Her heart stopped pounding, but she still felt drained. Back there she had almost become paralysed with fear and it hadn't entirely left her. She couldn't know for sure whether they were working for Kim, ordered to look out for her.

Logically, he couldn't possibly be looking for her – if so, why hadn't he come after her before now? He wasn't dead, that much was true; Koto's baby was proof of that. He was still alive. Had his interest in her diminished? Or was he merely awaiting the right moment. Her head ached with possibilities.

It also struck her that Luli had been evasive about her life when she wasn't looking after Dawn or the penthouse flat in Victoria House. The excuses for not being around now seemed just that – excuses – and she was vague about her absences, saying only that she was seeing friends though not admitting that those friends were in Kowloon.

Connor wouldn't be too happy to know she was frequenting that place, but Luli was a grown woman, an employee not a slave. She had a right to have a life outside her work and quite frankly it was nobody else's business.

All the same, it wouldn't hurt to have a quiet word with her. Kowloon Walled City was known to be a haunt of opium dealers and other criminals. Kim Pheloung, the man who had once played a major part in her life, had known it well, had lived there, and even though it had changed, could no doubt still find his way around.

Information would have filtered back to him and he would have found Luli. That's how it was in this dark, damp place. Everyone was watched and information was as good as cash.

She attempted to rein in her fear. There could be any number of reasons why he hadn't come after her. She'd last seen him just as the war was drawing to a close. He'd had plenty of time to pursue her and hadn't. Unless he had not yet arrived back in Hong Kong. Unless he was still in China – Koto said she had come from there, but it might not be the truth.

A deep shiver flowed through her body. The night was suddenly colder, her world not as it had been. The feeling of security she'd entertained since the end of the war felt punctured and broken. Koto had not been impregnated by a ghost and was adamant that Kim was the child's father. That fact alone confirmed that Kim was alive. Koto had no reason to lie.

According to Yang, Connor's long-serving bar manager, Kim had been executed by the Chinese for wartime collaboration with the Japanese and she had embraced it as fact because there was no reason not to. Now everything had changed.

With hindsight she could see how vulnerable she had been when he'd first whisked her away at the very point when she was being processed to enter a POW camp. Just days before that, her treatment at the hands of a group of enemy soldiers had almost destroyed her spirit. She had needed somebody to make her feel safe, to be cherished within the walls of his house and have his arms and his glossy body aiding the healing process.

She'd been fascinated by his sheer exoticism and even now she shivered at the memory of his body, his piercing eyes and the feeling of safety that he'd given her. In those early days she had not realised he was taking advantage of her vulnerability to mould her into his own creature, no more than a puppet that only he could control.

As wide boulevards diminished into narrower roads and alleys, she kept her gaze fixed on the bobbing hat of the rickshaw driver, noting a bite-size piece had been taken from the shabby straw. There was some amusement in surmising how this might have happened. A child, perhaps? A dog? No. More likely a rat gnawing at the brim whilst the driver slept. A silly way to occupy oneself maybe, but preferable to looking back at the walled city where an ugly part of the past had exploded into the present.

'Damn him,' she muttered.

Light from a wall-mounted copper-framed lantern fell down over the door of Connor's Bar, an improvement on the backlit sign when the bar was first opened.

What would she say to him? He'd be alarmed, afraid for her, insist on hovering over her shoulder, have her live here or even insist she have a bodyguard trailing around after her. He certainly knew the right people to provide one – and might even leave Yang to run the bar and do it himself. She didn't really want that.

Taking a firmer grip on her battered brown bag she paid the driver and was about to get down from the rickshaw when she suddenly changed her mind.

The driver eyed her quizzically as she sat back in the seat staring ahead at the darkness of the alley, her thoughts fighting one against the other. Tell him or not tell him?

She reconsidered the consequences to her actions and decided she was being too hasty. She had to build up to it. She had to think things through and work out what would be for the best. Besides, she feared what he would do – seek Kim out and deal with the man once and for all.

Chapter 5

Connor phoned about halfway through the morning on the following day.

'I'll be over at seven. Will that be OK?'

'Seven?'

'You invited me over for dinner. I take it the invite is still on?'

She threw back her head and closed her eyes wishing she could go back to bed and sleep. Going back to bed was easy enough, but sleep? She'd hardly slept all night.

'Did you hear what I said? Is anything wrong?'

Tonight. Tonight was the night. Not over the phone.

'Seven will be fine.'

'I should be on time, but if I'm not please don't start without me.'

She laughed lightly at his humorous manner.

After that she barely heard what he said as she rehearsed in her mind how she would tell him the dire news; a slow lead in or a short sharp staccato, like a sudden outburst on a trumpet – hardly staccato; more of a blast.

'I'm looking forward to this evening. I could do with putting me feet up away from the bar, Kowloon and Yang. I've never known a man for gossip like Yang. He should have been born a woman. I told him so.'

'Isn't that a bit unfair?'

'No of course not. He doesn't mind a bit when when I call him Widow Twanky.'

'I meant, don't you think it's a bit unfair on women in general?'

There was a pause. She could imagine Connor slapping that broad, intelligent forehead of his once he'd realised what he'd insinuated.

'That isn't what I meant, darling. I'm thinking of the pantomime dame. Not a real woman at all.'

'That's a black mark against you, Connor O'Connor.'

'Will I still get fed this evening despite my cardinal sin or do I have to say half a dozen Hail Marys first?'

'No, just promise here and now to do the washing up.'

'I stand contrite.'

She laughed. 'You've never been contrite in your life.'

She sat thoughtfully once he'd gone. Today she had come directly down from her flat to her office and had not been outside. Inside Victoria House had to be safer than being outside. It was easier to guard her safety inside. Outside was a different matter. Outside she was vulnerable.

Somebody had brought her in a cup of tea. She couldn't remember when. She took a tentative sip. It was cold. Grimacing, she set the cup back in its saucer.

Stretching her neck, she rubbed at her back and closed her eyes and readied herself for the next patient, then

63

started as she saw Colonel Warrington's face and heavy body appear from around the linen screen.

'I'm glad I caught you,' he said, pulling up a chair and making himself comfortable.

'I don't recall us having arranged a meeting.'

'We didn't. I was in the area and took it upon myself to drop in.'

No apology that his visit was unscheduled and she hadn't invited him to sit down.

Her back and neck were stiff enough, but now stiffened some more.

'I haven't time for this. I've more patients to see.'

He tugged at his trousers with both hands before crossing one leg over the other, a gesture designed not to disturb the razor-sharp crease down the front of his trousers.

'Can I ask again how you feel about Korea?'

'Politically, geographically or as a likely holiday destination?'

Although he smiled at her sarcasm it was too much like a sneer. Humour, she decided, was not part of his make-up.

'Let me run the details past you. Japan occupied Korea from just after the First World War. Now they want independence which of course has resulted in some infighting. The UN is trying to prevent things escalating, but some parts of Asia are a powder keg of anti-colonial feelings. The Chinks aren't helping the situation, of course, and neither are the Ruskies.'

'You mean the Chinese and the Russians.'

'That's what I said.' In a way it was what he'd said, but there was no mistaking his derogatory tone. 'It's no big surprise that it's a powder keg.'

'Communism threatens.'

'The world is changing. I believe it's called self-determination.'

'No. It's communism. Pure and simple. A threat to capitalism and everything we hold dear.'

'Nonsense. Look at India. It wanted independence and has achieved it. Britain knew it had to be done. And no communism.'

'It won't last.'

'Yes it will. The wind of change, I think somebody said. France will have to do the same too with French Indochina.'

The colonel made a guffawing kind of noise before attempting to put her right.

'France is not a soft touch. She will hold onto her colonies.'

'At any price?'

He covered his mouth with one gnarled hand and cleared his throat.

'I cannot expect you to understand. It is a matter of pride. That's the way they are. France is keen to reassert herself on the world stage. I've spoken to a few French diplomats. They're insistent on making up for lost time. Anyway, they're like the US. They want to keep Communism at bay.'

Her eyes flashed. 'Are you insinuating that nobody else does?'

'Britain is very casual about Communism.'

It was obvious that he held rigid and rather clichéd views on most countries and his browbeating was beginning to annoy her.

'Colonel, you didn't come here to discuss the political situation.'

He fingered his loose bottom lip and frowned, his gaze fixed on the cardex of patients she kept on her desk.

'It has to be a woman, of course.'

'So you told me.'

'The nuns would not be comfortable having a male doctor.'

'They'll have male patients.'

'Yes. But sick men do not pose a threat.'

Rowena resisted the urge to roll her eyes.

'You're very persistent.'

'It will advance your career.'

'Perhaps I have no wish to advance my career.'

The colonel shook his head and grinned in a slightly patronising manner.

'Of course you do. You are proud of what you have done. I mean, just look at this place.'

He spread his hands to indicate the building they were in.

'I'm quite happy here.'

'But the world moves on. There are new battles to be fought. New waves of refugees in need of your help.'

She looked out of the window into the garden where chrysanthemums had once grown. Kim had loved the flowers with their big bright heads and heavy blooms. She'd had the lot cut down because they'd reminded her of him. Even now she turned her head away from gardens where they grew.

'I have a daughter. I can't go.'

The way he stared at her was unnerving.

'I have a daughter too.' He leaned forward, his hands clasped in front of him. 'I have to say you'll be killing two birds with one stone if you do go over there. I'll admit to a personal reason besides my patriotic duty. You're the woman for the job. I knew it right from the start, what with your modern ideas and suchlike.'

Something about the way he said it made her tense.

'She's a nurse. I want you to bring her back from there.'

Her jaw dropped. 'So this isn't about me taking this post.'

'That too. I really think you're the best person for the job. If you go I'd like you to take her a message.'

'Why don't you write to her?'

'I want somebody there to persuade her to leave that godforsaken country.'

She found his surly attitude downright offensive. 'I can't believe I'm hearing this.'

'Hearing what? It's a simple enough request, goddammit! I'm asking you to help me get her out of there.'

She frowned. 'And what if she doesn't want to leave? What then?'

His expression darkened. 'If she doesn't I'll disown her. Tell her that.'

She knew he meant it and it chilled her to the bone. 'I'm sorry...' She shook her head more vehemently this time. 'I don't think I can help you. Get somebody else.'

He shifted in his chair, again tugging at the immaculate crease of his trousers as he recrossed his legs.

'I don't want anyone else.'

'Well you're going to have to find somebody else. My life is here. I can't help you.'

It was water off a duck's back.

'I'll cut you a deal. You take up the post and I'll donate a portion of my family's wealth into Victoria House. Think what you could do with more funding; have a proper office, not some impromptu division behind a screen. A new elevator. An extension to the building taking it out into the garden. P'raps have an operating theatre. A proper one. I'm pretty sure there are times when you need something a bit better than what you have.'

She thought of the babies she'd delivered out on the steps or in the foyer – even in front of her desk. What wouldn't she give for something better? Everything.

He'd wrong-footed her. Incoming money could do so much good. Despite her dislike for the man and her reluctance to take up the post in Korea, he'd sowed seeds of confusion. She couldn't dismiss his offer out of hand.

'That's very generous of you, though it seems now this is more about your daughter than any philanthropic tendencies on your part.'

'I'm not going to deny it. I'll give you a letter to take to her. To be opened by her when you get there. The letter will make everything clear. She'll tell you what's in it.'

Rowena frowned. She fancied there was even more to the story, that it was more than just persuading his daughter to come back. However, seeing as she had no intention of going she would not pry further.

She shook her head. 'I really don't think—'

'Before you refuse out of hand, there are other issues here that you should consider. I've spoken to some members on the board of trustees who are perhaps... upright Christians. Old school morals and all that.' He studied his fingernails which were pink and handsomely manicured. His eyes flashed up at her again. 'You're an unmarried mother. You must know that not all of the stuffed shirts on that committee approve of you. I've been called to that board at times. I listened. Stuck up for you. Hinted at the circumstances. Hardly your fault... a casualty of war, and that's besides the opium dealer you got involved with.'

Her anger boiled over. She sprang to her feet. 'How dare you!'

'Easy, easy!' He lifted his hands, making them flow across in front of him as though he were smoothing the waves on a lake. 'I took your side.'

'How very generous of you, though it smacks more of blackmail to me.'

'Get down from off your high horse. You know how people are. They gossip and have personal prejudices inherited from past generations.'

'Yes. Mostly people who spent the war thousands of miles away keeping up standards on the home front – their standards – pre-war bigotry nurtured in the safety of the Home Counties – not out here. Not until now!'

She spat the words out like bullets.

Warrington stared at her from either side of an aquiline nose.

'I've seen your file. Your history. There are other things...'

'What things?'

'Your pedigree.'

'My grandmother was Indian. From Bombay. So what?'

He made a kind of so-so movement with his head. 'So was my great-grandmother, though a different sort of Indian. Navajo, I believe. But that was way in the past and it's the present that matters most. This Irish guy you're involved with...'

She cut across him. 'Connor and I are planning to get married – when the time is right. We divide our time between my flat and his place.'

'Going to Korea is bound to help rebuild your reputation and influence the committee.'

'And what about my time in Japan? At Hiroshima? Doesn't that count for anything?'

The moment she saw the spit of triumph in his expression, she knew she'd said the wrong thing. His gaze dropped yet again to the file. Quite frankly she wished it would burst into flames leaving nothing but ashes and no information at all, but no doubt everything was in triplicate. Somewhere, another copy existed.

'You were dismissed from there for undermining orders and giving information to discredited parties.'

'You mean journalists. People were dying. It was only right that the world should know. Anyway, I would have thought my disobedience in the aftermath of one war would count against me getting posted anywhere else.'

'Are you a Communist?'

'No. I am not.'

His sandy-coloured upper lip bristled with military precision. He looked at her steadily and for a moment a look of sadness entered his eyes. It existed only fleetingly, flashing past like a meteor crashing to earth.

'I'm glad of that.'

He got to his feet, both hands – strong hands – pushing down on the chair arms.

He fixed her with a cold hard glare. 'I want my daughter back from there, Dr Rossiter. Before everything comes tumbling down like a pack of cards. It will all be explained in the letter I give you. For her eyes only – and then for yours.'

He put on his cap and nodded at her before disappearing behind the linen screen, the sound of his boots echoing in the outer foyer.

She sat there after he'd gone, not quite understanding why she felt so numb. So apprehensive. Until yesterday she had condemned his proposition out of hand. Hong Kong was her haven – or had been. Yesterday she had learned that the most frightening and the most beautiful man she had ever met was still alive and she could no longer take her safety for granted.

Duty called so although it took some effort, she pushed her misgivings aside. She had a clinic waiting and paitents' who needed her.

At the end of the day, tired and feeling she'd done her best for her patients she took the creaking lift to the top floor. No longer preoccupied with diagnosing disease and treating wounds, old memories and fears resurfaced. If only the lift would go faster. She needed to feel safe again. The prospect of going through that door had rarely been so welcoming. Her steps quickened, her hands trembled as she jammed in the key and turned the handle.

The door firmly shut behind her, she leaned against it until her heart had ceased banging like a drum. The familiar and well beloved was here in front of her. This was her refuge and tonight, more than ever before, it was much appreciated.

Over time she'd made this place her own, finding modern

furniture, curtains and paintings reflecting her own taste rather than the more flamboyant furnishings Kim Pheloung had favoured.

Details of that first time she'd come here had faded with time, but tonight they came back to haunt her.

He'd been waiting outside the hospital, had offered her breakfast, brought her back here where he'd even provided slippers for her aching feet. She recalled the cold look in the eyes of his grandmother. It was she who had opened the lift door, welcoming her grandson and totally ignoring her, tottering around on bound feet.

All gone. Or so she had thought.

After a bath and pouring herself a drink, she stared out of the window. Before her eyes new buildings were rising from the remains of the old. Beyond them ships lay at anchor in the harbour, both the dark water and the city speckled with polka dots of light, so many more lights than in years gone past.

Despite the influx of refugees Hong Kong had recovered quickly from Japanese occupation and seemed set on becoming an even bigger cog in the world of finance than it had been in the past.

Horns sounded from ships at anchor in the harbour, their lights splashed around them like fallen moons, and all around them, dotted like stars, were the twinkling lanterns on sampans and Chinese junks.

Despite everything that had happened, Hong Kong was her home, thanks in no small extent to Connor and her own dedication to her profession. Was she being paranoid in thinking that Kim Pheloung would seek her out and try and resume where he'd left off?

Her blood ran cold at the thought of how he'd tried to control her, mould her into the creature he wished her to be. Other women had been taken to pieces and restructured by him. The challenge was in doing the same with an educated woman, one brought up in a different world with different values. She'd been lucky. With the help of Luli and Koto, she'd managed to escape.

A shiver ran down her back like iced water. She rubbed at the goose pimples on her arms and looked down at the view.

'Don't be silly. You're being paranoid.' Her words were whispered but saying them out loud seemed to diminish the fear that was constricting her mind. Up until now there had been no fear, no haunting vision lurking like a dark shadow just beyond her sight. Sharing the dire news with Connor would help enormously. She really should have done it earlier, but having him standing in front of her, like a bulwark against all comers, he would be her strength and her shield.

Seeing him this evening would be more than it usually was and she couldn't wait for him to arrive. She would tell him what had transpired and all would be well. It had to be tonight. And what about Colonel Warrington's offer? Should she tell him about that? It seemed trivial compared to the news about Kim and yet deep down she couldn't help feeling that it mattered a great deal. Why, she wasn't quite sure.

The smell of dinner was in the air, the table was laid and she'd helped herself to another glass of wine, sipping it thoughtfully whilst working on the small speech she intended deliverying, firstly about Kim and then about Korea.

She would laugh and say, 'Fancy thinking I could be persuaded to go there. I think I've had more than enough of war.'

He came in wearing his own troubled smile, his violin case tucked beneath his arm. With a weary sigh he set it down on an armchair.

Perhaps it was down to her nervousness that she pounced on it and propped it against the wall. 'Don't put it there. It's for sitting on.' Her voice was crisp, her manner abrupt.

There was a questioning look in his eyes, then he smiled as though her sudden fastidious manner amused him. 'OK.'

Their eyes met as she passed him a measure of decent red burgundy she'd been given by one of her French colleagues. She could not hold his gaze and although she smiled, she could see the quizzical look, the faint frown that told her he knew something was troubling her.

Wine passed their lips. A hint of awkwardness persisted. He turned away, picked up his violin, placed it on the edge of the walnut cocktail cabinet and then glanced at her.

'OK if I put it here?'

'Of course it is. I just didn't want either of us to sit on it.'

She did her best to sound flippant.

'Then I'll play you a tune.'

He gave her a quick peck on the cheek and after taking a deep draught of wine, tucked the violin under his chin and picked up the bow.

She sat on the arm of the sofa. His eyes followed her, always searching, always incisive.

'Been working too hard?'

'I'm sorry. Just a little tired.'

'Is that all?'

'Isn't that enough?'

'Probably. Never mind, my darling, music calms the troubled breast... Relax.'

Cupping her glass in her hand she slid from the arm and made herself comfortable against the sofa cushions.

With gentle persuasion, he drew out a tune; the sound like gossamer on the air, fragile and poignant. The words ran through her mind, Connor's own version that he insisted was the right one.

My love's an arbutus
By the borders of Lene,
So slender and shapely
In her girdle of green.
And I measure the pleasure
Of her eye's sapphire sheen,
My love's an arbutus on the borders of Lene.

He looked at her over the strings of his instrument and the bow. The tune was softer now and his eyes were fixed on her face. 'Are you thinking the words?'

'More than just those words. Other words. Everything.'

'What do you mean by "everything"?'

'Everything is you. Connor, you're a refrain that stays in my mind.'

His eyes met hers over the top of the sliding bow and the curved gloss of the violin, the shape of which he compared to the body of a beautiful woman. A woman like her.

'When I hear your music or sing what you sing to me, you are with me even though you might be a thousand miles away.'

'As I once was.'

His voice was music to her ears, yet there was tension. She was choosing her moment; as for Connor, he was waiting, aware that something was going on.

This stiffness between them was uncharacteristic. Their habit, after all these years, was still to embrace and kiss passionately, barely controlling the desire that still burned in their bodies. By not allowing that desire to smoulder and spiral to the surface, each knew the other had worries.

Telling him all that had happened was proving more difficult than she'd envisaged so she parried his unspoken question with her own.

'You're worried about something,' she said as the last note drifted away. 'I can tell.'

'Funny, I was thinking the same about you. You didn't sing. You've got a fine voice. You should sing more than you do. It exercises the larynx.' He pointedly cleared his throat.

She shrugged. 'Overwork.'

'That's nothing new. There's something else. What's troubling you, girl?'

She frowned, looked down into her glass and immediately wanted a refill.

'I read your mind,' said Connor as he refilled her glass. 'Which is something of a change. You're always reading mine.'

'So what do you think I'm worried about?'

He took a sip of his own glass then chewed at his lips as he thought it through.

'Your brother back in England.'

'Certainly not.'

Clifford and his wife had declined to give her and Dawn

a home immediately following the end of the war. She still seethed at the last letter she'd had from him, angered by his blatant refusal, '*we already have one half caste child in this village, and having another, even of a different race, might not be a good idea*. Reading between the lines she herself would have been welcome. All she had needed to do was put the child into an orphanage or have her adopted by 'some of her own people'. That's what he would have suggested. He just hadn't got it that Dawn was part of her, so should therefore be one of *her* people.

'Is it true that there's a war brewing?'

'Ah!' He threw back his head. 'We're talking of Korea. Do you know, I met Koreans in the war but hadn't a clue as to the longitude and latitude of their country. Thought it was further south. It's up north with China and Japan as neighbours.'

'Do you think they'll call you up?'

He arched his eyebrows, seemingly surprised by her question.

'I can refuse.'

'Will you refuse?'

'I'm old enough to be able to. Don't worry.'

He replaced the violin in its case and swigged back the rest of the wine.

She felt his eyes on her when she poured herself another drink.

'It's good wine,' she said by way of an excuse for drinking so much – and she was drinking more than she usually did. Dutch courage, even though the wine was French.

'The wine's fine. Your worries are… worrying. It might never happen.'

'I hope it doesn't. Hard to believe that anyone can be contemplating war after such butchery and fifty million dead.'

She noted a deepening of the frown line across his brow, his deep blue eyes like patches of weed just below the surface of the sea. She could feel the intensity of his gaze, studying her in a bid to find some way in to what she was thinking.

Her mouth was dry, but she managed to utter the pertinent question. 'Have they called up the reservists yet?'

He shook his head. 'The regulars are already there, but it won't be enough. China is pushing the Koreans to reunite what would become a satellite Communist country.'

'So there is a possibility of you going.'

'They'll call the younger men first, boys of eighteen, only lately using a razor. More young men! Good God! Couldn't somebody have worked out a settlement to suit everybody?'

He slammed down his glass so hard that the stem broke. A small cut oozed blood.

'Damn!' He looked down at it with surprise.

Rowena took hold of his hand. His eyes softened with surprise as she covered the cut with her lips in an attempt to stem the blood flow.

'There's something else,' he said quietly.

She didn't look up but continued to suck at his wound, her tongue licking her lips.

When she failed to answer he took hold of her shoulders. 'There's something on your mind and it's not just about the possibility of me going away to fight.'

Suddenly his eyes glowed with hope. 'Are you pregnant? I won't be going anywhere if you are. Compassionate grounds. Now wouldn't that be something.'

She shook her head. 'No. I wish I was.'

He stroked her hair, her cheek and her chin, lifting it so she couldn't help but look into his eyes.

'So don't tell me that hangdog expression is about nothing. I know you better than that, darling.'

'I'm just worried about you.'

'That's nice of you, but I've known you long enough to know there's something else. I can see it in your eyes. Come on. Spill the beans, as the Yanks say.'

She took a deep breath.

'The powers that be, in the person of Colonel Sherman Warrington, came to see me today.'

Connor frowned. 'What did he want?'

'He's offered me a position in Korea. At first he assured me it would be of benefit to my career – especially in the eyes of the UN observers. Perhaps also to the trustees of Victoria House and the Red Cross.'

'I fancy there's a big but to this.'

She smiled and hung her head. 'You're right. It's more than that.'

'Tell me, and if you say that he's made you an indecent proposal, I'm likely to lay down my violin and pick up a machine gun.'

'Nothing like that. The Red Cross have a need for a doctor, and he asked if I would be interested.'

'And you said you wouldn't be interested.'

'How do you know I said that?'

'Because you have commitments here and I'm one of them.'

'I'm being pressurised. I felt there was something else to his proposal and there was. His daughter's a nurse. He wanted me to go there with a view to delivering a letter and persuading her to leave. That's what made me think there's a war about to start and he wants his daughter out of there.'

'Ah! I see your point.'

'What does that mean?'

'He thinks there's trouble brewing and he's probably right.'

'That doesn't sound very promising.'

'So where is this place?'

'It's a convent near Seoul, the capital. They've specifically asked for a woman doctor.'

His frown deepened. 'I'm not going to ask you not to go there because I know you'll make your own mind up. I've never dictated to you before and I'm not going to start now.'

'Thank you. He's very persuasive.'

'What about Victoria House? They won't want you to go, surely.'

Affection tugged at her heart. In Connor's opinion she was the best doctor ever and nobody could not want her. Even though she'd mentioned friction with the trustees, he'd refused to believe they could actually do without her. She loved him for it.

She shrugged. 'He seems aware that the board of trustees might be very relieved if I go. He's even talking about donating money to Victoria House if I accept.'

Connor's eyebrows lifted in surprise. 'He sounds desperate.'

'And nastily persuasive. Apparently there's been gossip about me being an unmarried mother, and whether I was suitable for the job. There's also gossip about our relationship – sultry nights in my bed or yours.'

His smile was broad. 'That should keep their blood pressure up.'

'It's not funny,' she said and smiled through the pout she pasted on her lips, at the same time tasting his residual blood.

Connor laughed. 'Old blokes and old bats. I bet some of them have never seen their wives in the nude. Turn their light off prior to a quick fumble beneath their nightgowns.'

His own smile faded. No amount of humour was going to smooth her troubled brow. Normally they would both laugh at what he'd said but not tonight.

'The board of trustees might be persuaded to remove me. Some are of the old colonial set who don't think women should work once they marry – especially if they have children.'

'Then that's settled. We get married – if that helps.'

Rowena turned her head away from him. 'We said we wouldn't. Not until we had to.'

'My God, can you hear what you're saying? If the old memsahibs with their big hats and small minds heard you say that, then you'd be out of a job quicker than you could say get knitting.'

She grinned. 'You know I can't knit.'

'Ah, it's disappointed I am. What kind of a homemaker does that make you? I'm a man who appreciates knitted socks. Anyway,' he said, his expression tightening, his eyes turning darker. 'I won't let you go to Korea. And don't let anyone tell you that war won't happen, and that even if it does it's bound to be over by Christmas. We've heard all that malarkey before. Nothing was ever over by Christmas.'

She wrapped her arms around him and laid her head

against his shoulder, breathed in his smell, caressed the cloth of his jacket.

'When will we learn?'

She felt the heat of his palms through the thin fabric of her dress and was aroused. His hand moved up to smooth her hair. She closed her eyes, and horrific as it was, she was glad that Korea had given her an excuse to look worried if it meant having her concerns smoothed away like this.

Her sigh hinted at relief and drew his attention.

'Cheer up, sweetheart. You won't be going off to Korea if I've got anything to do with it.'

'There's something—'

'Shhh!' He sniffed. 'Is that dinner I can smell becoming well done?'

'Damn!'

The moment was drowned out by the sound of saucepans and plates clattering, her attention temporarily transferred to the braised fish with rice and pan-fried vegetables, a mixture of bean sprouts, chestnuts and other exotic ingredients she'd bought from a street stall.

The delicious smell of fish sauce she'd made herself from shellfish flavoured with herbs and spices floated on the air in a pungent mist. Breathing in the smell was almost as satisfying as tasting it.

Connor found a replacement glass and poured the wine, filling both his and her glasses two thirds of the way to the brim. The bottle was empty.

Once they were sitting with food-filled dishes in front of them, she became aware of him looking at her as though realising that there was something else on her mind.

He raised his glass. 'I meant it about getting married. It would have to be a twenty-four-hour licence.'

Rowena wrinkled her nose behind her open palm and laughed.

'People will think we have to.'

'We would have anyway if we'd stuck to the original plan of waiting until you were expecting.'

Their laughter dissipated as the disappointment they'd harboured for years locked their eyes.

Somehow they'd both expected starting a family to be easy and when it proved otherwise had consoled themselves that at least they had the fun of trying. As the months and years went on they talked less and less of the reasons why it might never happen, leaving unsaid that the starvation and deprivation in the war years had perhaps done unseen damage to their bodies. Perhaps it would never be possible to have children. But they did have Dawn and even though Connor was not her natural father, he treated her as though he was.

'I was glad to hear that Dawn is coming home. I've missed her.'

'So have I.'

His face darkened and his bottom lip sucked inwards as he reached for a piece of bread. She knew immediately that he was keeping something from her.

'Connor. You've got something on your mind too. What is it?'

'Oh. Nothing much,' he said with a toss of his head

'Tell me the truth.'

He turned his attention from the wine to the food,

fingering the bread into crumbs, dipping it into the sauce without actually raising it to his mouth.

'Connor?'

'Thinking about us and the future. Don't want to run a bar for the rest of my life.'

His brow furrowed into a deeper frown that made her pulse quicken, the sound of blood flowing faster in her ears.

She looked searchingly up into his face. 'What is it?'

He sighed and threw down the bread, smacked his hands together like an act of finality.

'The old man across the road – the blind man?'

'What about him?'

'The conclusion is that he was murdered. His neck was broken by an iron-hard hand.'

She gasped. 'How terrible. Do they know who did it?'

He shook his head. 'All they know is that he acted as a lookout for criminal gangs. He might have looked as though he was blind, but he was far from it.' He paused, reluctant to tell her the rest but aware that she needed to be alert. 'McCloud thinks he was employed to keep an eye on the comings and goings at the bar, perhaps to watch one person in particular. Whoever paid him to do it no longer needed him and didn't want him opening his mouth, it could be… Darling? What's the matter? You've gone white as a sheet.'

It suddenly felt to her as though all the air had been drawn from the room. Her hand rested on her throat, gasping as she took in what he had said.

So she told him about Koto, her pregnancy, and the fact that Kim was the father, and far from being dead was alive and kicking, and perhaps ready to take up where he'd left off.

They sat up until the early hours without finishing a second bottle, half the food going cold and congealing on their plates.

'I wasn't going to tell you what McCloud had to say.'

'I wasn't sure about telling you about Koto simply because I could hardly believe what she told me. I didn't *want* to believe what she told me.'

Connor slumped back on the unfussy sofa that was of a straight-backed modern design.

'I feel I should run and hide, but far from here. Perhaps even back to England.'

'We might anyway. Depending on what happens.'

'And when it happens.'

Connor grunted. 'That's for tomorrow.' He glanced at his wristwatch. 'Or today, depending on how you look at it. Come on.' He helped her to her feet. 'The dishes can wait.'

Chapter 6

The sight of her bare buttocks as she shuffled to the edge of the bed aroused him almost as much as her nakedness had aroused him the night before. Unfortunately neither of them had slept well. Still, watching her tripping lightly to the bathroom was adequate recompense for not sleeping. He lifted the bedclothes and eyed the length of his body. What chance for sex, he thought.

The sound of splashing water followed. He held her pillow against his face and breathed in the scent of her skin. They'd made love the night before but the thought of doing so again had entered his mind. All he needed was for his body to follow suit. Unfortunately it didn't look as though that was going to happen. She was off to work and he was getting older and not quite up to the job.

He sighed and, resigned that ambition was not matched by ability, he began to ease his own way out of the bed, swinging his legs over the side.

'I think it's best you come and stay with me. I can protect you better there,' he called out.

She came out from the bathroom rubbing at her face with a white towel, the rest of it hanging in front of her but hiding nothing.

'I can't possibly do that. You know I can't.'

'Then I move in here.'

'You've got a business to run.'

'I've got Yang.'

'And what will you do when I'm called out to a patient? Trail along behind me?'

He shrugged his naked shoulders and pulled on his shirt, began buttoning it.

'I can help. I can roll bandages – or something.'

'It will be "something", especially if it's a woman in labour.'

'I could pretend to be a doctor – or something.'

'Another of your somethings that just isn't feasible. And before you suggest it, you can't be a midwife either.'

'Once I've sorted it with Yang, I'm coming back over to stay with you.' His voice took on a lighter tone. 'At least it will give the board of trustees something to talk about.'

She let the towel drop to the floor and began to put on clean underwear, a girdle, slid stockings up her legs and fastened them to the rubber pop-button suspenders.

Connor said nothing. Despite the bad news he followed the stockings sliding up her legs like a second skin. He glanced at his watch. Too late to suggest going back to bed but at least he could hint at what she was doing to him.

'Are you doing that on purpose?'

She let her skirt drop over her hips and pulled up the zip. 'What?'

'You're a veritable femme fatale,' he said, getting to his feet. 'Dressing in front of me like that.'

'I won't ask whether you'd prefer me getting undressed in front of you.'

'You don't need to ask that. You know the answer.' He kissed her whilst relishing the curve of her hips beneath his hands. Like the shape of a violin.

She looked her usual confident self. Over the years he'd learned that she was good at looking confident even when she was not.

'Tell me you'll think it over about me moving in with you. Promise?'

'I will, but really, Connor, we have to be realistic and not become paranoid, though I must admit I was feeling that way. I've seen nothing of Kim and nobody has actually seen him...'

'Except Koto.'

'Except Koto. She's seen him since conceiving. He wanted her to get rid of the baby, but she ran so he must still be alive.'

Rowena began brushing her hair but stopped after just a few strokes. 'That means she's left her son behind. I'm thinking he must be in safe hands or she wouldn't have come to Hong Kong. I feel for her, I really do.'

Connor pulled up his trousers and tucked in his shirt. 'Promise me that if you do hear anything from him, if there's the slightest chance of him abducting you again, you let me move in. OK?'

There was an intense look in her eyes, so strong and so incisive that he couldn't hold her gaze.

'I've thought it through. The fact is, Connor, that if he

was going to abduct me surely he would have done so by now. He's had five years to come after me.'

'Unless he's only just come back to Hong Kong or is elsewhere. Koto didn't say he was in Hong Kong, did she?'

Rowena shook her head. 'No. She did not, but I can't help feeling...' Her eyes darkened as she attempted to seek an answer. 'Perhaps he's only just arrived back in Hong Kong. Even so, it begs the question why now? What's changed?'

Connor shrugged. 'Perhaps something. Perhaps nothing.'

It was sundown and the dying rays of the sun gilded the century-old buildings opposite Connor's Bar with a pink blush which made them look almost brand new. They looked clean too, the stonework washed by the storm, and even though it was days ago, water still dripped from half-formed gutters and the balustrades of jutting verandas.

It was a sight Connor had seen many times before and on those occasions the experience had been enjoyable. Life too had become more relaxed once the past with all its brutality had been buried in time – until now.

The house opposite was now empty. Rumour had it that the daughter had refused to live there since the death of her father and had gone to live with relatives in the New Territories.

Yang reacted with outright shock when Connor told him the news about Kim, and that he would be spending more time with Rowena.

Yang assured him that he would keep a lookout and ensure the bar would continue to thrive. He also apologised.

'I truly believed the news that he was dead, Connor. It was

a very reliable source. One of his own men. One who has now mended his ways and works for the United Nations.'

'And those who do business on the shady side, Yang. What do they say?'

He shook his head. 'His name is not mentioned. Dead men's names are not spoken of. It is unlucky to do so.'

'But dead men don't father children.'

Yang looked embarrassed, his thin dark eyebrows forming a deep V. 'This is true.' He shook his head. 'I do not understand. I was assured of his death. He went back to Shanghai too many times.'

'This man who works for the UN, can you give me his name?'

'Yes. He is called Ling Jones.'

Now it was Connor who raised his eyebrows. 'His name's Jones?'

'Yes. Ling Jones. Ling is his family name, of course, and his personal name is Jones. He only kept half his Chinese name. He took the name Jones to honour his grandfather. His mother told him that his father had been a sailor with the Royal Navy and came from a place called Cardiff. Do you know this place, boss?'

Connor nodded. 'Yes. I do.'

'And the family Jones. Do you know them too?'

'Not personally, though I have to tell you, Yang old friend, that there are a lot of them in Cardiff. Hundreds if not thousands.'

He didn't have time to explain that Jones was as common a clan name in Wales as Lee was in the Chinese community.

Connor decided he would pay this man a visit despite his shady background. Even criminals and enemies could be useful; he'd seen that proved when the victorious British had used the occupying Japanese forces to keep order in Hong Kong at the end of the war.

'No matter.'

He thought about Nan Po, the man who had appeared to be blind. Nobody had suspected him of being anything else. Thus everyone had moved freely, including Rowena.

Where there was one lookout there could be many more. Somebody following. Somebody *in situ* over at Victoria House, perhaps.

No matter Rowena protesting that she didn't need a bodyguard, he intended staying close to her. The bar would be fine with Yang though he wished there was somebody else to give extra support.

Connor's Bar was not the same as it had been before the war. The decor had been modernised but still had a Chinese theme, low lighting, red lanterns and cane furniture with deep padded cushions replacing the old stuff that opium addicts had once relaxed on.

Golden dragons writhed on two black lacquered screens set on either side of the bar. Behind one was the door to his private quarters. Behind the other was a thicker door barring the way to a room with thick carpets, a blackjack table, roulette, and a table specifically for card games.

Admittance was limited to members who could afford the membership fee, and the serious gamblers of Hong Kong definitely could. He'd initially suspected that the old man had been watching one of these, reporting back to somebody anticipating blackmail or even kidnap. It could be either and they certainly had a choice of wealthy and powerful people. Bankers, government officials, rich

Chinese merchants and those whose business interests were not entirely legal liked to unwind with a drink and a card game or a spin of the wheel. The news that Kim was still alive altered everything. It was very likely that Nan Po had been watching Rowena.

Keeping close to Rowena was not going to be easy. He needed the help of the Hong Kong police and there was only one member of that august group who could be guaranteed to keep a close watch on the place. So where was he?

His wristwatch told him that barely a quarter of an hour had passed since the last time he'd glanced at it. Eventually, as dusk descended and the lights went on all over Kowloon, a dark green Land Rover skidded to a halt outside, sending a cloud of dust and grit spinning out from beneath the deep tread tyres. Brandon McCloud got out from the driving seat, slammed the door shut and strolled into the bar.

Connor reached for the bottle of Glenmorangie he kept just for the high-ranking police officer and poured him a drink.

Brandon, like himself, had been a soldier, though in a different strand of the armed forces. Having served in the military police on demobilisation, he'd made a sideways move and risen swiftly through the ranks of the Hong Kong police.

'You should be one of us,' Brandon had said when they'd first met. Connor had shuddered at the thought and knocked back a measure of Bushmills best Irish whiskey to help drown the sour taste in his mouth.

'I've had enough of taking orders. I prefer to give them,' he'd said, nodding to where a white-jacketed waiter was showing a high-ranking civil servant and his mistress to their favourite table.

Brandon downed his drink like a man denied a dram for a week – which was hardly likely. Brandon was Scottish and as such figured it part of his patriotic duty to keep the whisky industry going.

Connor poured a refill without asking whether he wanted one.

Brandon nodded his thanks, frowning over the depths of his thoughts.

Connor looked him up and down.

'You've lost weight.' He wanted to know what was going on with the investigation, but first to put the man at his ease.

'It's the job. The worry.' Brandon rubbed at his stomach. 'The doc said I'd get stomach ulcers if I didn't lose some weight.'

'So you've cut down on food.'

Brandon flashed him a defensive look. 'Well I'm not going to bloody cut down on drink. That is sacrosanct, my friend, bloody sacrosanct!'

He downed the second glass so quickly it couldn't have touched the sides of his throat.

Connor had known him long enough to estimate fairly accurately that he was ready to talk. He would also know what Connor wanted him to talk about.

'Any news on the old man's death?'

It worried him when Brandon gulped down the third drink and then kept his eyes on the empty glass. He felt his stomach muscles tighten. Intuition, as his old mother would say. Something bad was about to be said.

'It's difficult to get information. You know how it is here. Anyone daring to talk is likely to be found floating face down in the harbour. But we did get a piece of information from a source we've used before. The old man was an uncle – or some kind of relative – to a bodyguard working for a shady character who used to be a big gang boss in Hong Kong before and during the war. Used to control most of the opium trade, apparently. You've been here a while. Ever come across him?'

'Kim Pheloung.' Connor fingered his glass, his eyes downcast.

Brandon looked surprised. 'You know him?'

'Knew him.' Now it was Connor's turn to down a stiff whiskey – Irish, of course – before giving him a short resumé. He explained about the bar in the days when Yang had owned it but failed to keep up with paying protection money. Pheloung had come down on him heavily, threatened his life. In desperation Yang had sold the bar to Connor and his old friend Harry Gracey who, being members of the ruling British elite, were more difficult to intimidate. He went on to tell Brandon about Pheloung's obsession with Rowena.

'I wouldn't hold that against him. I could easily get obsessed with her myself if I didn't know how good you might be with that kukri you keep behind the bar.'

Brandon nodded at the curved knife glinting from its hanging place. The piece was genuine and had once been used by a member of His Majesty's Gurkha Rifles, strong and wiry men from mountainous Nepal who had made something of a career fighting in the Far East for the British Empire.

Connor refilled his glass.

'I've heard a rumour that he's alive, which is a shame. I'd much prefer him dead. Do you know for sure that he's back in Hong Kong?'

Brandon shook his head. 'No. I haven't come across him.'

'If I know anything about Kim Pheloung he will be attempting to build up his old empire. He's not the sort to give in easily. I had heard he was executed by the Chinese for collaborating with the Japanese just a while back. I would have thought if they'd spared him we would have heard from him by now.'

'Unless he was forced to join them, allow himself to be brainwashed, re-educated, as they like to say. Might have become a changed man.'

Connor frowned. 'No.' He shook his head. 'He might have appeared to change, but on his terms. He might very well have changed them. Kim was – and perhaps still is – very much his own man. The Chinese might have met their match.'

Brandon frowned. 'From what you say it seems strange that we haven't punched his ticket – or at least heard of him.' He shook his head. 'No. The name isn't mentioned in the whirlpool of Hong Kong crime, I'm afraid. At least, not lately, though he has a history so we do have a file.'

Connor noticed Yang behind the bar, eyes downcast, but obviously listening to every word.

Brandon was making other suggestions.

'According to the file he disappeared for some time. Rumours abound that he fled to Japan then French Indochina. I believe he has family in Saigon. A mother and three brothers so we're led to believe. Their father was Malay, though, but he's no longer around. Died on the Death Railway, so rumour has it, and that's perfectly believable. We go on about eighty thousand Allied troops dying on that railway but it pales into insignificance when compared to the quarter of a million Malays, Siamese, Burmese and suchlike. Enough people to fill a city.'

Having sounded forth like a minister of the Kirk on a Sunday morning, Brandon suddenly noticed that Connor's face had drained of colour.

'Connor. You look as though you've seen a ghost.'

Connor nodded. 'Nobody really knew his pedigree. The name Pheloung sounds foreign but I'm not sure that it is. My guess is it never was his real name. It's all part of the subterfuge, you see – he will be whatever he has to be to get what he wants. He used to have a house in the walled city. Yang experienced the exploitive side of his nature. He was the biggest opium dealer in Hong Kong. I know that for a fact,' he added, suddenly feeling sick to his stomach. His friend Harry had become an addict and Rowena had attracted Kim's unwelcome attention; two reasons for wanting to kill Kim himself.

Brandon frowned. 'He might still be there in the walled city. That's where all thieves, cut-throats and murderers hide. It's like a rabbit warren and getting bigger. There used to be less than two hundred living there now it's thousands and still growing.'

'He'd taken over one of the houses that used to belong to a Chinese administrator. I suppose it's still there amongst the shanty town that's sprung up there of late.'

'Well, all we know is that one of your customers was of interest to somebody – only so far we don't know which of your customers was being watched or the identity of whoever was paying the old man. It might not have been your friend Kim.'

Connor listened, wishing he didn't feel so helpless and had answers: number one being Kim Pheloung's whereabouts.

Thanks to Rowena he knew so much more about the man. Even now he could feel her body shaking beneath his hands, her head on his shoulder, voice half muffled into the pillow as she related what it had been like to be his creature. One minute she was imprisoned in a POW camp, and the next living in Kim's house in Shanghai, but a prisoner all the same. Kim Pheloung is or was a psychopath. 'He collects women in the same way that other people collect butterflies,' she'd whispered against his shoulder.

Traps them, thought Connor, and couldn't help comparing him to Victorian collectors who'd pinned live butterflies to velvet mounts, beautiful creatures trapped behind glass.

His thoughtful silence attracted Brandon's attention.

'There's something you're not telling me. What is it?'

Connor fingered his glass. He wanted to say this right but at the same time he was in a hurry to catch the ferry and join Rowena in her penthouse flat.

'I know for a fact that Kim Pheloung isn't dead.'

He went on to tell Brandon about Rowena being called to Kowloon Walled City and delivering Koto's baby, Kim's baby.

'She shouldn't have gone in there. That place is nothing but a damned cesspit.'

'She's a doctor – and headstrong.'

Brandon smiled and finished his drink.

'I don't think you need worry about this bloke seeming

to have come back from the dead. He's definitely not the big cheese in Hong Kong at present. The *taipan* of crime, the new *luoban,* is called Fu Chan.'

Connor frowned. 'Fu Chan! Sounds like a character from a cheap crime novel.'

Brandon threw back his head and laughed. At the same time he reached for his drink.

'You're thinking of Fu Manchu who was a villain, and Charlie Chan who was a private detective. I do enjoy a good detective novel.'

Connor grinned as something totally absurd struck him. 'I can't believe that a real cop like you reads pulp fiction.'

Brandon reached for his hat and his swagger stick.

'Every man deserves a little light relief. The reality is grievous, Connor. I only wished I could solve cases like Sherlock Holmes. I know what you mean though, and there is evidence to suggest that it isn't his real name.' He frowned. 'We've heard him called by another name – Koos Maas.'

'Dutch?'

'Possibly.'

'It sounds more realisitic.'

As Connor fingered his empty glass, an odd feeling of disappointment came over him. He'd been convinced that Kim had returned to Hong Kong and taken over the reins of every racket, including the lucrative opium trade. From what Brandon had told him, this just wasn't so. There was a new man in town. His joke about the man's name receded. Using a combination of the names of two characters from fiction was amusing, but whoever this man was, he was far from being a laughing matter.

'So have you met this new crime boss?'

Brandon shook his head. 'He's like a spider in the midst of the web, too far inside to be seen. Quite frankly we haven't a clue what he looks like. We heard a rumour he was some kind of invalid – though what kind we haven't a clue.'

'Kim was far from that.'

'That was then.'

Chapter 7

The woman approaching the ferry that would take her across to Hong Kong looked nervously about her. She was dressed in a padded knee-length coat, warm woollen trousers and shoes with thick soles. Despite her sturdy footwear she walked unsteadily, as though she had an impediment in her shoe, perhaps in both shoes.

One of her arms was wound around the small bundle of humanity carried papoose style against her chest. In her free hand she carried another bundle made out of a sheet, its four corners tied together and forming a rudimentary handle through which she had slipped her pale white hand.

Dawn was breaking over the arrival of the first ferry of the day but she did not raise her eyes to welcome the warmth of the rising sun, but kept her head down, her face hidden behind a silk scarf that an older woman might wear.

Taking small careful steps up the gangplank she breathed a sigh of relief when the rough boards of the deck were creaking beneath her feet.

Her body remained tense, her shoulders squared until

three short blasts on the ship's horn signalled that it was moving backwards, before another single blast signalled it was going forwards and out into the channel.

With the sun warming her face, she gazed towards the growing conglomeration that was Hong Kong, where new buildings were growing like weeds along the shoreline.

The baby mewed in her arms and a pair of tiny hands clenched into pink fists as though she was ready and willing to fight her way through the world.

The closer the boat got to Hong Kong, the more the woman relaxed, smiling as she found a bench to sit where she exposed her nipple to the baby's hungry mouth.

'There, my child. Not long now. We will make our way to our friend Luli. She has a place for us.'

Kowloon was behind them. Hong Kong was straight ahead.

There was much noise around her, the shouting of dock labourers as they caught the ship's thick hawsers thrown to them by the crew. This was the first time she'd ever been on a boat so she found everything quite fascinating. Over the pale mound of her feeding breast, she eyed the people around her; men and women on their way to work for companies or the colony's administration, children in the company of a nanny on their way to the more exclusive schools on Hong Kong Island.

All around her was noise, people speaking, their breath like mist on the morning air.

Briefly her gaze landed on a thickset man in black, a cigarette hanging from the corner of his mouth which he threw into the black water just before the ferry bumped against the quay.

Luli had scribbled a map so she could more easily find her way to the refugee camp – a sister camp to that on Kowloon, hastily converted from old army barracks. She'd memorised the map and knew she had to bear left and then right.

People bustled past her on all sides, like a tidal wave flooding out through the main gate onto a wide straight road with smaller ones branching off like twigs from a tree trunk.

Initially spurred on by the sense of danger, her energy was now beginning to sag, the weight of the baby plus her bundle straining her arms, and she tottered on feet which she'd attempted to bind to please Kim Pheloung. It had pleased him for a time, wanting her to feel acute pain in order to prove her love for him.

Grey buildings to either side of her, ramshackle balconies clinging to their fragile walls, became etched with the gathering gold of the rising sun. This is a good omen, thought Koto, forgetting that only a few years past a flag depicting the rising sun had induced fear in the populace of both Hong Kong and China.

The crowds persisted all the way to the camp, pressing around her, speeding up her footsteps to such an extent that her toes and the bones of her feet felt close to breaking point.

She was far from being the only refugee pushing their way forward, fanning out from the orderly crocodile the guards were trying to get them to form.

A hum of harried comments went on around her. The baby stirred in her arms. She kept her eyes fixed on the entrance, praying that the doctor who had delivered her baby would vouch for her, keep her safe.

Steadily, bit by bit, the column of hopeful people shuffled forward, their closeness pressing, their smell cloying.

Just as she tried to turn her head, somebody else pushed in behind her, their body even tighter against her than the last one. A woman caught hold of her arm and pulled her sideways.

She asked after the health of the child. Koto responded that she was OK. OK was the word everyone was using since the crushing of Japan. Very Western. Very American.

For a short time she was propelled away from the press of bodies, her ribs expanding against the swift inrush of air. The entrance was just a few feet away now and her heart thudded at the thought of passing into its relative safety. Most people would regard being enclosed by its high walls a great imposition. She did not, for in here she might find safety.

A few more steps…

Just as she got to the gate, a scuffle broke out behind her, a wall of bodies crashing into the back of her and pushing her forward.

The camp guards heaved their rifles onto their shoulders and shouted for order.

When nothing happened they shouted a warning and, when that failed to produce results, fired over their heads. People screamed and headed in all directions, now mostly away from the wall.

A chaotic crush surrounded her, so tight she felt her ribs were being crushed. Suddenly there was a small relief as a gap was created by a man behind her. She looked round, meaning to thank him, recognised him from somewhere and instead of smiling, grimaced, tried to run, but his hands were big and strong.

She didn't scream or shout at him to let her go because it would do no good. All she could do was wait her chance, but when it came he was ready for her.

His big ugly foot stamped hard on one of hers. Even though she no longer bound her feet to please Kim, the pain was sudden and excruciating. She cried out, barely managing to use her bundled belongings to cushion the baby as they both fell to the ground, and flinging herself sideways so she didn't fall on top of the baby.

The glint of a sharp blade flashed in front of her eyes. 'I come to you, my ancestors,' she whispered, sure that this was the last day of her life.

The baby and the cloth that had held her to her mother's breast fell forward, the ragged ends evidence that the cloth had been sliced from around her neck. Hands with thick fingers, palms as round as a rice bowl, caught the newborn like a mango in his brutish hands. One of his hands still held a knife.

Koto prostrated herself, arms outstretched above her head. 'Please! My baby!'

He jerked his chin. 'Get up. Follow.'

A look of utter relief swept over her face as she raised her eyes. The baby was crying, but thankfully still alive.

She hurried after the man who carried her child, taking three small steps to every stride of his, her heart quaking with fear.

Hurrying as she was, her breath was like a stabbing pain in her chest.

'Please. Slow down. Please?'

Daylight was swallowed up as a narrow alley ran into another that was even narrower, until at last it was only wide enough for the broad-shouldered man in front of her to move sideways.

Finally he stopped in a dead end, a high wall in front and brooding buildings on either side. The smell of human excrement mingled on the air with spices and lilies. Above them a strip of sky wound like a ribbon between the buildings.

Koto trembled as she was pushed in front of him and before a closed door which was painted so dark a green it was almost black and blended with the walls to either side of it.

A cat meandered across the threshold, the limp body of a rat hanging from its jaws.

Her abductor glanced briefly at it before transferring the baby to one huge hand almost as though he was about to throw it into a basketball net, or worse still to the cat, thus providing a larger feast than the one it was presently holding in its jaws.

Without a word being said, Koto knew she was obliged to follow this man. The life of her newborn was literally in his hands.

Connor tracked down Ling Jones working in the kitchens of the UN command. Although combat troops from other countries were present, the majority of army and diplomatic personnel were American.

He'd known even before arriving that getting in wouldn't be that easy so he'd prepared himself a cover story. He believed he'd located Lee's father, a Welshman from Cardiff who he christened David Lloyd Jones. He congratulated himself on the name. It sounded genuine and at the same time slightly memorable.

'I thought Ling might like the details,' he said with brimming confidence.

The guard eyed him as though he was carrying a time bomb in his pocket but loosened up on noting his rank and army reserve status on his identity card.

'A father, you say.'

Connor nodded. 'Jones Ling's father was Welsh. Hence his surname being Jones.'

The soldier grinned and shook his head. 'You know that's always thrown me – the surname coming before the first name – Christian or otherwise.'

'Chinese custom.'

'You got it.' He shook his head some more as he handed back the identity card. 'He'll be an outside auxiliary support – kitchens, cleaners and general maintenance. Let me check.'

He rifled through a sheaf of papers attached to a clipboard hanging from a hook in the guard station, stopped at the third or fourth one in – it was hard to tell which.

As if he couldn't quite believe what he was seeing, he unhitched the clipboard from its rightful place and took a closer look.

'Kitchen worker. Would that be right?'

'I suppose it must be.'

Another bout of headshaking.

'Well not any more. He took off two days ago.'

'Took off? Took off where?

'Don't know, bud. He don't work here any more and that's for sure.'

Connor frowned. He hadn't allowed for this and although he was inclined to ask the soldier to take another look it was really grasping at straws. There was only one more question that might – just might – bear fruit.

'Do you have an address?'

The fresh-faced soldier who looked to have spent little more than a year in uniform, shook his head.

'Not my department. You need to speak to the office that deals with alien employment. I'll give them a ring and see if they can fit you in.'

'I would appreciate you doing that.'

Phone clamped to his ear, the soldier looked bored as he waited for somebody to answer and turned to conversation.

'Couldn't help notice that you're a sergeant in the reserves. Saw much action in the war?'

'Plenty.'

The soldier's eyes shone with enthusiasm. 'Hey, that's great.'

'Not really.'

'But you were there, right? In a real war.'

'It was real, all right,' Connor answered grimly.

The young man beamed with admiration. 'Killed plenty, I bet. Wish I'd been old enough to fight in that war. Missed all the fun.'

Fun! That was the last word Connor would have used to

describe what he'd endured, what he'd seen and what he'd lost.

Old images were resurrected. He felt sick to his stomach, wanted to grab hold of the greenhorn and shake him till his eyeballs fell out whilst telling him that it wasn't exciting, it was sickening, dirty and nasty. He didn't want to talk about it; wouldn't want to talk about it for a very long time. He shared those memories with few people.

Rowena was the only person who knew some of what he'd gone through, mostly because they had been in similar situations at the same time. They'd both seen how brutal humanity could be.

He bit back his anger. The nausea subsided.

Somebody at the other end of the phone suddenly answered and the soldier almost snapped to attention even though he couldn't be seen.

'Corporal, there's a man here wanting to get in touch with one of our kitchen operatives.'

It was a woman on the other end, and no big surprise. Quite a few administrative personnel were female nowadays.

There was a pause as she asked a question.

'Jones Ling, Corporal.'

A remark from the other end.

'Yes, Corporal.'

He put the phone down.

'She says she has to check her files and also check with her superior – apparently it's a security thing. Wait a minute and she'll ring back.'

The soldier persisted in asking him about his wartime experiences until he was called outside where a food delivery truck was waiting to be checked before entering.

Connor was relieved that by the time he returned the phone was ringing and he was given directions.

'I'm to escort you. Nobody is allowed to just wander around this place, even a war hero like you.'

'I wasn't a hero.'

'Sure you were. You all were. And I want to be just like you.'

'I don't think you would. I was a prisoner of war.'

The rest of their acquaintance continued in silence.

A woman appeared wearing the neat light khaki uniform of an American female soldier.

The young man saluted her. 'Corporal Coy.'

'Wanda Coy,' said the firmly built young woman, as she shook Connor's hand with as much vigour as any man, totally ignoring the puppy-dog looks of the guard who had escorted him to her.

'Connor O'Connor. Thanks for fitting me in.'

'It's a pleasure.' Her expression was pained when she glanced at the guard who had brought him to her. 'That's all, Private. On your way.'

Blushing to his hair roots, the soldier took the hint.

'An avid admirer?' asked Connor.

'Missing his mom,' replied Wanda Coy, her chin doubling when she chuckled into her shirt collar.

Wanda Coy was far too inferior to warrant an office to herself but was one of twenty or so other clerks, secretaries and typists, their desks arranged in rows equidistant from each other. It occurred to Connor that each desk had been allotted exactly the same space – two feet from the one in front, the one behind and the one in the row to either side of them.

Down at the far end was a series of offices, some with opaque glass windows reinforced with wire. He could tell by the bobbing heads that the occupants of those offices were sitting and even from this distance he could discern black and white notices on the doors. Without needing to go closer he knew that names and rank would be stamped in black on a white surface. Like pedigree bulls or horses, the officers got a stall to themselves while lesser ranks were herded together like sheep or cows.

Curious, and keen for a break from stamping documents and typing memoranda, a number of staff glanced in his direction. The women's interest lingered longer than that of the men. All the latter wanted was to be done with stamping and out on the town. The women were more interested in the possibility of being asked out by fresh company from the guys they worked with.

'I understand you're after the address of a guy named Jones Ling who used to work in the kitchen.'

'That's right. I understand he left just a few days ago.'

Wanda fingered a pile of files and pulled one out from about halfway down.

'Damn. I've only just pulled that file and now it's half buried.' She shook her head. 'You just cannot believe how much paperwork is generated in this place – half of it a waste of damn time.'

She looked up at him and grinned. 'I never used to swear before I joined the army. It keeps the grunts at bay. You know what men can be like, being a sergeant and all.'

'That's right, Corporal.'

Her smile widened. 'Please. Call me Wanda.'

'Wanda. So do you have this man's address?'

'Can you tell me why you want it?'

'I need to check if a mutual friend is deceased. I thought he was, but now I'm hopeful that perhaps he's still alive.'

'A wartime friend?'

He nodded. 'I had hoped to find him here and get it sorted. Your help would be much appreciated.'

'Of course.'

She flicked open the file, read what was there, copied the details onto a piece of paper and handed it to him.

'Best of luck. Hope you find out for sure about your friend – one way or another.'

Connor glanced at the address before folding the paper into quarters and tucking it into his breast pocket.

'Are you sure about this?'

She nodded. 'It's the address he gave us. Is there a problem?'

'Thanks for your help. It's much appreciated.'

There was the sound of a door slamming shut some way down the end of the office, but he didn't look round. It didn't concern him. In one way he had what he wanted. In another way he did not.

Wanda Coy tapped her teeth with the end of her pencil and decided that the rear view of Connor O'Connor was just as good as the front view.

'Corporal?'

'Sir.'

She sprang to her feet and gave a sharp salute. It wasn't often that anyone caught her off guard. This was one of those few times and it just had to be him – Colonel Sherman Warrington.

Normally his eyes were a frosty blue, but they now appeared much darker and gave her the impression she was being skewered.

Looking straight ahead away from that hard look came easy. She'd perfected the art of letting whatever he said or did wash over her.

'What did you give him?'

His question surprised her. She'd expected, if anything, that he would firstly have demanded the man's name.

'An address, sir. He's looking for a man who used to work in the UN kitchens. He thinks he might be able to clarify whether an old wartime friend is alive or dead.'

She felt the coldness of his stare though it worried her less now. He had taken her by surprise, but her confidence was already beginning to reassert itself.

A clerk from another department added two more files to the unwieldy heap already in place. It slipped slightly which necessitated her using both hands to pat it back into place.

She presented a blank expression. 'Is there anything else, Colonel?'

'Yes. If he comes here again I want him referred to me. Is that clear?'

'Of course, Colonel Warrington.'

She saluted sharply.

Once he had stalked back to his office she heaved a huge sigh of relief and sank back into her chair.

Maisie, a red-headed girl from New York City who had stopped chewing gum until the colonel had gone, grinned at her from across the gap between them.

'That was short and sweet.'

'Warrington is only bearable in small doses.'

'You don't fancy him then?'

'Are you kidding?'

The front and back of Connor O'Connor's physique was imprinted on her mind, but even so she couldn't help wondering at the colonel's attitude.

'I can tell you right now, honey, that not everyone feels like you. I've heard he's got a new woman.'

'He's married.'

'Since when has that ever stopped a guy from straying? I'm telling you, he's a glutton for dames and the more the merrier.'

Wanda picked up her pen and prepared to get back to the pile of paperwork.

'Yeah, yeah. Another guy away to play with every little Suzy Wong he can get his hands on.'

Maisie leaned closer and lowered her voice. 'Not Warrington. Some men can't get enough of them, and you have to admit those slim figures and glossy black hair are pretty enticing for guys used to high-school girls and girlfriends just like their mum. But not him. He's not tempted. He never goes near Asian women. He hates Asians – all of them. I've heard him say so, though I'm sure you already know that.'

Wanda shook her head in disbelief. 'I've heard him say so too. Strange for a guy who I understand volunteered to serve here.' She shrugged. 'Still. He must have his reasons.'

After taking a quick look round, Maisie blew a bubble which popped quickly, a sign for her to get back to work.

Wanda did the same. She was feeling warm inside and

very hopeful. She'd written Jones Ling's address on the front of the piece of paper she'd handed over – and her own on the back.

Back in his office Sherman Warrington reached for the phone and dialled a number.

'I want to see you tonight.'

She agreed immediately, just as he knew she would.

'And bring that statement with you.'

She prevaricated. She didn't want her name mentioned. He had to promise her that it would stay locked in his drawer until long after either he or she had left for home. In the meantime he would listen to her gossip, her eyes bright with anticipation, waiting for him to say the magic words that she was the woman he'd been searching for all his life. He'd divorce his wife for her, he'd set up home anywhere in the world she wanted to be.

In his opinion it was a very true saying that a woman's way to love was through sex and a man vice versa. The dames got it in their heads that if they gave in on the sex front, a man would love her forever. That's what they thought it meant. His lips curled in a contemptuous sneer. Sex was great. Women were stupid

He had his own reasons for getting involved with her, his own mission to attain. The great advantage about being in military intelligence was being privy to personal information. He could ask anything of anyone, manipulate events, sow seeds of dissent and dissatisfaction – all of it for his own ends, his own coldly calculated revenge.

Chapter 8

It was the porter who found the baby left on the steps of Victoria House.

'It's a girl,' said the duty nurse who had undressed it whilst awaiting for Rowena to examine and give it a clean bill of health. 'But not a newborn.'

Rowena sighed. 'The mother must have had her reasons, poor soul. Never mind. Let's see how healthy it is.'

She smiled down at the child as she placed the end of the stethoscope on its chest, then froze.

The nurse noticed.

'Anything wrong, Doctor?'

'The child has a birthmark.'

'Yes. I noticed it too. It's heart shaped. Pretty really, but still a blemish.'

Rowena knew what the nurse was getting at. A lot could be read into a blemish – even something as commonplace as a birthmark.

'Is it that bad?'

'That depends on the hour of birth and how much the mother is willing to pay for a reading from a fortune teller.'

Rowena finished her examination. There was nothing untoward. The child was in good order, fed, warm and clean – she'd not doubted it would be otherwise. What did concern her was that Koto had not given any sign of abandoning the baby. She'd seemed loving and pleased that she'd given birth to another child and determined to defy Kim no matter what.Her blood racing, she shook her head.

'I need to go up to my flat a moment. I won't be long. Can you deal with this until I get back?'

'Of course, doctor.'

Luli was dusting a dark green porcelain Buddha. The Buddha usually made her smile and helped lift her spirits or ease her tiredness because he seemed to smile back. Always smiling, always serene, a bit like the *Mona Lisa*. But not now. She had no doubt that the baby was Koto's, but where was Koto? What had happened to her?

Luli looked surprised to see her. 'You finished, Dr Rowena?'

In response to Rowena telling her to call her by her first name, Luli couldn't quite do it. Rather than stick to the more formal Dr Rossiter, she had taken to calling her Dr Rowena.

'No.'

Sensing something was not quite right, Luli stopped what she was doing, a wary look in her eyes.

'A baby was left on the steps outside last night. The porter found her this morning.'

'Oh. Poor baby.'

'It was Koto's baby.'

Luli's mouth dropped open. 'Koto's baby?'

'She had a birthmark on her right cheek shaped like a heart. Do you recall me commenting on it?'

Luli sank down into a chair, the duster twisted in her hands. She shook her head in disbelief.

'She love baby. I do not understand…'

Her voice trailed away as though some sudden realisation had come to mind.

'What is it, Luli? Why would she abandon her baby?'

For a moment Luli was completely still. Then she shook her head vehemently.

'No. No. Not her. Not Koto.' She looked up into Rowena's face. 'Him. He made her do it.'

Rowena steadied her gaze. Luli was probably right. Koto had been forced to give her child away but had left it where she knew it would be looked after.

Connor was disappointed. His visit to the UN headquarters had been pleasant enough thanks to Wanda Coy, but disappointing. There was no point in dashing to the address he'd been given seeing as he knew it to be the empty house opposite his bar.

His disappointment and confusion made him surly. Even the happy-go-lucky porter outside Victoria House received nothing more than a grunt of recognition.

As usual Victoria House was crowded with sick people and crying children and the smell of poverty reminded him of a house he'd once entered that had been boarded up for years, the dust smelling of dead things, vermin and emptiness.

A nurse barred his way from entering the inner domain. 'She's busy.'

'I need to see her. It's a matter of life and death.'

She pulled in her chin and eyed him suspiciously.

'Honestly,' he said, purposely softening his manner.

She took him to where she was tending a child with ringworm, applying a powerful-smelling fluid from a ribbed bottle that he immediately associated with poison.

She did not glance up at him but kept her eyes focused on the small child whose head was covered in pale purple rings. His mother was nodding to everything that Rowena said to her in Cantonese even though it was quite possible that Cantonese was not the woman's natural dialect.

Although aware of his presence, Rowena did not look up at him until she was finished. Finally both child and parent left, hand in hand.

'Give me a minute,' Rowena said to the nurse who smiled, raised her eyebrows and winked before disappearing.

'I need to speak to you.' Connor took off his hat.

Rowena was already on her feet, washing her hands, readying herself for the next patient.

'You'll have to make it snappy. Some of these people have been here since five o'clock this morning and more keep coming.'

'Then I won't try and make love to you.'

He grinned.

Rowena merely flashed her eyes.

'Not even a quick hug?'

'No. I'm on duty.'

He knew she meant it. It was her habit to avoid human contact when she was wearing that white coat of hers

– mainly for hygiene purposes of course, but also as though it were a badge or shield that set her apart from the world.

'I thought I'd better keep you up to speed on current events.'

'Oh.'

She kept up her façade, tidying things, preparing things, glancing at written notes. Irritating, but he pressed on.

'I've been making enquiries about Kim Pheloung. I went to the man who told Yang that he was dead, but the address I was given has to be false.'

Rowena frowned. 'How do you know that?'

'It's the house across the alley where the old man was found with a broken neck.'

The stuffy office seemed suddenly cold. She looked down at her hands, such white soft hands. It always amazed him how these hands, her hands, were so capable of making life better for sick people. Now they seemed blurred and out of focus.

She kept her face turned away. 'This man – is it really necessary to locate him? I mean, in all honesty, if Kim is alive and wants to get to me, he will.'

'You're right. I would have thought he would have. But there's still time.' He dared to reach out and touch her. 'Is something wrong?'

She stayed still, rested both hands on the metal side cabinet and heaved a big sigh.

'A baby was left on the steps outside this morning. It was not a newborn and it had a heart shaped birthmark on its left cheek. I've seen that same birthmark before. She turned and looked directly at him. 'It was Koto's baby.'

His eyes widened.

'Well that's a surprise.'

'A very big surprise. I've spoken to Luli. She was as surprised as I am. Koto would never abandon her child unless somebody forced her to do so.'

When she raised her eyes to meet his, he thought he would drown in them. They seemed huge, much larger than usual.

'It could be a warning, a message to you.'

'That he's coming?'

'It could be.'

Although she tried her best to hide it, he saw her shiver.

'Well that settles that.' His fingers played with the brim of his hat, turning it round and round until he was back to where he'd began. 'I'll go back to the bar, pick up a few things and return later.'

Her stance was stiff, her look forthright. 'No. I didn't agree to you moving in.'

'Rowena, I need to stay close to you.'

'Let's look at this logically. You don't know for sure that it was me Nan Po was watching and we don't know for certain that Koto really didn't change her mind.'

'It's the most likely reason for him being there. I can't think of anyone else he could have been working for and neither can McCloud. He certainly didn't discount it. In fact he thought it was highly probable once I told him the whole story.'

She looked at him askance. 'The *whole* story?'

'Me darling girl, I had to. He needed to know all the facts. Anyway,' he went on, 'I've got a few days off and Yang is perfectly capable of taking care of things.'

'So who was this other man who gave the house across the way as his address?'

'A man named Jones Ling. Half British, half Chinese. He used to work for Kim and now he's disappeared.'

'Why is he so important? How does he fit into this?'

Connor rolled his head and turned his eyes heavenwards. 'Yang knew him and that at one point he'd worked for Kim. Perhaps he knows where Kim is hiding out. There's no point in entering the walled city unless you know where to look. It's not as it was. It's like a rabbit warren in there.'

'There's every chance that he's not in there at all. Perhaps he's living in Shanghai.'

'Rowena, he *paid* Nan Po to watch you. Don't you understand that?'

'There's no need to shout.'

'There's every need. Please, Rowena. For God's sake listen to what I'm saying.'

He saw her wince and was unrepentant about shouting.

'I'll make no excuse for raising my voice. I'm concerned for your safety.'

Rowena folded her arms and shook her head, at the same time looking down at her shoes. When she looked up at him it was his turn to wince.

'Connor, at some point you will have to go back to the bar. And what then? I doubt McCloud could spare two men to stand outside my door on a permanent basis – just on the off chance that Kim comes calling. Besides, you still have to ask yourself why should he come now? He's had years to make his presence known. But he hasn't.'

He hung his head, hating to admit that she had a point. All the same, he was just as determined as she was.

'After a few days of putting up with me here, you can come over and stay with me – where I can keep an eye on you.'

Rowena let out an exasperated sigh. 'And I will feel like a prisoner all over again. Don't you think we're being a bit paranoid? Maybe it wasn't me that the old man was watching. Maybe you're missing something – McCloud is missing something. Can't you check who else was in there that night?'

He frowned and tried to think. This was hardly virgin territory. He'd been over the possibilities in his mind over and over again. His bar, and more especially his gambling den, was popular with both Chinese and foreigners – especially service personnel and civil servants. Brendon McCloud was one of them.

'I don't keep a written record. I can't check.'

Rowena pulled in her chin like a nun confronted with gross indecency. 'Connor, that's ridiculous. You should have a membership list – you know you should.'

His proud brow furrowed like a schoolboy who's been chastised for scrumping apples. Both his records and accounts were in a mess and he wasn't inclined to sort things out. Running the bar meant just that, not the scribbling of details in dusty old ledgers.

'I need to get somebody to sort it out. In time…'

'You've had enough time. You've had years to sort it out. For goodness' sake, Connor, get a grip on things! You're a man aren't you, not a mouse.'

'Well that's a bit below the belt.'

Rowena immediately regretted her comment and roped her arms around his neck. 'I'm sorry. I didn't mean that to sound the way it came out.' In an effort to emphasise that she really meant what she said, she slid her hand around the nape of his neck and brought his lips down to meet hers. He came willingly.

'Am I forgiven?' Her voice was as smooth as silk.

'This time.'

'I'll make it up to you later.'

'Now there's a thought.' He smiled.

She read his mind and saw the same scenario herself. They were definitely on the same wavelength. Bed was the very best place in which to make up without actually saying anything. A mere touch coupled with a look of outright desire said more than words could ever say.

It had always amazed her that for a big man he was extremely gentle, his touch light and his movements sensuous. Their bodies seemed capable of speaking without words, easily reading the desires of the other until mutual satisfaction was achieved.

'Well?' he said between nuzzling her ear and stroking her chin.

'Connor,' she whispered. 'Everyone's watching us.'

'There's nobody else in here.'

She nodded towards the flimsy screen. 'No,' she whispered back, her voice husky with affection and much more besides. 'But in this case the walls really do have ears.'

He let her go and said he would come back later.

And so he stayed that night and everything seemed extremely secure. No violence of any kind came knocking at their door.

In the morning there was fresh coffee and a fried breakfast for Connor.

With her back against the sink and sipping hot black coffee, Rowena looked at Connor.

'What will you do today?'

'Look after you,' he said as he mopped up egg yolk with a slice of toast.

'How will you do that?'

He wiped his hands and then sipped his coffee. His eyes met hers.

'My plan was to sit in your office.'

She shook her head. 'No. Too intimidating for the patients. They'll think you're HKP.'

'I could stand guard outside.'

Rowena put her cup to one side. She was aware that he wasn't looking at her, but thinking.

'A penny for them.'

Her heart seemed to stop when he looked at her sideways, blue eyes beneath a lock coppery hair.

He got up from the table, stood in front of her and placed his hands around her waist.

'I don't want you to be frightened.'

'I am, but only a bit.'

'I'm thinking that I've made the wrong move. I need to have a rethink.'

'In what way?'

'I've taken up a defensive position when really I should be on the offensive. I should be out there looking for him.'

'You made a start with this man Jones. Anyway, isn't it McCloud's job to do that?'

'He's one man, not an army.'

Luli chose that moment to come in to collect the dishes. She said good morning to each of them with a happy smile – that is until she saw Rowena straighten, move away from the sink and look as though she was about to ask her something she might not wish to answer.

'Luli. Put those dishes down. I want to speak to you.'

Luli sucked in her lips and did as ordered. 'I know nothing about the baby,' she said. 'It was not me who left her on the steps.'

'I know. That's not what I want to talk to you about.'

Connor was on alert, coffee cup raised to his mouth but not missing a thing. It was Luli who had led Rowena to Koto in the walled city.

'Luli, is Koto still in the place where she gave birth?'

The girl's dark lashes brushed her cheeks nervously as she shook her head.

'No. She is gone.'

'Are you sure of that?'

Luli nodded again.

Connor saw the girl's nervousness and decided she was hiding something that was not necessarily connected with the abandoned baby. 'I hear you know people in the walled city, Luli. Can you tell me who they are?'

The perfectly formed almond eyes, as gentle as a doe, fluttered again. 'Just… friends.'

Connor eyed the girl's moon-shaped face and glossy black hair. He'd known Luli for almost as long as Rowena. They both regarded her as loyal and having a big heart, but

Connor was having second thoughts. The reason she wasn't saying anything was down to her nature. She was devoted and loving and also a trifle gullible. With the right handling she could be persuaded to do almost anything – as long as she was led to believe that she was helping others.

One particular suspicion sat stubbornly at the forefront of his mind, though at this juncture he had no intention of pursuing the matter. There was a far more important question waiting to be asked.

'Did Koto tell you the whereabouts of Kim Pheloung? Do you know where he is, Luli?'

The girl was like a rabbit caught in the headlights of a fast-moving car. The moment didn't last. She shook herself out of the imagined spell and shook her head vehemently.

'Koto did not tell me.'

Connor closed the gap between himself and the girl.

'Koto didn't tell you, perhaps. But you know, don't you, Luli? I can tell by the look in your eyes.'

The scared rabbit look was replaced by a deeper one of human fear. This time when she shook her head her hair flew around in a thick mop of blackness, her face ashen.

'Girl, you tell us or you tell the Hong Kong police. Which is it to be?'

For a split second Luli's eyes were wide with fear. After that her movements were fast. She bolted out of the room.

Connor moved to follow her but Rowena grabbed his arm.

'Leave her.'

'Leave her? She knows more than she's letting on.'

'You frightened her. You should not have mentioned the police. You know their reputation isn't exactly honourable.'

His look was intense, his eyes blazing into hers. 'She didn't want to tell us the names of her friends in the walled city.'

'Does that matter?'

'Rowena. Think about it. Koto knew where to find her and trailed her here to Hong Kong – and to you and the beginning of that trail had to be in China, specifically Shanghai. The old city is full of illegal refugees smuggled in by gang bosses, either for money or to work for a pittance. There's a chance that Luli is involved in the trade.'

She shook her head in disbelief. 'No. I won't have it. I refuse to believe it. Luli works for me. She takes care of Dawn. She loves Dawn.'

Something about Connor's sudden and prolonged silence made her look more intently into his eyes. They seemed darker than usual, contemplative, as though some worrying secret had burst like a balloon inside his head. In that moment it felt as though her breath was a mass of tiny needles stinging her throat.

Finally she voiced what was in both their minds. 'He knows that where there is Luli there too am I. He can find me at any time.'

He said nothing, his eyes still locked with hers and the thoughts in his mind open for her to read.

She took a deep breath and spoke the thoughts he had not put into words.

'Dawn. He can find Dawn too.'

Chapter 9

'Big night tonight,' declared Barbara Kelly.

The comment barely registered. Rowena's thoughts were elsewhere.

'I'm sorry, Barbara. My head feels full of feathers this morning.'

'I was referring to the Trustees Ball. Are you going?'

There they were in her mind, an amalgamation of higher up physicians and surgeons from all over Hong Kong, along with those who frequented the Jockey Club and sat on various influential committees.

'No.'

'You should.'

Rowena gave her a telling look. 'It's couples only.'

'Well you and Connor are a couple. Aren't you?'

'He wasn't invited. So I'm not going.'

'Oh!'

She didn't go into detail. It was none of Barbara's business, but the fact that Connor had not been an army officer but a sergeant major, one of the *real* fighting men, was one of the reasons he had not been invited. Rowena suspected a secondary reason was the common knowledge that they slept together but were not married. The fact was, the more that people expressed their disapproval, the more both she and Connor dug their heels in. They were doing what *they* wanted to do and not bowing to how others *wanted* them to be.

'Not my scene,' she added. 'So how's your love life, Barbara?'

She was only mildly interested in Nurse Barbara Kelly's romances, but they did form a pleasant diversion from the daily grind.

Barbara blushed and fluttered her eyelashes. 'It's going well.'

'Is this beau of sufficient means and status to be invited to the ball?'

'I think so. Oh dear,' she added suddenly glancing at her watch. 'I'd better go and give the baby her feed.'

Rowena knew she was referring to Koto's baby, who at present had no official name. When asked if she had any preference she'd said that she hadn't. Deep down she was half-expecting Koto to reappear and claim her child.

It was an hour or so later when Dr Grelane pushed open the door of the room that was more usually used to examine pregnant women and asked if he could have a quiet word.

'In private, if you don't mind.'

Rowena nodded at the Chinese nurse who had been sterilising instruments. 'I'll finish off here, Nurse.'

Whatever he wanted to say was obviously for her ears only and somehow she didn't think she would like what he was going to say. Thankfully it wasn't likely to take very long. This was one room that wasn't cut out for long meetings. There was only one chair. Most of the space was taken up by a flimsy obstetrics bed complete with a set of adjustable stirrups at one end, a headrest at the other. It had been made sometime in the twenties and was due for replacement once the money stretched to it.

After a quick glance round, he chose to stand looking out of the window, a dark shape blocking out an oblong of light, with one hand resting on the sill, the other in his pocket. She assumed that he was leaving her to take the chair, but she refrained from doing so. Dr Simeon Grelane was one of those people she preferred to meet eye to eye, on the same level. If she sat down he would tower over her which she would find intimidating.

She counted the seconds until he deigned to turn round and confront her. He looked unsettled that she hadn't sat down and began drumming his fingers on the steel table in front of him as though he was practising for a concert.

'You have something important to say?'

The fact that she spoke first seemed to annoy him. He stopped playing an imagined piano concerto and frowned.

'I had a call from a Colonel Warrington. He's an advisor to the UN – or something like that. He told me he wants to requisition your services and mentioned Korea.'

'Yes.'

Though her heart was beating like a drum, she purposely kept her response monosyllabic. At the same time she wondered at this odd turn of events; what purpose had the colonel hoped to serve by relaying this information to Dr Simeon Grelane?

'I thought it only right to inform you that the trustees of Victoria House will not stand in your way.'

'No.'

His eyebrows shot up.

'No? You don't want to accept the position?'

He sounded very surprised and also a little disappointed.

'Is there any particular reason you don't wish to go?'

'My work is here.'

She noticed the slight inclination of his head, the conniving look in his eyes, and knew he was disappointed with her answer. From the very moment he'd arrived less than a year ago, she'd recognised his ambition and felt uncomfortable around him. He wanted her job. He wanted control of Victoria House.

He took a deep breath. 'I will stress again that the trustees would be quite willing to let you go. Not that you haven't made a big contribution to Victoria House—'

'Hah! A pretty big contribution seeing as I set it up in the first place.'

She could almost hear the grinding of teeth when he clenched his jaw and took measured breaths. She herself was furious.

'Nobody disputes that and as a woman you have coped extremely well. However, your work is hands-on. It is felt that different skills are now needed, somebody willing to work behind the scenes, coping with the rigours of management incurred by our new association with the United Nations and all that that entails.'

Rowena folded her arms and clenched her elbows, as though such things could hold back her temper.

'And a woman isn't capable of that? Is that what you're saying, Simeon?'

He clutched his chin between nicotine-stained finger and thumb as though he were seriously considering this as a matter of some importance. She wasn't fooled. He'd made his mind up. He wanted her gone. The whole point of this interview was him thrashing around to persuade her to go. It was also to emphasise that he was a better man for the job than she was – man being the operative word.

'I was just—'

'I have work to do.'

Impatient to leave his presence she spun on her heels but had taken only three steps when he shouted at her.

'Wait.'

Her face aflame, her eyes glittering with anger, she turned to face him.

'Simeon, I really don't know what's triggered this situation and why you want me carted off to Korea. Please don't deny it. We've been aware for some time that things will be changing around here. Up until now nobody has voiced any doubts about my adapting to a new situation and then suddenly, there it is, I am no longer fit for supervising Victoria House, the job I've been doing for some time.' She frowned. 'Colonel Warrington and his offer is aired and it's a window of opportunity to get rid of me. That's your prime objective, Simeon – and please, don't deny it. And before you run away and make plans to succeed me, please note that I was asked, but have turned it down. I don't want to go to Korea. My home, my family and my job are here.'

Simeon shifted from one leg to the other, looking down at the floor, shuffling his feet.

If she expected that to be the end of it, she was sadly mistaken. Simeon was on a mission.

'There is no doubt that you are ideally suited for such an appointment. The trustees feel that the tenure of your current position is open to discussion.'

'I might have the same opinion about them. I was instrumental in appointing the board of trustees.'

'You did, but only under sufferance. After all, this place was requisitioned after the war. It doesn't belong to you.'

Her face burned. 'It doesn't belong to you either – or the board.'

'I know, I know. It's all properly recorded. The previous owner was killed by the Japanese.'

The knee-jerk reaction to say there was a possibility he might still be alive died in her throat. The situation was complicated enough. She said nothing.

Taking his cue from that and considering her cornered, Simeon carried on.

'There are a number of issues counting against the possibility of you undertaking a management role, number one of which you have a child…'

Her stance was defiant. 'You have three.'

His expression was sickeningly smug when he nodded over his folded arms. 'Yes, but I am a man and their mother looks after them. And, of course, we *are* married.'

'Dear God…'

Rowena looked at the ceiling then at him. If heaven was on the ceiling it wasn't helping her much.

She moderated her voice, each word carefully pronounced so there would be no misunderstanding of what she was saying.

'This is nineteen fifty. The world is changing for a lot of people and that includes women. They are unwilling to be tied to the home as they were in the past and are as capable as men of holding down a professional job. My daughter is well cared for and my private life is my business. Now please excuse me. I have work to do.'

She pointedly stood against the door, her fingers resting on the handle.

'Goodbye, Simeon.'

He looked less than pleased, the corners of his mouth downturned.

'Perhaps we can talk again, but I would urge you to consider the offer. The United Nations pays well.'

'Are they paying you?'

For a moment he looked as though he was about to explode, opening his mouth but nothing coming out.

Once the door was closed behind him, she flung her pen onto the steel table where it rolled the whole length before coming to rest against the kidney dish holding the instruments.

She bristled with indignation as she marched back to her sanctuary behind the linen screen, thinking back over the years to when she had first come here, to a time when there was no refugee facility, just an exotic man and his strange grandmother with her bound feet.

Barbara Kelly poked her head around the screen.

'Doctor, you look as though you're more likely to kill somebody than cure them.'

'You could say that.'

'Cup of tea?'

She nodded, kicked off her shoes and slumped into her chair. 'That will do for now.'

The clattering of cups and the boiling of the kettle silenced Barbara's chatter. As she sat there seething, a question came into Rowena's mind.

'Barbara, have you heard a rumour about me being shipped off to Korea?'

'I don't think so.'

Barbara tossed the answer over her shoulder, her attention seemingly focused on getting the boiling water into the teapot. The action seemed casual enough and Rowena dismissed the impression that she'd seen the nurse's shoulders stiffen.

'There,' said Barbara placing the cup and saucer on the desk, a beaming smile on her face. 'Milk and no sugar. Fancy a digestive?'

Rowena shook her head. At first she looked at the tea then noticed Barbara's pink face.

'You're blushing.'

'Oh.' Barbara placed a graceful hand on her cheek. 'Just a bit hot, that's all. It must have been the steam from the kettle. Stood too close to it.'

Later that evening when she was doing her best to read a decent novel, her thoughts returned to Barbara and her flushed face. She also reconsidered her response regarding Korea. She hadn't answered one way or another. Not yes, not no, but 'I don't think so.'

Perhaps she'd ask Barbara the same question tomorrow – then reminded herself that Barbara's name wasn't on the duty roster for the next day.

This whole Korean thing was getting out of hand. Tomorrow was her day off too. It wouldn't hurt to beard the lion in his den – to pay Sherman Warrington, the instigator of this unsettling suggestion, a visit and ask him why he was undermining her position at Victoria House.

'What's his purpose? His real purpose?'

There was only one reason she would go and that was to escape her past, primarily Kim Pheloung. She was bearing up well, the fear deeply buried and controlled by throwing herself into her work. However, it might not last and she didn't just have herself to think about. She had to think about Dawn. If Kim did surface there was no knowing what he would do.

Sherman Warrington smoothed back his hair, adopted a welcoming look and shouted 'enter', his eyes gleaming with triumph. He smiled, recalling her highly principled manner on the first occasion they'd met. Not so much now, he thought. Things had occurred – and more things would occur. Eventually she would capitulate to his suggestion... just a little more leverage.

Today the white coat of the medical professional had been replaced. She was wearing a pair of tight-fitting yellow trousers that stopped mid-calf, a white blouse with a V neck and an upright collar that brushed her jaw. He didn't notice what she wore on her feet because her face, glowing, honey-coloured and healthy-looking, held his attention. So did the soft skin exposed above the neck of the blouse. Much to his disappointment there was no sign of her cleavage so he kept his attention fixed on her face.

'Please,' he said, waving at the wraparound chair on the

other side of his desk. 'Take a seat. Would you like coffee? It's the good stuff. Shipped in special. I won't drink anything else.'

'No thank you.'

She perched forward on the chair as though she'd decided that the meeting wouldn't last long and she'd take flight as soon as it was over.

She'd decided to be straight to the point, to speak her mind before he'd had the chance to speak his. As it turned out he got in first.

That's the kind of man he is, she thought as she listened to him bragging about how great his coffee was, far superior to anything she'd ever tasted. The message was that nobody had coffee like he did. Nobody had or did *anything* as he did.

'Now, to what do I owe this pleasure?'

She'd expected him to start persuading her to accept the Korean assignment and she'd had her answer ready. He'd wrong-footed her, expressed pleasure that she was here.

Her feathers weren't ruffled just yet. She took a deep breath. 'I was wondering when you require somebody to fill this post in Korea – unless it's already been filled, of course.'

Suddenly the colonel's persona seemed more relaxed.

'It hasn't. As I've already said it's a closed order – whatever that means – so they'd prefer a female doctor. Are you a Catholic?'

She shook her head. 'No.'

'Oh well. Never mind. Being from a Christian country is near enough. They can't have everything.' Leaning forward he clasped his hands in front of him and looked her straight in the eye. 'I'm glad to hear you've changed your mind.'

'I didn't say I had changed it entirely, but I am considering it more favourably. You did say there was a chance I could take my daughter?'

'She's female. They have a school. I don't see a problem.'

Her chin jerked in a pert nod. 'I see.'

'Might I enquire as to why you're reviewing this posting more favourably?'

'No. You may not.'

'Ah.' He sat back in his chair. 'I'll take it that it's personal.'

'I didn't say that.'

'Whatever you want. I'd like a definite confirmation before the end of the week.' He paused. 'That dinner invitation still stands.'

'I'll have to decline. There's a lot to do if I decide to leave Hong Kong, and almost as much to do if I stay.'

He grunted that he understood. 'You may recall I asked you to look up my daughter.'

'Yes. You wanted me to persuade her to come home.'

'Her name's Sheridan. Did I tell you that?'

Rowena took a deep breath. She couldn't remember whether he had or he hadn't, but she wanted to get to the point so decided he had. 'Is she your only child?'

Every sign of warmth and welcome left his face. 'She is now. My son died for his country.'

'I see.'

His voice and his gaze seemed to drift away. 'He was worked almost to death on the Burma railway – the Death Railway as it came to be called.'

'I'm sorry. So many men died.'

'He got through to the end. Then he was killed.'

His voice and demeanour were icy. It was as though the

room and its occupants had been buried beneath a glacier. This, she decided, was a man who needed to talk about his loss – even if only in a small way. She started with a small question.

'What was your son's name?'

'Sherman. Same as mine. Sherman Ross Warrington Junior. My grandfather fought with General Sherman. A great civil war general who subdued Georgia. Have you heard of him?'

She nodded. 'Yes. By name if nothing else though I did hear that he marched through Georgia destroying and killing as he went.'

The colonel looked at her as though she was a little mentally deficient in not knowing more. His tone was casual but his eyes were rock hard.

'Some call it that. I call it a move that achieved final victory. My grandfather named my father Sherman. My father named me and I named my son. My daughter is named Sheridan – as near as dammit to Sherman as I could get with a girl's name. I want to pass on that tradition to a grandchild. That's why I want her back here – at any price.'

Rowena brushed away her suspicion that Sheridan might want to stay away, and for a reason she hadn't quite worked out yet, though outright dislike and subsequent estrangement from her father was a distinct possibility. Still, she wasn't here to evaluate his reasons for wanting her to go. She had her own daughter to worry about.

'I think I might have that coffee now. If you don't mind.'

Whatever dark thoughts lurked behind the watery blue eyes seemed to lift. 'Sure. Sugar? Cream?'

'Just black, please.'

He poured hers plus one for himself then eyed her as he might a candidate for interrogation.

'Can I ask you something?'

At least it wasn't a demand.

She took a sip of her coffee. He was right. It was good.

'What do you want to ask me?'

'Are you going to marry the Irishman?'

'I don't think that's any of your business.'

'You're right. It's not. I apologise.'

He glanced at his watch.

'I've got a meeting shortly so we better make this quick.'

'Is that what you say to Barbara?'

His jaw dropped. Now she'd wrong-footed him, and took him completely off guard. It was just a guess as to the identity of Barbara's latest Romeo. To her astonishment she'd hit the bull's eye.

He quickly collected himself.

'My personal life is no business of yours.'

'Oh, I don't know. Romantic dalliances are indeed personal, but not when they affect one's work.'

She was clutching at straws. Barbara had not failed in her work. She presumed he hadn't either.

'Barbara is something of a romantic. I wouldn't like to see her hurt.'

He shrugged and smiled like an eighteen-year-old who's just lost his virginity.

'She's a grown woman and my wife's back in Maryland. We're about to get divorced.'

'I'm sorry.'

'Don't be. It's by mutual consent. She accuses me of being married to the army. She was never cut out to be an army wife. We rubbed along OK until Sherman was killed.'

For a moment he seemed lost in his thoughts as though he was trying to get them in some kind of order before relating them to her.

'Sherman's ship was sunk and then, as I've already mentioned, he was captured and ended up working on the Death Railway.'

She nodded. 'Yes.'

'Went all through the railway to its end at a place called Three Pagodas Pass. That was where the Japs were going to kill them all – wipe out the evidence. Then the atomic bombs got dropped and everything changed, except the news didn't get through to a contingent of Korean army soldiers guarding my son and his colleagues. The Japs had occupied Korea for some time and it was their habit to get them to do most of the dirty work. They used the Korean women in their comfort houses and the men they used to guard prisoners of war – on a par with the *kapos* in the Nazi prisoner-of-war camp. Less than soldiers, a bit better than enemy prisoners. In their opinion the men were ignorant peasants and the women were whores.'

His surly tone was curdled with hate and sickened her to her stomach. She disliked his attitude and was inclined to say that he was being unfair but, recognising a man who wanted to share the details of his loss, she checked herself. Many people still hated the old enemies. It would be a long time before the hatchet of hatred would be buried – if ever.

He was musing, hands clasped over his tightly muscled

stomach, his gaze drifting to the nondescript scene through the window – a contingent of Chinese men being escorted by guards to wherever physical labour was required.

It was as though he didn't see them, his mind being somewhere else.

'Pretty name for a place. Three Pagodas Pass. Ugly things shouldn't have happened there, but they did. They killed him and the other guys with him. The war was over, but news travelled slowly. They killed him. Hours after the event, the news arrived that Japan had surrendered. Too late for my son.'

He fell into silence. A nerve twitched in his jaw as though he was chewing it all over and there was pure hatred in his eyes.

'Your daughter knows this?'

'Of course she does, but it didn't stop her going off. Felt she was called to it.' He tossed his head and repeated the words through clenched teeth. 'She just had to do it.'

'Nursing is an admirable vocation.'

He raised his eyes to meet hers and for one moment was unreadable. It made her feel as though there was something she just wasn't getting but she did suddenly feel sorry for him. His loss was so great. She'd feel the same if anything happened to Dawn.

'I can understand you wanting your daughter to come home from there.'

And you need her.

He was bitter but she was unsure as to whether he was lonely. He was not the type of man who either sought or embraced company – at least not on an emotional level. His like of women was purely sexual. She couldn't regard him any other way.

He brought his gaze back into the room. 'I can't persuade her to come home.'

'Then something very special must be holding her there.'

It was as though flesh and blood had suddenly turned molten lead to solid iron, hard and brittle, all warmth now cold steel.

'Nothing that can't be jettisoned.' His jaw remained tense, his lips barely parting.

'How does her mother feel about her being there?'

'Her mother's disinclined to leave the States. Travelling unnerves her. Not all women are like you, Dr Rossiter.' He paused and frowned slightly as he searched for the right words. 'You're capable of sorting out this whole mess with her. That's why I chose you.'

'I haven't agreed to go.'

His logic, the way he appeared to be cloaking something else behind this request, was confusing. She sensed he was still telling her only half the truth.

'But you will,' he said in a satisfied manner, leaning comfortably back in his chair. 'You will. Give it a little time. I'm sure you will. You're the right person for the job. Nobody else can do it.'

His statement was delivered like a promise or some kind of prophecy – as though he knew future circumstances would force her to go.

'I sense you're wavering. Understandable, seeing as you might have reached the end of the line at Victoria House.'

'I might still have a place there. I deserve a place there.'

She left his office feeling as though her soul had been laid bare and that the possibility of her staying at Victoria House was just that – a possibility.

'It's not fair,' she muttered through gritted teeth. Of course it wasn't but since when had the world been fair?

The colonel had also laid his soul bare, but nothing he'd said had fully explained why he wanted her to go there. Warrington was an incisive man, assessed what he saw and made up his mind. On that count alone she refused to give in to his bullying.

She needn't have come, but the fact that she might shortly lose her job was reason enough, though there were others. At the back of her mind she was worrying what might transpire as regards Kim Pheloung, not just for herself but for her daughter. Dawn, the child she had come to love, was at the centre of her universe and had to be protected.

Fleeing to somewhere else, if only for a while, might have to be considered. She was frightened of Kim finding her, yet not wishing to leave a place she'd come to love. The sights and smells of Hong Kong had become part of her. So too had Connor O'Connor. The difficulty, if she did decide to go, was telling him.

Wait and see what transpires, she told herself. If nothing happens I stay. If something threatening happens then I go.

The wind was coming from the west that night, bringing with it the warm smell of mainland China and the grit of the Gobi Desert. Layers of grey and mauve cloud lay like damp gauze across the glow of the western sky when

Rowena Rossiter drove her car onto the ferry that would take her across to Kowloon.

A group of sailors already the worse for drink made a number of suggestive comments that went over her head.

'Too posh for the likes of you, are we?'

Another of the sailors repeated the comment, though louder this time.

On becoming aware that they were addressing her, she turned her head. 'I'm sorry. Did you say something?'

Realising that their suggestions hadn't been heard let alone responded to, they were about to try again when a pair of young women rested their arms on the guardrail close to them, giggling as they eyed the twinkling lights that were swiftly coming their way.

Thankfully they left her to think her thoughts as she attempted to find her way through the maze of questions twisting and turning in her mind.

Once the ferry had docked, she started the engine and turned the car's bonnet along a route she knew well.

The main thoroughfares were ablaze with neon lights. The alley in which Connor's Bar was situated had a lesser glow though was still brighter than it used to be before the war.

She parked the car quickly and dashed in.

Yang tried to say something to her as she passed, but she ignored him and found Connor. He was tuning his violin, playing a few random notes until he got it right. On seeing her the random notes became a recognisable tune, their favourite tune, 'Star of the County Down', the tune he'd played her when they'd first met when he'd changed the nut-brown hair of the girl to raven-black hair – his homage to her.

'I need to talk.'

Connor's expression was implacable.

'Come on through.'

She followed him up the stairs to his apartment where the smell of new wood prevailed thanks to the rebuild that had taken place after the war.

French doors with metal frames led out onto a balcony that looked over the narrow alley below. At present the wooden shutters were wide open and the smell of greenery, dust and a salt-laden sea wafted in with the breeze.

He brought out his fiddle from under his arm and leant it against a glazed green dragon, the bow slotted into a crack in the dragon's head.

'Sit down.'

She didn't sit down. 'I feel a little—'

'Sit down. You're making me nervous.'

He pressed her into his sturdy but overstuffed sofa, eyeing her speculatively though not pushing for an explanation. Connor was a man who took things slowly. That way he reckoned on the facts being clearly relayed.

He said nothing more but poured gin into a glass then squeezed juice from half a fresh mango into it.

'Drink this.'

She took a big gulp, then another.

After pouring one for himself he sat down beside her looking thoughtful and waited.

She clutched her glass with both hands, wishing he would ask her a pertinent question. When he remained silent everything she wanted to say poured out like rain from the sky. She told him about Colonel Warrington, about how confused she was feeling, thinking there was some ulterior motive for him to want her to go to Korea.

'And so does Simeon Grelane,' she said finally.

'I can understand that. Grelane wants to take over at Victoria House. Right?'

'Right.'

'But this colonel – he's pestering you.'

She nodded.

She slumped back further into the sofa and shook her head.

'I just don't know why all this pressure.'

'It has to be something to do with the UN administration. You know how it is; they gear everything for their own ends, run everything along their own lines. That's got to be it.'

Rowena frowned, her hands tightening around the glass tumbler.

'I just can't help thinking there's something else going on. One thing I do know is that my nurse, Barbara Kelly, is having an affair with him.'

'I expect they discussed you and she praised you to high heaven.'

She shook her head again. 'That doesn't seem to be enough of a reason for wanting me to go to Korea and meet up with his daughter. There has to be something else, but I haven't a clue what it is.'

'Come here.'

He put his arm around her and brought her against his chest, kissing the top of her head, then her forehead and finally her lips.

'Does that feel better?' he asked.

She smiled, nodded and said that it did.

'The trouble is,' she said after he'd poured her another of the alcoholic and refreshingly fruity drink, 'that I could cope with it better if I wasn't looking over my shoulder, expecting to see Kim Pheloung treading in my footsteps.'

'"For close behind a fearsome demon treads…"' Are those the right words? Sorry, I'm no poet.'

'You're more or less right. *The Rime of the Ancient Mariner*. Only he's no mariner. He's murdered, Connor. You know it and I know it.'

He ranged his arm along the back of the sofa. 'Nobody seems to know where he is. I think we can forget him – at least for now.'

He didn't tell her any more about Jones Ling disappearing. He didn't tell her that he suspected that at some point the man's body would be pulled from the harbour.

Chapter 10

Three times a week it was customary for the girls at Queen Alexandra's School for Girls to take a stroll out of the school gates and into the town or out into the country. On this particular day the teacher was in a hurry and had some personal shopping to do before going out on a date that evening with a handsome silk merchant she'd met at an uptown bar.

Chattering like a flock of magpies, the girls were enjoying this foray into town more so than usual. They'd even been allowed to take a portion of their pocket money in case they too were moved to buy something for themselves.

Street traders carrying panniers, housewives, children and soldiers on leave all jostled for space in the narrow alleys, sometimes dividing the girls from their colleagues.

'Hold hands,' shouted Miss Dare, their teacher.

It was too late for that. They divided, came back together and divided again. That was when Dawn Rossiter heard somebody call her name.

'Dawn. I have a gift for you.'

She turned round, expecting to see a friend of her mother's or of Luli, their house servant.

The lady who gave her the doll was very pretty, wore a silky tunic and trousers and had a warm smile, but she did not recognise her. Neither did she notice that her smile was not matched by her eyes which showed no sign of emotion or that she had the sweet-smelling tang of opium about her.

The doll filled Dawn's eyes. She was dressed in a red silk dress over matching red silk trousers and her porcelain face was brightly painted, her eyes outlined in black and her lips and cheeks were the same colour as her dress.

'Tell your mother that it is a gift from an old friend,' said the pretty lady.

'Which old friend? Can I tell my mother a name?'

The pretty lady smiled. 'Tell her it is from Kim.'

Dawn studied the garishly painted doll before looking up to ask the woman if the gift giver was a man or a woman, but the crowd through which the woman in red had appeared now surged in a thick blanket of humanity. There was no sign of her.

The woman swiftly forgotten, Dawn held the doll by the ankles at an angle to her chest in order to scrutinise it more fully. The truth was she wasn't keen on dolls but had no wish to appear ungrateful to this woman who smiled so prettily and had mentioned it being a gift from a friend of her mother. She preferred books or things that could move of their own accord like clockwork trains and animals, novelty things that made her wonder how they worked.

Back in the dormitory she shared with three other boarders, she propped the doll up against her pillow. One of her friends, Belinda, who was keen on dolls, stroked the silky dress and poked at its rosy cheeks.

'Don't you want it, Rossiter?'

'I don't like dolls.'

'Can I have it?'

Dawn thought about it. The woman had said it was a gift from a friend of her mother, a person named Kim who she didn't know, so would it matter if she didn't mention receiving it to her mother? Would she care if she gave it away to somebody else? Not if she didn't tell her about it.

Belinda was eyeing the doll with undisguised desire, her lips twitching as she searched for some way of getting hold of it. At last she had the answer. They would swap unwanted gifts. 'My mother gave me a box of Turkish delight. She had them sent out from a store called Fortnum and Mason. I'll do you a swap.'

'You've been eating them.'

'Only the top layer. The bottom's still there – well most of it. I ate one from there. That's all.'

Belinda was a generous girl and had already shared out some of her bounty sent by her mother among her school friends, girls who had found warm friendship with each other in the absence of close family. Dawn had enjoyed sucking the sugar off the sweet cubes of white and pink and her mouth watered at the thought of having the rest at her disposal.

Dawn nodded her head avidly. 'OK. Bring me the box. We'll swap now.'

Belinda dashed off and swooped on the cabinet at the side of her bed.

Solemnly, the two little girls held their swap in their right hands, handing over at exactly the same moment.

'I'm taking her to bed tonight,' Belinda declared, hugging the doll to her chest.

'You can do as you like,' said Dawn with a saucy grin. 'I'm tucking the Turkish delight under my pillow. I'm going to eat them all night.'

'You'll be sick.'

'No I won't.'

Lessons, the evening meal and a warm bath were followed by prayers and then to bed, the everyday routine of Queen Alexandra's School for Girls; goodnights were said, lights were turned out.

Whispered conversations lasted only for a short time. The school day was long and both their energy and excitement were spent. Slats of soft moonlight filtered through the wooden shutters. All was peaceful – at least for an hour or so.

The usual snuffles and murmurs of sleeping schoolgirls were suddenly rent asunder by a loud scream followed by another and another, loud enough to bring a prefect running, loud enough to rouse the housemother from her bed, her hair a mass of rags meant to make her hair curl.

Lights were switched on. The housemother and prefect gasped. The girls, including Dawn, were out of bed huddled with their arms around each other, eyes wide as they took in the terrible scene. Belinda was still screaming, the doll in pieces, and Belinda's arms oozing blood.

It was early morning when Rowena got the message.

'There's been an incident.'

It sounded as though the headmistress was licking her lips in an effort to banish the dryness from her mouth in order to speak.

She swiftly got out of the bed, the ivory-coloured phone clutched tightly in her hand.

'What do you mean, "incident"?'

Her body turned cold as she listened, too shocked to comment.

Finally, 'I'll be right there.'

Connor swung his legs out of bed, reached out and grabbed her arm.

'What is it?'

She explained it quickly and succinctly, the message condensed into as few words as possible.

'I'm coming with you.'

She dressed quickly.

'We have to catch the first ferry.'

'We will.'

Disturbed by the sound of feet clattering down the wooden staircase, Yang was waiting for them at the bottom of the stairs.

'Look after things until we get back,' Connor ordered.

Yang did not press for an explanation but simply closed the door behind them. Something was wrong and that was enough for him.

'Do you want me to drive?' he asked.

'No.'

The car started first time. Connor leaned across and switched on the car's headlights.

'Sorry.'

'There's every reason for swearing but not for saying sorry.'

The windows misted up. It was cooler outside. Connor pulled his coat sleeve down over his fist and rubbed at the windows. She remembered to switch on the windscreen wipers which flicked over the screen, scattering moisture, the rubber squeaking. Apart from car noises they travelled silently

Queen Alexandra's School for Girls had been built in the early twentieth century for the daughters of colonial administrators and army officers. Pale sandstone formed the quoins around the main structure of red brick. Steps led up to its Renaissance-style façade, arches of stone supported on dark pink marble. Some who'd seen the Doge's palace in Venice commented on its similarity. Rowena had never been to Venice and had always thought it beautiful, but not today. This morning, with dawn still only a flicker on the horizon, she wished she could fly.

She left the engine running and ran up the steps. Connor turned it off and taking two steps at a time followed her in.

A house matron, a faded blue dressing gown thrown over a voluminous cotton nightdress, a grey plait lying weightily over her shoulder, was waiting for them.

'Come this way.'

The headmistress, Miss Charfield, in a state of night attire similar to the matron, was standing over Dawn who was sitting in a chair with both hands around a mug of hot cocoa from which she was taking quick nervous sips.

Miss Charfield, was a stalwart woman of a little under six feet tall. Rumour had it that she'd been a brigadier at some point in her life. She was certainly not the type to be easily flustered and even now she was keeping a stiff upper lip. Her forthright gaze strayed only momentarily to Connor and then swiftly, without acknowledging his presence, she addressed Rowena.

'Nothing like this has ever happened before. We've had girls have accidents and fall sick before, but never something as cruel as this. Your daughter was given the doll by a woman in the crowd who said it was a gift from a friend.'

'A gift?'

Miss Charfield's lips made a chewing motion as though she were about to spit out something particularly bitter. 'On the surface it looked to be just a rag doll, but it was far from that. I cannot imagine anything so horrible but have to conclude that this was a premeditated attack. It couldn't be anything else.'

Feeling as though her blood had turned to ice, Rowena placed a protective arm around her daughter. Connor leaned on the desk, eyes narrowed, his attention focused on Miss Charfield.

'What makes you say that?'

Her breasts heaved over her clasped hands.

'Because of what your...' She was about to say daughter, but looked at him and changed her mind. 'Because of what Dawn has told us about a stranger – a woman – giving her the doll.'

Not quite understanding what was going on here, Rowena shook her head. Connor looked as nonplussed as she did.

'What is it about this doll?' she asked whilst feeling Dawn's glossy hair beneath the palm of her hand.

The headmistress's face was grave.

'Somebody gave Dawn the doll and she passed it on to Belinda who took the doll to bed. During the night she rolled over onto it.' The headmistress shuddered. 'Unfortunately it was made of glass and broke easily. It crushed beneath Belinda's body. She has a number of lacerations and had to be taken to hospital. Hopefully they are not too serious, but one cannot be too careful. Queen Alexandra's has a duty to its pupils.' She glanced at Dawn then back to Rowena. 'The whole experience is quite sickening and, indeed, Dawn has already been sick. Under the circumstances I think you should take your child home for now.'

Rowena exchanged a swift look with Connor then sank down so she was level with her daughter's face. She took the half-finished mug of cocoa and handed it to Connor who placed it on the desk.

He watched her, wanting to intervene, but it was not his place to do that. Dawn was Rowena's daughter and her responsibility and although question after question plagued his mind, he had to leave it to her.

Rowena's grey eyes shone into her daughter's face. 'Darling. Think carefully. You said a woman gave you the doll.'

Rowena felt her small body shaking against hers.

Dawn nodded.

'A pretty Chinese lady gave it to me. She was wearing a red dress too just like the doll.'

'Did she say what her name was?'

Dawn shook her head. 'Only that the doll was a gift to me from an old friend and to make sure I tell you the friend's name.'

Rowena felt the colour drain from her face. She didn't

look at Connor to ascertain his response. She knew it would be much the same as hers.

'The name of that old friend – do you remember what it was?'

When Dawn nodded Rowena felt a lurching in her stomach as though she too was about to be sick.

'Kim. She said his name was Kim.'

Rowena stood up. At the same time she held on tightly to her daughter's hand. 'You're right. I have to take Dawn home with me.'

The headmistress agreed that it might be best. 'Matron bandaged Belinda's wounds before she was taken to hospital. All our attention has to be fixed on her. Her mother's in Australia at present with her father. He's a diplomat.'

Side by side, Dawn in between them, they left the school silently. Neither had any doubt that they were thinking the same thoughts. It had happened. Kim was back in town!

Rowena drove away from the school, chilled from head to toe, intermittently assuring her daughter that it was a one-off incident that wouldn't happen again. The fact that the woman had been pretty and was wearing a red dress froze her to the bone. Kim had always insisted she wear a red dress. It was no coincidence. It had to be Kim.

Belinda had been unfortunate. The main fact at the heart of this was that Dawn had been the intended victim and there was nothing to suppose he wouldn't try to hurt her again. Revenge. It had to be revenge.

'It was meant for Dawn,' she said to Connor once she saw that Dawn had fallen asleep on the back seat. His eyes remained focused, unflinching, on the road ahead. There was no real knowing what he was thinking. Finally he spoke.

'It was a message to tell you that he's here.'

Her heart raced as though trying to escape this situation whilst her mind tried to cope with some terrible consequence.

'He won't stop there. He'll send more messages like that.'

'Possibly.'

'So what can I do?'

His hands tightened on the steering wheel.

'Leave Hong Kong. It's all you can do.'

'I belong here. What about Dawn going to school, what about you?'

He gave her shoulder a reassuring squeeze. 'We belong together. Wherever you go, I go. That's all that matters.'

And keeping Dawn safe, he wanted to say, but held back thinking he might mention events to McCloud though unsure of what good that might do. He'd heard a rumour that Brandon was involved in corruption. There were always rumours of corruption in the Hong Kong police, some of which were true.

Rowena hadn't spoken. Her face was frosty still.

'Has Luli returned?'

Numb with desperation, Rowena shook her head. 'No sign of her.'

Connor carried Dawn from the car to her own little bed. The cold light of daybreak was gradually turning the sky from indigo to pewter and an orange strip of light was defining land from sea.

The slowly rising sun was only an illusion of warmth. Rowena felt as cold as ice. Even with Connor's arms around her, she was finding it hard to sleep. Suddenly, tending to the flood of refugees was no longer as important as it had been and her first instinct was to flee the threatening danger. If anything happened to Dawn she would never forgive herself and Kim would find her here. He could do it easily.

'You're tense.'

'I feel like ice.' She rubbed at her arms and gained no warmth from the bedclothes that covered her or even the warm body lying beside her. 'Understandable, don't you think?'

She felt the muscles harden in the naked arm that lay across her. Her tone had been abrupt yet she felt no regret because she had none to give. Fear had drained her. Dawn's safety was uppermost in her thoughts.

Connor combed her hair with his fingers, normally a very pleasant act that made her purr like a cat. Not tonight though.

'I have to get away from here.'

'You could go away up in the hills for a while. Just until we catch him.' He didn't mention how difficult that might be. Nobody uttered his name. Nobody knew of his whereabouts. The old criminal hierarchy had changed. The only name he was getting was Koos Maas, which sounded Dutch.

Rowena sighed. 'It's not far enough. Hong Kong is too small a place. And it's an island. It's easy to be trapped on an island.'

He kept silent as his fingers softly worked their way through her hair, thinking his own thoughts which she knew instinctively matched her own; how far did you go to keep those you love from harm?

'McCloud has promised to look into providing a couple of rozzers to protect you.'

'McCloud's men cannot be with me every hour of the day and before you suggest it, neither can you. And Yang can't be expected to run the bar by himself. It's busier than it used to be – and more complicated.'

It was true. The wartime bar had extended into the next property and the casino had filtered into a series of old storerooms at the rear of the building. And there were extra staff which Yang regarded as a slur on his competence: 'I not need others. I can do everything.' Thanks to his less than convivial behaviour, they didn't stay around for long.

Connor lapsed into silence as he considered what she'd said, knowing it was the truth but unwilling to admit to it.

They both turned onto their backs, staring at the ceiling as they considered the possibilities and assessed what the other was thinking – and planning.

At last Connor brought the mutual conclusion out into the open. 'You're going to accept the posting in Korea.'

'Only if I can take Dawn with me.' She half turned towards him. 'I'm sorry. It's all about Dawn. But it won't be for ever. It can't be. Do you mind awfully?'

She shivered when he stroked her shoulder and looked at her. Even in the dim light of their bedroom she could see worry flickering in his eyes.

'In that case I'll volunteer to go. If war doesn't happen and peace breaks out – well, I'll cross that bridge when I come to it.'

'You sound very casual about it.'

'I'm not. I'm very serious. I've thought it through. If our

friend Colonel Warrington wants you there in that hospital, he might be able to swing it so that I'm there too.'

'Connor, it's a convent!'

'OK.' She felt the roughness of his chin scrape against her neck, his breath warm and moist against her ear. 'I'll make sure I shave every day. Once I'm wearing a habit, they won't know any different.'

He'd intended lifting the mood with some humour and he'd succeeded. The thought of a man the size of Connor wearing a nun's habit and trying to hide a perpetually stubbly chin made her laugh. It was the first time she'd done so that day.

'I don't think you'll get away with it.'

'I don't think I will, but you can bet there's a UN force in need of men close to that convent. It's a hospital, isn't it?'

'And the bar? Yang can't run it by himself.'

He made a rumbling noise deep in his chest.

'You sound like a bear growling.'

'I'll sort it.'

'You need a miracle.'

'You're right. I do. I haven't done much praying for years but I can't see the Lord turning me away just because we haven't been in contact for a while. I can't recall ever asking him for a miracle. But now I am so if he's to maintain his reputation with me, then I think he should oblige.'

Chapter 11

Mrs Kate Brodie was short, slight and quick on her feet. Her eyes were as blue as those of her brother, Connor, and her hair the same coppery brown though being longer was far more unruly.

The blue frock she wore had once strained tightly across her breasts and belly, but that was in the days when her chief duty in life had been to minister to the needs and rotund stomach of Seamus Brodie. Thanks to his love of fatty bacon, buttered spuds and fried bread, he had left her a widow at twenty-four years of age. He had also left her a forge where he'd shod horses and mended motorcars, tractors and practically anything made of metal.

Having no skill in such tasks herself, she had sold the business on for a considerable sum of money. Once that money was in the bank she looked round at the old house he'd inherited from his mother, noted the heavy furniture, the drab chairs and the old-fashioned lace curtains that had dimmed the daylight to a barely endurable gloom, and decided it had to go.

During his lifetime he'd refused to get rid of any of his mother's furniture. Kate had been tempted to take the whole lot outside and burn it on a big bonfire. Of Victorian vintage and mostly made of mahogany, there was no way she could possibly carry any of it very far. Even the old wind-up gramophone was too heavy for her to lift, so instead she'd got two men from Dublin to take the lot. She'd also sold the house to a woman of low repute, an act she knew would have her mother-in-law turning in her grave if she knew. Molly Brodie had instructed her son that if he died without issue everything was to be left to the Church. It filled Kate with great joy to overturn that instruction.

On a whim she had decided to leave Ireland and spend some time in London. Whilst there she had wandered into Chinatown and been mesmerised by the colourful shop fronts, the chatter of crowds, the rows of ducks hanging in rows from hooks outside and inside the shops.

It would be wonderful to go somewhere just as colourful. She considered Europe but after a long war decided it would be as drab as the British Isles. Not only that but her brother, Connor, was in Hong Kong and that could be as interesting and colourful as Chinatown.

'I'll send him a telegram,' she exclaimed, stopping dead in the middle of Regent Street.

For a moment that was indeed what she was going to do because that was what the old Kate would have done. Arrange things. Give him a warning. Act the good girl.

Standing there, the crowds passing her on either side, a smile slowly spread across her face. The new Kate could do as she liked when she liked. She no longer had to conform. She would surprise him.

So here she was stepping off an aeroplane. In order to see as much of the world as possible, she had taken a steamship for most of her journey, stopping off at exotic places, the names ringing with strangeness: Lisbon, Naples, Cairo, Columbo, Singapore. It was in Singapore that she'd bought a ticket for a flight to Hong Kong, so excited to be doing something most people only dreamed of – if they dreamed at all.

She pulled her hat more firmly onto her head in order to shade her pale complexion. Her lips parted in wonder. This place was exactly as she'd imagined it, full of colour and noise, a world away from the smell of hot iron and villagers whose idea of travelling was a once-in-a-lifetime trip to Dublin: to go any further afield, really abroad, meant London.

After going through passport control and customs, she stopped just outside the entrance, suitcases leaning against her legs as she rummaged in her handbag for her brother's address. A bar. Connor's Bar. Well it would be, wouldn't it. Not that she'd hold that against him. In her mind's eye she imagined him playing the fiddle while somebody else did the work. Not that he was work shy; just above that sort of thing.

Her eyes swept the taxi rank. She wanted to try a rickshaw but it was late afternoon and she knew from reading a pre-war army information booklet that she had to cross the water to Kowloon.

'You want taxi, missy?'

'Yes. I need to catch the ferry to Kowloon. So glad you speak English,' she said to the taxi driver as he swept up her suitcases and bundled them onto the back seat.

His cheeks ballooned in his fat face when he smiled.

'You English have been here for long time. Have to speak it to make money.'

'Yes. Of course you do.'

Travelling on the ferry was nothing compared to a sea-going passage where one saw nothing for days except a vast expanse of ocean. At least on the ferry she did have sight of land both in front and behind her. On checking her watch, which she'd already altered to local time, she could see it was five o'clock. Kate prided herself on getting small details right. The big things depended on small things.

She employed another rickshaw driver on the other side who looked very similar to the one on the Hong Kong side. Perhaps they're brothers, she thought.

'Connor's Bar. Do you know where that is?'

The rickshaw driver's big teeth flashed in a wide smile.

'Yes, missy. Me know Connor's Bar.'

Kowloon was noisy, but she loved it. This was where I was meant to be, she said to herself and grimaced when she thought of the forge and the village where it always seemed to be raining and people were drab and spoke of nothing and did nothing except get drunk in the pub and confessed their sins on Sunday.

It was sunny here and although she kept the brim of her hat down, she was enjoying the warmth, the smells and the mix of tongues and people.

The alley was narrow and the buildings on each side were tall and flat-fronted. Off-duty servicemen eyed her as she alighted from the rickshaw, her suitcases falling out behind her.

'I do,' said the rickshaw driver, diving to pick up her cases.

'All right. You do.'

She bustled ahead of him into the relative coolness of the bar, her eyes gradually customising to the shadowed interior.

Heads turned, eyes looked her up and down – she ignored them all.

'Ah!' There he was with his back to her. Even though they hadn't seen each other for some time, she recognised her brother immediately just by the width of his shoulders and the way he held himself.

She felt the rickshaw driver hovering at her shoulder, waiting for her instructions as to where he should place her suitcases.

'Just there should be fine,' she said, indicating the spot behind where her brother was standing.

At the sound of her voice Connor turned round – and his jaw dropped.

'Bloody hell.'

'Well that's no way to greet your long-lost sister, Connor O'Connor.'

Connor noticed the cases.

'You've come to stay?'

'Hello, Kate. Lovely to see you. It's been such a long time…'

'It has. What are you doing here?'

'You know Seamus died. I wrote to you.'

'You didn't write that you were coming over.'

'That I didn't, but I was in need of a bit of adventure in my life and here I am.'

Becoming aware of the rickshaw driver hovering at her elbow, she snapped open the brass clasp of her handbag and paid him.

The driver fingered the Hong Kong dollars before grinning, nodding and heading for the door.

'Did I give him too much?'

'Possibly.'

'A bar.'

'Do I hear disapproval in your tone?'

'Does it make money?'

'Yes.'

She looked tellingly down at her cases then at him.

'That's good to know. So, Connor. Is there any room at the inn?'

It was nine o'clock in the morning and raining when Rowena phoned Colonel Warrington to say she would accept the posting to Korea.

'But only if I can take my daughter with me.'

He agreed immediately. Although she had suggested mentioning his name to Warrington, Connor had insisted he made his own arrangements.

'A few British regiments are going as part of the UN force. I'll go direct to them.'

She had signed off duty when Sherman Warrington exited the rickety old lift outside the door of her penthouse. It surprised her to see him there and her tone turned surly. Hadn't he exerted enough pressure?

'I don't receive people at home unless they're invited.'

'This is private business. I wanted to speak to you alone. I have a letter I want you to pass to my daughter. I have the utmost faith in you,' he said to her. 'A modern woman in a modern world.'

She wasn't quite sure what he meant but, willing to let the remark pass, took the bulky envelope. She weighed it in her hand, guessing there to be three pages at least.

'It seems you have quite a lot to say to her.'

'Call it fatherly advice.' He glanced beyond her to the open bedroom door.

'Already packing, I see.'

She half turned. Dawn was standing in the doorway.

'Mummy, can I take Winnie?'

Dawn was holding aloft a teddy bear which wore a pink dress and had a ribbon tied around one ear. As far as Dawn was concerned, Winnie was definitely a girl's name. Luli had made the dress and Dawn had tied the ribbon around the bear's ear.

'Of course you can.'

She saw her daughter's smile freeze as her gaze alighted on the uniformed colonel.

'My daughter, Dawn. Say hello, Dawn.'

'Hello.'

The colonel said nothing but stared coldly before turning back to address Rowena.

'I've arranged a flight to Tokyo for three days' time and a flight from there to Seoul. Good day.'

His departure was as abrupt as the sudden change in his manner. The grating of the lift grille his final salute. No goodbye.

Dawn's pearly teeth showed through her parted pink lips and she looked taken aback.

'That man doesn't like me.'

Rowena crossed the room and hugged her daughter close to her heart.

'I don't think he likes anybody,' she said.

As she caressed her daughter's silky black hair a little of the tension seemed to leave Dawn's shoulders, calmed by the perceived safety of her mother's arms. Rowena guessed that, like her, Dawn had instinctively interpreted the hate in his eyes. She shivered. It wasn't just the danger from an old lover she wanted to escape. There was also Sherman Warrington, a man she hoped never to see again.

Connor's sister Kate had breezed into their life with all the vivacity of a typhoon in May; brisk, indomitable and totally unexpected.

There were only a few days until Rowena and Dawn left for Korea and Connor too had received his call-up papers.

It had seemed only proper to arrange for his sister to meet Rowena before they left. 'This is Rowena,' he said to her. 'My fiancée. And this is Dawn.'

Kate looked from her brother to Rowena and back again. 'So how long have you been engaged?'

'Quite a while,' said Rowena and couldn't help blushing. 'I'm a doctor. We will get married at some point, but…'

'No need to explain,' Kate said in her brusque manner. 'If I'd have known what a drain a husband could be on a woman's freedom, I would never have bothered. Do you like mutton stew?' she suddenly said to Dawn. 'It's got dumplings in. And I've made apple pie and managed to get my hands on some cream. Or rather Yang did. Would you like that?'

'She's formidable,' said Rowena to Connor once his sister had taken Dawn under her wing and proceeded to shower her with substantial meals. It was also very noticeable that Yang was in awe of Connor's sister – or perhaps even a little terrified.

'Aye. 'Tis a wonder her husband lasted so long. She can't stop herself from feeding up everyone she cares for, but be in no doubt it isn't her only skill. She can more than count a shilling; she can turn it into a pound quicker than the governor of the Hong Kong bank.'

His eyes were downcast and but there was an odd lightness about him, as though fresh thoughts had entered his mind that had not been there before.

'You're going to leave her in charge while you're gone.'

It was a statement rather than a question and once again he was surprised and also pleased that she could easily read his mind.

He smiled wryly and a merry twinkle came to his eyes.

'Yang could do with a hand.'

A concerned frown creased her brow.

'What about the gambling? What about some of your more shady customers?'

His wry smile became a knowing grin.

'They'll be fine once they know not to cross her.'

It was a novelty for Dawn to board a plane, her teddy bear tucked under her arm and Luli too was excited though nervous. Rowena had carefully considered taking Luli, but reasoned that she would need someone to look after Dawn when she was carrying out her duties in the hospital. Dawn was used to Luli and loved her. Dealing with a stranger would be more taxing. Despite everything, Luli was bound to be the best bet. Connor accompanied them to the airport saying that as he'd had some input into extending the runway back in the Japanese occupation, it was only right that he take a look at it.

Within sight of the terminal he clasped Rowena's shoulders and held her so close to his chest that she was forced to look up at him.

'I won't say look after yourself because I know you will. And if you don't this young lady here will write and tell me all about it.' He patted Dawn on the head. In response she gave him a hug and the three of them hung there, a small family unit, two off on an adventure right away, the other in a few days' time.

Then they were gone.

He held his fingers to his lips as he watched the plane take off, as if in that way the taste of her kiss would remain that bit longer.

Outside in the blinding light of the noonday sun nothing had changed. Taxis and rickshaws were still jostling for space, arguing over their place in the queue. Traders selling food and woven baskets barged in front of anyone whether they looked interested in purchasing or not. Some people bought just to get rid of them.

He looked around him and was about to raise his hand to summon a rickshaw when he saw a face he thought he knew.

He frowned. The man was swarthy, dressed in a traditional manner, black tunic and trousers, white-soled shoes. His hair was tied back in a long queue, worn as a proclamation of belonging to a criminal gang.

'Where you go, sir? Where you go?'

A hustling rickshaw driver pulled up in front of him just as he was about to head in the direction of the black-clothed man.

When he next looked the man was gone. There was nothing else to do but head for Kowloon, the bar and his sister's stodgy food.

Brandon called in just after six in the evening, threw his swagger stick onto the bar and ran his right hand over his dry lips.

Connor nodded at Yang who duly produced two shot glasses, filling each to the brim with a measure of Bushmills Irish whiskey which Brandon knocked back in one.

'Have you heard the news?'

Connor shook his head and drained his glass. 'No.'

'The UN are pulling out of Korea. There's only a smattering of troops being left there.'

Connor sighed. 'And there's me all packed and ready. The powers that be don't change much, and that's for sure.'

Brandon agreed with him.

'So it could be that you won't be going.'

'I've heard nothing to the contrary. Anyway, we haven't got that many troops there. We'll be only a token force – until something big happens.'

Brandon shook his head. 'I hope nothing happens. Let the Chinese and Russians have the bloody place. Most people have never heard of it, so why should we bother?'

'Politics,' said Connor and reached for his violin.

'A bit more music to soothe the savage breast,' muttered

Brandon. 'Well, I suppose that's as good a remedy as anything.'

It was a few days later when the news came that a few reservists, including himself, were likely to ship out. Just as Connor had guessed, the small contingent of which he was part was being sent to Korea as a token force. Defending the south from the north was being left to the Korean army.

'Two days and I'll be leaving,' he said as he tuned up his violin and prepared to tuck it under his chin.

'Then you might as well party,' suggested his sister, her strident tone almost causing Yang to drop a fresh bottle of Bushmills. 'And you're the copper,' she said on first meeting Brandon McCloud, looking up into his face as if accusing him of some heinous crime. 'Are you a singing and dancing one?'

'I am a copper, as you put it, though neither a singer nor a dancer.'

'My sister,' said Connor.

'A pleasure to meet you, ma'am.'

'I'm not your ma'am. I'm Kate orCatherine if you must. I answer to both.'

Brandon's jaw dropped.

Kate took no notice but sang along to her brother's rendering of 'Molly Malone' in a voice that could crack the windows.

Chapter 12

His breath seemed to still in his chest as the gangplank was heaved away onto dry land, a poignant moment which had never affected him so severely before. It was as though a cord had been cut, an umbilical connection to a past experienced and a future yet to be endured.

As the ship nosed into the wide waters of the ocean, a pea-green nausea prevailed on the faces of those of his colleagues who had not experienced a rolling sea since the long voyage from Southampton to the Far East.

Setting aside his initial amusement at tough boys being sick, he got up from the dining table and called for attention.

'My bonny boys! You'll not be fighting your way out of a paper bag going on like this. Go out onto the deck and get some fresh air. Stare at the horizon. Go on. Fill your lungs. I guarantee you'll be downing whiskies tonight and reel like drunken sailors.'

One by one, like a trail of worried ducklings, they followed him out onto the deck. The sea was rolling in green humps. One minute they were at the bottom of a trough and the next on the peak, on a following sea that took the ship up from the stern before letting it drop, the bow of the ship pointing skywards.

The wind was salty fresh in their faces, deep breaths were taken and hard stares fixed on the horizon. It worked for some, their faces turning from pea soup to snow white – as good a sign as any that they were getting over it. Others merely heaved their dinner into the sea, vowing never to eat another thing again and walking home to Britain, Australia or wherever else they had come from, anything rather than go to sea ever again.

By the time Hong Kong had sunk out of sight he was by himself, leaning over the guardrail with his hands clasped and his gaze fixed on the spot where the familiar territory had been. He wished he could turn back time as easily as he could the old metal alarm clock that had stirred him to action back in Connor's Bar.

There were things he'd wished he'd done before leaving – before Rowena had left for Korea. That, he told himself, was when the pair of you should have got married. Never mind that about *having* to, about the risqué naughtiness of getting her pregnant to force their hand. He didn't need his hand to be forced into marrying her. He'd loved her for ever and nothing was likely to change that.

Connor's Bar had been lively the night before she'd left, the joviality aided by Connor himself playing on his fiddle and Rowena, a little tipsy from a bottle of champagne he'd bought from a contact at the French embassy, singing at the top of her voice.

'And to my pride, standing at my side, is the star of the County Down…'

She'd been so drunk that she'd got the words wrong, but it didn't matter. All that really mattered was keeping the sound of her voice inside his head.

He'd sung the song again on the night before he'd set sail even though she wasn't there. In his heart she *was* still there. She always would be.

A loud shout woke him up that same night. At first he blinked into the darkness thinking that he no longer had his bedroom to himself. As his dream came back in bits and pieces, he'd realised that he'd been the source of the shout, calling out for his star of the County Down.

The undulating waves between the ship and the vanishing island made him want to stretch out his hand and follow the curving movement, so similar it was to the curve of her hip, the slighter slope of her thigh.

Closing his eyes he took a deep breath, wishing it was her hair and her body he was smelling and not the salty sea air. In an effort to hold onto the memory he narrowed his nostrils and closed his eyes.

'Bracing, don't you think?'

He opened his eyes and looked at the man who had interrupted his most intimate thoughts.

Father Mark had dark eyes and black hair. When they'd first been introduced he'd said he was born on the island of Malta in the heart of the Mediterranean.

Connor had asked him what in the world he was doing heading for Korea.

'A challenge, Sergeant. Malta is a small island with a captive audience, you might say. I'm on my way to administer to a number of our mission convents. A volunteer was asked for, so up shot my hand. I've always wanted to travel.'

He felt the priest's eyes appraising him, wondering no doubt whether he was still as unflinchingly Catholic as the country that still tinged his spoken English with pronounced vowels.

'Are you a married man, Mr O'Connor?'

'Almost.'

'That's a cautious answer. Or cryptic. Depending how you look at it.'

'She's very dedicated to her job. She's a doctor.'

'Ah! Very commendable. The hospitals in Hong Kong seem very good. Expensive, but good.'

'She doesn't do much at the private hospitals. She runs – or ran – a medical station for refugees. It's something she's been doing for some time.'

Speaking about her to a total stranger was very comforting, like a lifebelt to hold onto in the stormy seas that lay ahead.

'Is that so? It must be hard for you to leave her behind.'

'I haven't. She left for Korea before I did to take up a position in a convent hospital near Seoul.'

'Did she indeed!' He seemed most impressed. 'Poor souls. Fleeing homes and wars constitutes a great deal of Asian life. We have to do what we can to help where we can and perhaps bring solace to troubled souls both north and south of the thirty-eighth parallel.'

Connor gritted his teeth in a bid to hold back what he would like to say which would no doubt bring offence. Father Mark noticed.

'It may surprise you to know, Sergeant, that the Church has a large flock in Korea. The first mission was set up sometime back in the last century – not by the

Catholic Church unfortunately, but we caught up pretty quickly.'

'I didn't know that.'

'Never mind.'

He paused. Connor continued to stare at the sea but was aware of the priest studying him before he deigned to speak again.

'Are you going to Seoul?'

'That's the plan. I'm part of Colonel Warrington's United Nations contingent there to oversee and evaluate – whatever that means.'

'I hope for your sake it means exactly what it says. Observe and evaluate. We certainly do not want any more fighting.'

Resting his arms on the curved teak of the ship's side rail, he clasped his hands together. No, he did not want to fight. He'd done enough.

'Would your lady be going to the Carmelite convent of St Catherine?'

'Yes.' Connor's manner had turned brusque. He wanted to be alone with his thoughts.

'That's one of ours and not too far from the United Nations enclave. You should be able to meet up.'

Connor smiled and looked at the priest, noticed his eyes were twinkling mischievously.

'You held onto that bit of information, Father.'

The priest beamed. 'I thought it wise to wait until you had sifted your thoughts and collected yourself.' He touched the brim of his hat in the manner of a salute. 'I'll be holding a service later this morning – I managed to bring two bottles of communion wine with me. Will you be taking communion?'

Connor shook his head. 'No.'

'I'll be taking confession straight after.'

Connor turned to meet the priest's direct gaze. The twinkling hint of mischief was still there, almost as though he knew that it had been years since his last confession and, God knows, he had plenty to confess.

'I won't be doing that either and it's a long while since I set foot in a church.'

'You served in the war?'

'Yes. I did. I was hoping never to see another. I might not be so lucky second time round.'

'Neither might I in my mission, but there, we still have to do our best, don't we?'

Chapter 13

KOREA

'We're only twenty-five miles from the dividing line between North and South Korea. Did you know that?'

'Yes,' Rowena said in a distracted manner. She was finding it hard to concentrate on what the mother superior was saying. The green tea provided in small clay bowls was unsweetened so did little to revive her after her long journey.

'You'll find it strange at first. It's not quite Chinese and not quite Japanese either. People do tend to lump them altogether.'

'I was aware there were differences. I worked in Japan at the end of the war.'

The robed woman smiled kindly and nodded. 'So I am given to understand.'

Korea was tagged onto China, a jagged promontory pointing like a finger at the island of Japan. The costumes were different, the women wearing full-length dresses or voluminous ankle-length bloomers. Their houses were built in a style of their own and the Korean people had their own customs despite the incursion of latter-day invaders trying to make it otherwise.

'Come along. I'll take you to your house.'

Taking hold of Dawn's hand and leaving the tea unfinished, she followed the tall upright figure of Mother Immaculata Conceptua out of the main gate of the convent and down a narrow pebbled alley.

With staggered neatness, the pretty houses with their tiered roofs and neat portals ranged on either side of the pebbled slope.

'There's no key,' said the saintly woman as she pushed open the door. 'Nobody has keys. Everyone trusts everyone else and in all my years here I have never heard of anything being stolen.'

'That's good to hear.'

The door entered into one large room that seemed surprisingly warm considering there was a cold northerly blowing outside.

The nun pointed at the fireplace, the hobs and the cast iron pot hanging over the central glow.

'The fire is lit so the floor is warm. Water is heated behind the fire and fed into pipes in the ground. The Koreans are rightly proud of their ingenuity. Few European houses have such a fine facility – not since the Romans.'

Rowena pushed misgivings to the back of her mind and focused on what was being said.

'There are two bedrooms. One for you and one for your daughter. There's also a bathroom.' She grinned. 'Please don't expect it to be anything like what you're used to, but I'm sure you'll manage.'

The man who had followed them pushing a cart piled with their baggage bundled past them, grunting with exertion until at last he let the bags slide onto the floor.

Rowena was momentarily distracted by her daughter's unruffled interest in everything and wished she too could entertain the same level of excitement. With typical childish exuberance, her daughter had taken everything in her stride, flying on an aeroplane, leaving the familiar at such short notice and landing in a strange country, a different country and being greeted by a woman wearing clothes religious women had been wearing since the Middle Ages.

She was totally accepting and very excited, the opposite end of the spectrum to how Rowena was feeling, which was resentment, mostly. Being forced into anything did not sit well with her. Even now, as the nun droned on with an abridged history of Korea and the Christian religion, she found herself wondering if she'd made the right decision. Remembering the episode with the glass doll, the probability that Nan Po, the old man opposite, had been watching her, and that Koto had got to her through Luli, were valid reasons for coming here. But no sign of Kim. Just the threat of him, somewhere, just out of sight.

'I did the right thing,' she whispered to herself.

'Of course you did, my dear. I'm sure you'll enjoy our small infirmary – as much as an infirmary can be enjoyed.' The mother superior had heard and misinterpreted. Rowena did not correct her. Her life in Hong Kong was her own business and she was keeping it strictly to herself.

'You have very good hearing,' Rowena remarked.

The nun beamed. 'It comes from seeking out those who whisper in periods of enforced silence.'

'You do that? The enforced silence, I mean.'

'We do. It's one of the disciplines of our order.'

'I'm sure I've made the right decision.'

The nun smiled and said nothing.

Dawn came dashing in from the kitchen, a biscuit tin rattling in one hand, its lid in the other. 'I've found cookies,' said Dawn.

Rowena was glad of the interruption.

'They look delicious, darling.'

Mother Immaculata Conceptua assured them that they were delicious and home-made.

'By Sister Henrietta. Our food is supposed to be plain and simple, but we can count on Sister Henrietta to tempt us occasionally.'

'And you allow yourself to be tempted?'

'We only succumb to very small temptations. Now come along. Let's get you settled in.'

The hem of her habit swept the baked clay floor. The furniture smelt of beeswax and a small vase of flowers was set on each window sill, including each bedroom.

'Is this my room?'

The prioress laughed lightly.

'Your daughter is very excited.'

'Yes. It was her first time in an aeroplane.'

'You flew here? I came here by boat – so long ago now.' A dreamy look came to the nun's eyes.

Rowena looked around her. Everything was quite plain and the rooms were square. Such simplicity evoked a calm she had not expected yet realised she craved. Parting from Connor had been hard on both of them but she'd consoled herself that it wouldn't be for long and asked him if he thought so too. 'Of course. Let's hope so anyway.' The look in his eyes betrayed that he wasn't quite sure.

The smell of things growing came from outside the window along with the aroma of something pungent and herb-laden.

'I've never been there, but I perceived Hong Kong to be a very bustling place.'

'Yes. This is far quieter.'

Mention of Hong Kong brought a whole plethora of thoughts to the front of her mind, Connor mainly, but also the things that had happened immediately prior to her leaving, this time not the frightening things but the unexpected steps that had brought her here. Thinking of those steps and the initial offer from Colonel Warrington brought to mind the envelope the colonel had given her and his request for her to make contact with his daughter.

Now was as good a time as any.

She looked towards the hospital. 'I believe there's an American nurse here named Sheridan Warrington. Her father asked me to look her up.'

Mother Immaculata blinked as though she'd said something surprising. 'Her father asked you?'

'Yes. He did. Is she here?'

A nod was accompanied by a disquieted expression. 'Yes. She is here.'

'I'd like to meet her.'

'Well now,' said the prioress with a sudden heaving of her chest. 'Perhaps I could send her along to you. Once you've settled in. I'm sure she would be delighted to have a quiet word, especially seeing as her father asked you to introduce yourself.'

She detected a quizzical look as though the prioress knew something she didn't.

'I'd like that.'

Tucking her hands into her sleeves, the prioress smiled and gave Rowena a reassuring look.

'I can see that you were in two minds in coming here and will assume you had good reasons for so doing.' She shook her head sadly though her natural beaming smile remained fixed on her face. 'I cannot assure you that you will be happy here. It is for all of us to find our happiness – wherever it may be.'

Once the prioress had left Rowena made a big effort to put things away, some deep urge wanting everything to be spick and span and look as though she'd truly put down roots in this place. In reality she felt a great need to keep busy rather than face the reservations and the aching knowledge that it would be some time before Connor's body was lying beside her.

Dawn delighted in helping, chattering away about the trip over on the aeroplane and asking when they could do it again.

'Perhaps quite soon,' said Rowena, and sincerely hoped it was so.

She also stated her intention to be an air hostess when she grew up.

Rowena listened and said she thought it would be a very good idea. She'd said much the same thing when Dawn had declared her intention of becoming a doctor, a teacher, a chef and a soldier. At one point she'd even mentioned becoming a nun, but only after seeing *The Bells of St. Mary's*, starring Bing Crosby.

★

It was not happiness she felt as she attempted to familiarise herself with the hospital, its hinterland and this country. The building itself was far less imposing than that of Victoria House with its pillars and pediments, testament to the past power of colonial days. From the outside the roughly plastered walls of St Catherine's Hospital looked plain and unrelentingly austere, though there too hung a history. At some point, perhaps in an endeavour to lessen their plainness, they'd been painted in a rust brown colour. The weather, the winter cold and the rainfall had dribbled the paint into uneven stripes, like the slab-sided body of a starving tiger, or copious tears running down drab cheeks.

Inside was less austere, the cold white walls relieved by a series of niches each containing a plaster statue of saints Rowena did not recognise.

The convent was separate from the hospital behind a high wall unrelieved by a window or aperture of any kind. At one end of the enclave a square bell tower peered above the clay tiles like a long-necked bird craning above its nest. In one place the starkly plain walls were relieved by a pair of beautifully carved wooden doors that looked as though they should be set in a Norman arch at the entrance to a European cathedral. Closer inspection proved otherwise. Birds, dragons and other mythical beasts vied for territory with sword-wielding warriors and ladies with delicate faces wearing voluminous dresses. The doors expressed age and a grounding in old religions and legends, but were certainly not Christian in origin.

The prioress was a mine of information on the country and their surroundings, including the living accommodation, and continued to visit them for a number of days.

'I wanted to check that you're settling in.'

Rowena made tea, listening politely as the mother superior imparted more information on their immediate surroundings and Korea in general.

'These houses are very comfortable. Are they very old?'

'Not really. No more than a hundred years. They're called *hanok* houses and were originally occupied by peasant families who farmed around here, but following the Japanese occupation, they found more lucrative work in the city centre. Have you been there yet?'

'No. Not yet. I wanted to get to find my way around the hospital first.'

'And settle in. Oh dear.' She flapped one hand dismissively. 'I do apologise for wittering on. I enjoy imparting information. I used to teach geography and history before I joined the order. I still do if given the opportunity. We only have a small school and two sisters who teach in it. We are primarily here as nurses – though it is nice to keep one's hand in.'

'It's a beautiful country and so are the people. The houses too,' said Rowena. 'I much appreciate all you've told me. Most informative.'

It occurred to her that if she was to stay, she needed to learn more about this place, and perhaps in time would like it more and settle her ongoing disquiet. The buildings were indeed quite beautiful, similar to Chinese in style, clay tiles laid on top of wooden posts. The curled ends – subdued swallow tails in comparison to Chinese pagodas, still gave the impression that if magic words were uttered they would leave the roof, take to the skies and fly away.

Dusk had long fallen and darkness seeped like spilt liquid across the sky. She sat on the wooden bench set below her front window, breathed in the sweetness of blossom and nodded at one or two of her neighbours who eyed her with respectful curiosity.

A young Korean man stopped, smiled and spoke to her. 'You are Dr Rossiter.' It wasn't a question.

'Yes. I am.'

'Good. My wife and I will call in on you shortly – if that is convenient?'

Glad of the prospect of visitors, she didn't hesitate to respond that she'd very much welcome their visit.

He bowed his head in a courteous gesture. 'I look forward to it, Doctor.'

She watched him stride off up the lane, wishing he could have stayed longer.

As the night air turned colder, she left her seat and went inside.

Dawn had already gone to bed. Mother Conceptua Immaculata had sent a message earlier that day saying that Dawn would be welcome to start at the convent school whenever she felt ready to do so. Dawn had expressed her impatience, asking why it wasn't possible for her to start straight away.

A compromise had been reached. The day after tomorrow was suggested and accepted.

The day after tomorrow was also Rowena's first day. A new duty rota had been created, to which she would adhere and play her part.

Perhaps it was some kind of omen that she felt the urge to pick up the colonel's letter, finger it and wonder what it contained. Whether it was or not, the following day saw the top half of Sheridan Warrington appear above the bottom half of the stable-style door.

'Hi. I'm Sheridan.'

Her smile revealed pure white teeth. Her eyes sparkled. She was blue-eyed, blonde-haired and fair-skinned, wholesome in every way.

Exactly what I expected, thought Rowena as she opened the bottom half of the door and let her in. Then took a second look.

'Oh. How wonderful.'

What she hadn't expected was Sheridan's rounded belly. Her eyes fluttered back to her face and she smiled.

'Sheridan. How lovely to meet you.'

'You too. Dr Rossiter, isn't it?'

'Call me Rowena.'

It was only as she invited her in that she saw the man behind her, the same one who had promised that he and his wife would visit her.

Sheridan's white teeth flashed and her blue eyes sparkled as she introduced him.

'This is my husband, Jung. Lee Jung. He's a chemist and only allowed to come within these hallowed walls to collect me. I've just finished my shift. Not that I'll be doing it for much longer,' she said, smiling yet again at the same time as landing a series of affectionate pats on her stomach.

'I always keep a promise,' he said on shaking her hand. He glanced lovingly at his wife. 'We both do.'

Warrington had not mentioned that his daughter was married and pregnant and it surprised her. For now she made no comment about this and concealed her surprise. Lee Jung's open look and dancing eyes were both disarming and likeable. He never stopped smiling.

'And who is this pretty girl?' Sheridan bent low enough so that her blue eyes were level with those of Dawn.

'My daughter.'

She said it in the defensive manner she fell to at times, anticipating the flash of disapproval. On this occasion it was absent. Sheridan beamed lovingly at Dawn, all the time keeping her hand over her stomach, looking at Dawn then turning her head to smile fondly at her husband.

The message was clear, as was the depth of their shared happiness. Their child too would be a mixture of East and West.

Luli hovered in the background and bowed as she was introduced.

'Luli has been with me for many years. Can I offer you tea? English style, I'm afraid, and taken with a little milk.'

'Just so long as you have biscuits.'

'I'll get those,' Dawn piped up, delighted they had visitors and keen to impress in the hope that they would visit again. She followed Luli out into the kitchen. A mixture of Chinese and English mingled with the clattering of crockery.

Rowena turned her attention to her guests, their conversation centring on the hospital, Sheridan outlining the work they were doing while her husband's fingers lay lightly on her hand, his attention fixed on her face every time she spoke.

'We're very glad you've come. It's quite a luxury having another doctor here.'

'Another doctor?'

'Why yes. Dr Mercier does a very good job.' Sheridan frowned. 'Didn't anyone tell you there was another doctor here?'

Rowena shook her head. 'No. I was told there was a great need for a female doctor seeing as it was a convent hospital. Your father...'

At mention of her father, Sheridan's face darkened. 'Oh yes. My father. I didn't know you'd met him.'

There was no doubting the bitterness in her tone.

Dawn set a plate of biscuits out before them next to the teapot.

'I've counted ten, so that's two for each of us and two for Luli.'

The biscuits were neatly set around the edge of a large plate. Luli smiled happily at being included.

Pouring tea, doing anything, gave Rowena time to think. The colonel had been precise with the details, leading her to believe she would be the only doctor here and, as a female, imperative that she took the posting. What reason would Colonel Warrington have not to tell her there was another doctor? It didn't make sense.

Cradling her cup with both hands she took a small sip of her tea, declining to take a biscuit from the plate Dawn was passing around. The plate was emptied, Dawn bagging two for herself and insisting Luli also had two.

Dawn followed Luli out into the kitchen at the promise of more biscuits, presenting Rowena with an opportunity to talk freely.

She asked for more details about Dr Mercier.

'He's been here for three years.'

'He's a man?'

'Most definitely.' Sheridan's face clouded over. 'What did my father tell you?'

'I believe he left some things out. In fact it appears that I've been lied to.'

'By my father.'

Rowena sighed and set her cup down on the lacquered table which had stout legs inlaid with mother of pearl.

'He said the nuns specifically requested a woman doctor because men were not allowed into the convent grounds, and that included the hospital.'

'What?'

Husband and wife shared shocked expressions.

Finally Sheridan shook her head, the cheery disposition replaced by anger. 'This is intolerable.' She frowned. 'I believe you specialise in the field of obstetrics.'

'Yes, but over the years I have had to muck in with other things. Victoria House, where I work in Hong Kong, caters for refugees.'

'So Mother Superior told me.'

Husband and wife suddenly became subdued, their fingers interlocking, their eyes fixed in mutual concern.

A sudden thought came to her. 'Was she expecting me? A woman doctor?'

Sheridan shook her head. 'I'm not sure. Well, only when she knew you were coming. I got the impression it was kind of sprung on her.'

Rowena was perplexed. She took a deep breath, her

thoughts reeling. 'It sounds as though she didn't exactly ask for me.'

'I don't know, but she did seem a little surprised to receive the news.'

It was Jung who voiced the obvious conclusion to his wife.

'Your father had something to do with it? There was some reason he wanted Dr Rossiter to come here?'

Her face clouded over again. 'You're right. There has to be an ulterior motive.'

Sheridan ran her hand down over her belly, her eyes downcast. Finally, she heaved a big sigh as though she was gearing herself up to face whatever lay behind this.

Rowena thought this the right time to mention the letter.

'He asked me to bring a letter for you.'

'Did he indeed?'

Worried looks were again exchanged between husband and wife.

'One moment.'

Being alone in her bedroom where the letter was propped up beside her travel clock gave her time for momentary thought. Fleeing Hong Kong for her daughter's safety – even if only for a short time – had seemed a useful option, an opportunity to take a breather, but should she have made more in-depth enquiries? She was now faced with the fact that the situation was not quite as the colonel had intimated.

Their fingers brushed briefly when she passed Sheridan the letter. They were cold as ice.

The bright and golden girl who was Sheridan Warrington – now Mrs Jung Lee, held the letter in both hands as though feeling its weight. Jung placed his arm around his wife's shoulders and gave her a reassuring squeeze.

'Go on. You have to open it.'

Sheridan held his gaze for a moment before giving Rowena a direct look, her jaw firm, her lips unsmiling. 'My father is manipulative and self-centred,' she said suddenly, addressing Rowena. 'All my life he's called the shots – his idea of running a family. On his terms.'

Rowena eyed the envelope uncomfortably.

'I hear your mother's divorcing him.'

Sheridan covered her eyes with one hand. 'That's not true! How could he say such a thing?'

A single sob made her whole body reverberate with a single shiver.

'My wife's mother took her own life,' explained Jung as his hand gently caressed Sheridan's shoulders.

Rowena caught her breath. Disliking Colonel Warrington had been an easy thing to do. He'd come across as domineering so his daughter's manner was hardly surprising. It now seemed he was also a liar.

At first it looked as though Sheridan was going to open the envelope carefully, inch by inch so she might delay whatever demands her father was making. But suddenly she seemed to come to an instant decision, ripped the envelope open and tugged the letter out.

Rowena felt a dull ache behind her eyes when she saw Sheridan interrupt her reading, glance up at her thoughtfully before resuming.

Jung was reading over her shoulder. An icy stillness came to his face as his eyes followed the words.

Finally Sheridan looked up. Her blue eyes had lost their warmth.

Rowena waited, her feeling of apprehension billowing with uncertainty.

'Have you any idea of what this letter contains?'

Rowena shook her head but knew without being told that whatever was in the letter was as much to do with her as with Sheridan.

'Read.' Sheridan's hand shook as she passed her the letter.

Rowena bent her head and began to read. The words sprang from the page. Her breath squeezed from her lungs.

Sheridan,

Despite your attitude on the last time we communicated, I'm going to give you one last chance.

I am sure that once you are back in the USA you will rebuild your life and realise that you have no loyalty to your husband. I have spoken to a lawyer friend and he believes divorce to be only a formality. It would be done and dusted in no time.

Once the wheels are in motion I will welcome you back though with one proviso; in order to completely wipe the slate clean, there must be no child of this fateful union. We want no one to know of your temporary lapse of common sense. It will be as if this alliance had never happened.

Dr Rowena is a woman of outspoken views on birth control and abortion. She is also an acclaimed obstetrician. With her help you can eradicate the past...

She stopped reading, looked up and shook her head in disbelief.

'I don't know what to say.'

Sheridan looked at her grimly. 'My father often leaves people speechless. But I think we all know what he's getting at.'

Rowena lowered her eyes back to the final paragraph.

I want a grandchild born of good American stock to inherit my name, another Sherman Warrington. A child fathered by a man of the same race who killed my son, your brother, will not do. However, I'm not going to beg you. If you decide not to carry out my wishes, then you are no longer my daughter. I would prefer to leave the family wealth to an animal charity than leave it to a child of mongrel blood. If you choose to go your own way, then you are entirely alone and dead to me.

Regards, Your father, Sherman Warrington

The silence was solid enough to cut with a blunt knife.

Rowena folded the letter into three, her hands shaking with the effort.

When she tried to pass the letter back to the recipient, Sheridan shook her head and refused to accept it. Jung took it from her shaking hands. His open expression had darkened. It was almost as though the vile insults had aged him by a whole decade, perhaps more. He briefly scanned the other paperwork attached to the letter before folding it all up and placing it back inside the tattered envelope.

'I can't do what he's hoping I would do.' Rowena shook her head again, the words tight in her throat as though she were about to vomit. She frowned as she tried to figure out why he would have thought she would be willing to carry out an abortion – unless he knew of her views. The only way he could know was a third party, somebody to whom she'd voiced her opinions passing on the information.

Sheridan was a little calmer. 'I wouldn't agree to it even if you were willing.'

Rowena eyed the blonde young woman and the dark-haired young man whose affability had vanished in the face of the colonel's vitriolic attack. The love that existed between the two people sitting opposite her was touching and also tragic. There would be no kind grandfather to welcome the newborn into the world, but at least there would be the two of them. To her eyes their love looked boundless.

Dawn came bouncing in to ask if anyone would like another biscuit.

'Just one each,' she said, bending forward slightly with her hands on her knees.

Luli loitered in the doorway behind her, glancing pensively at Jung as though unsure what to make of this man who sat so confidently with his blonde American wife at his side.

Jung helped Sheridan to her feet.

'I think we'll forego more biscuits on this occasion. We should be going. Perhaps you can save some for next time?'

Dawn nodded. 'All right.'

Rowena also got to her feet. 'I'll be at the hospital tomorrow. Will you be on duty?'

Sheridan stated that she would be.

Rowena placed her hand on Sheridan's arm. 'You must believe me, I never for one moment realised your father's intentions. I can't imagine where he got the idea that I would help you abort your child. I wouldn't do that. I *cannot* do that.'

Sheridan's eyes were glassy, her chin firm as she attempted to hold back heartbreaking sobs. 'You weren't to know you were being bullied into coming here.'

Rowena blinked and shook her head. She felt compromised, awkward and downright sickened by the colonel's intentions.

'I would still like to know where he got the idea.'

Their parting was awkward and it was hard to feel sunny following such a blow to one's self-esteem and reputation.

'Sheridan, I'm so sorry about this.'

She saw Jung's hand seek and fold over that of Sheridan. His voice was soft and gentle.

'It's not your fault.'

'I'm embarrassed and upset. If I had known his intentions…' Sheridan hung her head and brushed a tear from her eye.

'My father is a law unto himself. He trades in secrets and having his finger on the pulse of everything that's going on. It's his job to know what people are thinking and doing. I try not to think of some of the underhanded business he's involved in. Intelligence gathering – and more – are his stock in trade. And he likes things done his way.'

'He's in army intelligence?'

'Very much so. He's in charge of subversive operations. God knows what horrible people he gets involved with.' She shook her head. 'I don't want to talk about it.'

'I only wish…' Rowena closed her eyes and shook her head.

'You wish you'd stayed in Hong Kong. I can understand that. I would prefer the letter had never arrived and that my father didn't feel how he does about Asian people.' She shrugged. 'Perhaps if my brother hadn't got killed—'

Jung interrupted, his voice soft and soothing. 'You're tired. Time to go home.'

His arm around his wife's shoulders, they began to take slow steps away from her house and make for their own.

Jung called out over his shoulder. 'Goodnight, Doctor. No doubt we will run into each other. And by the way, you have a very lovely daughter.'

'Thank you.'

Sheridan threw a weak smile over her shoulder, her warmth subdued and her eyes fluttering with unspoken thoughts.

It wasn't until the house and all in it were snuggling down for the night that she found time to think deeply on the matter. The pillow was cool beneath her head. The only light was momentary, bobbing from a lantern bouncing on a long pole held by a nightwatchman whose job was more about chasing off vermin than burglars.

She watched the light bouncing over the ceiling until it was gone. Outside a nightingale burst into melodic evensong. Unseen by the nightwatchman, something on four legs skittered over the roof.

In that vague period between full wakefulness and falling

asleep, she imagined herself back at Victoria House, slipping her shoes off, slumping back in her chair and Barbara offering her a cup of tea.

Barbara!

Her eyes snapped open. Barbara and her new Romeo. Sherman Warrington was single and a known womaniser. Barbara was an eternal romantic, always believing that the next one was *the* one, the mystical Prince Charming with whom she would live happily ever after – as if such a thing existed outside the pages of a fairy tale.

Could it be that Barbara had relayed their conversation regarding contraception and abortion to this man? Had she done it willingly or had the colonel prised the information out of her, the basis of a plan forming in his mind?

Surely not! He was Sheridan's father and the baby she was expecting would be his grandchild. Rowena reminded herself that love and hate were comparable bedfellows. Both could drive a person to the point of obsession.

Suddenly she felt terribly alone and in need of somebody to talk to. The bed was only big enough to take one person. Even so, she stretched out her arm and rearranged the pillows. Its bulk was nowhere near hard enough or big enough to replicate Connor O'Connor, but when she closed her eyes it was him. In her mind he was telling her not to worry. He wasn't that far away and would be with her as soon as he could.

Chapter 14

Connor had made up his mind to dislike Korea but found himself pleasantly surprised.

The docks differed little from any other dock in the world, smaller than Hong Kong, but big enough to accommodate the ships that were bringing in an army from all over the world.

The people were friendly and dressed differently from either the Chinese or the Japanese, mostly in white, the women wearing long white tunics, open at the front to display voluminous white pantaloons, colourful cummerbunds around their waists. Older men sported black broad-brimmed hats and ankle-length tunics, whereas younger men were more inclined towards Western-influenced clothes.

Away from the docks, thatched single-storey houses rolled like fields of wheat as though they were blowing towards the distant mountains. It was here that the air tasted like alpine water, as fresh as a mountain spring.

Soldiers with nothing to do gossiped like women about what might or might not happen and whether the high command and the politicians would instigate a war, all for reasons they didn't quite understand. All they cared about was not loafing around and although there was some bravado coupled with their wish to fight someone – anyone – it was easy to talk about fighting – far easier than actually doing it.

Inaction led to a number of units being sent back to posts all over the Pacific when it seemed as though nothing would happen.

It all changed when, on 25 June, the North Koreans crossed the thirty-eighth parallel. The fighting men sent home were instantly recalled and the threat became a fear rather than just a rumour.

There were few seasoned soldiers in his old unit, mainly because so many had been killed or were too old to be recalled. Under the command of the United Nations, an international force had been formed, meant to repel the North Koreans, though the United States, being able to throw more money and therefore more men into the furore than anyone else, were in the majority.

The sweet air and the smell of blossom were obliterated as the skies over the airport turned black with troop-carrying planes. The *chock-chock-chock* sound of helicopter blades filled the air, their outlines like a swarm of hornets roused from their nest.

Some miles from the shore aircraft carriers and warships of many nations jostled for space.

Despite being taken by surprise, enlisted men tended to believe that this was just a glitch and the mightier powers of the Western world would have the situation under control in no time. They were well equipped and well trained, fresh from the occupation of Japan and other former enemy territories.

The local headquarters was based in what had been a school, typewriters clicking like manic grasshoppers in the main hall, maps stretched out on the walls and the lower panes of the windows painted over as an aid to secrecy.

Not being of a high enough rank to be party to command decisions, Connor promised himself to keep his head down, lead his men and follow orders. He didn't trust the high command and neither did he believe that this war – which seemed to have come to full fruition – would be over in a very short time. It wouldn't. His experience taught him otherwise.

Getting home was more of a priority to him these days than it had ever been. He had promised Rowena that he would not get himself into any trouble. It was against his nature to curb his tongue and not state the truth of a situation. Neither was it in his character not to volunteer for dangerous – and overly adventurous – missions. People who had never experienced the camaraderie of a fighting unit couldn't begin to understand the bonding between men on dangerous missions. It was all about mutual support and yes, perhaps even a little mutual daring, egging each other on to carry out the bravest actions.

Infantry and artillery moved northwards towards Seoul, a long column winding like a khaki snake in the direction of the capital of South Korea. He felt the tension in the air, heard the ribald remarks of young soldiers who barely knew how to shave, recounting their exploits of the night before in the local bars, dance halls and brothels, their last leave before battle began in earnest. He listened grim faced as they boasted of how much they were looking forward to giving the enemy a bloody nose if they kept coming south.

Young soldiers, their tongues fuelled by the testosterone raging through their bodies, would not know how it was until they'd experienced wartime mayhem for themselves. He too had been full of gab and garbage at their age but that was before he'd been spattered with bone and brains, before he'd stuck a bayonet into a man's guts.

On arrival in Korea, hastily arranged training regimes, designed to get them battle-ready had been swiftly organised before they were sent on manoeuvres – long route marches intended to test both men and equipment before being ordered all the way north.

Being only twenty-five miles from the border they could only go so far north before going south again, east, then west and all the time within sight and sound of continuous gunfire.

They covered thirty miles the first day, north at first, then south east, taking in the city of Pusan and other towns on the way. Twenty-five the next, zigzagging back on their initial route march through the rich paddy fields of South Korea. Somebody mentioned it being like a mystery tour, a coach trip to who knows where. Only in a way they did know where. They were being marched up and down the country to get fit, not to sightsee. In time they would travel north, directly into the battle zone.

Everywhere they went the air smelled of jasmine, tepid water and sweating water buffalo. Some people who'd chosen to stay put in their humble abodes rather than flee south eyed them impassively as they had other conquerors, disinclined to show loyalties that might get them killed. A few brave souls waved and welcomed them in Korean, Japanese or Chinese. A teacher in a village school spoke to them in English, though not warmly.

'You didn't come here and get rid of the Japanese until the war was over. They were here for many years before then.'

There was no point in apologising, especially when he added that Korea should be one country again, not divided by latter-day conquerors, a consequence of the Second World War.

Finally they turned north and things were beginning to get serious. By the third day Connor knew things would not – could not – go as well as either the high command or his young soldiers hoped. Various nationalities made up the core of the army, urged into action by the United Nations. There were bound to be differences, not least on the language front, though English formed the core lingua franca. A Kiwi radio operator gave him more bad news.

'Our radios aren't compatible with the Yanks' radios.'

'Explain.'

'They operate on a different frequency.'

'Then get on their frequency.'

'It's not as easy as that.'

The radio operator went on to explain the technicalities which had Connor rubbing at his tired eyes and fearing that things could only get worse.

Not being on the same frequency was one problem he disliked but could contend with even if it meant going back to sending messages by despatch rider. Other problems concerned the rumours flying around.

'Nothing to worry about. We're going to nuke them so won't need to fight.'

On the surface Connor poured contempt on that particular rumour. Inside he wasn't so sure. General MacArthur was Supreme Commander, a hawkish man who gave no quarter and had never forgiven the enemy in the last war for banishing him from the Philippines – which meant he would adopt an overkill strategy if he thought it worthwhile.

'Hey, Sarge. Do you think we might get some leave when we get to the next town?'

He was asked the same question at least ten times a day by ten different men. He answered in exactly the same way.

'Only when we've seen some action – if we see some action.'

The smarter houses he'd seen closer to the coast were replaced by meaner ones with mud walls and straw roofs. On looking inside one abandoned by its owners, he saw hard, baked-mud floors which were surprisingly warm beneath his feet though there was no fire burning. A Korean interpreter explained the system, heat coming from a single fireplace connected to pipes running beneath the floor. The fire was now only ashes, but residual heat remained.

'Interesting.'

It was interesting but although he was learning more of this country every day, he knew better than to get too complacent.

There were plus sides to his posting. Muscles that were beginning to turn flabby were now hardening. His stamina had improved. He could at least keep up with the bright-eyed boys of his battalion.

At night he looked up at the stars and wondered how Rowena was getting on. He'd thought he would have had some leave by now, enough time to travel to the other side of Seoul and see her. Thanks to the sudden attack by the

Communists, things hadn't turned out like that. From the moment he'd arrived the army had taken over his life.

On closing his eyes he could smell her, as fresh as the night, filling his nostrils like the scent of the surrounding fir trees. Close by he could hear the gurgling of a mountain stream and was reminded of her laughter, her voice when she sang with him.

In memory of her, until they could meet again, he hummed the tune he regarded as hers. From the very first time he'd met her and for ever more, she would always be his 'Star of the County Down'.

His humming was overheard. 'I know that song. You sing it and I'll play it,' said a man with a mouth organ.

Connor didn't answer. Some human instinct, the ability to smell danger inherited from men who had walked the earth when it was young, made him spring to his feet. He could see the dark mountains. He could see trees, some of which no longer seemed so still, the lower branches wavering as though windblown. Yet no wind ruffled his hair or bent the flames on the camp fire. Not close up. Only in the distance, against a sky that seemed to throb as though the land beneath it was on the move.

Others had noticed it too. Orders were shouted. Men began moving. A scouting party came rushing in, their faces flushed and their eyes wide with terror.

'They're coming. They're bloody coming!'

All hell was let loose. Nobody needed any further explanation. The North Koreans were heading south faster than predicted.

The still night was shattered by the sound of gunfire.

Chapter 15

Life in the convent carried on, ruled by routine and the absence of anything noticeably different. Rumours of what was happening further north were, for the most part, kept at bay by the thick walls surrounding the convent and the hospital situated close by. No casualties had come pouring up the hill and through the double gates. It was as though everyone was holding their breath. What could not be seen was not real until it was laid out in front of them with all its inconveniences, disruption and horror.

One thing they had learned was that during the pre-invasion inactivity, the military had withdrawn to Japan, as though winning the Second World War had made them somehow immune from any other conflict. Within days of the outbreak of war, armies of the Western powers were suddenly thick on the ground, the very air above their heads vibrating with the sound of war planes.

'What else can we do but trust in God and carry on,' declared the mother superior.

Rowena understood what she was saying. The thunder

of field guns and the crack of rifles and machine guns were sometimes heard above the hum of the city, though never above the peal of bells calling the nuns to their devotions.

'The form of the service is unchanged. The nuns are trusting in God to sort things out,' said Sheridan.

'What if the DPRK are beating at the walls?'

Jung smiled, looked at his wife and ran his hand down her back.

'Don't let the habits fool you. There are lions underneath. They're brave. They won't leave the convent unless they'd forced to.'

'Let's hope they won't have to.'

Their manner lightened, purposefully pushing away their concern. In its place they made Dawn the centre of attention. Jung gave her a doll dressed in traditional finery, her porcelain face beautifully painted, a soft blush on her cheeks.

'Not like the other one,' said Dawn, her eyes flickering as she raised them to meet those of her mother.

'No, darling,' said Rowena, at the same time wishing the day would come when the glass doll that had bloodied a school friend was entirely forgotten.

Over delicious-tasting food, Rowena asked Sheridan how long she'd been in Korea.

'Five years.'

'And have you always been a nurse here?'

Sheridan's long blonde hair flowed like silk as she shook her head. 'No. I fled life at home when the family received the news of my brother's death. We were all devastated. He was a great guy. We were twins. It felt as though somebody had cut me in half. I railed at everyone, blamed modern society for killing him. It changed my father, releasing a beast more at home in his intelligence work than in the family. He became the iron man, insisting everything was done his way and woe betide me or my mother if we didn't fall in with his wishes.'

Sheridan sighed. 'I wanted peace and quiet and the relative calm of an older world, certainly not the one I was born into. I wanted no radio, no newspapers and certainly not my father. Nothing of the modern world. So I came here. That was immediately after the war ended.'

'So you weren't a nurse back then.'

'Not when I came here and I didn't come here to be a nurse. It was the vocation chosen for me by the mother superior before I took my final vows.' Sheridan's kind eyes met her grey ones. 'I first came here to join holy orders. I was a nun.'

In an odd way the news wasn't that surprising. Sheridan had a naturally kind and serene disposition. Rowena could well imagine her as a nun, and certainly as a nurse.

'I learned nursing. It's the mainstay of the order rather than missionary work or teaching though we do—' she corrected herself, 'they do some teaching, as you know, but they are rather like the old Knights Hospitallers – dedicated to helping the sick.'

Rowena expressed her surprise. 'You were a novice but took final vows. It must have been difficult to leave.'

Sheridan nodded. 'Yes. There were obstacles, but they were not insurmountable. I received the call to take the veil and that's what I thought I wanted to do, that it would be my life for ever.' She looked at Jung. 'But that was then. I thought I wanted to hide myself away and ponder the reasons the Lord took my brother to his heart, then my mother and turned my father into a monster. You see,' she said, turning her clear eyes back to Rowena, 'I can even understand my father's attitude to anyone foreign. I chose the veil of a nun in order to carry on living. He chose hatred. It's all that keeps him going. His son is dead. There is no one to whom he can pass his name and keep an unbroken chain continuing from the past and far into the future. That was what he wanted.'

'But you're having a baby – a grandchild.'

Jung interceded. 'Not one that would suit him. He wants a grandson who would remind him of his son, not of his son's killers.'

Rowena considered this. It seemed excessively cruel. She realised sending her here had been a last-ditch attempt to make his daughter conform to his wishes. He did not want a mixed race child. He wanted one fashioned in his own image.

Rowena bristled but held back what she was thinking. Sheridan's father knew that Dawn was of mixed race. He also knew that her daughter was the result of being raped. She pushed aside the chilling memory that at one time she had asked the camp doctor to abort her child. Warrington would not have known that, but perhaps he'd guessed...

'What did he think of you becoming a nun?'

Sheridan's smile was cryptic. 'Almost as bad as marrying a Korean and getting pregnant. He threatened to come and drag me out, and he did come, but the sister guarding the gate explained he could see me but only in the visiting room and then not alone. He thought I had gone crazy – like my mother,' she said more softly. 'I regret not being there for my mother. She lost my brother and then lost me. My father had been lost to her for years. It came as a great shock when I heard that she'd taken her own life.' The last words were barely above a whisper.

It was a pleasant evening and Rowena liked these people. Once they'd eaten, Jung poured a little French wine into their glasses – even a splash into Dawn's glass. Before Dawn had a chance to take it, he diluted it with a good measure of water.

'The French say children should get used to wine. Especially French children. It is part of their heritage. But only a little to start with,' he explained amiably.

There was a terrace at the back of the house overlooking a pond. Sweet-smelling flowers grew around shiny-leaved shrubs in raised beds. Two stone benches were set either side of the pond. Dawn squealed with delight as a bottle-green dragonfly landed on her shoulder. She gave chase when it flew off and went looking for more.

'So how did you meet?'

Sheridan and her husband exchanged loving looks. Their hands, resting on the stones, were touching gently as though to press more firmly would set them on fire.

'Jung is a pharmacist and often visited the convent. As the leading nurse, we were often in conversation together. As time went on something inside me seemed to break. It was as though the barrier I'd built around myself was tumbling down.' She laughed lightly. 'I suppose you could call it a whirlwind romance.'

'Will you never go back to America?'

'Stateside?' Sheridan shook her head and suppressed a shiver. 'I don't think I can do that. This is my home now. My baby has roots here.'

Rowena trailed her hand in the pond and watched as the fish circled and dived until finally deciding that she was no threat, then shook her head, an act of disbelief.

'I can't believe that your father didn't mention that you were married when he asked me to look you up. He didn't mention about the baby either, as though he thought I could somehow convince you to destroy... your baby.'

There was the sound of a carp falling back into the water after snapping at a fly.

Their attention strayed, but only momentarily.

'When I wrote to my father about Jung he raged about me being a whore, not a nun at all. He told me that if I didn't get a divorce, he would have Jung killed.'

Her gaze was steady. 'He's in such a position to do that.'

Suddenly feeling very cold, Rowena took her hand from the water. 'I see.' She cast her mind back to her conversations with him – the things he'd said about Koreans.

It wasn't often she was stuck for words, but this was certainly one of those moments.

'Do you have a sweetheart, Doctor?'

The change of subject warmed her slightly and she managed to smile.

'Please call me Rowena. And yes, I do. His name's Connor. We're hoping to marry. When we can.'

'And your daughter? Did you adopt her?'

'Sheridan, that's prying,' said Jung.

'Oh sorry. I didn't mean to be rude.'

Rowena's eyes strayed to where her daughter was some way distant, leaning over the pond talking to the fishes.

'It's all right. She's my daughter. I don't know the identity of her father and neither do I wish to know. He's most likely dead. It was wartime. The circumstances were...' She paused, swallowing the memory as though it were a lump in her throat. Even after all this time it was a difficult question to answer. In times past she had turned her face away, intimidated by looks of disapproval that were sometimes real, sometimes imagined. On this occasion she managed to hold her gaze. 'I never knew him. Not his name. She was conceived on Christmas Day, 1941. I don't know—'

'Please.' Jung held up a hand, palm outwards. She saw pain in his expression. 'I know what happened on that date. Bad things happened during the war.'

She smiled sadly at him. 'Yes. You're right.'

He smiled. 'But good things can come of bad. Dawn is a good thing, I think.'

This, she decided, was a very astute and sensitive man. She found herself envying Sheridan having her man by her side. She wished she did, but God knows where Connor was at this moment. Back in Hong Kong he'd made a promise to find her, his own departure held up by events – troops being held off until decisions were made. She missed him dreadfully.

'Connor is in Korea somewhere. I don't know where, but hopefully we'll meet up at some point.'

Just mentioning his name brought back the small details of their last meeting, his affection, his concern for her safety but also his sense of duty. Swallowing her fears, she'd smiled and stroked his lips and caressed his tumbling hair wondering how long it would be until it was stripped to an innocuous short back and sides.

The tension that had sat like a demon on her shoulders fell away as the plane had soared away from Hong Kong, first to Tokyo and then to Korea. She'd felt lighter once the threat from Kim was left far behind, along with the island that had long ago become her home. The only consolation was that Dawn was safe and she and Connor would meet up whenever the chance presented itself which as yet had not happened.

Dark replaced dusk and at this time of year, the days were sunlit, darkness falling later and the air humming with insects.

Dawn had ceased chasing dragonflies and was now paddling her hands around the water lilies and speaking in a soft voice to the fish, enticing them to come to the surface as she might entice a dog to eat out of her hand.

Rowena got to her feet. 'It's time we were going.'

'It's been a pleasure having you here.'

'You and your beautiful daughter,' added Jung.

'The air here smells so fresh,' said Rowena, lifting her eyes to an indigo sky that was scattered with stars.

Sheridan looked up too.

'I want my child to see these wonderful stars.'

Her voice was full of awe, almost as if this was the very first time she'd ever seen such a sky.

Jung placed a reassuring hand on her shoulder, his face full of concern.

'Our first child will see such a sky and so will all the others we make together.'

She gently touched the hand that lay on her shoulder.

'Why are there wars?' she asked pensively, to which Rowena answered, 'To make the peace seem more precious?'

Jung shook his head.

'Nothing has happened yet, and maybe it won't. Anyway, we have a large well-equipped army that's quite capable of holding back the enemy.'

'I hope that is so.'

'Of course we do.' Jung said it convincingly and not without a hint of pride, which was touching seeing as his father-in-law, an officer in that modern international army, would prefer that he was dead.

The air was mellow as they waved goodbye to the tall willowy blonde and her shorter but muscular husband, and wended their way home to their traditional house where the floor was warm and swallows were already building nests in the grooves between the tiles.

'They're very nice people, Mummy. Don't you think so?'

'Yes,' said Rowena. 'They are.'

Inside she wanted to cry.

Chapter 16

Fighting finally began in earnest and war became as it always had been, confusion as much a part of its make-up as shelling, falling bombs and sporadic fire exchanged with a largely unseen enemy.

Pyongyang was heavily bombed, but the fighting on the ground to the south continued. Only the city of Pusan, a large city in the south-east of the country, seemed to be holding its own.

The countryside all around Seoul had become a battleground, a hit and miss affair of ground gained only to be lost again.

Under the circumstances things had gone well enough, though problems always arose in a multinational military manoeuvre, the business with the radios on different frequencies being just one of them.

Connor and his battalion – bloodied and sullen, staggered back to the outskirts of Seoul well aware that the DPRK was not far behind them.

The debriefing was fast and not without a few hard

words exchanged between Connor and the US contingent sitting in judgement on what he had to say.

'They're right behind us and if we don't act swiftly Seoul is lost.'

'Nonsense. We're bringing in fresh troops.'

'I take it these will be men taken from the occupation force in Japan?'

'Do you have a problem with that, Sergeant?'

'They're a peacekeeping force. Mostly new recruits that have never seen any action. Sir.' The last word, the formal address, was added casually as though it was the last word he would have used for any of those sitting before him.

Jaws locked and the eyes that regarded him hardened. Connor was summarily dismissed and told to hold fast and stay in touch.

Once he'd closed the door firmly behind him, he stood seething. He would not – could not – move from his belief that a lot of dying would ensue before the incoming troops earned their spurs.

'Sergeant O'Connor?'

Colonel Warrington had approached him unheard. The very fact that he was here surprised him.

He saluted as was expected of him, though reluctantly. It was down to this man that Rowena was here and you, he thought, like a bloody lovesick fool, followed right behind her.

'Sir.'

'You look surprised, Sergeant Major.'

'I wasn't expecting to see you here, sir. I understood you were based in Hong Kong with the UN delegation.'

'Let's just say I got tired of sitting behind a desk.'

Warrington was smoking a fat cigar, his eyes steely through the pungent smoke.

'I want to speak to you. Come on through.'

Connor followed him along a cool passageway into his office. Warrington sat in the upholstered chair behind his desk. With a flick of his wrist, he indicated the chair immediately opposite.

'Cigar?'

Connor took one, rolling it between his fingers as he tried to guess what this was all about. Warrington had a reputation for getting things done and was rumoured to be involved in the more unsavoury aspects of spying and subterfuge. What was he after?

The colonel didn't offer him a light.

'I'll keep it for later.' It slid easily into his top pocket. Wondering at the thinking behind this treatment, he locked his hands together in his lap and waited.

'Your doctor friend is at St Catherine's – though you probably already know that. I take it you're going to see her?'

'As soon as I'm able.'

'Are you taking her out to dinner?'

The idea seemed slightly ridiculous in the heart of a war zone, but wasn't exactly impossible.

'I hardly think I'll have time for that.'

He spoke tightly, wondering where this was going.

'I can bypass the chain of command and get you to the hospital pdq. How would that be?'

Connor blinked.

'I do know where it is.'

'But you need a jeep and possibly a driver so if the need arises you can get back here.'

'I'm a serving soldier. I have duties—'

'I can alter those duties.'

Connor could hardly believe what he was hearing. In response he gritted his teeth and pointed out that although he desperately wanted to see the woman he loved, he had a duty to the young men under his command whose lives depended on his experience of that other war.

'St Catherine's is only ten miles away. You could be there and back in no time.'

'If the DRPK aren't hammering at the gates by then.'

'They could be.'

Those three simple words made his blood run cold. Seoul would be taken, along with most of South Korea.

'Are there any plans to evacuate?'

He nodded. 'There are. I want you to tell both your doctor friend and my daughter that I will send my personal driver to pick them up – that's if they want to abandon their vocations. I should think they will once you explain the situation.'

'That's very generous of you.'

'Of course it is, but I recognise your need and I have one of my own too. My daughter's there. I want her brought back here safe and sound. Is that clear?'

'Is this an order?'

'Of course it is. I'll fix it with your superiors and organise transport and requisitions for weapons. Do it as quickly as you can.'

Chapter 17

The man had been in the hospital for three days, slipping in and out of a coma thanks to a debilitating growth in his stomach.

He moaned when she pressed his abdomen around the periphery of the growth. His eyes flickered open and rolled in his head.

There was nothing she could do to save him, but she could help alleviate his agony.

'Another shot of morphine.'

Sheridan, duty nurse today, pointed out what she already knew. 'We've only a little left in the cabinet.'

Rowena nodded and carried on tending the wound. 'Then we use it sparingly.'

Jung had been doing his best to maintain a drug supply, but it was obvious the war was affecting his efforts. Their stock was running low, but they were doing what they could. However, maintaining a certain standard was tiring.

Rowena swiped at her tired eyes with one hand and passed Sheridan a clean dressing with the other.

'I'll leave you to it. I'm slipping outside for some fresh air.'

Sunset bled into the clear sky. A perfect end to a perfect June day if she ignored the sound of gunfire that appeared to be coming closer. The sounds of war faded and the day became more perfect when she saw him, striding towards her, his uniform reltively clean and his smile lifting the craggy face she knew so well.

The fatigue left her aching bones. Not a word was said as they embraced beneath the scented boughs of a frangipani.

Their kiss was long and lingering. He gazed into her face as though searching for some feature that wasn't there any longer.

'I've missed you.'

'Have you been in action?'

He smiled faintly but his brow was furrowed with concern. 'I can tell you that I have but it has to remain a secret. The folk back at base are paranoid about giving away our secrets – not that I think we really have any – unless you count throwing all at the enemy and getting ourselves killed!'

She touched his lips. 'Don't say that, Connor. Please don't say that.'

He sighed and for a moment put a little space between them though still held onto her. 'I'm aiming not to get myself killed – if I can possibly avoid it. Anyway, I'm here for a reason. We can't hold the enemy back.' He frowned and at the same time, she felt his grip on her arms intensify. 'Civilians are to be evacuated. Sheridan's father is here. He's sending an embassy car to collect you and your little group, including his daughter.'

'I don't think she knows he's here. It'll come as something of a surprise.'

'Getting out of here is top priority.'

'It's that bad?'

'It's that bad. The UN forces are falling back to Pusan.'

As the news sank in she flicked a finger in the general direction of the hospital ward. 'I have to tell everyone.'

Sheridan was sitting on a chair in the little nook that served as the nurses' rest room. Three hard wooden chairs and an ancient bamboo table were squeezed into the tight space. A battered kettle sat on top of a single gas ring fuelled by methylated spirit. Bone china cups, fragile and beautifully painted, hung from brass hooks.

Sheridan was bent over her rolled-down stocking as she applied cream to a burst blister on her ankle.

On hearing Rowena enter, she looked up and smiled. 'I thought you'd already left.'

'I'm just about to. Connor's outside.'

'Lucky you! I'd like to meet him.'

'I think you should. He's brought a message from your father. He's in Seoul.'

Sheridan's head jerked up.

'He's here?'

'You didn't know? He didn't tell you?'

She shook her head, her lips pursed tightly.

'You might as well hear it directly from Connor.'

Sheridan followed her and after a brief and rather restrained handshake, Connor explained in more detail.

'Apparently the enemy has broken through. All civilians

are being airlifted out. Your father's sending a far for you both.'

For a moment Sheridan froze and the smile dropped from her face

'I'm not sure I believe him.' She shook her head. 'I won't go.'

'Sheridan. You have to think of the baby.'

Sheridan's face, which usually seemed to shine like sunlight, was now as grim as November.

'He'll force me to get rid of the baby – one way or another. Once I'm back in the States he'll arrange for it to be adopted. I'll never see my child again.'

'No.' Rowena shook her head. 'He's your father and once he sees the little mite, he'll be smitten. Trust me. I've seen such situations before, and anyway, Jung would never allow it.'

Sheridan shook her head emphatically. 'I don't believe that. You don't know my father like I do.'

Connor stood silently. Judging by his stern expression, he too didn't believe Warrington would be persuaded.

Sheridan sighed, hanging her head and at the same time massaging the nape of her neck.

Rowena glanced at Connor, wishing he looked more optimistic. He didn't, so she went on trying to persuade. 'We're in the middle of a war zone, Sheridan. It's only natural for him to worry about you. Perhaps this could be the chance to make up and he's taking that chance.'

Sheridan's eyes flashed and for a moment the bright blue seemed green as the sea.

'No. That's not what he wants.'

'Yes on both counts.'

Rowena sank onto a chair. It still irked her that the colonel had never mentioned anything about his true reason for wanting her here. For the umpteenth time she deeply regretted sounding off about contraception and abortion in front of a witness. Her anger with Barbara still burned deep inside.

She reached for Sheridan's hand. 'Come on. I want you to meet Connor.'

'And have him persuade me?'

Rowena sighed and eyed Sheridan anew. 'You're frightened of him – your father, I mean.'

She nodded. 'Look. Give me time to think this through.'

Suddenly, Connor was there, filling the doorway.

'Ladies, I could wait no longer. The suspense was killing me. Am I interrupting anything?'

'Of course you are,' said Rowena, plastering a smile onto her troubled countenance.

The introductions were short and sweet but Sheridan regained a portion of her happy expression.

'Your father's providing the transport to the airport, the rest is down to Uncle Sam. You can fly to wherever you want to go – anywhere that's safe and suits your fancy. You don't have to go back to America. From Tokyo you can go anywhere in the world.'

Jung was informed. Gunfire sounded in the distance, adding impetus to his insistence that yes, of course they must leave.

'Only if you go too.'

'I'm a civilian. Of course I will go.'

It was a big relief to everyone that Sheridan was finally

convinced. As civilians they would all be able to leave the country and flee to safety.

'Seoul is surrounded. It's not going to be easy to get out. All we hold now is the airport. It wasn't easy to get here, so don't think the car is likely to be here tomorrow or the next day. They have to clear a pathway through first.'

In the gathering dusk Connor held Rowena in his arms. 'You could come with me now if you like – I can probably squeeze Dawn and Luli in too. It's only a jeep, though. The limousine for you all arrives tomorrow.'

She shook her head. 'I'll await the car as ordered – just in case Sheridan wavers. At times I don't think she's as confident as she makes out. Do you mind?'

'Of course I do. But I know from past experience you'll do what you want to do. You're an independent woman, so you are, but that's probably the reason that I love you.'

Her arms tightened around him. 'You're going now?'

'I've a war to fight.'

'Where?'

'I can't tell you that. You know I can't.'

'Stay alive, Connor. Please stay alive.'

Darkness was falling when Connor and his driver left for the dangerous journey back to Seoul. The sky to the north glowed orange with shellfire and even though the heavy artillery was some distance away, the smell of cordite drifted on the air.

The jeep ricocheted between potholes. A lone buffalo stumbled across the road in front of them then headed down the bank and into a rice field.

Connor leaned forward. Livestock were usually shut in at night. Normally of a placid disposition, this one had looked frightened and moved faster than he'd ever seen one move before.

Colonel Warrington had been true to his word and provided him with a driver by the name of Joe. On the way to the convent he'd chatted amiably about his folks down in Alabama and his relief to get away from there and sample the delights of a different world.

'Man, I've never seen such pretty girls. Like china dolls, so fragile they look as though they might break in two if you gave them an almighty hug.'

To Connor's mind, this wasn't beyond the bounds of possibility. Joe was built like a bear.

He'd still had plenty to say when they'd first left St Catherine's, but now, only a few miles from Seoul, had fallen to silence.

Some way off to their left came the sound of a gunshot, followed by a few more.

Joe put his foot down, the jeep leapt forward, and Connor reached for his revolver.

His eyes skirted the blackness beyond the rice paddies. For the moment they were passing through open ground where an attacker would be seen, unless they were laid full length in the wetness or against the banked up earth between the field and the road.

Every muscle in his body tensed as with narrowed eyes he peered into the darkness for the slightest sign of movement. Very soon the fields gave out to a wooded area, the section of road blacker than any they had so far gone through.

There were no further gunshots. The resultant silence was

like a held breath. The sound of the Jeep's engine and the squealing of the springs when Joe failed to evade a pothole set his teeth on edge.

Joe muttered under his breath as they careered into the tunnel of trees, his foot heavy on the gas.

His nerves on edge, Connor turned this way and that, waiting for whatever might be here to come at them from out of the darkness.

Halfway through the tunnel of trees, three quarters of the way through, the more open country enticingly lighter up ahead.

Just a few yards and they would be out.

A single gunshot cracked out of the darkness, followed by another, then another.

Connor fired into the blackness, at the same time seeking a flash of gunfire from the attackers to give him direction.

The Jeep swerved from side to side, Joe's effort to avoid bullets rather than potholes.

The road evened as they crossed the line from the tunnel of trees and out onto the open plain.

Connor began to breathe a little easier. The trees had provided good cover for their attackers.

'Done it, boss.'

Joe sounded jubilant.

Against his better judgement Connor began to lower his revolver. His action proved premature when a shot rang out and he felt the thud of a bullet enter his arm.

'Damn!'

The gun fell from his hand and onto his lap. He didn't need anyone to tell him that the bullet had shattered his arm. The pain was agonising, more so when another shot got him in the upper thigh.

With Connor crumpled at his side, barely able to contain his agony, Joe grabbed the gun from his lap and, with one hand on the wheel, began firing over his shoulder.

The Jeep bounced onwards. Whilst Joe kept on firing, Connor gritted his teeth against the terrible pain and leaned across to help steady the wheel with his left hand, his body bent almost in two until the pain took over and he began to slide into unconsciousness.

Joe squeezed the last ounce of speed from the Jeep which turned out to be enough to leave their attackers behind.

In a cloud of dust and debris they finally reached the UN compound where an unconscious Connor was offloaded by medics. After that everything was a blur except for the burning fear that his attackers had veered away from the heart of Seoul and were heading for St Catherine's.

Chapter 18

Another day dawned and still the very sky seemed to roll with the sound of what seemed like distant thunder, its blueness scarred with dark grey and bright orange.

Worried eyes turned northwards and throats were constricted by the unspoken dread that the war was getting closer.

Rowena's throat was as tight as anyone's. There was little to be seen from the narrow window of the ward, but still she stared, fearing for herself, for her daughter, for everyone.

Standing beside her, Sheridan placed a protective hand over her swollen stomach. 'Is that what I think it is?'

Rowena nodded. 'I thought the promised car would have been here by now. I think we need to make plans.'

'What if it doesn't come? Where do we go?'

'That's what we need to check.'

'With my father. Go direct to him,' blurted Sheridan then changed her mind as to who exactly should be contacted. 'With somebody. Anyone that knows.'

'Come on. We need a telephone.'

There was only one phone and that was in the main office. Rowena raced there, closely followed by Sheridan, leaving a nun and a Korean nurse to carry on.

The door, an ugly old thing fashioned from metal with wire-enforced glass in its top half made a screaming noise as she flung it open.

Dawn. She had to get Dawn out of here. How ironic that she'd supposed this to be a place of safety from the phantom that was Kim Pheloung.

Lee Jung came rushing in behind her and grabbed the phone before she did.

Phone slammed tight against his ear, he barked questions in the native tongue and looking perplexed and worried by the answers he was getting.

As he replaced the phone in its cradle, he turned his worried face to her.

'It's happened. The rumours are correct. The DPRK are surrounding Seoul.'

She knew DPRK meant Democratic People's Republic of Korea. The north was on the move, and were determined to grab back what they considered theirs – the whole of South Korea.

Jung's face glistened with sweat and his kind eyes were black with fear.

'Where's Sheridan?'

'I'm here.' Her face drained of colour and using both hands to lean on the door frame, Sheridan appeared; her eyes like saucers, her face as white as milk.

Jung went to her and gripped her shoulders. 'We have to get out. *You* have to get out.'

'No.' She shook her head vehemently.

'Yes. Everyone I spoke to is terrified. Some are heading out of the city to Pusan. Some say the Communists are coming this way and that they will take Seoul. Others refuse to believe it. But we must believe it, Sheridan. Do you understand what I'm saying?'

'But where do we go?' She looked at Rowena. 'Connor said my father was sending a car.'

Rowena sighed. 'He did. I thought he would be back straight away.' She feared the reason he might not have returned, but kept it from her face. At a time like this she had to be positive. 'We need to find out how bad things are from somebody with their finger on the pulse.'

She exchanged a knowing look with Sheridan's husband who in turn took a deep breath as he waited for his wife to do likewise and hold her terror at bay. 'Can you phone your father?'

Sheridan's face crumpled. 'Do I have to?'

'We need to know how much time we have and whether that car he promised is coming.'

She shook her head. 'I can't. I just can't. Jung, please don't ask me to phone him.'

'But your friend Connor said he was sending a car to get us out of here.'

Her expression remained tense. 'He'd prefer me to be dead.'

Jung shook his head and his expression betrayed his pain and the truth of what he said next. 'No. He would prefer me to be dead.'

Rowena felt enveloped in tragedy. She had no doubt that he would also most likely prefer the baby to be dead too.

'Let me do it.'

She pounced on the phone, got the operator and demanded in a tone that was far sharper than normal that she be put through immediately.

She was passed from one soulless voice to another, first one army telephonist, then an officious army corporal, a woman whose tone became sympathetic once she was told her reason for phoning. Finally she was passed to the colonel's personal administrator who put her through. His clipped manner was unchanged.

'Dr Rossiter. I know why you're phoning.'

For a moment the throaty roar of a low flying aeroplane drowned him out.

'I'm sorry. Can you repeat that?'

'As you can hear, we've already got planes taking off.'

'With civilians? Are civilians being airlifted out?'

'Only if they want to go.'

'I was told you were sending a car. Your daughter is ready to leave now. Right now. As her doctor, I have to insist that she is given priority.'

Rowena glanced at the size of Sheridan's stomach, then her fearful face. Jung wore an intense look and she could tell he was apprehensive of the verdict from a man who openly hated him.

'Are you travelling with her?'

'Yes. There are also a number of nuns and other medical personnel.'

'Has she read my letter?'

'Yes.'

'Have you read my letter?'

'Yes.'

There followed a leaden pause.

'And?'

'We need to get her to a hospital.'

'Ah! Yes. Of course you do.'

She'd been purposely vague. She had skimmed over any reference to terminating his daughter's pregnancy.

'She needs the pristine environment of a quality hospital.'

A pregnant pause as he assessed what she was saying to him. Not that she would specifically carry out such an operation, but that certain standards had to be met. Her heart was in her throat.

'If you can get your things together I'll make sure your names are on the passenger list. But no natives. Is that clear?'

She realised he meant Koreans but could not bring herself to believe that Jung, the father of his unborn grandchild, would not be allowed aboard.

'How do we...?'

'As promised I'll send a car for you and my daughter. Buses for the nuns and other medical staff. The car should be with you shortly, then the buses. Tell everyone to get ready.'

An abrupt click signified the call was ended. She'd wanted to ask him if he'd seen Connor, but he hadn't given her chance.

Silence was thick on the air when suddenly the phone jangled and made them all jump.

Rowena pounced on it. 'It's for me.' It turned out she was right. Connor's voice was full of urgency.

'I'm being airlifted out. You need to get here. Fast.'

'You're being airlifted?'

It seemed like a miracle, until the probable reason hit her.

'I've been injured. Just a flesh wound. Hobbling a bit, that's all. Can you get here?'

'Yes. Colonel Warrington's arranged for us to have seats on the plane and he's sending a car to pick us up.'

'I'll be on the same flight. I'll look out for you. It'll be the last one. You know that, don't you?'

She said yes without really taking in what he was saying, probably because she couldn't quite believe it to be true. Civilians needed to be airlifted out of the war zone. She shivered, remembering all too well what could happen if they were caught by enemy troops.

Luli's moon-shaped face turned as pale as silver when told of what was happening.

'We go back to Hong Kong?'

'Tokyo first, then Hong Kong.'

Dawn took the news in her stride. Despite the panic going on all around her, she was excited that once again she would soar into the sky and land in an entirely different country.

'I like flying,' she said in a very adult manner.

In amongst all this havoc, the rushing backwards and forwards, the air of outright panic, the doors of the convent remained closed, the nuns nursing in the hospital keeping relatively calm as though they were somehow a fortress and could withstand whatever was to come.

'These are stout walls,' Rowena remarked to the prioress after telling her that buses would be sent to rescue all Western personnel, 'but that won't stop them.'

Sister Immaculata Conceptua was dismissive. 'We're not leaving.'

Rowena did her best to persuade her.

'Do you realise what might happen?'

Just uttering those words alone were enough to bring back terrible experiences from that awful Christmas Day in 1941.

The nun's expression remained one of serenity. 'I am well aware. Christ is our armour. We will not leave here unless we are thrown out.'

Rowena considered the comment both clichéd and ill-considered, but stopped herself from saying that the enemy might very well do a lot more than throw them out. Field artillery and machine guns were perfectly capable of piercing even the most splendid armour. Desperate to convince the prioress to leave, she tried again.

'The buses are our best way out.'

Mother Immaculata Conceptua was resolute. 'The sisters and I will say prayers to the Blessed Virgin and ask for both protection and guidance. The way will be shown to us.'

The first sign that things were moving in earnest came within the hour. A bus came trundling into the yard, a cloud of dust behind it and two UN army outriders on motorcycles in front of it. The colonel had been true to his word.

A man wearing a uniform and carrying a clipboard leapt down the front steps from where the driver sat.

'I've come to pick up non-Korean nationals who are too sick to walk. Can I speak to the doctor in charge, please?'

'I'm Dr Rossiter. Perhaps you'd like to follow me.'

There were twelve non-Koreans in the wards and thirty-four nationals. Some of them were South Korean army.

As the sergeant from the bus wrote names on his clipboard, Rowena's eyes were on those who would not be going, mainly members of the South Korean army suffering from malaria and a number of other sicknesses. Some of them were delirious and barely able to sit up in their beds.

As she stared, darkness seemed to descend all around her and she was back in that other time and another army. Christmas decorations twirled in the draught from an open door and the soldiers in the beds were not Korean but British, Australian and Canadian. Short, stocky figures ran between each bed. She heard screams, saw again the bayonets thrusting into helpless men. Even when they were lifeless, the screams continued. Even after all these years she could still hear them ricocheting around her skull.

She suddenly became aware that the sergeant was saying something to her and jerked back to the present. The images faded.

'Doctor. Did you hear me? I've listed everyone entitled to board the bus.'

'What about the Korean soldiers?'

He shook his head. 'Sorry. I have my orders and there's only room for so many on the bus.'

Informed of what was going on, Sister Henrietta, both a nun and very well-trained nurse, sank to her knees between the beds, bowed her head and clasped her hands in prayer.

Another nun was shepherding the half a dozen pupils from the convent school into the ward.

Dawn ran to her and Rowena hugged her close.

Out of the corner of her eye she espied Sister Henrietta, still on her knees praying. This was one rare moment when she too felt like getting down on her knees and saying a prayer. The unimaginable had happened.

Despite her urging, the nuns were still adamant that they would not be leaving the convent.

'We have to be here for the sick and wounded being left behind. They need our care.'

'Come on, dear,' she said softly and kissed the top of her daughter's head. 'We need to pack. Just one suitcase, I think. We have to be quick.'

An unspoken message passed between her, Sheridan and Lee Jung. All that mattered was getting away.

It seemed the suitcase was too small and she was trying to take too much. Things kept spilling out and no matter how hard she pressed down on the lid the clasps refused to fasten.

Annoyed, she smacked her hands down hard on the irksome brown leather.

'I don't think I can get much else in here.'

'I can help,' said Dawn.

'Is your case packed?'

'Yes. Luli and I are sharing.'

Dawn bounced onto the bed then sat on the lid. The clasps clicked into place.

'Clever girl. Better get going.'

For a brief moment Rowena stood in the doorway looking back into the cosy house where they had spent so little time. It should have been a place of safety but events on a wider stage had caught up with it.

'Goodbye,' she whispered.

'Mummy.' Dawn was tugging at her skirt. 'We have to go.'

'Well you seem in a big hurry.'

Dawn smiled. Her eyes sparkled. 'I want to go on the plane again.'

Despite everything Dawn's blithe comment made her feel that bit lighter. Her daughter was prioritising things in her own way.

Sheridan and Jung were waiting for them outside, their faces flushed and anxious. Jung was carrying what looked like a new suitcase in one hand and a carpet bag in the other.

With barely a word the small party hurried to the main compound of the hospital.

Rowena noted that the gates were now tightly shut and soldiers of the South Korean army stood guard with weapons raised.

Unlike the solid wooden gates of the convent, the hospital gates were of wrought iron and through them she could see the faces of frightened people. There were demands to be let in, shouts, screams and the sound of crying children. Helicopters hung in the sky like black spiders, swooping off in diverse directions in pursuit of goodness knows what.

Rowena hugged Dawn tightly as they waited in their huddled little group, feeling privileged but also guilty that they would get out when most of the people clamouring at the gates would not.

The crowds at the gate surged forward as the car appeared. Extra guards, their weapons cocked and ready for action, began beating at them with the butts of their rifles, pushing them back so that the car could get through and the gates could be opened.

The black bonnet of the official-looking vehicle, a UN flag fluttering on either side, pushed its way through. It was of the kind used by embassies to ferry diplomatic staff, not khaki like the ones used by the army. The colonel could certainly pull strings at a very high level, thought Rowena.

Perhaps it was seeing Sheridan's blonde hair blowing in the wind that made the driver head straight for them and park just feet from where they were standing. A cloud of yellowish dust rose like smoke into the air. The driver got out and addressed Sheridan directly.

'Colonel Warrington's daughter?'

'Yes. With family and friends,' she said quickly.

She sounds scared, thought Rowena, but then, we're all scared.

The driver opened the passenger doors. Rowena, Dawn, Luli and Sheridan clambered into the back. Lee Jung was about to get in the front seat when the driver's arm sprang across and stopped him.

'Excuse me, sir. I'm only scheduled to pick up four people.' He eyed the note he held in his hand. 'Can I have your name?'

'Lee Jung.'

'He's my husband,' Sheridan added.

Not convinced, the driver sucked in his lips as he eyed the list for a second time. 'I don't appear to have you listed.'

Watching with one arm around her daughter and the other around Luli, Rowena felt the apprehension in her stomach turning to fear.

'He's my husband. You can check with my father, Colonel Warrington.' Sheridan was beginning to sound panic-stricken.

At mention of her father's name, his attitude changed. 'Get in, sir. We don't have much time.'

Jung sat up front with the driver, everyone else squashing

themselves onto the rear seats that faced both forwards and backwards.

They drove to the gate where they stopped and waited for it to open. The guards came together in a solid wall, bracing their weapons across their chest, ready to beat back the frightened people with their children and their bundles still seeking refuge from what was to come.

Aided by beatings and shots fired into the air, the crowd fell back, the guards opened the gates and lined up side by side to form a barrier, allowing the car to drive through.

Breaks occurred in the soldierly lines as the press of terrified humanity attempted to push through, hands scrabbling at the car windows until it had picked up speed. Even then terror gave wings to the feet of those running behind the car, crying, screaming and begging to go with them.

The atmosphere inside the car was sharp with tension. Rowena hugged Dawn more tightly, praying that they wouldn't be too late to board the flight that would take them to safety.

Every so often Jung glanced over his shoulder at Sheridan. Her face was white and her flesh taut over her cheekbones. He did his best to comfort her, assuring her that everything would be all right. They would soon be out of here.

The roads were becoming packed with men, women and children, their homes piled high on oxcarts, their animals tethered behind.

The tide of people eddied around them, parting like water as the car nosed forward. Some shouted and waved their fists. Clashes seemed to be occurring with uneasy regularity.

At first she couldn't work out why fights were breaking

out, until it occurred to her that not everyone was heading away from the enemy. Some were heading towards it, mostly the more mobile who took great strides or rode bicycles.

She tapped Jung's shoulder and pointed it out to him.

'Some people appear to be heading north towards the army. Am I right?'

He looked over his shoulder at her, his face lined with concern.

'Not everyone supports the government in Seoul.'

She nodded feebly as though she understood when in fact she didn't really understand at all. Following the end of the Second World War and the defeat of Japan, who had occupied the country since 1912, the victors, notably Russia and the USA, had divided the country in two. The north as a protectorate of the new Communist China, the south as a Western enclave, had seemed an excellent compromise at the time.

'I thought everyone agreed to the country being divided.'

Jung shook his head. 'Families have been divided – children divided from fathers, mothers from sons. There was hope but now there is not.'

An uneasy silence reigned yet again.

Rowena closed her eyes and buried her face in her daughter's hair. Luli looked nervous. Sheridan laid a protective arm over her stomach, rested one foot upon an upturned suitcase.

A cloud of yellow dust rose from beneath the car tyres as it came to an abrupt halt at the entrance to the airport which was heavily guarded by troops of the United Nations.

The driver wound down the car window. The gap was

immediately filled by the face of an American soldier who looked to be barely out of high school.

They were asked for their names which were ticked off a list fastened to yet another clipboard. The soldier's yellow-stained finger ran down the list. He counted the names then counted the heads inside the car.

'What was that last name?'

'Lee. Jung Lee.'

The soldier exchanged a quick word with the driver who confirmed that Jung's name wasn't on his list either.

'He's my husband. He has to be on there,' called a very worried Sheridan from the back of the car, her voice bordering on hysteria.

The driver backed up her claim and suggested they check with Colonel Warrington.

'No time.' The guard waved them on through.

The tension that had accompanied them all the way from St Catherine's was still with them, but lessened at the sight of the aircraft waiting there on the runway.

The driver helped them out with their luggage and pointed them in the right direction. 'You'd better hurry. Through there to have your papers checked.'

They ran to where more uniforms were checking and stamping papers, Jung carrying both his own and his wife's luggage.

Ahead of them a family group of Korean nationals were turned away and immediately broke down, screaming and crying that they had worked for the American forces and would pay the price if they were left behind.

Members of their own army were called to escort them

back across the concourse and outside to whatever fate awaited them.

Then it was their turn, first Rowena, then Dawn and Luli, then finally Sheridan. All were stamped and told to hurry along and to take their luggage with them. They took only a few hesitant steps, then paused and waited until Lee Jung's papers had been stamped.

Even as they waited, Rowena felt a lurching in her stomach, a sense of foreboding that brought a lump to her throat.

The words she'd suspected hearing were finally spoken.

'I'm sorry,' said the official looking directly at Jung. 'Your name isn't on the list. Non-Korean nationals only.'

'He's my husband,' shouted Sheridan who had already left the small group to return and stand like a rock beside Lee Jung.

'I'm sorry. The last plane to Tokyo is for non-combatant, non-Korean nationals. You're welcome to carry on, Miss—'

'Mrs. Mrs Lee Jung!'

Sheridan's face looked as hot as her voice.

Rowena sensed her terror and sense of helplessness. She could not leave her to stand alone.

'Look,' she said, addressing the official whose expression gave no sign of either emotion or giving in. 'A number of nuns were scheduled to fly on that plane. They were guaranteed seats but declined to leave so there are definitely spare seats.'

The official shook his head. 'I'm sorry. They've already been allocated, besides which, the rules are very specific. Non-Korean nationals only.'

'But he's married to an American.'

Again a shaking of his head. 'Wives of non-Korean nationals are allowed, but not husbands.'

'That's ridiculous! He'll be killed if he stays here.'

'I'm sorry—'

Sheridan lashed out, knocking the clipboard from his hand. 'My father is Colonel Sherman Warrington. He'll vouch for my husband.'

The official's expression made Rowena's stomach crawl. It was obvious that he knew of Sheridan's father, but more than that it was more than likely that Jung's omission from the list had been deliberate.

'I have my orders.' His lantern jaw seemed cast in iron.

'My father's orders,' said Sheridan weakly swiftly coming to the same conclusion.

Jung reached for his wife's hand.

'Go,' he said softly.

She shook her head. 'No. I won't go, not without you.'

The military police were getting impatient. 'Please. Can you all move along, please? The plane is waiting to leave.'

'I'm not going.'

Sheridan's voice was strong again and there was no doubting the love burning in her eyes.

That look was enough to tell anyone who cared to see that Sheridan would not leave her husband behind.

Finally she shook her head. 'Forget it. Give my seat to someone else. I will not leave my husband behind. You can tell my father that. Don't forget. Colonel Warrington. Remember his name.'

At first the man seemed a little put out, but he recovered quickly. 'It's your choice.'

Rowena looked at Sheridan's stomach and Sheridan looked at her.

'I'm frightened,' she whispered, her fear directed at Rowena. 'I'm so frightened.'

Rowena recognised a pleading woman when she saw one. She wasn't asking her to stay, not in so many words. The country was about to be torn apart. How would a new mother survive here, especially an American national surrounded by hostile forces? Jung was a good man, but he wasn't a midwife.

'I'm frightened too, but I'm not going,' said Rowena suddenly. 'I'm staying with you.'

'You don't have to,' said Jung. 'My wife is going on the plane. I insist.'

'I'm sorry, Jung. You can insist all you like, but I'm not going. I know I promised to love, honour and obey you, but this is one occasion where that last vow is going to be broken.'

Perplexed but determined, he attempted to push her towards the plane, but Sheridan resisted.

'Darling, I'm sure I can sort this out. Now get on the plane.'

The two of them looked so compatible yet also so vulnerable.

Sheridan stood her ground and shook her head, her jaw raised defiantly.

'You need a proper hospital—'

'There's one here.'

'I'll stay with her until we can get her into a hospital then get the next flight. Luli. Take Dawn on the plane. Connor is already on there.'

Luli didn't wait to be told twice but took hold of Dawn's hand and began scurrying across the tarmac. At the same time their cases were taken by uniformed soldiers who urged them to run to the aircraft.

Rowena watched, divided as to whether she was a fool or too duty-bound for her own good. She was watching her daughter leave. Was she so wrong to stay with Sheridan who was beginning to fall apart before her tear-filled eyes?

The small figure of Dawn and the larger one of Luli were the last passengers to be allowed on. Dawn waved from the top of the steps, a small figure caught up in world events. The aircraft door of the ageing Dakota that would take them to Tokyo slammed shut behind them.

Her gaze lingered. The reality was that the plane's propellers were already in motion, yet in her mind was a half-formed vision of the door reopening, of Dawn and Luli framed in the doorway, Connor smiling and waving behind them. It was all a big mistake. There was no need to fly away. Home was here and they could all be here.

The plane wobbled as it turned to taxi down the runway, heading for the far end where it would turn, increase its speed and like a silver stork soar into the sky.

She felt Sheridan and Jung's presence along with her own foolishness. She could have left. Sheridan could have returned to the hospital. The nuns would take care of her when the time came for the baby to be born.

Connor was on that plane and probably feeling hurt, surprised and angry that she had not boarded along with her daughter. She hoped he would forgive her and understand why she had opted to do this. In a way it was for children like Dawn as much as for anyone else. They deserved the best treatment when entering the world and she knew for sure that Connor would keep Dawn safe in Tokyo until he knew that Kim Pheloung was no longer a threat.

In the meantime, Sheridan was looking less pale and although not her normal self, some of her confidence had returned.

'Rowena, I am so very grateful. I can't believe you're doing this. Your daughter is on that plane, but what I do know is that I will be in safe hands – when it finally happens – when the baby is born.'

Rowena kept her lips tightly clenched though her eyes were moist with tears. 'It's for that reason that I feel obliged to stay with you. I was in a Japanese prisoner-of-war camp when Dawn was born. Someone was there for me and for her. I feel the time has come for me to do the same for somebody else.'

When they looked at each other it was as though they were all sharing the same thought. There was fear but also solidarity of spirit.

The plane was no more than a dot against the cumulative cloud formations piling like mountains towards the south-east. In time it would reach Tokyo.

Hand in hand and with slow deliberation, they turned away, three disappointed people preparing themselves for whatever happened next.

All around was noise, hustle and bustle, people thronging to the roads using any vehicle with wheels that still turned, any engine that still worked, a water buffalo with enough strength left to pull a cart piled high with meagre belongings and miserable people.

Before very long they found themselves caught up in

the flood of refugees heading out of the city. None of them doubted what would happen next and it was a while before anyone spoke.

'I shall never forgive my father. Never!'

Jung did his best to reassure her.

'What's done is done. First thing first, we go back to the convent. At least we will have food and shelter there, also time to work out what to do next.'

'And the faster the better,' added Rowena, her eyes scouring the verge, the ditches and any patch of open ground for some form of transport.

'A handcart would be most useful,' she said to Jung.

'You expect me to get into a handcart?' Sheridan sounded totally contemptuous of the idea.

'I'm your doctor and it's my considered opinion that you've walked far enough.' She tried to sound jovial, but it wasn't easy.

'We should have asked the driver who took us to the airport to oblige us with a return journey,' Jung suggested.

'I think he got on the same plane as my daughter. More people are going to want to leave, Western embassies for a start.'

She remained on alert for any type of transport – a taxi or even a lift on a bullock cart. There was nothing. The whole country seemed to be on the road and packed with people.

Seething with anger at what the colonel had done energised her, though her feet were sore and her single suitcase was weighing her down. The man was a monster, as bad as Kim Pheloung but on a different level – or perhaps not that different at all. How could he be so cruel as to leave his own daughter and grandchild to whatever befell them? The soldiers of the north would show no mercy to the daughter of an American officer. He must know that.

There was no doubt in her mind that he had wanted his daughter on that flight, but had purposely engineered the procedure so that her husband would be left behind. He had banked on her doing that and on Jung insisting she took the flight. Obviously he did not know his daughter as well as he thought he did. Sheridan would never abandon Jung, and vice versa.

Rowena tried not to regret her decision to put her professional duty before her personal responsibility to her daughter, but the pain persisted. It was as though one half of her soul had been torn away. She imagined Connor sitting on that plane, his arm and leg heavily bandaged and forbidden to move whilst he waited for her, for Dawn and Luli. Worried and panic-stricken, he would have pounced on Luli, getting angry as she told him the truth. She could imagine Luli clinging on to a tearful Dawn as the reality took hold that her mother wasn't here, sensitive to Connor's barely controlled anger.

The afternoon had fallen into early evening by the time St Catherine's came into view. The sun was setting, burning like a golden halo behind the top of the bell tower.

Sheridan also noticed it. 'Look,' she said, her voice gentle and full of wonder. 'It reminds me of an icon of the Virgin Mary. No longer a bell tower, but the Holy Mother watching over us. It's a good sign. I'm sure it is.'

It was a typical thing for an ex-nun to say, and it caused

them to pause, catch their breath and raise their eyes to the sight, though details of the upper part of the bell tower were indistinct, like a face that is in shadow or silhouetted against something much brighter.

'I do hope it is a good sign,' murmured Rowena. 'I really do hope so.'

Mother Immaculata Conceptua waved to them from the top of the convent steps. The entire conclave was no longer an oasis of calm. The big double gates were thrown open to the mass of humanity who had come there seeking sanctuary. Whether they would find it or no was another matter.

Nuns, nurses, postulants and laymen were helping patients leave the hospital and enter the convent, some of them complete with their beds or in wheelchairs. Others were slung between porters.

With a pang of fear Rowena realised the prioress had made the hard decision to abandon the hospital in the hope that the thick walls of the convent would help preserve their piety and their people. The hospital, with its metal window frames and brittle glass, was vulnerable to modern weapons. The convent less so.

'Come along,' shouted the prioress. 'Quickly.' Her jaw dropped when she saw Sheridan. 'Sister Therese...' On realising the mistake she had made, addressing Sheridan as though she was still a nun, she hastily apologised. 'I'm sorry. I haven't slept for twenty-four hours. I can't sleep.' She frowned. 'Why are you here? I thought you had seats booked on a flight to Tokyo.'

'They wouldn't let us on the plane,' said a tearful Sheridan. Her husband wound his arm around her shoulder.

The prioress nodded. 'I see. Well never mind. The more the merrier.'

'We're safe now,' Jung said to his wife.

The sound of a plane climbing into the sky sounded from overhead. Rowena looked up, swallowing her sadness as her eyes followed its progress. Like the other plane she'd seen take off, it was heading south – towards Japan. Theirs would be the last plane to fly out. Suddenly she felt terribly alone.

More people kept coming, funnelling into the compound of the Catholic mission, men with worried faces, women carrying children, their earthly belongings bound up in battered suitcases or Gladstone bags, even in sheets roughly ripped from their beds. A lot of them were Westerners, administrators, bank clerks, managers of bi-partisan businesses that had thought establishing a base in Korea had been a very good idea.

There were people everywhere, crumpled lumps of humanity huddled into small spaces that allowed them to cling together in tight family groups.

Aided by a harassed-looking young priest, the nuns were doing their best to provide spaces to sit if not to lie down, but the mission was small and once the chapel was full, people were resigned to sitting on the steps and in the compound outside.

Bundled up with luggage, children, chickens in wicker baskets and a pig on the end of a lead, those who had sought sanctuary seemed to give a collective sigh of relief, even more so when the gates closed with a dull thud and a great bar locked into position.

Walls and gates constituted a barrier, leaving only a square of sky above and the very tops of dark green pines.

Anyone who had been imprisoned couldn't fail to fall back on memories they'd prefer to forget. Rowena was no exception. The same memories had been skirting her mind ever since she'd heard that the enemy were coming south and no matter how hard she tried to push them away they kept resurfacing.

The circumstances didn't help. She was penned in, the walls were thick and she could see nothing except the very tops of trees and the odd roof or two. Nothing else except sky, no houses stretching away to those pale mauve hills; the comparison with a Japanese prisoner-of-war camp was all too real and it wasn't easy to override the dark memories.

'At least your child is not caught here. It is good that you sent her away from the evil that threatens us. She was meant to go and you were meant to stay. God moves in mysterious ways.'

The calm eyes of a Carmelite nun she knew as Sister St Paul met those of Rowena and although she did not possess the devout beliefs of these women, she did respect them. Since she'd first arrived here, it never failed to impress her how both calm and intuitive they were. Sister St Paul could indeed be correct that she was meant to stay here, after all, where better for a doctor but administering to those in need? She would make herself useful.

She took her stethoscope and thermometer from her bag and headed for Sheridan and her quiet little spot in the shade of the tree.

'How are you feeling?'

Sheridan was sitting on an upturned wicker basket that was usually used for laundry.

'I'm fine.'

Jung was holding her hand. He looked up at Rowena. 'I'll take care of her.'

Rowena glanced at the thermometer. At least her temperature was normal, but the sound of her heart was more worrying. It wasn't the right time to ask her if she'd ever had rheumatic fever or any heart condition. There was no point in making a bad situation worse, so she smiled at her, told her everything was fine and cast her eyes over the other people sharing the compound.

'Is anyone injured? Does anyone need a doctor or a midwife?'

There were murmured responses and a few raised hands for which she was glad. At least she could keep occupied and shove the worries about Sheridan to the back of her mind.

Amongst many others, she tended a small boy with ringworm, son of an attaché from the Swiss embassy. The whole family had failed to make the last flight and got caught up in the mêlée of fleeing humanity.

Heatstroke, fatigue, palpitations in the breasts of older people, fears for children, nervous anxiety; it was all there rippling like a terminal disease through those gathered.

The nuns handed out water along with hastily intoned prayers and, like them, she did her best with limited resources.

Sheridan was sitting with her eyes closed, head tilted back and resting on the wall behind her. At a distance it appeared her lips were trembling, but on getting closer she heard her repeating over and over again how much she hated her father and how she would never forgive him for his obvious intention to separate her from her husband.

Jung continued to do his best to soothe her.

'We will get through this. All will be well.'

'I shall never forgive him. Never! He wanted me to get rid of our baby! Can you believe that? He specifically sent Rowena here to carry out an abortion.'

'She wouldn't do that.'

'But why did he think she would? I'm beginning to think my father is quite mad.'

'He's a traditionalist. He planned what his family should be. You upset his plans.'

'So did you.'

Aware of a shadow passing over them, Sheridan opened her eyes. Both she and her husband looked up into Rowena's face.

Sheridan eyed her quizzically, though there was a bleary look in her eyes.

'You wouldn't have done it, would you?'

'She doesn't mean it,' Jung said apologetically to Rowena and patted his wife's hand. 'It's the worry – and the disappointment,' he added softly.

'What Jung means is that deep down I keep hoping that my father will relent and change his mind, invite us to visit, tell us how much he's putting into a college fund for his grandchild…' Her voice faded away. Her hair veiled her face in thick strands as she shook her head. Rowena guessed she was gritting her teeth in an effort to prevent sobs falling from her mouth.

Rowena got down on her knees then squatted on the edge of the woven basket and clasped her hands together.

'I'm not going to say that his rejection doesn't matter. To you it matters a very great deal. He's your father, but if you can understand this, he's at your back, behind you. This child,' she said, patting Sheridan's very obvious lump, 'is what's in front of you.' She smiled. 'You can't miss it.' She'd meant it to be funny, but Sheridan's expression was unaltered. Rowena carried on. 'Boy or girl, it's your future. The baby will take you forward and sad as it may be, your father will fade into the background. But it's his choice and there's nothing you can do to change that. Nobody can instruct anyone to destroy your baby. That decision is purely down to you and Jung.'

A strange look passed over Sheridan's face and made Rowena realise what she'd just said.

'I didn't mean that I would do it,' Rowena added, flustered now and not wishing to convey that there were circumstances in which she would carry out an abortion. 'I do believe the day will come when the procedure will become legal for those who need and want it. I also feel that at some time in the future there will be a better method of contraception than there is now.' She shrugged nonchalantly. 'But that's something for the future, certainly not now.'

Jung and Sheridan exchanged confused glances. Rowena sensed where this was going.

'I think your father heard of my views through a third party.' She averted her eyes, at the same time taking her time to sit cross-legged as she worked out what to say next. 'I recall a night back in Hong Kong. In the midst of a typhoon a baby was abandoned, the mother running off just after she'd given birth.' Sensing Sheridan's interest, she carried on with what had happened that night. 'Three babies were born that night. Two boys and a girl. The girl was abandoned. I felt sorry for the child but also for the woman who no doubt had a whole sampan of hungry mouths to feed, and a girl being of less value than a boy, the baby was left behind. I was angry. I didn't blame the woman for making such a drastic choice. She couldn't help getting pregnant. That was when I think I may have said too much about women getting worn out having big families that half the time they couldn't feed. I stated that things had to change.' She stopped right there and thought how innocently she had voiced her opinion without realising that her views would reach the ears of Sheridan's father.

'Somebody told him?'

She nodded. 'I failed to work it out before I left. Someone on the hospital board, I think.' Not the truth, of course, but she was loath to tell her the truth. She was pretty certain that it was Barbara Kelly who had relayed the information, but if she did tell Sheridan it would also come out that Barbara was seeing Sheridan's father. Matters were already more complicated than she would like. For the moment at least she would let sleeping dogs lie.

'Everything changes and medicine is no exception,' said Jung. 'In my short career I have seen many great advances, the most momentous of which was penicillin.'

Rowena agreed with him. 'I thought the world had changed too. Now I'm not so sure.'

He nodded. 'Ah, yes. Also the world.'

My world too, she thought which had changed irrevocably for her back in 1941 when the Japanese had invaded

Hong Kong. Neither she nor her friend Alice Huntley had foreseen how quickly things would change and how cruel war could be. This war, she decided, would be no different and Sheridan would need every ounce of her strength – and her undoubted faith – to get through it and, for that matter, so would she.

The convent dispensary was quickly running out of basic medicines, but there were bandages and rather a lot of kaolin and morphine normally used for bad cases of diarrhoea and dysentery. By letting the kaolin sink to the bottom of the bottle the residual morphine could be used for pain relief.

Only the very young slept through the night, the adults fretting on what might happen next, straining their eyes and ears in an effort to ascertain whether the sound of gunfire was getting closer. Being taken prisoner was a constant of conversation.

Sheridan was no exception.

'What was it like to be a prisoner of war?'

A cold rush of blood made her hands tremble, but she recovered quickly.

'It was hell on earth, but I survived.'

'Will we survive?'

'Believe me, Sheridan, I will not let it happen to me again.'

'That's what Jung says. He won't let it happen.'

'At least you have something very special to look forward to. Another two months and your waiting will be over.'

The chapel bell unexpectedly doled out a single note. Heads turned to that direction. Normally it would ring to call the nuns to prayer, but there was no room for prayers on account of those fleeing the mayhem outside the towering walls being crammed inside. As the single note faded away the mother superior appeared on the top step of the mission between two rather grand Palladian pillars, a conspicuous show of devotion given by a father on his daughter taking her vows many years before.

The mother superior was a tall woman and had a voice as clear as a bell, both of which assets helped her gain everyone's attention.

'*Mesdames et messieurs. Bienvenue.* Our order was founded here in Korea to bring the peace of Christ to this nation. We hope to return to that role once the present conflict is over. In the meantime you are all welcome here, though I must inform you that our food rations are not extensive, so if any of you have brought your own supplies, I would ask that you consume those first.' She smiled and bowed her head slightly. 'Our provisions are equivalent to the three loaves and five fishes our Lord fed to the multitude, and I wish I had his skill to make it go further. However, we will do our best to ensure everybody is fed.'

Just as she finished there was the sound of explosions followed by the cracking of rifle fire. Anxious looks passed between the holy sisters and fear buzzed from one frightened civilian to another.

Sheridan stopped seething over her father. Like everyone else she'd become aware of a far more serious situation.

The three of them had already consumed what food they'd managed to bring with them, mostly rice cakes and slivers of chicken plus some fruit. It was enough. Fear had dimmed their hunger.

'Where are the Americans? Where are the United Nations?'

Jung looked at both women with worried eyes. 'They didn't think this would happen. They trusted on the diplomatic process and believed what they were told.'

'Do you think Seoul will fall?'

He looked away from Rowena's question and she instantly felt queasy. Her chest tightened to such an extent that she thought her lungs would burst and beads of sweat broke out on her forehead. The prospect of being caught in a similar trap to the one she'd been in before was harrowing.

The sound of gunfire reduced to a low rumbling some way off, but perhaps closer than it had been. Sleep tonight would yet again prove elusive.

There was little in the way of beds, most people making do with a suitcase or rolled up coat as a pillow and covered by a blanket supplied by the nuns.

It was summer so the night was relatively warm. Rowena only hoped that they weren't still here in the winter. She'd heard they could be very cold indeed. Siberia wasn't that far away.

All night the guns thundered. By morning the convent inmates were bleary eyed and very hungry though there were some who refused food.

The nuns attempted to encourage everyone to eat. 'Whilst we still have food. We all need to keep our strength up.'

Rowena remarked that she hadn't heard the bell calling the nuns to chapel that morning.

Sheridan said nothing but just looked at her with frightened eyes. Her look was easy to interpret. The situation had to be serious if the bell had not sounded. It didn't mean that the nuns hadn't attended chapel, just that the pealing of a bell might attract unwanted attention.

Suddenly there was a huge explosion which made the walls of the convent tremble.

A cloud of dust fell from the outer wall that skirted both the convent and the hospital. The guns definitely sounded closer now.

The fighting outside the walls continued. Their ordeal went on. Food supplies were just about holding out, but they couldn't remain behind the stout walls and heavy gates indefinitely.

Rowena helped out where she could; keeping busy a proficient barrier against fear and depression.

The convent school carried on, the children as glad to be occupied as were the nuns and the medical staff. During the day everyone seemed to be walking on glass, alert to every explosion, every gunshot. Nobody expressed out loud just how close the enemy was to the city. At night, in an effort to snatch a little sleep, they blocked their ears with plugs of cotton wool or covered their heads with cushions, blankets or heavy winter coats.

It was a few days later, on Friday 30th, that the guns fell silent and they discerned other sounds. Anxious eyes looked from one to another.

'Why has it gone so quiet?'

The question was asked in a whisper but answered swiftly. 'They're here, or if not here, they're not far away and they're meeting no resistance.'

The man who answered the question had been a diplomat

at the British embassy who had got left behind because he'd been on holiday up in the mountains and hadn't got back in time for the last flight out.

Their worst fears were founded the following morning. The sun was barely warming the ground when there was the sound of vehicles outside, men shouting, followed by a loud hammering at the convent gates.

Fear-filled eyes became more terrified. The nuns stood for a moment, all looking at their prioress for leadership, their hands tucked inside the sleeves of their habits.

'Open the gates!' The demand came from outside and was repeated two or three times.

Her back stiff, her expression steadfast, the prioress nodded. In response two nuns went forward to lift the heavy beam. Everyone watched as the gates swung back and there was an intake of breath at the sight of the fighters of the DPRK filling the gap.

Rowena stayed close to her two friends. Inside she was sick at heart. Outwardly she stood tall. One thing above all others filled her with resolve; even if she was taken prisoner, she would not remain that way. Whatever it took to get home, she would do.

Sheridan addressed Rowena. 'You should have left when you could.'

Rowena shook her head. 'I couldn't leave you.'

Jung kept close to Sheridan though Rowena could see he was on edge, wanting perhaps to bear on his fellow countrymen that he was Korean and his wife was pregnant.

'Too late now. What day is it?'

Sheridan shook her head. 'I don't know... is it the thirtieth?'

The thirtieth. It had been five days since the northern army had crossed into South Korea. Their progress had been frighteningly swift and opposed only by the South Korean army. The Western powers had been caught off guard and very quickly overwhelmed.

Just like Hong Kong and Singapore, thought Rowena.

It seemed like hours but was only minutes, an interval when those inside the convent walls and those outside eyed each other up and waited for someone to make the first move.

The first move fell on the mother superior who stepped forward and spoke to the man who appeared to be in charge.

'Welcome to St Catherine's, a place of prayer, peace and charity. I'm afraid we have no food to give you and there are no fighting men, only wounded.'

The grim-faced man, his jaw as square as the corner of a doorframe, eyed her and those around her. He looked indecisive and did not seem to have understood what she'd said. He called a man to his side and said something. The man looked at the mother superior, smiled and said, 'Good morning.'

'Good morning.'

'Nice day.'

'Good Lord.' Rowena rolled her eyes. It was fairly obvious that the man in charge had asked for somebody to translate. It was equally obvious that the chosen translator had only the most minuscule knowledge of the English language.

The prioress tried speaking French which only resulted in a blank stare at her, then a helpless look at the commander whose face was getting redder by the minute. Finally he slapped the man and pushed him back with the other men.

Jung stepped forward, his arms raised above his head.

'No. Jung. No.'

Sheridan's entreaty was softly spoken but Jung was already on his feet. She hung onto his raised arm.

'I have to help,' he said quietly and gently removed his wife's hand from his arm.

'Stay. Let him do it.' Rowena took his place, her arm around Sheridan.

There was a rattling as weapons were raised towards Jung who had taken maybe half a dozen steps. Once in position, he bowed and informed the commander in Korean that his English was excellent and he was willing to translate.

The man's dark eyebrows beetled above sunken eyes that appeared to be just deep hollows above gaunt cheekbones. He snapped a series of questions, the first of which seemed to refer to Sheridan. Rowena guessed he was telling them that Sheridan was his wife. The commander's glance stayed on her for a moment. It was hard to tell whether it was out of appreciation for her fresh-faced looks and blonde hair or simply because he couldn't quite believe that a Korean had opted to wed an American girl.

More questions were barked and although Rowena had no knowledge of the language, she guessed they were about who all these people were. The nuns in their habits were self-explanatory, but there were Europeans here plus an American Presbyterian minister and his family. These they seemed most interested in.

Sheridan, who understood a good deal of what was being said, translated.

'They're going to interrogate everybody, Americans first. They're also going to search the convent. He says it's because

South Korean soldiers hide in convents. Jung has told him there are none and that there had been some injured soldiers in the hospital, but these had been discharged when they heard the DPRK were coming.'

The commander laughed and said something. In response his men laughed too.

Sheridan translated again. 'The commander remarked that the southern soldiers had not been discharged but run away, that they'd been running all the way from the thirty-eighth parallel.'

Something else was said. Jung looked agitated. He glanced at his wife then back at the commander.

Rowena felt a shiver run through Sheridan's body and heard her whine, 'Oh no. Please, Jung. No!'

She tightened her grip on Sheridan's shoulders.

'What did he say?'

'He needs a translator all the time now, someone who can speak both English and French and insists Jung goes with him so he can assist in the interrogation of prisoners.'

There was no point in asking if the fact that his wife was pregnant would alter the commander's decision and allow him to stay. Jung nodded, bowed stiffly from the waist. He was not given the chance to kiss his wife goodbye.

The commander waved a hand at the group of nuns and their statuesque mother superior. Jung spoke directly to her.

'The commander asks me to inform you that he will be back to interrogate everyone here. In the meantime guards will be placed outside for your own safety and two will stay inside to search for deserters.'

'There are no deserters here,' said the mother superior

with a firm uplifting of her chin. Her firm manner cut no ice with the commander.

Jung explained further. 'They say they want me to go with them to everywhere there are still foreign civilians in the city. I am to assure them that they will come to no harm.'

The mother superior raised her hand in a blessing.

'May the Lord keep you safe.'

Jung nodded his appreciation. 'Thank you, Reverend Mother.'

He gave Sheridan a wistful look followed by a smile that had no need of words but said everything about his love for her.

With slouched shoulders, his water bottle over his shoulder, he followed the dirty, dusty and ill-dressed army out of the gate. His wife's eyes stayed on him until he was lost in the mêlée of men, then she sobbed and her head fell onto Rowena's shoulder.

Guards were placed outside the convent gates and another two inside. The latter two exchanged quick words with those outside before charging into the convent to search for so-called 'deserters'.

A wail of dismay and fear went up from the civilians gathered there, all fearing for their lives.

Sheridan hid her face more deeply against Rowena's shoulder.

'They're going to kill us.'

'No they're not.' She hugged Sheridan with both arms. 'They're not going to kill us. They're off searching for valuables, not that they're likely to find much in a convent administering to the poor and sick. They're going to be very disappointed.'

She smiled to herself at the thought of their disappointment. When they finally emerged from their search, it was clear they had helped themselves to the food larder. Exchanging words with the guards on the outside, they swapped places, two more guards going in to see what valuables they could come up with. And so it went on.

Every so often they walked amongst those in the yard and even into the chapel where more people were congregated. They stood at the back of the chapel looking bemused, laughing and making fun, as the nuns went through their devotions. Only when the nuns began to sing did they fall silent, listening enraptured though not understanding a word.

Less food, more guards; imprisonment but in a different country and under different circumstances; this time she'd chosen to stay.

Sheridan woke up during the night, crying that her husband would be killed and then she would be all alone in the world.

'Shh,' Rowena soothed her. 'You're not alone, Sheridan. I'm here with you until Jung comes back and very soon all will be well again – just you wait and see.'

The truth was that she didn't know if and when things would be well again. Neither did she know whether they would ever see Jung's cheery face. All they could do was hope.

Chapter 19

HONG KONG

The runway was long and Tokyo airport was busy coping with military flights including huge numbers of fighters, bombers and supply planes, their shadows black and volatile. In ever increasing numbers, helicopters, their blades flashing like swords above their menacing bodies, swarmed like locusts.

Despite all that they were in the air within minutes.

Connor was beside himself. There had been no sign of Rowena and although Luli did her best to explain things, her lower lip was shivering and her words jumbled.

'Mummy says she has to stay,' murmured Dawn with tear-filled eyes.

'Why?'

His bark made her jump and Luli did the same. She hated flying and he knew it would be some time before he got any sense out of her. In the meantime Dawn was settling down, her nose pressed against the aircraft window.

'Goodbye, everyone.'

She waved out of the plane's round window. Luli was

sitting with her eyes closed and her hands over her ears. She was also muttering a prayer that Connor thought he recognised though it had been an age since he'd entered a church and recited some form of litany.

He did not want to leave and had asked to stay but his requests had fallen on deaf ears.

'No more fighting for you, old son. Back to Blighty.'

'I live in Hong Kong, not Britain,' he'd said grimly.

'Then you're going back to Hong Kong – via Tokyo.'

He'd been settled enough when he'd checked with Warrington and been told that Rowena would be on the same plane. Back home to whatever they had to face – together. It was with a sense of purpose and high spirits that he'd boarded the plane. Everything had changed.

He watched the clouds flitting past the aircraft windows and now and again caught glimpses of the green paddy fields far below. Rowena was still down there somewhere, and here he was flying through the clouds and feeling as though he was smothered in his own personal cloud, a big black one that was pouring rain down on his head. They'd been torn apart in the last war and here it was again. There and then he vowed it would be the last time. Once they were reunited from this dilemma he would not be parted from her again.

It was late afternoon when they touched down in Hong Kong. Dawn, who had so enjoyed flying in her mother's company from Hong Kong to Japan and then onto Korea, was subdued.

Connor knew the reason was that she was missing her

mother but there was nothing he could do about it. He was missing her too. More than that, he was wondering what awaited them though he believed it would take some time for Kim Pheloung to hear on the grapevine that they were back. He consoled himself that Dawn was only a target for Kim when she was in the company of Rowena. Rowena was and always would be the object of his intimidation.

His arm ached but not badly enough and he was still limping from his leg wound. All the same he did his best to assist with loading the luggage into a taxi. Luli and Dawn clambered in the back. He got in the front with the driver who gave him a cursory glance then suggested there was plenty of room in the back.

'I prefer the view from here,' he said. 'All the way to the ferry.'

The driver swung his gaze back to the view ahead, but every so often Connor glimpsed the sideways glance, the questioning look.

At the quayside he found a phone and rang the bar. It rang for some time before being picked up.

'Yang. It's me. I'm about to get on the ferry. Collect me at the other end.'

'Boss! Sure. Good to hear your voice. I'll be there and if—'

'Connor. Is that you?'

His sister had snatched the phone from his barman's hand. He could imagine how it had been since she'd moved in. Yang would certainly have had his wings clipped. Kate liked to be in charge.

'I'm at the ferry with Dawn and Luli. We need collecting.'

'What about Rowena? Isn't she with you?'

'No. I'll tell you all about it when I get there.'

'You'd better.'

No further details or words of welcome. His sister didn't waste time on too many words. She was a woman of action and always had been.

'"Glad you're home" would have been nice,' he said to himself.

However, there was no time to be grim faced. He felt a great need to reassure Dawn that everything would be all right even though her mother wasn't with them.

As promised, Yang was waiting, sitting behind the wheel of a dark blue car that he hadn't seen before.

'Yang. Old friend. Have you come into some money?'

'Not my car, boss. Mrs Kate's car.'

'My sister's bought a car?'

'She said my car was not classy enough to pick up guests when needed.'

Connor frowned. 'What guests?'

The alley in which Connor's Bar was situated had always been on the gloomy side. In the little time he'd been away it had brightened considerably thanks to a neon sign and numerous lights festooned across the house opposite. No longer was it neglected and peopled only by an old man and his daughter; the smell of cooking made his stomach rumble.

On reading the flashing neon, he became instantly informed of the reason for this. *Katie Yang's Chinese Restaurant*, and underneath, *Traditional Chinese Cooking*.

'I've been away too long,' Connor murmured.

'I'm hungry,' declared Dawn, her nostrils moving in response to the glorious smell.

'And I'm curious that so much has changed in the short time I've been away,' muttered Connor, his eyes taking in the newly painted house, noting the clean courtyard and the potted bamboo gracing it and the first-floor balcony.

Yang eyed him nervously. 'Mrs Kate in charge.'

'She was.'

Connor clenched his jaw and although his leg pained, helped Yang with the baggage. He would hold back the questions until they were inside.

'Well look at you all. I'm thinking it's food you'll be needing,' said Kate with a toss of her head. She showed not the slightest hint that anything was wrong, or indeed that anything had changed. Like everyone else who entered her life he was expected to accept anything she did – and he was damned sure that this was all down to her.

'It's explanations I'm needing,' he said as he set down the cases. 'And rooms ready for these two.'

'That's not a problem,' said his sister with customary bravado. 'Your own room is aired. The girls can have my room. I've one going spare over the road which I hadn't expected to be going spare. All the other rooms are out. This one got cancelled at the last minute.'

'Luli. Do you remember the way?'

Luli said that she did. The two girls disappeared into the corridor behind the bar. He waited for the trudge of their feet ascending the stairs before turning his attention back to his sister.

'Do you want me to ask the questions or are you going to give me the details right now in your own words?'

'Just to clarify matters, this bar is still yours,' Kate declared defiantly. 'You'll find the takings are up and the customers happy. The restaurant over the road complements the bar. There's no bar over there, and just so there's no misunderstanding, the place over the road is mine. I heard it was up for rent so put in me bid, so to speak. You may recall I had money from the sale of the old place back home. Over the road is my business. The building over there was falling down with neglect, and filthy too. And it wasn't magic that brought the place up to scratch. It was hard work. My hard work.'

Her defiant look stayed planted on her face, her eyes unblinking and her chin thrust forward as though she were inviting him to throw a punch. Not that he would. She was a woman and his sister and no pushover. Besides that, he'd always thought she had a good head on her shoulders, a fact her late husband had chosen to ignore. He certainly wouldn't be one to knock it off!

'You didn't take long getting it up and running.'

'I did not. You might say, Connor, that as an independent woman I'm like a greyhound let out of the trap. There'll be no more getting married for me, I can assure you of that, but I do know how men's minds work. I've plans. The restaurant attracts sailors and the girls they fall in love with over here. I'm fulfilling their experience of the exotic – along with the girls, that is.'

Connor looked at her in alarm. 'What kind of girls?'

'Their girlfriends! The ones they bring here. Not the other kind, Connor O'Connor. How could you have thought such a thing of your sister?'

'And the rooms?'

'Itinerant workers – professionals, mostly, working for the banks and the shipping companies. Hong Kong is going up in the world. There's money to be made here, Connor, and I'm not shy about claiming my fair share.'

She eyed him sagely.

'Your arm's well bandaged. Got caught in the line of fire, did you?'

'It comes with the job.'

'That it does and no doubt you'll be telling me in your own good time. Now you've asked your questions, there's some I have for you; first off, the whereabouts of Dawn's mother. What happened?'

Suddenly beset by weariness and despair, he hung his head and rubbed at the sudden throbbing in his injured arm.

His sister noticed. 'It'll keep until later. Now go and get settled in. You look shattered, so you do.'

He sighed heavily and reached for his kit bag.

'You've an injured arm. Here. Let me.' She slung the kitbag over her shoulder.

It still surprised him that she was mighty strong for a small woman, but once she had the bit between her teeth there was no stopping her.

'No wonder you ended up married to a blacksmith.'

'He was used to handling wilful mares.'

Despite his fatigue, a smile crept onto his lips.

'Shall I be getting your fiddle out for later?' she asked as she let the kitbag roll onto his bed.

'Not tonight.'

'No. Of course not. We need to talk.'

★

It was late when brother and sister were sitting with drinks in front of them, Kate letting him sink two or three whiskeys before setting to with her questions.

His eyes strayed to the space between them where, despite him telling her not to bother, lay his beloved violin.

'You might need it once you've unburdened yourself. Now drink up. There's a bottle of Jameson's waiting for your attention.'

He smiled and emptied his glass, the liquid reassuringly warm as it hit the back of his throat.

Kate waited patiently, sipping at her drink without once dropping her gaze from her brother's face.

He decided to relate his experiences one at a time so began with his injury, building up to telling her about Rowena and spilling his feelings.

'You're right. I got in the way of a bullet. It was always on the cards that I would.'

He went on to tell her about the country, the people and his observation that the Western powers were not fully engaged with Korea's problems.

'It's a country that had the misfortune to be divided by diplomats. Once the Japanese had been ousted it was a case of trying to please everybody. Then some bright spark, thinking that was it and peace would reign for ever, withdrew the majority of the peacekeeping force. The DPRK, North Korea, saw their chance and the Communists surged south and there weren't enough armed forces personnel to do anything about it.'

'So you didn't see who shot you.'

'You're asking me if I shot him.'

'Of course I am. An eye for an eye. That's my motto.'

Connor shook his head. 'I've no idea. I can count on one hand the times I've looked the enemy – any enemy – in the eye. So I was invalided out.'

'But that's not all. You don't want to tell me the most important bit.

Their eyes met. They were so alike, both liked to get to the point without unnecessary preamble.

He paused before answering. 'You're right.'

'What's happened to Rowena? Did she feel duty bound to stay, or…?'

'She's alive, and yes, it's about duty. She always was one who couldn't separate her professional side from personal.' He frowned. 'I'm trying not to worry, but it isn't easy.'

After Kate had poured more fiery fluid into his glass, he explained what had happened in more detail, Dawn and Luli coming onto the plane but not Rowena.

'I'm afraid for her – very afraid.'

He went on to tell her the basic story, the facts that he knew prior to Rowena's departure and the bits and pieces he'd gleaned from his short meeting at the convent as well as Luli's testimony.

Kate looked puzzled. 'She'd only just met this American girl. Why do you think she stayed? There has to be another reason.'

Connor shook his head. 'Nothing concrete that I can work out except that it was this woman's father who first asked her – almost ordered her to go there.'

'So what was his reason?'

'I don't know. She wasn't going to go at first, but then something happened that changed her mind. It scared her. Scared me too.'

Kate's eyebrows rose. 'You're going to tell me what it is?'

Head bent over his drink, he told her the history of their involvement with a man named Kim Pheloung, of his criminal activities including extortion, bleeding Yang dry in the days when he'd owned Connor's Bar. He went on to tell her about Kim's obsession with Rowena, what had happened in the war.

'We thought he was dead and then something happened to make us think otherwise. Rowena was scared he'd come after her.'

'And did he?'

Connor nodded. 'He used to own that house over there.' He jerked his head in the direction of his sister's new business venture.

'But that's not the scary bit.'

'No.'

Kate's face visibly paled when he told her about the glass doll.

'Jesus, Joseph and Mary!'

She threw her hands over the lower part of her face. For a while she said nothing, her eyes full of thought.

Not wishing for another drink, Connor reached for his fiddle, gently caressing its sensual curves, and was reminded of Rowena, the indentation of her waist, the rise of her breasts, the sweep of her hips.

He tried a few notes, tuned it a little, then slid his chin onto the rest and lifted the bow.

His arm felt stiff and there was pain, but he wouldn't let that stop him. After flexing his arm, straightening his elbow, the sweet strains of 'The Londonderry Air' lifted like a whisper from the silky strings.

He waited for Kate to sing the heartfelt words of a woman waiting for her man to return from war, but she sat there, stiff as a poker and staring disbelievingly into space

Oh Danny Boy, the pipes, the pipes are calling...

He played on, in need of music to soothe his soul and help him think. He wanted to go back to Korea and find Rowena. Somehow he would, but it wouldn't be easy. Kate could look after things here and he didn't think Dawn would be in danger. It was Rowena Kim was after. It had always been Rowena. Yes, he would go to Korea.

As the notes finally died he saw something he had not ever seen before. There was fear in his sister's eyes and a pallor to her face.

He laid down the instrument and asked her outright what was troubling her.

'This man. This Kim Pheloung. I think we may have had a visit from his henchmen. They wanted money – a share of the profits.'

Now it was Connor who let fly with a string of blasphemies.

'What did you do?'

'I lost my temper. Told them if ever they crossed my threshold again I'd blow their brains out.'

'You've never fired a gun in your life.'

'It can't be that difficult.'

Connor placed his hand on the bridge of his nose and rubbed at his eyes.

'Good God.'

'I'm betting they won't come back.'

'I'm betting they will.'

Although he was dog tired, sleep didn't come easily. His

plan had been to get back to Korea by whatever means possible, find Rowena and bring her back. That particular option was now out of the question. The thugs, whoever they were, would be back and, much as he wanted to be reunited with the woman he loved, he could not leave family and property in danger. He had to stay and the first thing he would do in the morning was contact his Scottish friend in the Hong Kong police. Not that he could do much unless he caught them in the act, but at least it would be a start.

Chapter 20

Korea

The thundering of heavy tanks came to an end, replaced by an eerie silence.

Although she was not as devout as Sheridan, Rowena made a point of accompanying her to mass. Her prayers were for her husband. He had gone with them under duress and they both hoped that his usefulness as an interpreter meant he would survive.

Having finished looting the convent and finding nothing of any great value, the guards had returned to their duties though it seemed resistance had fallen away. From some way off came the sound of sporadic gunfire and also that of cheering crowds. The south, Rowena decided, had fallen in with their brothers from the north.

First thing in the morning and at sundown, it became Sheridan's habit to sit outside, her eyes fixed on the entrance where the gates were now left wide open. When the weather was dry she sat in the sunshine. When it rained she sat on a pile of logs that had the advantage of having its own little roof.

Rowena brought her food and at the same time checked her over, deftly feeling for the first signs that the baby was getting ready to be born.

It was at six in the evening a week later when a bedraggled Jung appeared at the gate, deposited there from a huge American sedan jammed with Communist soldiers. The car drove off with a screech of brakes, a cloud of dust and banter between those in the car and the guards at the gate.

Jung staggered forward looking totally drained.

Sheridan gasped and tried to get to her feet.

Rowena restrained her. 'Stay there. I'll get him.' The American minister helped her.

'You OK, guy?'

Jung answered that he was. 'I'm just tired and very hungry. Do you have anything to eat?'

Rowena said she would get something. 'The nuns have thrown the last of their rice into a huge pot along with a lot of other things.'

'Sounds delicious.'

Rowena grinned. 'You might not say that once you've tasted it. They threw in everything they had left. Come on. Let's get you fed and then you can tell us what's going on – after you've given your wife a big hug, that is.'

Jung hung onto his wife as though he would fall to his knees which, given his condition, was very likely.

Sheridan held his upper arm as he ate and every so often they exchanged coy looks. It was also very noticeable that both had tears in their eyes.

'That was certainly most welcome,' said Jung once he'd finished the meal – the rice made more substantial with the addition of both dried fish and tinned meat – a thick soup that only a hungry man could fully appreciate.

He'd gulped down a mug of water before eating and now swallowed a second through his dry lips, the mug trembling in his shaking hands.

He savoured the dregs before speaking.

'They prided themselves on being able to fight on an empty stomach. Seeing as I was only employed as a translator they expected me to follow suit – which I had to do.'

He went on to tell them about banks, churches, businesses and the more opulent private houses being subjected to looting. 'They took anything of value – even church candlesticks. Some of my own people helped them.' He shook his head. 'I feel so ashamed.'

'Don't be,' said a grim-faced Rowena. 'Any nationality is capable of cruelty. Believe me, I know.'

His eyes met hers. 'Some of them used to be my friends. Now I don't think I ever really knew them. They suggested that seeing as my wife was American, I should divorce her.' He touched Sheridan's hand and there was such gentleness in that touch, such love, that Rowena had to swallow a heartfelt sob.

'What do they intend doing next?'

Jung's eyes met hers and she disliked what she saw there.

'They will be here tomorrow to interrogate everyone. Not that they care what answers you might give. They trust no one – not even religious orders.'

Rowena sighed and rubbed at her face. She was tired because she wasn't sleeping properly, but then how could she when the world around her had once again been turned inside out?

'We need to tell the mother superior.'

Jung got to his feet, but faltered because Sheridan was clinging onto his leg.

'I'm frightened, Jung.'

He very gently prised her hands away. 'We are all frightened, Sheridan. Pray for all of us.'

She nodded. Her hands dropped away to be clasped together as she bent her head in prayer.

Mother Immaculata Conceptua listened silently, her pale eyes unblinking as Jung recounted all that had happened.

Shoulders tense with apprehension, Rowena stood at his back, impressed and also terrified of his recounting of what he had seen beyond the convent walls.

'The world has gone mad. Everything of value is being taken.'

As she listened, Rowena's gaze went beyond the reverend mother to the altar. The convent's only items of value were two silver candlesticks and a crucifix that normally sat on the altar.

'We've hidden them,' said the mother superior on seeing Rowena glance in that direction.

Jung's face was full of alarm. 'Don't let them find them. Refusing what they want can get you killed.'

In contrast, the face of the nun was totally calm and also full of courage.

'Whatever is in store for us, we will trust to the Good Lord to give us courage.'

It was always difficult to sleep, but that night was worse than usual. Along with her two closest companions, she cowered under a blanket, her eyes fixed on the fire and the pan of hot water they needed to make tea. Her gaze transferred to Sheridan whose head lay on her husband's shoulder. Her eyes were closed and although her face should have had colour thanks to the fire, she looked pale, almost grey. In contrast, Jung was staring into space, his gaze seemingly fixed on things in his mind and not in the here and now.

Rowena recognised that look for what it was. In a bid to spare his wife's concern, Jung hadn't been entirely truthful about all he'd seen.

After ensuring that Sheridan was sound asleep she took the opportunity to probe a little.

'Are they killing many people?' she asked, her voice barely above a whisper.

He nodded. 'Not all are killed. Some are intimidated, some tortured.'

'Foreigners?'

'Anyone who disagrees with their doctrine or hides valuables and anyone who has received a foreign education...' he glanced tellingly at his sleeping wife, 'or anyone who happens to be a member of the Roman Catholic Church.'

He hung his head in his hands, a man totally spent.

Rowena sighed. 'Let's see if we can get some sleep.'

They both sank back under their respective blankets, each aware that the other was only pretending to sleep, that visions of horror – both present and past – awaited them in dreams best avoided.

The enemy entourage came back halfway through the

following morning. A number of trucks and battered old buses rattled to a halt outside, men with guns alighted and began shouting at everyone to get to their feet, gather their belongings then line up outside.

All those who had found space inside the convent, including the sick, were hustled outside. Children and babies cried. Old folk, their legs too weak to stand for long, were supported by those who could stand.

Two young men, who couldn't possibly be much older than twenty-two, went to each person in turn asking their names, occupation and how long they'd been in Korea. Rowena accordingly gave her name, said she was a doctor and had been here for only a very short time.

They perused her papers with dour faces before returning them.

Jung answered for his wife in his own language. They answered him sharply, glanced sideways at his wife, their eyes sliding down at her swollen stomach. Jung responded, nodding in the direction of the trucks and buses and the men hanging around there.

Their papers were returned.

Rowena guessed they'd questioned his wisdom in continuing to be married to an American wife now that the DPRK was victorious.

'I told them I've been working for them as an interpreter, that I was ready to serve. They said they will call me if they need my help with the interrogations.'

A French diplomat proved to be a sticking point in their interrogations, the man flagrantly refusing to speak in English.

'He is not speaking good French. He is trying to trick us,' complained one of the young firebrands of Korean communism to his senior officer.

The diplomat said something to Jung who dutifully passed on his details to the two young men.

When he returned to Sheridan and Rowena he was smiling.

'The diplomat gave me more than his personal details. He also told me that a mass invasion is expected. He wanted us to know, which is why he pretended he did not speak English.'

'And the two young men couldn't really speak French?'

'That's about the size of it, but they are the vanguard of the DPRK and want us to think that they know everything.'

The day wore on. Food was getting scarcer. The nuns had resorted to boiling up a large pot of barley and throwing in everything that might give it some flavour.

'We cannot go on much longer feeding all these people,' Sister St Paul confided.

Rowena thought of the few tins lingering on the shelf in the little house up the lane and suggested going to fetch them.

Sister St Paul frowned. 'If they're still there. *Allora*! If only.'

The Italian exclamation added piquant humour to the dire situation and served to make Rowena think it really was possible to sneak out and see what she could find.

She suggested doing exactly that to Jung and Sheridan. Jung's face brightened at the prospect and although Sheridan thought it was a good idea, her natural exuberance was absent. She had previously possessed such a vibrant personality but in a relatively short time had become increasingly lethargic.

Rowena couldn't help being concerned. Her time was coming and the baby was sapping her energy.

She attempted a cheery optimism. 'We could do with having our taste buds tickled. Don't you think so, Jung?'

He eyed her knowingly, capturing the essence of her mood and motivation.

'I do.'

'I need to get past the guards. Perhaps if you keep them occupied...'

He nodded thoughtfully; then grinned. 'I could engage them in political argument. They do like imposing their point of view.'

'In other words you'd have to let them win the argument. Is there anything else you could do?'

'Let them fill me with holes?'

Rowena smiled wryly. 'That's not an option. You've a wife who depends on you.'

She thought of the three cans of condensed milk she'd left on the pantry shelf and frowned. Sheridan could do with something sweet and creamy to help her through what remained of her confinement.

She made her decision. 'It won't be that easy, but I think I should try.'

Jung eyed her thoughtfully.

Sheridan's eyes flashed open. 'Are you talking about getting to your house?'

Up until that point, she had seemed to be dozing.

'I didn't know you were listening. Yes, I'd like to get back and take the few tinned things I left behind in the larder – that is, unless it's already been looted.'

'It might not have been,' said Jung. 'They prefer to loot bigger establishments – especially banks.'

Rowena looked up to where more guards from the ragged array of transport were thronged between the open gates.

'I don't think it's going to be possible.'

'You could get out the other way,' said Sheridan, shifting onto her side. 'Though I'm in two minds whether you should. I wouldn't want anyone getting killed on my account.'

Both Rowena and Jung looked at her.

'What other way?'

Because Sheridan was heavily pregnant, it was easy to forget that she had once been a nun and knew the convent extremely well. It seemed a lot of subterfuge for a few tins of condensed milk but Rowena had easily convinced Jung that Sheridan needed it. Sheridan was more concerned about them risking their lives, but Rowena was determined. Sheridan was getting weaker and needed that milk far more than she realised.

The plan was simple: all three of them would enter the convent and make their way to the chapel. There was a small vestibule behind the high altar used by visiting priests and bishops for changing into their vestments. To the rear of the room was a door that opened into the visiting room which in turn had a separate door to a separate gate. When a nun had visitors – relatives, perhaps, come to advise of the passing of a family member – this was where they would meet. Once the meeting was over the nun would return via the chapel and the visitor would let themselves out through the other door.

★

The chapel was cool and almost empty except for a DPRK soldier standing in front of the altar with his head bowed and his hands behind his back.

Could he really be a devout Catholic?

Alarmed by his presence, they faltered, though for only seconds.

Rowena followed their lead, bowing her head and crossing herself, then clasping her hands as if in prayer.

'It has a lock on the inside,' whispered Sheridan in a tuneful way as though she was singing a litany.

The soldier glanced at them briefly as he made his way to the exit, his footsteps speeding and a guilty look on his face.

They waited until he was gone, breathing a sigh of relief when daylight flooded in through the door before it clunked shut.

'He looked nervous,' remarked Rowena.

'He will be in deep trouble if he's found out.'

Rowena moved quickly and silently, Jung right behind her.

Sheridan struggled down onto her knees and kept up the appearance of being at prayer. Hopefully she would still be alone by the time they got back and their sudden appearance from behind the altar would not give rise to any questions.

The aperture was cramped, smelled strongly of dust and was dominated by a wooden coffer where a spare altar cloth and a few priestly vestments were kept. Right opposite the curtained entrance through which they'd come was a simple wooden door. On opening it they found themselves in a circular room with roughly plastered walls and a single window some way above their heads. It contained two chairs upholstered in dark green brocade, the most attractive furniture in the whole convent, thought Rowena. Then something else struck her.

'They didn't come in here. If they had the chairs wouldn't be here.'

It was true; every room in the convent had been disturbed by their ferreting for valuables. This room was untouched.

Jung turned the heavy iron ring that held the door closed and opened it very carefully, just a few inches, enough of a gap enabling him to look both ways and check that the coast was clear.

'All clear,' he whispered.

Head down, Rowena darted forward. The door could only be opened from the inside, convenient for a nun to open it and her visitor to do the same and close it behind them. It would not open from the outside.

It was late afternoon and silence lay heavy on the air. Her head covered with a big hat and wearing Korean clothes, she kept low as she hurried along the alley and up the hill to the house.

When she got there she found that the door was open and the house cold. Little had changed. The dull rather ordinary furniture had hardly been disturbed, certainly not by human hands, perhaps only by a dog seeking somewhere to sleep.

She stepped further into the room, keenly listening for the smallest sound that would send her running.

The kitchen looked much the same as when she'd last seen it, a single pan hanging from a hook, a small kettle sitting on a trivet.

She remembered placing the tins far back on the shelf

in the highest cupboard – just in case I needed them. She smiled at the thought. This was that time.

Her heart pounding, she found a stool to stand on but still had to stand on tiptoe in order to reach the back of the cupboard. Fumbling around and stretching as much as she could, her fingertips located the three cans of condensed milk. Shuffling a little to the side of those she found another which, on pulling it forward, she found contained sliced peaches.

She couldn't help squealing with joy when she also came across a packet of tea, a jar of marmalade and a tin of corned beef. A small bag of rice and that was it. Everything was placed into the canvas sack she'd brought with her. It was time to head back.

As before, she kept low, her ears attuned to the slightest sound.

Her route back to the visitors' door took her around the side of the convent and away from the main gates but it was still dangerous. Keeping to the shadows thrown by houses and high walls, she kept low but fast, glad to see that the alley where the door was situated was in shadow.

From the front gates came the sound of male laughter, of motors being started, perhaps to ensure they were still capable of travelling. But where to? she thought. Is it for us? If it was she was fearful. Sheridan and a number of other people were not up to travelling very far and she really couldn't foresee everyone making their destination – wherever that might be.

Darting from one doorway, the overhanging eaves going some way to hiding her, she finally made the visitors' door, tapped on it and apprehensively waited for Jung to let her in.

There was no response.

She tried again then rested her ear tightly against the tarnished wood and thought she heard something from inside. Voices.

Panic pervaded her whole body. The tins and other items she'd found weighed heavily on her shoulder. She thought about going round to the main gates and using all her feminine wiles to get past the guards, but that seemed a far-fetched hope. The enemy were keeping everyone in the yard prior to their departure and hours had gone by. They would blame her for straying, in which case she might not be going anywhere. For the time being at least she lay flat against the wall, her heart thudding against her chest wall and her blood pounding in her ears.

Again she leaned her ear against the door and at first thought she heard nothing – then suddenly the door swung open and she fell inside.

A trio of angry faces looked down at her. The visitors' room had finally been discovered. Her first thought was whether Jung had been taken. And what about Sheridan?

She cried out as they dragged her to her feet. The bag was taken from her shoulder and searched.

'You stole!'

She staggered when he slapped her face.

'I did not steal! I went to my own house. I bought those tins. See? They're from Hong Kong. I came here from Hong Kong.'

'A foreign colony! You came here from a foreign colony to make this a colony! You a spy!'

'I am not a spy. I'm a doctor. I wouldn't know how to go about spying or creating a colony. I only know how to bring babies into the world. My friend is pregnant. She was at prayer when I left her, but she badly needs this milk.'

His eyes were dark with menace.

'Please,' she implored. 'If you have children you would understand. If you have a wife…'

Something shifted in his eyes, though not to any great extent. The menace swiftly returned.

'Everything belong to we, the people. We share everything. You will share everything.'

To her great dismay he took two cans of condensed milk out of the bag plus the quarter pound of Typhoo tea and the jar of Hartley's marmalade. It left very little, just the tin of corned beef, the tin of peaches and only one tin of condensed milk. She so wished it could be more, but refrained from begging just in case it angered him and he took it all.

The sound of scuffling and shouting came from the vestibule between this room and the altar. Jung appeared, struggling to throw off the two guards who were holding him. He immediately clasped his hands, bowed his head and sounded as though he was both explaining and pleading.

The man who had stolen her meagre supplies frowned angrily at him, shouted, pointed at the tins, at Rowena and finally at the bag.

Jung said something else, more plaintively this time, and sank to his knees.

The man who appeared to be in charge glared at him for a moment as though trying to make his mind up about what to do next. Finally he seemed to come to a decision.

Snapping his next words, he flung the bag at Rowena. It slammed against her chest but she held onto it grimly even though it now contained so little.

He shouted at her and waved his arm. She was to go with Jung, but not until he'd grabbed her arm again and spat a warning into her face.

The chapel was empty of supplicants but full of soldiers who appeared to have made it into a billet, sprawling out beneath the doe-like eyes of the simply painted icons.

Legs were hauled in as they made their way through the mass of uniformed men, Jung smiling and greeting them as though they were his friends rather than his enemies.

'What did you say to them?' she asked once they were back in the courtyard.

'That you had only been thinking of my wife's health and did not want me worrying about her when I had more interpretation work to do for the glorious North Korean Army. You were lucky. He might have shot you.'

Sheridan gasped with relief at the sight of them.

'Thank God.' She closed her eyes and Rowena was sure she muttered a small prayer of thanks for their return.

'Drink,' said Rowena after Jung had made two small holes in the lid of the tin of milk.

Sheridan shakily took hold of the can with both hands. Having had so little decent food of late, she should have drunk greedily, but she sipped only delicately, savouring each mouthful and insisting they also took a sip. Both of them declined.

'It's for you and Junior,' said Rowena with an outward show of gleefulness that she didn't feel inside. She was worried. In the last war food was more valuable than gold in the harsh environment of the prisoner-of-war camp. They were currently not in a camp – at least not yet. Even so, any kind of war resulted in shortages. Agriculture and supply lines were already in disarray. It was only a matter of time before they really felt its bite.

The moon rose and food was prepared, the nuns distributing what they could spare to those who had nothing left to eat.

Rowena had donated the tin of corned beef to their cooking pot, to which had also been added the last remaining vegetables from the garden. Even the tinned peaches went into the mix. The portions were small but warmed the stomach, the only addition a cup of water helping to fill the gap between the amount eaten and what was truly needed.

As the cooking fire died down and the stars filled the sky, Rowena looked up and thought of her daughter. Somehow the threat from Kim seemed far less than it had done. He couldn't reach her here and neither could he use Dawn to once again trap her in his spidery web.

Closing her eyes, she whispered a thank you, not so much a prayer but a deeply felt relief.

Jung and Sheridan lay under a single blanket. Jung had thrown an arm over his wife; such a protective gesture that it brought a lump to her throat. If Connor was here he would be doing the same; hugging herself ranked a poor second to having him here lying beside her. She so wished he was there, so wished they were together again. She squeezed her eyes tightly shut and tried to sleep. The whole world seemed asleep except for her.

She began to doze, drifting in and out of what was real and what was imagined. The night sounds were muted except when a handful of young Korean soldiers marched among them, pointing their weapons as though they intended shooting people in their sleep. It happened most nights, a primitive form of intimidation that at first had scared them but they'd since got used to.

One night changed her perception yet again. She thought that a cloud had passed over the moon until she heard a soft slow footfall, as though someone was being careful not to be noticed.

Unnoticed by Sheridan and Jung, the shadow that had fallen over her fell over them.

She started, a cry of fear catching in her throat as she raised herself up onto one elbow. Sensing he was being watched, the owner of the shadow froze. On seeing her he raised a finger to his lips signing for her to be quiet. Swiftly and silently he reached down and just as quickly straightened and was gone.

She couldn't tell for sure whether she was dreaming. Dozing into sleep could be such a blurring experience. Whoever their visitor was, he had done no harm, had urged her to be quiet and somehow it was oddly calming. Her eyes closed and she slept deeply.

The morning arrived very still and warm. Bees were buzzing in the convent vegetable patch unaware that their hive had been robbed of honey by enemies they didn't know existed.

Because she'd had so little sleep, Rowena awoke later than the others. On seeing Jung's smiling face she asked him what he was so happy about.

The pair exchanged a smile. Jung explained. 'Junior is being well looked after.'

'We have a guardian angel,' Sheridan added.

Jung patted the canvas bag. After a quick look round

he carefully slid something out. It was the two tins of condensed milk.

'The man who apprehended you also has an expectant wife. He is also a Christian and hopes his good deed will be repaid in kind to her.'

Everything changed just after noon. Rowena had helped the nuns distribute a very much diluted barley soup when a man of authority arrived in the courtyard. The men of the DPRK saluted smartly behind their commander, who Rowena recognised as the man they'd disturbed at prayer who had also returned the tins of milk – though not the marmalade and tea.

Sharp words of command were exchanged.

She could tell from Jung and Sheridan's face that the news was not good.

An order ran out in English.

'Get your things together. You have to leave here. Now. Right now. You have just one hour to get your things together. You leave. You must leave.'

Sheridan flung herself into Jung's arms. 'Where are they taking us?'

He shook his head. 'I don't know. Perhaps to Pyongyang.'

Rowena knew Pyongyang was the capital of the north. She also knew that she would not allow herself to be taken there.

'I won't go.'

'You have no choice.'

'Then I will await my chance. I will never, NEVER allow anyone to imprison me ever again.'

Chapter 21

Hong Kong

The news that a group of gangsters had entered the bar with a view to extortion came as a big shock.

Over a few early evening whiskies, Connor told Brandon McCloud the details.

'And before you ask, Yang didn't recognise them.'

'Is he telling the truth?'

Connor nodded.

A twinkling amusement came to Brandon's eyes. 'And is it really true that your sister ordered them from the premises?'

Again he nodded and a half smile twisted his lips. 'My sister can be a bit frightening at times.'

It was two days later when Brandon visited the bar again and Connor stood him a drink. Kate poured it, plus one for her brother and another for herself.

Connor looked at her. 'Shouldn't you be tucking Dawn in bed or something?'

'Shouldn't you? She's your responsibility, not mine.'

It had been obvious from the moment he'd returned that his sister wasn't going to stand aside from running either his business or her own. Neither was getting married again or starting a family high on her agenda. Kate had found her role in life and was turning out to be a natural businesswoman, tough and uncompromising; nobody was going to dictate what she should or shouldn't be doing.

Connor turned back to Brandon and asked him if he'd found anything out. Kate eyed the Scotsman as she might a puppy not yet housetrained.

Brandon took a sip of whisky, cleared his throat and stated what he knew – which wasn't much.

He firstly addressed Kate. 'The tattoos you mentioned – flowers, you said?'

'You know I did.'

'You're quite sure about that.'

'Yes, I am. I told you – it looked like a dahlia.'

'Or a chrysanthemum?'

She looked at her brother. 'Could be, but not so neat as one of those.'

'Then I think I know who we're dealing with,' said Brandon. 'They're members of the Ragged Flower Society.'

'Sounds almost horticultural,' remarked Kate with an air of contempt.

'Far more dangerous,' returned Brandon. He drained his glass then looked at it in a meaningful way. Kate frowned and pursed her lips.

'Get the bottle, Kate. We need our throats and brains well oiled.'

She poured another for them and one for herself. Connor had never known her to be much of a drinker, but that was back in Catholic Ireland. She was in Hong Kong now and did as she pleased.

'The gang leader is a man named Koos Maas.'

'It sounds like a Dutch name. Is he Dutch?'

'They weren't Dutch that came in here,' said Kate. 'Definitely Chinese, though the size of barn doors. But Chinese. Yes! So what do we know about this man and where can we find him?'

Brandon exchanged a look with Connor. He wasn't used to being hustled, but that was definitely what Kate was doing – hustling.

'In Kowloon Walled City,' said Connor before giving Brandon a chance to answer himself.

'I don't need to tell you that it's a labyrinth. He's in there somewhere at the heart of all that squalor.'

Connor wasn't sure what to make of all this. He'd been so sure that Kim Pheloung was behind the thugs who had visited whilst he was away. Kim had lived in the old city before and during the war, when it was little more than a compound. The only buildings had been ex-Chinese government and long abandoned, but Kim had had a house there. Now it seemed this new crime overlord had also made his home there, though it was a very different place than what it had been. Hastily erected buildings had resulted in a labyrinth of shambolic and haphazard construction.

'So we know a name and have a pretty good idea of where he lives, though he has to come out sometimes. That's when I'd like to confront him.'

'That's when I'd like to arrest him,' Brandon declared. 'According to my information he only comes out at night, and then only by car. Shady and elusive. We're going to keep an eye out for him.' He frowned. 'I dislike having a new man on the block without knowing what he looks like.'

★

It might not have gone any further if there hadn't been a phone call from a nervous-sounding woman. Kate took the call, her brow furrowing as she listened to the shaky voice on the other end.

'Would you tell him I'd like to speak to him?'

'Not without more information. For a start I'll be wantin' your name.'

There was a pause. Kate waited, her jaw determinedly set. She'd not utter another word until the other woman had spoken.

'My name's Barbara Kelly. I'm a nurse at Victoria House. Connor knows me.'

'Does he now!'

'I used to work with his... Rowena. I need to speak to him. I feel guilty, you see. It's all my fault. I need to speak to him.'

'As I said, he's not here, but if it's a heavy burden you're needing to unload, it's only right you should do it face to face. Come here. To Connor's Bar. You know where that is, don't you? Three in the afternoon.'

She slammed the phone down. She had the woman's name and enough details to go on if the woman didn't show up. The fact was, she wanted her to show up. The subject matter had intrigued her. Something she'd done regarding Rowena, something she felt guilty about. Was it possible she'd had an affair with her brother? He was a handsome man, a strong ex-soldier who could charm the birds from the trees when the wind was blowing from the right direction.

Whatever the cause, she was curious to meet this woman and hoped she would get here before Connor did. The woman sounded distraught and she thought she knew how to handle her.

'Putty in me hands,' she muttered to herself as she put out her cigarette in the tin ashtray that sat to one side of her accounts ledgers.

The business was doing well and she was very much enjoying her new surroundings, plus she had plans. Very big plans.

The woman wore a bright red dress scattered with big white flowers. Her sandals and handbag were also white and the pearl studs in her ears matched a single strand of pearls at her throat.

She entered nervously, peering through the blue smoke rising from a dozen or more cigarettes.

Admiring glances were thrown her way plus the odd ribald remark.

It intrigued Kate that she didn't show any signs of blushing, but perhaps as a nurse she was used to it. Sick men could rise to the occasion, even if it was only in their minds.

She told Yang to hold the fort whilst she went over the road to the restaurant.

Without bothering with introductions, Kate placed her hand on the woman's shoulder and firmly guided her towards the door.

'We'll go over the road. It's quieter there and I can hear you talk and hear meself think.'

The woman – Barbara Kelly? – looked surprised but let herself be manoeuvred.

The restaurant was not only quiet, it was cool and shady. A man was sweeping the floor, another polishing cutlery behind a fretwork screen emblazoned with a green dragon.

She ordered him to stop polishing and fetch them lemonade.

'It's home-made,' Kate said. 'My own recipe.'

The lemonades were set before them in dark green glassware.

'I'm not a priest, but you're welcome to confess. What have you been up to?'

'I didn't mean any harm...'

'You obviously know that war's broken out in Korea and that Dr Rossiter is stuck there. Is that what this is all about?' She looked the woman up and down in a bid to assess her possible attractiveness to her brother. The woman having an affair with him was the only possible reason for the visit – but she was open-minded. People and reasons could sometimes be surprising.

Barbara Kelly's eyes were downcast. 'I didn't realise I was doing any harm. I just thought—'

Kate held up a hand. 'Stop right there. A little background detail, if you please.'

She watched as Barbara's tongue licked her lips. The woman's guilt had dried up her mouth. She needed to do something before she spoke.

'I met a man.' She swallowed. Obviously she was finding this hard. She raised her eyes. The look could be interpreted as innocence or foolishness. Kate decided on foolishness. Many women had been fooled into thinking they'd met

Prince Charming, herself included. The man was a myth, the stuff of legend.

Barbara went on to tell Kate how this man, a Colonel Warrington, had been very interested in Rowena. At first he'd asked her general questions: was Rowena married, did she have children, where was she from.

'I told him about Connor, about Dawn, and how Rowena was very well thought of and that she also had very modern ideas...'

Kate frowned as Barbara's voice fell away and her eyes became overcast with guilt. So she hadn't been having an affair with Connor. It was something more complicated. Well, she was well able to sort that out.

'I take it you told him things that you shouldn't have mentioned and this had some bearing on Dr Rossiter.'

She nodded.

'I told him she was in favour of birth control and abortion. I also told him that she'd worked for the UN in Japan after the war and saw deformed children being born. Some of them didn't live for very long and those that did... well... I said that was probably what had shaped her views about abortion.'

She looked down at her white-gloved hands, the fingers fiddling with the clasp of her handbag.

Kate's frown deepened. 'Go on.'

Barbara cleared her throat. 'I knew he was trying to persuade Dr Rossiter to go to Korea – he was obsessed with getting her there – but didn't know why.' A disdainful sneer came to her face. 'I thought that perhaps he fancied her, but it wasn't that at all.'

'You had a good time with this man?'

She nodded. 'He took me out to dinner and suchlike, but then it stopped. He said he didn't have any money left for that. He was drawing in his horns – that's what he said, that he was drawing in his horns.'

'Then he dumped you.'

She nodded. 'He volunteered to go to Korea.'

'Was this following Dr Rossiter's departure?'

'Yes. He has a daughter there. He used to talk about her, how he had threatened to disown her if she didn't come back – and on his terms.'

'What did he mean by that?'

Barbara shrugged. 'I can't really say, but I did get the impression that she'd upset him in some way.'

Kate sat back in her chair. She was good at getting details into some kind of order, just as she had the accounts and organisation of Connor's Bar and the restaurant opposite. Not that Connor seemed to have noticed very much, glad to have someone who could take over the books so that he didn't have to do it. Typical, she thought. She'd done the same in her marriage; Seamus hadn't liked dealing with the day-to-day nitty-gritty of paperwork either. Keeping up-to-date records of the smithy had helped her achieve the very best price and if she could do that in an Irish backwater, she could do the same in a place that was definitely on the up.

'I was devastated when I heard that she'd got caught up in the middle of a war. Has there been any word at all?'

She looked genuinely worried.

'None. And no thanks to you.'

Barbara looked broken and Kate was glad.

'I'm not going to reassure you that we'll find her, because

I've no idea if we will. I'll leave the blame with you to suffer as you will.'

The other woman's face turned almost as white as her bag. Kate congratulated herself. Her instincts had proved correct with regard to her reason for coming here – yes, to tell what she knew, but also to garner some kind of redemption, reassurance that all would be well and that ultimately she would be forgiven.

Kate was not a forgiving woman. Even as a child she'd been known to harbour grudges.

'I think you callous and unthinking, Miss Kelly, so don't go expecting any forgiveness from me and mine. My brother and Rowena's little girl have been left adrift, thanks to you and this Colonel Warrington.'

The sudden redness of Barbara's neck flooded up into her face.

'I'm sorry… I'm sorry…'

She bit her lip and clutched her handbag with both hands.

Kate knew when she had somebody cornered and close to total breakdown.

'You are now. Why the devil didn't you think to ask why he was so interested in her views on such a delicate subject? Do you not have the slightest inkling as to how it's connected with him wanting her to go to Korea?'

Her face on fire, Barbara looked down at the nervous interlocking of her fingers. Kate judged her to be on the verge of tears – not that it would cut any ice with her. The woman was weak and Kate had little regard for such as her. No backbone. No credit to her sex.

Barbara shook her head disconsolately.

'I really don't know why he wanted to know about such

a thing. I thought…' She paused. 'Well, I didn't know really what I thought.'

Kate saw a slight blush creep to her visitor's cheeks and jumped to her own conclusion.

'You were sleeping with him and thought he wanted to know all this in case you should fall in the family way. Am I correct?'

Barbara kept her head down and didn't answer.

'Dear God,' muttered Kate, raising her eyes heavenwards with impatience more than reverence. 'Am I correct?' she asked again, this time loud enough to make Barbara start and sit upright.

Barbara nodded. 'Yes. I suppose so.'

'So if it wasn't for you, who was it for? And why did it result in Dr Rossiter going to Korea? What was there?' Her eyes narrowed. 'Who was there?'

Barbara took a handkerchief out of her handbag, dabbed at her eyes then blew her nose. Finally she raised her head and met Kate O'Connor's searching gaze.

'I think it was all to do with his daughter because she'd married a foreigner.' Kate's eyebrows arched high towards her hairline. An avid reader of detective novels, her favourite of course being Agatha Christie, Kate did as her favourite private detectives would do, evaluated the evidence such as it was and added a good dose of womanly instinct.

'His daughter's got herself into trouble and he wanted somebody there who knew their job and could relieve her of the little problem.'

Barbara looked at her more steadily. Her make-up was smeared but she was now in more control of herself.

'His daughter married a Korean.'

'That's what he told you?'

'No. That's the rumour. He never speaks of her and nobody else is allowed to mention her in his presence – so I hear.'

'She married a foreigner and he doesn't like foreigners.'

Barbara pulled at her gloved fingers without actually taking her gloves off. Kate surmised this attractive young woman had witnessed the colonel's attitude to the colony's ethnic mix of waiters, cab and rickshaw drivers, bank clerks and merchants.

Kate got to her feet, a signal that the meeting was over. 'I think that clarifies quite a lot. It's a pity you didn't mention all this earlier.'

Barbara took the hint, rising unsteadily to her feet.

'I thought I should let her man, Connor, know what had happened.'

'I'll tell him.'

'Tell him what?'

Connor was standing in the doorway, Dawn accompanied by Luli standing in the bright daylight behind him.

On seeing Dawn, Barbara caught her breath.

Connor eyed her quizzically.

'She's just going,' growled Kate. 'And the sooner the better. I'll be telling you all that she's told me. I only wish she'd told us sooner then you might not be a man alone with a child who's without her mother.'

Connor chose the wrong time to call on Brandon McCloud.

'There's a fire in a warehouse close to the waterfront. A

lot of casualties, I'm afraid. You'd better get in. We can talk on the way.'

McCloud drove the Land Rover as though the road was clear and not jam packed with people. On hearing the siren, most pedestrians were nimble enough to leap out of the way. Those that didn't were subjected to a torrent of expletives – some of Chinese derivation – delivered with a strong Scottish accent.

'Buffoons! Slimy sons of toads and serpents. Can't they tell I'm in a bloody hurry?'

Connor told him all that KateKate had told him. 'My money is still on Kim being alive and as cruel as ever though I'd much prefer him to be dead. On the other hand I'm beginning to feel much the same about Colonel Warrington. He's a man who operates in the shadows. He can pull the right strings.'

Brandon shook his head. 'A real snake in the grass. Getting at an innocent bairn in order to get his way.'

Connor had hardly slept since his sister had laid out her conclusion. 'Nan Po was in his pay. So was the woman who delivered the glass doll.'

'So it seems that your old adversary Kim Pheloung really is out of the scene.'

'It would seem so, or at least he's faded into the background, and seeing as you've not come across him, I'm willing to believe that.'

'This colonel's not in Hong Kong, is he?'

'He might be, though it's more likely he's in Japan.'

Both men fell to silence, Connor clinging onto the sides of his seat as the vehicle lurched forward, braked, grated gears and lurched forward again.

'No news from Rowena, I take it.'

Connor silently shook his head. The news from Korea was bad. The headlines in the newspaper reported only the more positive aspects of the war, but as an experienced soldier, he read between those favourable lines. Things were not going well at all.

'And no news yet of you being allowed back there.'

'No. Anyway, I've no wish to go back and fight. I only want to find Rowena and get her back.'

Brandon shook his head. 'I wish you well.'

'You can do nothing about Colonel Warrington.'

It didn't sound like a question but it was. Connor wanted some kind of revenge.

'I doubt it. In the meantime I've got this other item to chase down. This Koos Maas, though it's not proving easy to find him.'

They smelt the smoke even before they saw it billowing upwards, black and stinking of bitumen.

'It's a factory,' Brandon explained. 'A death trap of a place if I know anything about it.'

On getting out of the Land Rover their nostrils were assailed with another smell, far sweeter than the bitumen with which the floors and roofs were lined. More like a Sunday roast, thought Connor, and realising its source felt sick to his stomach.

It was some time before the smoke lessened though the smell remained heavy on the air. Blackened bodies with twisted limbs, their identities impossible to determine, were hurriedly laid in a single row.

The fire chief walked over to them shaking his head and wiping one hand across his sooty brow.

'How many?' asked McCloud.

The fire chief spat liquid carbon through his parched lips. 'You know the answer to that. Too bloody many.'

Connor also knew the answer. It wasn't the first warehouse converted into a factory that had gone up in flames. The export market in Hong Kong was growing – cheap goods headed for European and American markets. Labour was cheap and mostly illegal, drawn from the glut of refugees in need of employment, living and sleeping just yards from where they worked.

The conversation between Brandon and the fire chief was as depressing as the scene itself so he turned away. That was when he saw her. The woman's moon-shaped face was streaked with soot, but still he recognised her.

He looked all around, trying to work out where she had come from, and saw the narrow alley between the burning building and the next.

Despite the fact that debris was raining down, wooden beams, bricks and mortar falling in an avalanche of destruction, she had taken her chance.

Just when it looked as though she would run away, a fireman grabbed her arm, asking her where she'd come from and what the hell she was doing here.

'I'll take charge of her.'

The fireman glanced from Connor to Brandon and presumed they'd come together.

'She's all yours.'

The woman looked up at him with frightened eyes, confirmation that she had recognised him just as he had recognised her.

'You work here?'

She shook her head vehemently, tried to tug herself away, but Connor held on tightly, determined to hear what she had to say about a certain American colonel and his connection with her father, Nan Po.

'Do you remember me? I own the bar across the road from where you used to live with your father.'

Her eyes seemed to well up with fear and her face looked as though it was made of wax, not human flesh at all.

'Why was your father killed?'

The fear-filled expression was undiminished.

He asked her again.

She shook her head. 'I do not know.'

He looked away from her to the smouldering building.

'Did you work in there?'

She nodded.

'How did you manage to get out?'

She looked at him blankly. His eyes narrowed. 'You were at this end of the building.'

She nodded.

In his experience warehouses were built with a staircase at one end, sometimes two, but always at the ends of the buildings, the open-plan factory or warehouse area taking up the premium space in the middle. Offices were often adjacent to the stairs.

'You worked in an office. You were a manager. Yes?'

She said nothing.

He shook her. 'Tell me the truth. You were a manager. Weren't you? Tell me.'

Her face was expressionless when she nodded.

His gaze returned to the building, the blackened windows, the last dousing of water from powerful hoses going in through the empty windows and running down the stairs, meeting up on the ground floor and pouring out of the door.

'Who do you work for? Does Kim Pheloung own this factory? Do you work for him?'

A small frown creased her forehead when she shook her head. 'No.'

The answer surprised him. He had been so sure that she would say yes.

'Who arranged for you and your father to move into the house opposite me? Can you tell me that?'

'My father told me we were moving there.'

'And who told you to move out? There must have been somebody.'

Her jaw moved when she swallowed, gulping back her nervousness.

'The man from the army. The man who worked in the kitchens? Ling Jones?'

She nodded. 'Yes.'

He loosened his grip. So the man who had worked in the army kitchens and had been the fixer, but only the fixer. He was in no doubt that he'd been one of Colonel Warrington's informers, a pawn in his subterfuge operations, though on this occasion had been working in a personal capacity. He was also in little doubt that he would probably show up, though most likely floating face down in the harbour.

There was nothing else he wished to ask her, but once he'd let her go, Brandon grabbed her.

'Just a minute, young lady. I want a word with you. You're coming down to the police station with me.'

'No, no! Please. I must not go there.'

Brandon was unyielding but there was the ghost of a smile on his face when he looked at Connor.

'Note she said that she must not go there. That means if she does go she'll be labelled as an informer. Isn't that right, darling?'

If she'd looked scared before, it was nothing to how she looked now.

'So you might as well tell me here and now who you work for. You know it makes sense.'

She faltered; her mouth opening and shutting as she weighed up her options.

'Koos Maas,' she said at last.

'Ah,' said Brandon. 'Now we're getting somewhere. Koos Maas is this young woman's employer, which means he owns the factory which was no doubt overcrowded with people who had no business being here. I think it's time we paid him a little visit,' he muttered. 'Kowloon Walled City, here we come.'

Chapter 22

Korea

After only about fifty miles, they were turned off the ramshackle transport that had taken them from the convent.

'You walk.'

'The American Methodist minister tried to reason with the strutting stocky man in charge that there were women and children amongst their number, plus a number of the nuns were quite elderly.

He earned a lot of pushing and shoving for his trouble and then complained about their behaviour to anyone that would listen.

He addressed Rowena who had been dabbing the bruised cheek he'd incurred for his trouble.

'Well, don't you think it's appalling?'

'I've seen worse,' she said bitterly as she dismissed him. She took Sheridan's arm and, along with Jung, helped her down from the bus.

The soldiers insisted they left their belongings on the bus. 'We take them on for you. No carry anything when you walk. Walk faster that way.'

Nobody believed them, of course. They'd already taken personal property including watches, women's jewellery and even wedding rings plus whatever food that hadn't already been confiscated.

A bowl of rice and barley then they were on their way.

The sun beat down as the long column of tired people trailed along the narrow road between paddy fields. Those labouring there straightened on seeing these strangers who looked so different from what they were used to.

Overcome by curiosity, one or two shaded their eyes to get a better look.

One of their guards grabbed a nun by the shoulder, shook her like a rat, shouted and waved his weapon in the air. Another did the same with the French diplomat, though being a man and of stout stature, he didn't prove so easy to shake.

Rowena asked Sheridan what he'd said. 'He shouted to the people working in the paddies that these were capitalist lackeys intent on stealing everything they had, but that the DPRK would punish them and throw them into the sea whence they had come. He also told them that the French president was a warmonger and the pope a thief.'

They were pushed on for days, stopping only as the sun went down when water was passed round and sometimes even food. The only other meal was first thing in the morning. If they did stop at midday it was only to drink, though at one place they were shepherded into a building that had once been a school. Here they were given a meal of rice and dried fish flavoured with a little salt.

As they marched the guards sang Communist songs. At

night they did the same, moving amongst their prisoners, bellowing the same songs over and over again.

'This is torture,' remarked Rowena.

Jung informed her that she was quite correct. 'Their intention is to deprive us of sleep.'

'Is that so? Well, not if I can help it.'

She reached into the canvas bag and brought out one of the few sanitary towels she'd managed to bring with her. Another rummage around and she brought out a pair of nail scissors.

A bemused Sheridan watched her. Embarrassed, Jung looked away but didn't refuse when she gave him two small balls of cotton wool and told him to stuff them into his ears.

'We have to sleep. We have to conserve our strength. It's vital for our survival.'

It was a small act of defiance and known only to themselves. The men guarding them carried on with their raucous singing until their voices were hoarse and they were too tired to go on.

Small acts of defiance were morale boosting, but Rowena was resigned that it would not be enough to get them through this. Her greatest concern was for Sheridan. The excess weight of her advanced pregnancy was wearing her down and the lack of decent food and rest wasn't helping. On top of that her stoic constitution – which must have served her well when she was a nun, had been dented by her father's letter. Much as Sheridan loved her husband, it seemed to Rowena that there was a part of her still loyal to a domineering father and grieving for a dead brother. It wasn't beyond the bounds of possibility that her mother's suicide had played a part in her becoming a nun in the first place.

So far Rowena had managed to keep the tins of condensed milk in the canvas bag, which in turn she'd wore, hidden, beneath her clothes. A thin blouse would not have been enough to hide it, but Jung had passed her a spare shirt which was voluminous and did the job well.

She took only the smallest of sips herself, insisting that Sheridan have the lion's share.

'After all, you need to eat for two.'

Jung only pretended to take a sip.

'I'd prefer a beer,' he said, grinning as though he really meant it.

Sometimes they were forced to sleep outside. Thankfully, the good weather seemed set to last.

A man who had been an administrator with a British bank and had once served in the Royal Navy informed them that they were heading north.

'Towards the mountains. All we have to hope is that we're through them before winter sets in. Korea is on the same latitude as Mongolia and Siberia. It gets very cold.'

The first death wasn't long in coming. The Methodist minister's wife suffered from diabetes. As a consequence of this her ankles and feet were severely swollen. Every step was painful but nothing could be done. She'd run out of insulin and her request to obtain a fresh supply before leaving had fallen on deaf ears.

There was little Rowena could do for her without

medication and her feeling of helplessness increased as Mrs Rawlings began slipping into a diabetic coma.

All she could do was beg the guards to let her rest, but this too was denied.

'Walk. Walk. Everyone must walk.'

As her system became more unbalanced she stared around her in a state of confusion, asking where she was and what bus they were catching; how long it would be until the new house was built.

'We had a new house built some time ago back in the States when we were first married,' explained her worried husband. 'Her mind's gone back.'

Perhaps for the best, thought Rowena, knowing it could only be a short time until the woman lost consciousness – and then what would the guards do?

The answer came the following day when she finally fell to her knees, her eyes closed.

No matter how many times their Korean guards shouted at her to walk, she lay supine, not noticing when they nudged her ribs with the toes of their boots. Neither did she hear her husband's plaintive cries for mercy.

Foolish as it was, Rowena flung herself between the American couple and the guards who were already snapping at the triggers of their weapons, preparing to fire.

'This woman is sick. Without the proper medicine she will die. Please let her rest. I beg of you.'

The truth was that she didn't know how long it would be before the woman's organs began to shut down. Rest wasn't the real answer but it might be of some consolation to her husband that she could lie undisturbed in his arms as she took her last breath.

There were mumblings of disagreement before an officer took charge and gave the order to rest until the woman had recovered enough to go on. Rowena kept the fact to herself that she wouldn't be going on for much longer, but at least everyone would benefit from a rest.

There followed a shared sigh of relief and muttered prayers of thanks as the weary centipede of people sank onto the relative softness of the grass verge on either side of the road. The verge was only narrow and once night came down there existed the danger of rolling into a flooded rice paddy, but the cool water would at least give some relief from the heat.

The minister cradled his wife in his arms. Their captors looked on, including the man who had ordered the rest who she recognised as the same officer who had returned the tins of milk.

He turned his back, but heard her when she called out and thanked him. He turned round and their eyes met.

'My patient here is near her time. I do hope there's shelter where we're going.'

His gaze lingered as though he was digesting this information before looking away.

Later, when the moon was hanging low in the sky, he sought her out. Sheridan was sleeping restlessly, Jung sitting at her side soothing her forehead with a damp cloth.

Jung looked startled when he was addressed in French; after all, this particular contingent had professed that none of their number knew how to speak French. Rowena exchanged a surprised look with the French consul who had conversed with Jung. This man had understood everything that had been said. What was more surprising, he had not betrayed them.

Although Rowena had some knowledge of French, it was schoolgirl standard and not enough to follow what was said.

After the man left, Jung was frowning over his wife's sleeping form.

'He told me he had studied at the Sorbonne and had come back to Korea to teach. Unfortunately his family were in the north. He got caught up in its politics and had to toe the line. He asked after Sheridan's health. I told him she is not strong enough to walk much further and that it wouldn't be long before the baby was born.'

Even in the diminished light of the moon, she could see his expression and knew there was more to tell.

'He said their supplies were minimal and he couldn't chance giving us too much and that this was a forced march and would go on for some time. There would be no shelter until the very end – which is quite some way in the distance.'

Despite Jung's worried frown, she felt a leap of hope as she sought meaning in what had been said.

'Is he offering only us food?'

'I'm not sure.'

Jung shrugged his shoulders and pulled their shared blanket over him and his wife.

The sun was only just beginning to peek over the treetops when something unusual aroused her from sleep.

Weeping and words; that's what she could hear. On sitting up she looked over the humped forms of sleeping people and saw the figure of a kneeling man, his hands clasped in prayer. In an instant she knew who he was and why the prayer and the crying. His wife, Mrs Rawlings, had finally given up the ghost.

Sleepers glad to escape the reality of their predicament reluctantly raised their heads. So did their captors who, on seeing the source of the sound, stopped in their tracks.

Throwing back her blanket, she was about to go and give comfort, when Jung caught her arm.

'Don't.'

His voice was only barely above a whisper, but full of warning.

'They won't shoot him,' she said, shaking her head decisively.

'Only if he wants them to.'

His comment chilled her to the bone because she knew it might be true. How strong was the man's faith, she wondered, and how much had he loved his wife? If the answer was very much, then he would not wish to leave her behind.

He struggled to his feet, flung his arms in the air, threw back his head and bellowed to the sky. With a great flourish of whirling arms, he leapt into the air and there was the sound of a momentous splash as he jumped into the rice paddy.

She was on her feet immediately. 'No. He's not well…'

She was aware of Jung handing onto her skirt, determined she wouldn't go to the Reverend Rawlings' help.

The guards were young, naively full of political enthusiasm and keen to kill if it gained them greater kudos in the Communist party.

There followed the crack of a bullet leaving the barrel of a weapon, then a second and a third.

'Don't,' Jung said again. 'They're jumpy. Just scared kids, fired up with what they don't really understand.'

She let herself be held back. There was nothing she could do except follow her own advice and conserve her energy. Squeezing her eyes shut she tried to block the incident from her mind and seek pleasant dreams, but instead was bombarded with both old and new nightmares.

Dawn came in a rosy glow from the east. The woman's body was covered with a blanket then a layer of stones. It was done quickly. The husband was left lying face down in the paddy field where labourers were already picking their way towards him.

'The Koreans are an honourable people,' said the prioress. 'They will inter the body in a respectful manner.'

Up until this moment Rowena had seen little of the mother superior and asked how the other sisters were doing.

'Surviving and praying. That is all any of us can do.'

She picked up on the sudden hardening of Rowena's face.

'You look troubled, my dear.'

Rowena shook her head. 'Not troubled. Determined. I was a prisoner once before. I have resolved never to be one again.'

'And Mrs Lee?'

She referred to Sheridan by her married name – not the name she'd been known by in the convent.

'Thanks to these present circumstances, I fear the child will come early.'

'Food and rest. That's what she needs. That's what we all need.'

'I fear none of us will get it.'

'Then I will pray for her. For us all.'

Breakfast was as frugal as usual and once it was over they were prodded and pushed to their feet.

Jung protested when Sheridan was manhandled to her feet, spinning round quickly and giving the guard's shoulder a rough shove. Retaliation was brutal, the butt of the man's automatic rifle slamming into Jung's face. Blood trickled from both nostrils.

In a fit of foolish anger, Rowena sprang in front of him, shouting furiously at the young attacker who stared at her in amazement, not understanding a word and taken aback that she'd been brave enough to stand up to him.

As though suddenly awakened from a deep sleep, he sprang into action, raising his weapon, the butt readied on his shoulder, eye aligned to the sight and finger curving over the trigger.

She felt no regret for holding her ground even though it might result in her death, after which she might be flung into the paddy field for some woebegone villagers to find and dispose of.

Suddenly a strong arm broke the vision between her and the shoulder, a heavy hand slamming down on the rifle, altering its trajectory. A bullet left the muzzle and entered the ground just in front of her feet.

She saw their friend, the man who'd returned the tins of condensed milk, the one they'd started calling Can Man. His face was red with fury.

The younger man crumpled under the verbal onslaught of his superior to whom he was trying to explain what had happened. Can Man glared and said something, then his glare landed on them.

Sheridan was holding a scrap of cotton to Jung's face.

None of them had any idea what would happen next, but it didn't take long coming.

Everyone was ordered to start walking – except for the three of them who were told to sit back down on the grass.

Fear bound them together. Perhaps this was the moment. But at least we'll all be together, thought Rowena. She turned fear-filled eyes at Can Man. 'What are you going to do with us?'

He glanced at her briefly, said nothing and looked away, barking orders at everyone else. She needed no interpreter to know that he was telling everyone else to move along – except them.

He took a revolver from the leather pouch at his waist, waved it at the tail end of the long column and the guards bringing up the rear.

Rowena trembled. Sheridan buried her head in her husband's shoulder and murmured, 'He's going to kill us.'

The end of the column disappeared. Can Man looked down at them and shook his head.

'You give me no choice.'

They jumped as he lifted his weapon and discharged a shot into the air. It was followed by a short gap then a second shot, another short gap and a third, just as though he were carrying out three executions.

'I had planned to give you food before releasing you, but as I have just said, you give me no choice but to let you go now. You will find the Americans in that direction.' He pointed the muzzle of his gun towards the south-east. 'They may have arrived or they may not. You will have to take your chance. You have water?'

Rowena nodded soundlessly, unable to believe what she was hearing.

'Lie low a little while in case anyone doubles back. Get your breath. Then go. Head for the hills.'

Still amazed at their luck, they watched him stride off in the same direction as the raggle-taggle column of people before following his instructions and lying stretched out on the ground.

Rowena gazed up at the clouds, suddenly amazed at the different shapes, like boats gliding across a stunningly blue sea.

Despite being given a bloody nose, Jung was singing softly, Sheridan joining in now and again in tearful joy.

'I think half an hour has gone by,' remarked Jung.

Rowena got to her feet. 'He pointed in that direction. South-east.'

Jung nodded. 'That makes sense. The Pusan peninsula is in that direction. Plenty of room to land troops.'

'Let's hope there are a lot of them, and let's hope we can find them.'

Before leaving they checked what food they had. It was very little but somehow they just didn't care. They had another long march ahead of them and the prospect of freedom at the end of it.

'It's uphill for some way.'

'But downhill the other side,' laughed Rowena.

'Freedom and good companionship,' added Sheridan. 'Who could ask for anything more?'

Taking a cue from Sheridan's comment, Rowena burst into the song of the same name. It most definitely suited the occasion.

Chapter 23

Hong Kong

Connor studied the map of Korea spread out on his desk whilst listening to news of the war on the wireless. Not that everything said on there could be believed.

'Troops are presently advancing towards the city of Pusan... a number of casualties have been airlifted from the interior...'

He threw back his head, spitting expletives between his teeth. Getting back to Korea was impossible. Unless he had business there, he wouldn't be let in, and once there, where would he search for her? St Catherine's was a possibility, but there'd been severe fighting in that area and heavy bombardment. The place was likely in ruins.

The only way he could get back there was as a fighting man, and there was no chance of that happening until his wounds were healed. In the meantime he could at least do something to put his mind at rest on the home turf.

The wooden cabinet that looked like an ordinary cupboard, fragrant with the scent of resin, kept the moths off his clothes and hid the Luger given him by an American acquaintance who had served in the European theatre.

It broke cleanly. The barrel was empty, the bullets kept in a separate box. He loaded it quickly and clicked the bullets into place.

'And where do you think you're going with that?'

Kate had entered the room silently – like a cat, he thought, light on her feet, lighter still nowadays having lost the weight she used to carry.

'I've a mission,' he said, tucking the gun inside his jacket without the slightest display of guilt.

'And who's going to get shot?'

'Anyone who gets in my way,' he said grimly.

She looked at him with her chin down, eyes unblinking.

'You've responsibilities and I've plans for this family's future, besides which Rowena will expect you to be here when she gets back.'

He paused. A fleeting despair crossed his face then was gone.

'I'll be here,' he said, then set off to join Brandon.

Chapter 24

Korea

Their initial euphoria was short-lived. They were free to find their way to the American lines but their journey might have been more pleasant if it hadn't been for the mosquitoes.

'I'm being eaten alive,' Rowena muttered. The others were undergoing the same torture, hordes of the things all out for their blood. The waving of hands was not good enough. The only way they could escape them was to drape an item of clothing or blanket over their heads as they walked, but this was both hot and dangerous. The path they were climbing was narrow and uneven. Loose stones slid from beneath their feet. By sundown of the first day they were tired out, thirsty and hungry. All they had to eat was a little rice and some pieces of fruit and dried fish passed to them by their kind benefactor. It wouldn't last for long.

'I will go foraging tomorrow and see what I can find,' declared Jung.

Rowena suggested that wild garlic would be useful. 'Or a Korean alternative,' she added, at the same time flicking yet another bloodthirsty predator away from her face.

Jung knew what she was saying. 'I have heard mosquitoes dislike garlic. I will see what I can find.'

Daybreak came, Rowena woke up and Jung was nowhere to be seen. The mosquitoes were less, probably because they were replete with blood from the night before despite their prey hiding beneath the blankets. Somehow they always managed to find their way in.

Sheridan drank a little more of the condensed milk, washing it down with water. At her invitation, Rowena sipped a mouthful and both of them ate what remained of the dried fish and fruit.

Jung came back with the canvas bag over his shoulder which he'd hoped to fill with anything edible. The two women eyed it with interest.

'Did you find anything to eat?' asked Sheridan.

'Better than that. I found something that might prevent the mosquitoes eating us. I really think it is wild garlic.'

Rowena took a sniff. 'Smells like it.'

'Rub it on your exposed skin.'

He helped Sheridan, rubbing it on her arms, legs and face before doing the same to himself.

He'd also dug up some root vegetables and proceeded to make a soup, the first hot meal they'd had in days. Thankfully he also possessed a box of matches.

'I made a trade.' He grinned secretively. 'One of the guards wanted my lighter so I said he could have it in exchange for a box of matches. He was more than willing.'

'He could have taken it anyway.'

When Jung grinned he looked as cheeky as a nine-year-old, but what he said next added the wisdom of an older man.

'I know that and you know that but he wasn't much more than eighteen years old, still young enough to respect his elders.'

Rowena laughed along with Sheridan who kissed her husband's cheek. 'You are so clever, Lee Jung.'

Jung's eyes twinkled. 'I told you this before we married, Mrs Lee. That was back in the days when you couldn't get out of the habit of calling me Mr Jung.'

Sheridan explained what he meant to Rowena. 'I thought Jung was his surname, but in Asia it's common that the family name comes first then the given name.' Sheridan laughed at the memory though her laughter seemed short-lived, as though she just didn't have the energy to laugh for too long.

Rowena had observed she was losing weight, not surprising seeing as their diet was less than starvation level. She'd also noticed that every so often she winced and grabbed her stomach.

'It's OK,' she said on noticing Rowena's concerned expression. 'It's my stomach complaining that it could do with more food.'

Although Sheridan had done her best to sound reassuring, Rowena was not convinced.

The hot soup was totally consumed although Jung managed to conserve a few of the vegetables to eat on their journey. Once they were cooled he placed them in the canvas bag.

As the days went on, he foraged where he could. In his absence Rowena gave Sheridan her arm, especially when it came to climbing the steeper ascents. Luckily, the soles of her shoes were stoutly made and she was thankful she'd chosen such a serviceable pair with no heels and thick soles. Before setting out, Sheridan too had chosen flat shoes, a pair of dull black shoes that might have been in daily use back in her time as a nun.

Jung gave a great whoop of triumph on the occasion when he brought back a snake.

'Trust me,' he said, with great enthusiasm. 'A delicate flavour.'

Sheridan eyed it with disgust. 'An acquired taste, I would think.'

Rowena had seen all manner of things flung into food mixtures back in the dark days of her imprisonment at the hands of the Japanese so was totally accepting.

Whistling softly to himself, Jung skinned the creature and tossed it into the pot along with wild onions and a few roots and grainy heads of wild grass.

Despite Sheridan's initial reluctance to eat snake, both Jung and Rowena encouraged her to take a bite.

'You'll like it. It's just like chicken,' said Jung.

Sheridan blew on the hot piece of flesh, passing it from one hand to another until she'd gathered up her courage and delicately took a bite.

Both Rowena and Jung waited before eating theirs. Finally she swallowed, nodded and pronounced that Jung was right. It really did taste like chicken.

Unfortunately it was the last snake Jung managed to catch and his foraging was reduced to roots that needed boiling for hours before becoming soft enough to eat.

For two weeks or more the summer weather travelled with them. A bank of grey clouds swept low across the sky, filtering down through the trees. A thick mist was followed by heavy rain and the dry paths became wet with loose stones and slurry.

'I need to rest.'

Her body shivering with exhaustion, Sheridan laid her head against her husband's shoulder. Rowena took off her own blanket and placed it on the top of Sheridan's. Her eyes met those of Jung.

'She needs to rest. Perhaps we should stay here for a little while.'

Sheridan protested. 'No. I can manage.'

'Just a little while,' said Jung. Again she saw the worried look in his eyes and nodded. They would rest for just a little while, but both knew she needed serious medical attention. No matter her skills, Rowena would have preferred her to be in a hospital.

An hour later they pressed on. They were still ascending through woodland that had been pleasant during the dry period. The recent downpour had altered things but the fact that they could see the brow of this hilly country spurred them on. Beyond this brow they would begin to descend. In the meantime they continued to climb, their legs buckling beneath them on the slippery slope.

Their progress was slow and they were sinking ankle deep into thick mud – not much of a path at all. That was when it came to Rowena that their route was not a path formed by travellers but eaten out of the ground by a torrent of rainwater.

Exhausted, they finally had to concede defeat. They needed rest and food but only had the remains of the cold plant roots.

Jung reached for the haversack.

'No,' said Sheridan shaking her head. 'I'm too tired to eat.'

Jung started to rise. 'I will go and find more.'

'No, darling. You're too tired to go out and find anything else.'

Rowena too was exhausted and accepted that their fatigue was greater than their hunger so sleep was not too elusive.

The following day brought a clear sky. The sun had returned, warming the air and dappling the ground with images of dancing leaves. Steam rose in tenuous vapours from the branches of trees and shrubs and the birds were singing. Jung got to his feet, his arms hanging at his sides. With a shudder he roused himself to action and reached for the haversack.

Blinking back her weariness, Rowena looked up to the canopy of trees, their leaves a filigree of movement, green against blue sky.

'The birds are singing.' Her voice shook but she did feel considerably refreshed.

Jung grimaced in a humorous manner. 'I'm hoping one or two might have fallen from their nest.'

She saw his eyes wander to where Sheridan lay with her legs stretched out in front of her, her back resting against a rock, and they exchanged a searching look. Sheridan had just refused the very last piece of plant root. Having meat for the pot – whatever it was – would be extremely welcome. They badly needed some protein, if only to give them much needed energy.

Sheridan was fading, but Rowena held her tongue. Where there was life there was hope. Wasn't that the old saying? And yet in this instance her knowledge and instinct combined to predict otherwise. All they had left was hope, no matter how fragile it might be. Sending him off to find more food would give him that.

Her heart heavy, she watched him leave thinking how somehow his height had reduced thanks to the responsibility and concern lying heavy on his sloping shoulders. She kept her eyes on him until he passed from view, a solitary figure disappearing into the mist.

Sheridan's fingers brushed her arm, begging her attention. Rowena caught her breath. The once healthily rosy cheeks were sunken and her eyes circled with purple rings.

'I didn't want to say anything when Jung was here, but I think it's coming.'

The labour was long and painful. For three days Sheridan lay on her bed of pine, sheltered only by the nodding branches overhead.

'She needs a caesarean.' Rowena's voice was soft and low. Her forehead was beaded with sweat. She looked around her frantically as though out here, in the middle of nowhere, she might find the facilities she needed to make this possible. It was quite hopeless, of course. She didn't even have a scalpel. All her luggage, like everyone else's, had been left on the bus.

She felt Sheridan touch her. The sleeve of her blouse had fallen back in a silky ruffle revealing an arm that seemed all skin and bone. Her voice was barely audible and her face was creased with pain.

'Listen. Both of you. Please listen.'

Holding her hand gently in both of his, Jung was instantly reassuring. 'You're going to be fine.'

She smiled up at him and shook her head weakly. 'I'm not afraid to die. I am still of the faith. Do not weep for me.'

There was an underlying urgency to Jung's repeated reassurance. 'You're not going to die. You're not going to leave me. You can't. I won't let you.'

The brightest of smiles lit her face but was promptly replaced by a grimace and then an ear-piercing scream, so shrill that birds took flight from overhead.

Hours into the night it went on, until finally it was morning. A grey dawn became tinged with the orange glow of the rising sun. Her strength all gone, Sheridan lay there, her eyes closed, her mouth open, her body wracked with pain.

Suddenly she arched her body. No strength left for screaming, she let the baby come – but too fast.

There was nothing Rowena could do. The baby pushed its way out into the world, too quickly, savagely ripping the flesh of the perineum and staining the scented pine with blood.

The baby cried lustily. Rowena passed the child into the waiting arms of its father and turned her attention back to Sheridan.

'A girl,' said Jung, tears streaming down his face. 'We have a daughter.'

Sheridan barely acknowledged him. Her face was ghostly white, but despite the terrible pain from her injuries, she managed a sad, halting smile.

'A summer baby,' she whispered.

Leaves of the overhead trees danced in the sudden breeze

and her face was suddenly dappled with sunlight. She blinked in the sudden glow and for one precious moment her expression was reminiscent of the wholesome girl she'd once been.

'Summer. That's my name for her. Summer.'

Jung nodded enthusiastically whilst blinking the tears from his eyes. 'That's a beautiful name. A really beautiful name.'

Rowena, her hands sticky with blood, applied herself to what had to be done next. Cleaning her up was impossible. Her flesh was torn and she was haemorrhaging badly. She needed bandages, but they had none. A few items of underwear balled into a bulky sanitary towel helped staunch the bleeding but would never stop it. She had nothing to help. No needle, no thread, and even then the blood loss was so great she knew beyond doubt that a transfusion was needed.

Jung addressed her. 'Summer is a healthy baby, yes?'

'Yes,' returned Rowena and managed a smile.

The baby had been wrapped in Rowena's angora cardigan and put to her mother's breast where she swiftly found the nipple and began to suck.

The scene was soothing, almost hopeful. The birth was over but Rowena knew beyond any doubt that the worst was yet to come.

Wearied from lack of sleep and intense attention, she swept her hands over her face and rubbed at her eyes which felt as though they'd been stabbed with red hot pokers. They were gritty and tired but still hot tears ran down her dirt-encrusted face.

'I'm sorry,' she said falteringly and softly, keeping her

eyes lowered so she couldn't see the realisation of what she was, and what she was not saying, on Jung's gentle face. 'So sorry.'

She felt rather than saw his frown. He said nothing, didn't reassure her that she'd done her best or that there was nothing else she could do.

He might or might not know that she was blaming herself though deep down she knew very well that nothing was going to change what was about to happen unless a hospital suddenly appeared right in front of them. What she did blame herself for was her determination to escape, her resolve that she would never be anyone's prisoner ever again. Perhaps if they'd stayed with the others they might have come across a hospital, either enemy or ally, it didn't really matter.

There were good reasons to think that even in her heavily pregnant state, Sheridan would have survived, not least the American girl's cheery disposition. From their very first meeting Rowena had been impressed by her healthy skin, shining teeth, glossy hair and general exuberance. She had been, in fact, a picture of health.

Lack of food and comfort plus the journey into the mountains had weakened her. She had been in no state to give birth.

She heard Jung uttering words of love in both Korean and English.

Coming out from behind her hands she took in the beautiful scene of the baby suckling at his mother's breast. It was a familiar picture, portrayed in paint by the greatest masters throughout the ages, mother and child, the Madonna with the baby Jesus. But nothing, thought Rowena, was quite as beautiful as the real thing.

Sheridan lay perfectly still; the only sound her erratic breathing and the snuffling of the feeding child. Jung was stroking her forehead, a look of great sadness on his face.

She couldn't help but emit a painful gasp and ask herself whether it was truly possible that this vivacious young mother was close to death.

There followed another episode of breaths taken, a period of nothing, then her chest heaving with another snatched breath.

She exchanged a worried look with Jung who said nothing but moved his fingers to his wife's pulse. He shook his head, his eyes brimming with tears. As a pharmacist he had some idea of his wife's condition.

Rowena shook her head and whispered, 'She's lost too much blood. We need to get her to a hospital – any hospital.'

She looked around her as she had earlier, wondering if they could somehow make a stretcher from a pair of supple branches and carry her down the mountain. On reflection she decided the idea was hopeless. Carrying Sheridan down over uneven surfaces could result in an even greater amount of blood loss.

In her heart of hearts she knew beyond doubt that in the absence of modern medical facilities there was little hope of her surviving.

Death came more quickly than she'd expected. The young woman who had seemed as fresh as a summer breeze stopped breathing.

Rowena shook her, placed her hand on her chest, compressed, though she knew it was of no use.

The baby slept, still cradled in the cold crook of his mother's arm.

'I'm sorry,' she whispered.

Jung said nothing but bowed his head in prayer.

Mother, father and child; a sad trio indeed.

This, she decided, is a moment for privacy. In the short time she'd known them she had been impressed by Jung and Sheridan's loyalty and love for each other. This was a private family moment. She was an outsider.

She got to her feet, walked into the trees, breathed the air, looked up at the sky and wanted to howl in protest at everything that had happened. Regret and confusion hammered at her mind.

'It wasn't your fault.'

She hadn't heard Jung come up behind her.

'I can't help feeling responsible.'

'She should have taken the flight to Tokyo.'

Ah yes. Tokyo. Her father's doing.

Rowena sighed. 'Colonel Warrington has a lot to answer for.'

'She should have gone.'

'And leave her husband?' She shook her head. 'No. She would never do that. She loved you.'

She heard the springing of ground foliage and the breaking of branches and knew what he was doing but couldn't look. Not yet. She just couldn't bear to look.

She stayed where she was, feeling uncomfortably heavy as though the weight of the world truly was resting on her shoulders. More casualties of war. Another innocent life.

The past came flooding back and although Jung would have appreciated her help, she just couldn't bring herself to go back and see Sheridan lying so pale and still.

When she finally returned to the clearing Jung had covered the lower half of his wife's body with leaves and branches. The sleeping baby, replete with milk and warmly wrapped in the angora cardigan, was sleeping on a bed of pine nearby.

Jung was standing over his wife's half-finished grave. On hearing her footsteps through rustling leaves, he looked up at her.

'We haven't time to bury her and there are too many plants and roots to dig through.'

'And we don't have a spade.'

'No. We do not.'

She wanted to reach out and pat his shoulder, but hesitated, her fingers curling back into her palms. What could she say next? What was there to say in such dire circumstances?

It was Jung who broke the cold, empty silence. 'We must ensure that Summer survives.'

She nodded, looked at the sleeping child then at Sheridan and knew she was only half buried for a reason.

Wordlessly, he emptied the water from his bottle into hers. It should be enough now for only three of them. The water bottle was now a milk bottle. Summer had to survive. Her mother would want that above all else.

'I'll do it.' Rowena made as if to take the bottle. Expressing milk from a mother's breast was never that difficult. A woman's body was prepared to give all for her newborn, milk pouring out at the slightest provocation.

JEAN MORAN

In this instance she paused. It would be easy but she would not be the one doing it. Something about Jung's determined demeanour stopped her. This last, almost intimate moment, should be his.

Although the baby's first suckling had been vigorous, the deficit had been quickly replaced. Each nipple was already spilling milk, enough, Rowena reckoned, for at least twenty-four hours.

Jung passed her the precious cargo that would keep Summer alive for a little while.

Rowena hugged the milk to her chest before sliding the tin receptacle carefully into the canvas haversack. As best she could, she began helping Jung cover the remainder of Sheridan's body.

Her expression turned grim as Sheridan's father came to mind. He'd wanted her to abort the unborn child. Instead of that she was now going to her damnedest to save the baby's life.

Anger mixed with a whole range of other emotions. What a fool she'd been not to have understood his purpose. Along with that anger came another longer standing loathing: Kim Pheloung and his threat on her and her family. Her fear of him seemed to melt in the heat of her anger. She *would* get back to Hong Kong. Firstly, on her return she would give her daughter a big hug; after that one for Connor. After that she would seek out the man who had caused her to come here in the first place; not Colonel Warrington who she would most likely never see again, but Kim, the reason she'd fled for her life and that of her daughter. She would seek him out and once and for all cut him from her life.

All these things made her want to promise if not to God,

but to herself that if she was ever to lead a happy life these fears had to be purged from her soul. As a consequence of all these thoughts, she bowed her head in prayer.

'I swear I will face this man down and take my revenge. I will kill him.'

They were angry words, an oath based on fear but as sharp as the edge of a sword. She really meant what she'd said.

Once the whispered words were lost on the breeze Jung picked up his daughter, staring down at her wrinkled face as though he couldn't quite believe she existed.

Sighing, Rowena slung the canvas bag over her shoulder. Along with their greatly depleted bundle of food it also contained one single bottle of water for their consumption and a bottle of breast milk for the baby.

There was still sufficient daylight ahead of them to wind their way over the brow of the hill and down into the valley. According to their reckoning the city of Pusan had to be some miles in the distance. Hopefully the UN forces had landed there and with luck they might come across a convoy of troops.

The milk would not last for long. Their other hope was finding a place where they could at least find a wet nurse; somewhere they could leave the child and reclaim her at a future date.

For a moment they rested, ate a small morsel of dried vegetable, there being nothing else available as Jung hadn't managed to bag a fallen bird or even a scurrying rodent or slithering snake to bulk out their meal.

Summer was fed drips of milk from Jung's finger. The sight of him doing it made Rowena want to cry. She just had to look away.

Taking a sip of water, she tilted her head back and thought about her daughter, how it had felt, feeding her in depressing circumstances, though not nearly as bad as this.

Drowning in memories she regarded the sky lying like a blue lid over the valley. In the distance a flock of birds seemed to be flying in strict formation.

They had left the shelter of the trees. The land was more open here and the sunlight more intense. In order to better see the birds she used her hand to shield her eyes. The birds were coming their way, flying in a diagonal across the valley. As they came closer she heard the droning of engines. Aeroplanes.

Jung had seen them too. Even from this distance they could make out the insignia – a big star. American planes.

'Bombers,' he said, and although he said it softly she could hear the catch in his voice. The planes were a sign of hope. They weren't coming directly at them but at least it meant that a counter-offensive against the communists was in the offing. 'We need to press on,' Jung added.

The sight of the aeroplanes gave them renewed energy. If there were planes perhaps there would also be ground troops.

Night was drawing in and making their way downhill became more difficult. There were rocks on either side and very little flat space on which to rest. They both agreed that they would go on until they could no longer see their way.

Just before the situation became completely untenable, they came across a semicircle of space surrounded by rocks and rough grasses. It was far from ideal but they had little choice. Summer was wailing to be fed. Their route was bad enough in daylight, an indistinct downward slope winding around foliage and rocks. At night those obstacles would be hidden and they were carrying a child.

The cup-shaped space was too small to allow them to lie full stretch. After they'd eaten from their sparse rations and fed the child, they curled up into a foetal position, the baby asleep within the warmth of their enfolded arms.

Chapter 25

Hong Kong

Kate eyed her brother thoughtfully through a pall of tobacco smoke. She'd never smoked as a wife, never drank either because Seamus didn't approve of women doing either of those things. Never again would she allow herself to get into such a submissive situation. Nowadays she did as she liked.

Connor was sitting at the bar with his head bowed. Brandon McCloud – who thought himself a bit of a ladies' man – was sitting next to him. Usually McCloud would be throwing her a smile or a cheeky wink. But not today. They were sweaty, dirty and despondent. The raid on the walled city had not gone as planned. For a start they'd got lost, and secondly they'd come out empty-handed. The whole operation of finding this hotbed of criminals and, principally, this man Koos Maas, the man responsible for the deaths of many people in the factory fire, had been a total failure.

Connor caught her looking at him with that 'you should

have known better' kind of look. She got in first before he had the chance to comment.

'Taking a gun indeed, charging in there like Billy the Kid. The war's over, Connor. Things have changed.'

'Oh yes,' he said, his eyes glaring. 'And you would have me not do anything about the scoundrels that came here demanding a cut of the takings!'

His tone was harsh, but Kate was used to harsh tones. She could handle them. Anyway, she knew something he didn't know.

'They won't be coming back. The matter's been dealt with.'

Both men looked at her. It occurred to Connor that she'd grown by a few inches, but quickly realised it was just that she was holding her head high, her chin thrust forward.

Connor frowned. 'What have you done?'

She sniffed, adjusted her hat and pulled on her white, wrist-length gloves.

'You could say that I used my feminine wiles, but that would all depend on what you meant by that tired old cliché.' She stopped fiddling with her gloves, pulled them off and flung them onto the bar. She frowned. 'It seems that the owner is not long on this earth and is open to offers. So I offered.'

Connor frowned. 'Who told you that?'

'The bank manager. He more or less told me that whatever I own in future, I will no longer have any problems with gangsters involved in protection rackets. Far fetched I know, but men can change overnight when faced with their own mortality. I should know. My Seamus was a changed man when they told him he wasn't long for this world.'

She lost patience trying with her gloves and threw them onto the counter.

'Who needs gloves anyway? You can't grip anything with them damned things on. If my hands get rough and brown in the process of good honest work, then so be it.'

Connor positioned himself between her and the door.

'Where are you off to?'

'I've a business appointment.'

'What have you done, Kate? Hong Kong criminals aren't usually sorry for anything they've done. Death means nothing to them.'

Her gaze was steady. 'Oh yes it does, Connor. You saw death first hand yourself. You know how it can change people. Didn't it change you?'

He'd never admitted that anything about him had changed, yet deep down he knew it had. His sister was observant. She missed nothing.

He recalled the clever little girl she'd once been, always top of the class but obliged to leave school on account that, in their grandparents' opinion, all girls were fit for was to get married and bear children. Kate had done the former but had never been blessed with children and she'd worked in a shop before getting married. 'A domestic slave at home when single and married,' she'd pointed out when first arriving in Hong Kong and stating that she would stay.

He sidestepped to stop her passing. She raised a painted finger pointing it directly into his face.

'Mark my words, brother. The women are set to take over this world. You men have been running it for long enough. It's our turn now.'

So fierce was her look, so threatening her finger, that he

stepped aside. Despite his sister's formidable demeanour, he loved her almost as much as he did Rowena and her darling daughter.

'Just remember to fetch Dawn from school. It's your turn,' she shouted over her shoulder.

He caught Brandon grinning.

'She's a bit of a warrior, that one.' He raised his eyebrows. 'The sort of woman a man prefers to court than cross.'

Although inclined to agree with him, Connor did not echo his grin. His sister was up to something that he wasn't party to and he knew as sure as eggs were eggs that he'd have to wait until she deigned to draw him into her confidence.

Mr Gresham, the bank manager, welcomed her warmly, offered her a seat and asked her whether she'd prefer tea or coffee.

'Neither, thank you.'

She settled herself down in the chair and allowed herself to feel smug. Mr Gresham didn't offer beverages to just anyone, only the most valued of his clients, the ones who had shown adroit business sense. This was their second meeting. He'd been reluctant at first to see her, but had been under instructions from a man who owned a great deal of property; a man of power and influence. Gresham also feared him and the organisation he represented. But he'd made the offer as instructed. Now it seemed the deal was about to reach fruition.

'Let's get down to business, Mr Gresham.'

'Indeed, Miss O'Connor.'

She'd purposely decided to go back to her maiden name.

To her mind there was something about a mature spinster that inspired confidence. A widow, which she had only been for a short time, attracted pity and was generally considered slightly vulnerable. She was not vulnerable and disliked being pitied. There was a fire in her belly and she was stoking the flames.

Mr Gresham adjusted his spectacles as he perused her file. 'Your bank account relating to the restaurant and boarding house are showing very healthy profits – very healthy indeed.'

'That's what I'm here to see you about. I want to reinvest those profits.'

He took off his glasses and looked at her. 'Indeed, dear lady. And what have you in mind?'

'At present I am the leaseholder of those properties. I still pay a rent, though thanks to you, Mr Gresham, I have a very good leasehold arrangement.'

'I'm always pleased to assist a discerning client. Now what is it you have in mind?'

'I want to buy the freehold.'

His eyebrows arched and she saw a mercenary hardness come to his eyes. He scented a profit, a fee for negotiating this deal – if achievable.

'Well. That's quite a leap.' He scanned the account details in front of him. 'It would mean devolving yourself of all your profits, plus taking out a mortgage.'

'I didn't sink all my capital into the businesses. I still have a sizeable sum in a separate account – though not at this bank.'

Surprise dented his smug expression. She'd taken him by surprise, something that a good number of experienced investors did as a matter of habit. Even though he'd assessed Miss O'Connor as a shrewd woman, she was still just that. A woman.

Her feeling of bemusement did not show on her face, but she was thoroughly enjoying this. She had purposely kept the bulk of the money received for the business and property back in Ireland so she could play one bank off against another. If one didn't see their way to falling in with her plans and assisting her then she'd go to the other.

Mr Gresham licked his lips and smiled. 'If you could leave the matter with me, I will approach the owner and see whether he is interested.'

'Good.' Kate got to her feet.

'Have you any particular sum in mind?'

'I do, not that I'll be telling you, Mr Gresham, until the owner has told us whether he's interested or not.'

'Very good, Miss O'Connor. I'll pursue the matter immediately.'

Chapter 26

Korea

It was halfway through the next morning and there was no milk left. Rowena considered giving the baby water to keep her quiet, but feared infection.

She could see by the look on Jung's face that he was as anxious as she was. All they could do was soldier on, the baby wailing all the way.

Their steep descent had ended at last. They were walking through tough grass that whipped sharply at their legs. The flies and mosquitoes were still with them. In the far distance they sighted labourers working in the paddy fields. At last, thought Rowena, and although the baby was still yelling for food, at least there was hope. The people in the distance would help. She was sure they would.

Closer and closer they got to the figures working the fields, backs bent over the never-ending task of tending the growing rice, the mainstay of the Asian diet.

Just when she thought they were close enough to wave their arms and shout for assistance, the people tilted back their heads and looked skywards. Suddenly they were no longer tending the rice but racing towards the trees at the far end of the field. Behind those trees wisps of smoke rose from cooking fires. There was indeed a village back there. But why had they run? Every single one of them had disappeared.

Jung pointed. Holding the baby in one arm, Rowena stopped and shielded her eyes from the bright sunlight. A rattling whirring sound came to her ears and there above them was the same kind of helicopter she'd seen the day they'd gone to the airport. It hung like a black insect in the sky, like a huge mosquito but far noisier. Slowly, very slowly, it came closer and lower.

Jung ran forward waving his arms and screaming, shaking the thick stick which had aided him to stumble down the descending path.

Rowena screamed as a single gunshot ripped through the air and Jung fell to the ground.

Terrified for both herself and the baby, she flung herself to the ground, shaking and doing her best not to suffocate Summer who now lay beneath her, wailing for all she was worth.

The sound of the blades diminished and she heard voices, then footsteps coming her way.

'OK. Me not speak Korean, but you can get to your feet. Savvy?'

With her hand protectively covering the baby's head, she got to her knees.

'Yes,' she snarled in an icy tone, shaking with both anger and fear. 'I savvy all right.'

The two heavily armed men looked at each other as if to confirm they'd heard right. Suddenly one of them confirmed the patently obvious.

'She speaks English.'

She didn't care that they sounded puzzled or the fact that they were young and inexperienced. She could forgive them nothing. They'd shot Jung, an innocent man who had intended living the rest of his life for his tiny daughter.

'We are not the enemy,' she snapped, her eyes blazing. 'I'm a doctor and the unarmed man you shot was a chemist.'

'Hey, lady—'

'Don't hey lady me! He was trying to attract your attention because his child needs food and medical attention. His wife – his American wife, daughter of a US colonel, died back there giving birth to this child.'

Steeped in fury, she pushed past them, hopeful to see if she could do anything for Jung, yet instinctively knowing there was nothing.

She quaked with sorrow as they turned him over. His eyes were closed and his chest was a mass of blood-soaked cloth.

'Why?' she shouted. 'Why? He was the father of this baby. The baby's mother was American.'

They were young, probably straight from training camp. One tipped his helmet back and explained that, sorry, but his colleague possessed an itchy trigger finger.

She held her tears in check along with her anger. The baby, Summer, was all that mattered so although it was difficult, she reined in her explosive emotions and spoke in a calm and measured manner.

'I need you to get me to the nearest hospital. As I've just told you, the child's mother died. I've no milk to give her.'

The pilot jumped out from the cockpit seat. The helicopter blades were still now, though the engine still hummed with life as if impatient to get back into the air.

'Ma'am, I'm sorry for what's happened, but we will get you out of here. We're a fair way from a city hospital, but there is a field hospital close by.' The spokesman glanced at Jung then back at her. 'Does this guy have any relatives close by?'

'No. This child I am holding is the grandchild of Colonel Sherman Warrington. I think you'd better get me there pronto, don't you?'

They left Jung where he had fallen, their excuse being that the locals would bury him or they would come back for him when it was safer.

'Sorry, ma'am. We can't hang around. The North Koreans will have seen us land and be heading this way. We cannot be grounded here.'

In one way she was sad about that. In another she couldn't shift the feeling that Jung would be closer to his wife in her lonely spot back up the mountain.

Considering it was constructed from tents, the field hospital was an antiseptic oasis of pristine whiteness. Food for the baby was made up from dried milk powder they'd been distributing to local women, a small gesture aimed to win hearts and minds.

An army nurse offered to wash and feed the baby whilst Rowena ate something and organised a telegram to Hong Kong. She was instructed to keep it short and to the point.

```
Safe in US field hospital. .Being airlifted
to Tokyo. Home soon. All my love. Rowena.
```

She imagined the relief on his face and guessed he'd been trying to get back here, like some latter-day knight in shining armour, trampling everything in his way to get to her.

She smiled at the thought, then was interrupted by a nurse willing to loan her some clean clothes.

First she showered and then she slept. There was time enough to locate Summer's grandfather, though one thing was for sure, he wasn't anywhere near the front line.

She snuggled up to a pillow, kissed it gently and murmured goodnight. The baby had brought Dawn to mind and she badly wanted to see her daughter again though she was sure that Connor and his sister would look after her very well. From the very first Kate had struck her as an amazing woman, having travelled across the world to begin a new life. OK, Connor was there too in case she failed, but somehow she knew Kate would not fail in anything she did. In a strange way there were similarities between them. Connor's sister was a strong-minded woman who would never allow herself to be a drudge to a man ever again. In her case she would never be anyone's prisoner – foreign enemy or otherwise.

Once her credentials were checked, including those of Sheridan Warrington which she had thought to bring with her, it was relatively easy to track the whereabouts of Colonel Sherman Warrington somewhere in Tokyo.

'Would you like us to let him know you're coming?'

'No. I want to surprise him,' she said grimly.

The truth was she didn't want to give him the chance to move on without seeing her or the baby. She had not carried out his wishes so he had no further use for her and she wasn't sure what his response would be to Summer.

The plane touched down at six in the morning. The good folk at the medical station had concocted some kind of carrying bag for the baby and a clean replacement for the scruffy old haversack that had served them so well on their journey.

The adjutant back in Korea had been most helpful. She had two addresses for Colonel Warrington in Tokyo, both work and home. The most obliging young man had also arranged accommodation for her so that she and Summer could rest a little.

She looked down at the contented, crumpled face. Although barely a week old, her features were beginning to fill out and turn pink. She smiled and stroked the smooth forehead, touched the tiny hands. Summer made a mewing noise of contentment and pursed her rose-pink lips. Her hair was as black as Dawn's had been. Rowena felt tears in her eyes. No matter what happened next, she was determined that this child would have a good start in life. The big problem was going to be persuading Colonel Sherman Warrington to take responsibility for his grandchild. Nobody could resist her, surely?

Summer opened her eyes which were as blue as her mother's had been, her hair glossy and black like her father. The rosebud mouth seemed to be smiling up at her. She knew very well that it was most likely wind, but she smiled back.

'Your grandfather will be a hard man indeed if he doesn't fall in love with you.'

Chapter 27

Japan

Corporal Wanda Coy was considering applying for a transfer when Colonel Warrington told her that he'd requested she be allocated to his new command in Tokyo. Her counter request that she'd prefer to stay working with the UN contingent in Hong Kong was denied.

'You're part of my plan.'

She knew he wasn't kidding. Colonel Warrington planned everything out – who would do what job, where the desks would be in his new office and who would sit at it and what job they would do. That, she had long ago accepted, was how he ran his life. She shuddered at the thought of what his poor wife and family might have endured.

As for his attitude to her: 'Know your place, woman.'

Not Corporal. Not even her surname. And he never tried to hit on her. She wasn't fluffy enough; too athletic, too strong in body and mind.

'Going out with your girlfriend tonight?' he'd said to her.

'Yes, sir.'

She never elaborated because that would only confirm

that he was on the right track and have him deriding her even more, treating her as less human because she wasn't out of the preferred mould.

So here she was in Tokyo – no more than a glorified secretary in army intelligence and treated by him as something of an oddity, though she was at least of the same race. The only black American allocated to his unit had been swiftly transferred. Interpreters were the exception to his rules of white men only. He'd specifically asked for language graduates from American universities and was put out when most of them turned out to be Japanese Americans, but he was finally forced to accept that was the way things were.

Being a woman was in the same category as being of mixed race, though the colonel didn't care much whether she liked it or not here, and neither did he care if she disliked him. He insisted on having his way and there was nothing she could do about it. Revenge was something like a slow burning flame deep inside, but so far the opportunity to get her own back had not arisen. To know something about him that he wouldn't like her to be privy to would at least needle him. She would wait her time and surely it would come.

It finally occurred when the main gate reported the arrival of a woman carrying a newborn to see Colonel Warrington.

It was as if a rainbow had bridged her office from wall to wall.

'A woman, you say?'

'Yes. She has a baby with her.'

*

It had been a last-minute decision to bring Summer with her even though she had access to a very sweet Japanese children's nurse to look after her. Having thought deeply on the matter, she finally concluded that the colonel should meet his grandchild face to face and that she would likely only get one stab at doing this.

There was a very telling look on the face of the guard at the main gate. There was merriment in his eyes when he looked at the baby then looked at her and grinned.

'You a relative?'

'No. I'm not.'

'Ahuh!' He stroked his chin as he nodded, still grinning from ear to ear. 'Sure, lady. I'll give his office a call right away.'

He exchanged snide smirks with the other two guards. Rowena knew instantly what he was thinking. Barbara had made it plain what sort of man the colonel was and gossip wasn't easy to curtail, no matter who you were.

'Wipe that smirk off your face, young man. It's not my child. It's the colonel's grandchild. But don't tell him that. I want to surprise him.'

It was clear from their ongoing smirks that they didn't believe her.

'We won't be telling him, ma'am. We'll be telling the corporal. She'll inform the colonel and tell us whether to admit you or not. Can I have a name?'

'Rossiter. Dr Rossiter.'

The fact that she was a doctor seemed to alter things. The exchange of looks with his contemporaries was less derisive. She could be telling the truth. Whatever was said by the person on the other end of the phone wiped his expression completely. His cheeks turned pink.

'Sorry to keep you waiting, Doctor. Corporal Coy is expecting you. I'm to take you on through.'

There was no way she was expected, but Rowena didn't bat an eyelid, even though she knew for certain that she and Corporal Coy had never met.

The notice on the office door said Interior Security Administration. The guard saluted as he opened the door and didn't meet the look of condemnation from the dark brown eyes of the woman sitting behind a desk occupied by a typewriter and a tier of filing trays.

'Get me some tea and milk for the baby,' she ordered in a cast-iron voice.

'Just tea,' said Rowena. 'The baby's already been fed.'

Corporal Wanda Coy was well built with a strong chin and short hair. She wore no make-up and her chocolate brown eyes seemed to fill her face.

Rowena noticed a fleeting curiosity in them – and something else. It looked like purpose.

'The guard gave the impression that we've met before, but I don't think we have.'

'No. We haven't.' She glanced at the baby. 'You sure about the milk?'

'Perfectly sure. I fed her before we left.'

Wanda nodded solemnly.

'The baby's not mine.'

Wanda half smiled. 'You know what, at first I thought it might be. I know the colonel picks up women as frequently as a kid in a meadow picks daisies. Then he throws them away, but looking at you – well – you don't seem the sort. And you're a doctor?'

Rowena almost laughed. 'I'm no daisy, and this baby is the colonel's grandchild.'

'His grandchild!' Wanda sounded taken aback. 'I thought his daughter was a nun.'

'She was until she met her husband – her Korean husband.'

'Ah!'

'I'm afraid he got killed by friendly fire that wasn't so friendly.'

Wanda nodded.

There was a knock on the door and after Wanda had bellowed a hefty 'enter', an old Japanese man tottered in with tea. The smell of the hot liquid was enticing.

'Put it there. Thank you. I'll pour,' she said once they were alone. 'Now,' she said as she filled two cups. 'You'd better tell me all about it before the colonel gets back – if you don't mind, that is.'

Rowena outlined what had happened in Sheridan's life, leaving the convent and marrying Lee Jung. She did not go into the circumstances of her own journey from Hong Kong, the colonel wanting her to abort his grandchild. She did, however, touch on the reason she got stranded in Korea.

'Sheridan's father had not authorised transport out of there for his son-in-law. Sheridan refused to leave without him and I felt I should be there with her when the baby was born.'

Wanda frowned. 'Well that doesn't exactly surprise me.

He hates Koreans. Hates all Asian people. You know about his son being killed by Koreans at the end of the war?'

Rowena said that she did. 'I can understand his attitude, but I fail to understand his attitude towards his own daughter purely for falling in love with a Korean national.'

'It's no big surprise. Colonel Warrington hates anyone who isn't of his skin colour and background though he does sometimes suggest that he's descended from a Cheyenne war chief or something. But I think that's a lie. He thinks it sounds good and at least he's referring to a Native American – the first ones if you like. Gives him extra credit.'

'A complicated man.'

'A selfish, stubborn man. I sometimes wonder whether his son actually wanted to be in the army. It wouldn't surprise me if he did not, but what Daddy wants...'

Wanda pressed the nib of her pen down so hard on her blotting pad that it broke off.

'Sorry.' She smiled, as though she'd been stabbing the pen into the colonel's heart. 'He hates women too, though that particular dislike is confined to strong-minded ones that don't fall for his super-stud status.'

Rowena found herself warming to this woman and wondered what she was doing working here.

'You don't seem to like him much.'

'Not at all.'

'Can't you get a transfer?'

'He takes great pleasure in keeping me here against my will. We're at opposite ends of what we want in sex and relationships. We hate each other but he thrives on that.'

Summer began to stir in her arms. Both women looked

at her, Rowena with affection and Wanda with something approaching excitement.

It struck Rowena that she had not asked the baby's name. 'Her name's Summer.'

'Pretty name. Unusual though.'

'Her mother insisted. She was looking up at the sky. It was very blue and the sun had come out following days of rain. She died bringing her into the world.'

A respectful period of silence followed before Wanda spoke again. 'What do you have planned with regard to introducing her to the colonel?'

Rowena looked down at the baby before replying, watching with pleasure the tiny hands fold into fists as though she would fight her way through this world just as she'd fought her way into it.

'I thought that at first sight of her he would take her into his arms and make arrangements for her care.' She looked up to meet the disbelieving look in the corporal's eyes. 'Now I'm not so sure.'

Wanda shook her head. 'Hard of heart and soul is our colonel. He'll be back shortly. In the absence of anything stronger, drink your tea. You're going to need it.'

She'd only just drained her cup when Sherman Warrington barged in accompanied by a junior officer.

He swept his hat off at the door, flinched then froze at the sight of her and the bundle held in one arm.

'I'll catch up with you later,' he snapped to his junior officer, and closed the door in his face.

Wanda stood up and saluted then jumped in to explain. 'Dr Rossiter, sir. She's brought your grandchild back from

Korea. Her name's Summer and she's the sweetest little thing...'

Wanda's eyes glittered with triumph, undoubtedly taking pleasure from the colonel's discomfort, her words sweet but far from sincerely meant.

'You had no right!' His jaw was clenched, his voice low and cold.

She guessed that if there had not been a whole pool of army clerks beyond the glass-paned door, he would have bellowed at her. All the same, there was no doubting the fury simmering just beneath the surface.

Rowena unwrapped the silk shawl she'd wound around the child exposing Summer's sweet face, the glossy black hair, the small pink fists that looked ready to punch at the world.

'How dare you bring that mongrel here! How dare you!'

It was hardly the response she'd visualised, but in retrospect she should have expected it.

'Colonel, this baby is your grandchild. Your daughter died giving her birth.'

He drew himself up with gathered fury.

'Doctor, for two centuries my family have served their country and the army. We were proud to do so and my son would have risen through the ranks just like me, just like his ancestors. That will never happen now. My family has no future thanks to a bunch of Korean thugs. And then my daughter married one against my wishes. I said she would be dead to me if she went ahead. But she did go ahead and so she is dead to me...'

'She is dead. She died bringing this child into the world.

Do you feel nothing for her? Nothing for your grandchild?' Her voice bristled with anger and disbelief.

His eyes bulged and his bottom lip curled downwards showing his lower teeth. 'Nothing. Nothing at all. Now get out of here and take that brat with you. I've read your file, Doctor. You two are well suited to each other.'

'Oh. Because we're not bluebloods, not the thoroughbreds you so obviously prefer? Well guess what, Colonel, we are not horses! We're human beings. I should tread carefully, if I were you. A lot of you blue bloods are not quite so well bred as you make out. I wouldn't be surprised that if you went back far enough in your bloodline, you might find a few ancestors you didn't know you had. Were they slave owners, Colonel? Were they? Or were they the offspring of field hands, women taken by force?'

The loudness of her outburst boomed like a drum around the room. The baby in her arms stirred as though sensing the bad atmosphere around her and mewed in protest, the precursor to a bout of crying. She settled when Rowena rocked her.

There was no let-up in the colonel's anger. 'Two mongrels together.'

'And you, Colonel, you are the most repulsive man I've ever met.'

He turned abruptly away but only after throwing a look of fury at Corporal Coy.

'Well,' said the corporal once the door had slammed behind him. 'He'll be in one hell of a mood for days. Fancy another cup of tea?'

Trembling with anger, Rowena shook her head. 'No.'

Wanda Coy was beaming. It was as though a thunderstorm

had just passed and she'd escaped being struck by lightning or getting wet.

'You're wondering at my attitude,' she said to Rowena on noticing her puzzled expression.

'You look pleased with yourself.'

Wanda smiled. 'You bet I am. That guy has made it a mission to make my life a misery.'

'Why?'

Wanda's smile diminished. 'I'm a girl who doesn't go for guys. I like girls. And he knows it. He's referred to it every day I've worked for him, ensuring that my colleagues are men. Didn't you notice I'm the only female in this department? Never mind. It's a form of torture – at least he thinks it is, and he enjoys it. Now I've got something on him. He won't like me knowing. It might be that I'll finally get the transfer I've always wanted.' She tilted her head to one side. Her eyes sparkled. 'Or I might just refuse that transfer and stay on just to annoy him.'

'If it was me I'd prefer to go.'

Wanda nodded. 'You could be right. Come on. I'll take you down to the main gate and see if I can't get somebody to take you to where you're staying. Are you staying long in Tokyo?'

'I've made no further plans. I couldn't until I knew what the colonel's attitude would be towards his granddaughter.'

'Well you know now.'

'Yes. I do.'

Wanda stayed with her until the jeep she'd arranged came sweeping to a standstill.

'You live in Hong Kong?'

'Yes.'

'I suppose they have orphanages there.'

She glanced down at the sleeping baby, a tightness in her chest. 'Yes. They do.'

'I suppose it's all you can do.'

'Well, I don't suppose he's likely to change his mind.'

'Not a chance in hell of that. He's single-minded, I'll say that for him. He's also the most self-centred man I've ever met. Let me hold her while you get in.'

Rowena passed Summer into Wanda's welcoming arms. She waited, watching as Wanda cosseted the child close to her breast. For a moment it almost seemed she was about to unbutton her military blouse and press the baby's lips onto her nipple.

'You like babies.'

'I love them, and in time... who knows.' The look in her eyes was downright mischievous, like a little kid who's worked their way through a difficult maths exercise. 'Where there's a will, there's a way.'

Rowena relished the warmth, the smell of babyhood as Summer was passed into her arms.

'I hope you find her a good orphanage – best of all a good home,' remarked Wanda.

'I will. I'm sure I will.'

Chapter 28

Hong Kong

Connor stood next to his sister who in turn stood next to Dawn when Rowena finally made an appearance at her apartment at the top of Victoria House.

Connor followed the baby's progress from her arms to those of Luli. He seemed dumbstruck.

Rowena had waited for this moment, imagined how it would be. Not like this, she thought. I never dreamed it would be like this. Now the time had come she felt her face grow warm and knew her cheeks had turned pink. Like a girl, she thought. Like a virgin faced with the first love of her life. And there he was, standing there, tongue-tied, with questions written all over his face.

'Rowena. Oh my God...'

Finally his arms were around her and he was breathing in the smell of her hair, then kissing the top of her head, then her forehead, then her nose, her cheeks and her lips.

'I can't believe you're here at last.'

'It's so good to be back.'

'I made enquiries. I asked everyone I could think of.'

'I thought you would, but you know how it was there.'

'Difficult. Bloody difficult.'

'How are your injuries?'

He shrugged. 'Just a couple of grazes.'

'You got hit by bullets. I told you to steer clear of battles.'

'I forgot.'

His kiss was warm and she didn't care who saw it.

Kate, totally unfazed by their blatant show of affection, interrupted. 'The silly fool even tried to re-enlist – after he was invalided out, mind you.' Connor's sister gave her a swift half hug and patted her back. 'And by the looks of it you've got a few tales to tell.'

She was, of course, referring to the baby.

'Her mother's dead.'

'Well I didn't think it was yours…' She glanced at her brother. 'More's the pity.'

Summer chose that moment to let out a long wail of protest.

'I think she needs changing.'

'A baby,' remarked Dawn excitedly. She had grown enough in the last few months to be able to look down into the squealing bundle. 'Is it ours? Is it a girl? I would prefer a sister to a brother.'

'I will change her,' said Luli as she rocked the child back and forth, her face beaming with delight. 'It is good to have a baby again.'

Dawn expressed her intention to help.

Rowena held out her arms. 'Do I get a hug first?'

Dawn hugged her mother tightly. 'I missed you. I thought you were never coming back.'

'And leave you to grow up alone? I could never do that.'

Rowena kissed the top of her head.

'Can I help Luli change the baby?'

'Take her into the bedroom. And take this bag with you. You'll find everything in there.'

Connor finally relaxed his shoulders. 'I'm sure there's an epic story to be told and in time we'll hear it from beginning to end.'

She sighed and all the pent-up tension she'd lived with for the past few months melted away to be replaced by relief and urgent passion.

'I've missed you.'

He took hold of her hands, shaking his head as though he couldn't quite believe that the person standing in front of him was real and not a mirage.

'I've dreamed of you being home so many times, I'm still not sure it's real.'

'I'd prefer you not to pinch me. There's not so much flesh covering my bones.'

'You look good enough to me.'

'A few weeks of good food will do the trick,' said Kate. 'And before you mention Irish stew, no, I don't mean filling you with stodge – though of course you're welcome to it if that's what you really want. I've got a good chef in the restaurant. Our reputation is spreading. Just a pity we're here in Kowloon and not over on main island. Still, never mind all that. We need to catch up where we left off. It seems we had little chance to get to know one another before you went. We've lost time to make up.'

'We have indeed.'

'We've changed the baby,' said a triumphant Dawn. 'And we fed her. I found the milk and Luli showed me what to do.'

'We're not keeping her.'

Dawn's cheerful expression disappeared. 'Why?'

'She's not mine. She has a grandfather and... perhaps a family somewhere...' The words were swallowed along with what little knowledge she had. For a start she had no idea about Jung's family but knew for sure that Summer's grandfather would never claim the child. There were a few queries to be raised before Summer's future was sorted.

It was something of a surprise that Dawn was more enamoured of the baby than she was of her which made her feel slightly jealous. She'd expected Dawn to cling to her, to cry how much she'd missed her and make her promise never to go away again. But Dawn was besotted with the baby, a baby that wasn't theirs and would most likely end up at an orphanage.

She passed her arm around Dawn's shoulder and gave her a reassuring hug. 'Her name's Summer.'

'That's a lovely name. It reminds me of blue skies and sunshine. Did you name her that?'

'No. Her mother gave her that name. Her mother loved her very much, just as much as I love you.'

Dawn looked up at her, blinked then threw her arms around her. 'I've missed you, Mummy.'

Tears squeezed from the corners of Rowena's half-closed eyes.

'I've missed you too, darling.'

Without seeking Rowena's permission, Kate had made herself at home in the kitchen where the sound of pans clattered and the tinkle of cutlery left no one in any doubt that Connor's sister was preparing an evening meal.

In the short time of it being prepared and presented at

table, she related to Connor details of their being evicted from the convent and force marched through the paddy fields before gaining their freedom and making for the hills. She also told them about the officer who had helped them escape.

Connor frowned. 'Rumours have been coming in about more than one death march. It seems you were lucky enough not to be on the very worst one.'

'Perhaps it was because I was attached to a group of nuns.'

He shook his head. 'I doubt that. Rumour has it that the very first victim to be shot was an eighty-year-old nun.'

She threw back her head and although she was greatly saddened by the news of so many deaths, she sighed with relief.

'I want to forget, to concentrate on the future. I have to do that for everyone's sakes.'

'I suppose you do. I won't press you unless you want to elaborate. I went through enough during the last lot to appreciate where you're coming from.'

'I'm just glad to be home.'

Prayer-like, she clasped her hands together. They tingled, as though a great resolve had transferred from one to the other.

'I need you to tell me what's been happening here.'

He took a deep breath, his way of getting his thoughts in order before saying it out loud.

'Well, my sister's doing well. She's got quite a head for business – better than mine.'

'But the bar's doing well enough?'

'It rolls along fine.'

He took hold of her hands which seemed very small when cocooned in his, like a small animal hibernating in a warm burrow. She'd missed that feeling of safety, and yet she sensed he was holding something back. What he said next confirmed it.

'We've got a lot to talk about. But not now. Settle back in first. Hey?'

Although his smile was full of feeling, she wasn't fooled. The look in his eyes was not guarded enough to hide whatever was simmering inside. She decided to broach whatever was troubling him once they'd eaten dinner.

Over a cooked meal which Kate had brought with her, they all listened as Rowena recounted her experiences in Korea. At the heart of it was the fact that Colonel Warrington had purposely left Lee Jung's name off the list of civilian evacuees, Sheridan, his pregnant daughter, refusing to go without him and Rowena feeling it her duty to stay with the expectant mother.

Kate made the most comments, keeping the conversation to the more trivial aspects as to how the Korean people had treated her, what denomination were the nuns and whether they were able to maintain their dignity in such dire circumstances.

Rowena knew why she was leading the conversation, keeping things on a safe footing, sensitive to Dawn being in the room and wishing to protect her.

For her part Dawn exclaimed that despite her youth, she was quite willing to become Summer's new mother.

The outburst was unexpected and heartfelt.

Rowena looked at Connor and although he smiled, it was fleeting, and when he did speak it was only to comment on his one and only meeting with Colonel Warrington and also to relate how he had been injured.

They were all being cautious with what they were saying, like a dam holding back floodwater. The adult conversation continued in a brittle, polite manner until Dawn began yawning.

'You're ready for bed.'

Dawn didn't argue, but got down from the table and kissed everyone goodnight before heading for her bedroom.

Rowena went to tuck her in at the same time assuring her that she would not be going away again.

Summer's cry came from the small side room she was sharing with Luli. When she looked in on them Luli was feeding the baby from a fresh bottle she had fetched from the kitchen.

She looked up before Rowena could ask her the obvious. 'Everything all right, Dr Rossiter?'

'Yes. I think so.'

As she closed the door behind her the smile she'd given Luli disappeared and tension stiffened her shoulders. She sensed something was wrong, something neither Connor nor his sister were admitting to.

She went back into the living room of her penthouse flat, the scene of the far-off harbour filling her eyes.

Although darkness had fallen the spangled lights of the city provided a backdrop as good as any painting she might have cared to hang on the wall.

Connor had poured himself a glass of wine. Kate was gathering up the dishes but paused to make comment.

'And before you say that this is the help's job, she's got enough dealing with that baby. The little mite deserves all her attention until she's properly rehomed – preferably with an adoptive family. I never did hold with orphanages, even those run by nuns of me own faith. Cruel cows, some of them.'

It was hard not to smile. To say that Kate was outspoken was putting it mildly.

Rowena looked at Connor who was now lighting up a cigar.

'What's the matter?' she asked once Kate had gone to the kitchen.

He raised his head and his gaze was steady, unblinking.

'I've got some bad news.'

She felt a coiling inside as though a snake was living there and afraid to strike.

'Not more threats to Dawn.'

He shook his head. 'No. Not at all. In fact I'm beginning to think that our old enemy really is dead.'

'So what is it?'

He looked down into his wine glass, twirling it round and round by its stem.

'I'm afraid, my dear, that your beloved Victoria House has reached the end of the line. There's a new prefabricated refugee camp being built – state-of-the-art hospital too. Victoria House no longer fits the bill.'

Trying hard not to tremble, Rowena lay down her wine glass. 'I did have some idea this would happen. Dr Grelane said enough to set me on edge though under the circumstances I haven't given it much thought of late.'

Everything thrown at her before leaving for Korea now hit her like a tidal wave. The apartment wasn't exactly modern but the view of Victoria Harbour was to die for. This place also held a vault full of memories. Some of those memories were best forgotten, but she'd made a conscious effort to override them with moments of happiness.

Connor jerked his head at a long black unit inlaid with scenes of what the Victorians had considered Chinese life, inlaid with mother of pearl.

'The notices are on the sideboard.'

She got up from her chair and took a look at them, noting that the envelopes had already been opened.

Connor came to her side, his breath warm against her ear and his hand resting on her waist.

'I wasn't sure when you'd be back.'

Her eyes flashed up at him. 'Or that I would be back?'

She could see by the look in his eyes that she'd hit the nail on the head. He had feared her never returning.

'You were in a war zone. You should have got out when you had the chance.'

His voice had hardened. She perceived the anger he must have felt inside, sitting there on the plane, his arm and leg in bandages and seeing only Luli and Dawn coming aboard. The only thing that really surprised her was that he hadn't got off and gone looking for her.

The answer came even before she'd asked the question. 'There wasn't time to stop the flight. I did try but I was ordered to stay in my seat. And there was Dawn to consider.'

This was the first time she'd ever known Connor to be really angry with her.

'I had a duty to the mother of that child. I couldn't just leave her there.'

'You know that's not true.'

'Of course it's true.'

Only the fact that they still had company stopped their disagreement burgeoning into an outright fight.

He grabbed his jacket. 'I'll be heading home then.' He looked across at his sister. 'You coming, Kate?'

She shook her head. 'I think I'll stay and give a hand with the washing up.'

'Have it your way,' he grumbled.

The whole room shook as he slammed the door behind him.

Dawn poked her head around the door to the bedroom, holding her finger in front of her mouth.

'Shush. You'll wake the baby up.'

'Sorry, darling. Are you and Luli coping all right?'

'Yes. Of course we are. Shush,' she said again, not noticing or caring that Connor had gone. The door closed and suddenly Rowena felt all alone. Except for Kate.

'You really don't need to stay, Kate – oh sorry. I know you prefer being called Kate...'

'If my brother can call me Kate, so can you. You're my sister-in-law but just ain't got round to doing the paperwork.'

'Connor and I might never get round to doing the paperwork.'

'I don't think that's true. I don't think you believe that either and although he's being a bonehead today, he won't be tomorrow.'

Her head hurt. She placed a cool hand on her forehead. 'I didn't expect my homecoming to be like this.'

'It'll be fraught for a while – and bringing a baby home. Now that was a bit of a shock.'

Kate glanced towards the closed bedroom door, poured them both a glass of wine and sank onto a dining chair.

'Drink up.'

Rowena did as instructed then frowned. It was difficult to forget that Victoria House would soon be no more.

'I didn't expect to come back to the news that this old place was being vacated, though I did know it was on the cards, but I thought it would be years down the line, not so sudden as this. I'm not even sure who owns it any more. The trust has just used it.'

'And now it's moving on. Nice old building though. It's got a lot of potential.'

Kate was looking around disapprovingly as though the decor and furnishings weren't quite to her taste. There was also another look in her eyes, that was hard to interpret.

'You know, I think it's time my brother grew up and sold the bar. He's got responsibilities and it's time he took them more seriously. It isn't right him darting backwards and forwards between this place and his – not when there are children involved.'

'Dawn isn't his.'

'Sure she is. Not in the natural sense perhaps, but she is, for all that, his girl; I've seen the way he looks after her. He doted on her when you were trapped over in that place, took the time to help her with her schoolwork and made her laugh when he could – even when he himself was crying inside.'

She would never admit to having been upset by Connor's outburst, but now she was regretting not having run after him, sat down, just the two of them, and told each other how they felt. All of them had been over in Kowloon and she had landed on Hong Kong and naturally gone straight to her apartment at the top of Victoria House. Kate's suggestion that Connor should sell the bar held some sense if they were to make a go of their relationship. It was only a strip of water between them but if they were to tie the knot and form some kind of family nucleus it might well have been the Pacific Ocean.

'You need to get rid of that strip of water between you,' said Kate as though reading her mind. 'It doesn't make sense, you being here and him being there. How can you ever properly make a go of things?'

'Well. Perhaps it's me that should go over there to Kowloon or move somewhere close to the new refugee centre.'

'I don't think there's any need for that.'

Kate slapped her thighs and got to her feet.

'I will need a new roof over my head.'

'Will you be wanting to keep your job?'

The sound of Kate's warm Irish brogue made her think that she was missing something. Kate's tone sounded as though she was advising caution rather than merely asking a question.

Chapter 29

This time when Kate O'Connor visited the bank manager, the tea – served on a silver tray no less – arrived only a minute after she'd taken a seat in his office. She'd phoned only the day before stating in no uncertain terms that she didn't want to be kept waiting. The matter was urgent.

'Very nice tea, but I'm here on business. Do you have news for me or what?'

The bank manager coughed into his hand, at the same time shuffling some papers around in front of him.

'The vendor is not willing to sell you the freehold of your business premises, but is willing to do a swap in the manner suggested by you on the telephone the other evening. Quid pro quo, so to speak.'

She'd taken the phone call in private, keen that none of her family – including her brother – would try and alter her mind.

She glared at him, unblinking. A stronger man might have held her gaze, but Gordon Gresham was henpecked at home. He knew the power of a woman's look and the lash of a waspish tongue, but this woman possessed the manner of a man and demanded respect.

'Then the deal is done. Have you the papers?'

'Yes. I have.'

'Then I can sign them now. Strike while the iron's hot. That's my motto.'

She began pulling out her gloves. 'I've never come across a fountain pen yet that didn't leak ink over my fingers.'

'I assure you, dear lady, you will find this pen is of uncommon quality. I chose it myself.'

He handed her the pen. She got out her glasses and signed her name where indicated, first on the deed relinquishing the lease of the restaurant and boarding house, then on the purchase agreement for something she thought had far better potential.

'Very good,' said Mr Gresham as he blotted both sets of signatures. She noticed he was licking his lips a trifle nervously and guessed there was something else he wanted to say that she might not like.

'I know this might seem a trifle unorthodox, but the vendor has expressed a desire to meet you. He wondered whether you might join him for lunch.'

Kate sucked in her breath as she wriggled her fingers into her gloves.

'Now why would he want to do that?'

Mr Gresham smiled weakly. 'He is something of an eccentric. I believe he wishes to speak to you about another matter – your brother's bar.'

'I don't own my brother's bar. My brother owns Connor's Bar. It's his name above the door.'

'I do realise that, but all the same... if you could see your way...?'

She made a disagreeable sound as she glanced at her watch. 'I haven't got time to go gallivanting around all over this island. Couldn't he come in here for a cup of tea? You've always got a kettle on the boil when I come here.'

'For special customers, dear lady. Such as yourself, and Mr Maas. However, being informed that you are a lady to whom time is a very precious commodity and that you would prefer to pass him these documents for his immediate signature, he has sent a car to pick you up and take you to him.'

Kate didn't take two minutes to think about it. She wanted this all done and dusted in good time, but there was now another reason. Prices of property on Hong Kong Island were outstripping prices in Kowloon. Buying there now and selling the goodwill of her businesses was a rock solid decision. This man, Maas, owned much property in Kowloon and was willing to jettison his ownership of Victoria House, foolish as far as she was concerned, but each to his own. And now this. Could it really be true that he was interested in Connor's Bar?

She nodded curtly. 'I take it he'll be outside when I go through that door?' She jerked her head sideways, indicating the door she hadn't long entered by.

'Indeed, Miss O'Connor. If you would like to take these...' He handed her the sheaf of documents, the stiff paper crackling as he folded it into some kind of order.

Their parting was curt but professional. She was well satisfied. He had done everything she'd wanted him to do.

*

The car was black and had black windows. The Chinese chauffeur held the door open for her as she climbed halfway in then stopped and grinned at her reflection in the black lenses of the sunglasses he was wearing.

'Can you see to drive through those?'

She pointed at the sunglasses.

He said nothing. What little of his face that she could see was inscrutable – unsmiling and hard as stone.

She sucked in her breath, smelt beeswax polish and peered into the inner gloom. The car was almost as dark as its windows. She could see the shape of the man she knew to be Koos Maas but little in the way of features. He was just a black mass taking up half of the rear leather seat.

Besides beeswax she smelled sandalwood but also something else, something antiseptic that reminded her of hospitals and injured bodies.

Not one to be intimidated and certainly not by smells, she passed him the paperwork.

'I've done the honours. It's now for you to sign.'

'I will do so.'

The sound of his voice made her pause for breath; silky yet intermittently she heard a short, sharp rasp. She recalled an old man who'd got caught up in the troubles in Dublin. One nostril had been sliced open by a bayonet and from then on his speech had been broken in places by a breathless gasp.

Well I'm not about to ask him for details, she thought.

'So why am I here?'

The car had not moved – a good sign as far as she was concerned. This interaction with the man Koos Maas would be over and done with quickly and she could get on back and begin arranging to pull out of Kowloon and onto Hong Kong Island.

'Will you tell your brother I will give him…' A rasping sound, then a hurrying on. 'A good price for the bar.'

'Why don't you tell him yourself?'

The rasping erupted then dissipated. The smoother voice was back.

'I have my reasons. Take this.' He passed her a sheaf of paper which she recognised as some kind of contract. 'Get him to sign it. Bring it back to me.'

'What makes you think I can persuade him?'

A snorting followed by a series of rasping sounds. 'The deeds to Victoria House are yours if you persuade him.'

'That wasn't the deal.'

'It is now. The bar was my first business venture. I would like it to be my last. I am not usually given to sentiment, but the building housing the bar once belonged to my mother. My strength is dying. I am dying. It is easier for me to concentrate my businesses in Kowloon.' He paused, caught his breath, tried to say something then collected himself. Finally he said it.

'Tell him that if he sells me the bar, I will never set foot on Hong Kong Island again. I promise this on the souls of my ancestors.'

Kate thought about it. Whilst Rowena was trapped in Korea, Connor, slightly the worse for drink, had confided to her that back in the war they'd been under threat from a ruthless leader of a criminal gang, and feared he was hunting them. She'd also heard tale about the old man employed to keep watch on them from the house she had turned into her own very profitable business venture.

'So you won't be employing any more old men to spy on Dr Rossiter?'

Again that terrible rasping sound, the frantic gulping of air.

'I do not know what you mean.'

'Oh come on. That was bad enough, but getting one of your women to pass a glass doll to a child. That was pretty low.'

She knew it was nothing to do with him, but she wanted confirmation and certainly wasn't going to leave him feeling he'd got one over on her. Kate O'Connor preferred to be in the driving seat and took flak from no one. If it unnerved him a bit, then so much the better.

His sigh was deep then convulsive, a frightening gasping for breath.

'I did neither of these things, but if it helps Connor make up his mind, then I am grateful for whoever did do these things.'

He fell then into an apoplexy of frenzied coughing and wheezing. 'Go,' he finally managed to rasp. 'Go.'

As he waved his hand, the car door opened. The driver reached in, placed a meaty hand on her shoulder and pulled her out.

The car door shut with a reassuring and luxurious sound. The chauffeur went round to the front of the car. That door also closed leaving her looking at her triumphant smile reflected in the blacked out glass of the rear window.

Chapter 30

The trustees were settled around a table at the Hong Kong country club sipping at their gin and tonics whilst perusing the items set down on today's agenda. They were, for the most part, people who had found the wealth and status in a Crown Colony that they wouldn't have enjoyed at home.

'Shall we proceed to item five on the agenda…?'

The chairman had a bald head, loose jowls and smoked a large cigar. He'd preened like a peacock when someone remarked that he looked a lot like Winston Churchill.

'Yes, Mr Chairman. Regarding the height of the wall around the new refugee hospital.'

'But surely as a hospital it doesn't need a very high wall…'

'Some refugees are terribly contagious, dear lady,' said the chairman, leaning back in his chair as he regarded her through a haze of blue smoke over a rotund midriff and straining waistcoat.

'I know that,' retorted Mrs Isobel Dillon-Brown, the wife of a high-ranking official who had lived in the Far East far longer than most of those seated at the table. 'But surely we have to consider unnecessary expense...'

'Totally necessary.'

'But until Victoria House is sold...'

The chairman cleared his throat. 'Victoria House was requisitioned during the war from its original owner. We have an agreement with that original owner – fifty-fifty. He seems quite happy with us receiving half of the proceeds of sale and has even found a buyer and signed all necessary contractual documents.'

'A philanthropic man, by the sound of it,' added a Colonel Cross, a man with a reddish complexion that somehow went with his name.

'Albeit a foreigner,' remarked the chairman. 'Still, money is money, wherever it's coming from.'

Raised voices sounded from beyond the rose-red lustre of the double doors. Heads were turned. The chairman looked along the length of his cigar, a frown crumpling his domed forehead.

Before anyone could say anything, one of the handsome double doors opened and Dr Rowena Rossiter strode purposefully into the room. She was dressed for battle in a female version of a sharply cut business suit. Her jacket was tailored and nipped in at the waist. It was teamed with a narrow calf-length skirt. Her shirt was white and set off with a narrow black bow. Her shoes were black and so were her gloves. She was hatless, her hair tied back and just the smallest of pearls twinkled in her earlobes.

The Chinese doorman was extremely apologetic. 'I'm sorry, Mr Chairman, but she refused to go away.'

Rowena felt their eyes upon her. Some were hostile beneath grim eyebrows. Others were assessing her attractiveness.

'Dr Rossiter.' Isobel Dillon-Brown got to her feet and extended her hand. 'Welcome back. How very nice to see you again.'

Rowena tried to recall where they'd met – obviously some time before her sojourn in Korea. Mrs Dillon-Brown enlightened her.

'I read your paper on the merits of family planning. It was very informative.'

A murmur of disapproval ran through the male assembly. The woman's forthright manner made Rowena smile. She quite liked seeing the male gathering looking downright uncomfortable. She knew exactly what they were thinking, that the subject of family planning should be whispered amongst women and preferably out of their earshot. It was female business, nothing to do with them.

The woman carried on.

'I take it you've heard about the new hospital and refugee centre. It was the old barrack blocks but the renovations are going along very well. I suppose you would like to know what's happening with Victoria House?'

The woman's face was completely open, though Rowena detected a twinkle of mischief in her eyes. She was going all out to make these men feel even more uncomfortable.

The chairman's jowls quivered and ash fell from his half-spent cigar as he cut across.

'Mrs Dillon-Brown... this person has no business attending this meeting, and therefore—'

'Oh, but I think she has, Mr Chairman. It was Dr Rossiter

who set up the refugee centre within Victoria House just after the war, so I think she has every right to be here. Why, she knows more about the place than we do.'

'That doesn't give her the right to come barging in—'

'Just in case you didn't know, Dr Rossiter has just returned from Korea and for a while endured the privations and cruelty of one of those horrendous death marches we've been hearing so much about. That was after she was taken from a hospital in the city of Seoul. She knew nothing of the sale until she got back. I think it only fair that we hear her out. Am I seconded?'

The chairman, whose face had reddened considerably, hadn't taken his eyes off Rowena from the moment she'd entered the room. 'I'll second that. Let's hear what this charming lady… doctor, has to say.'

Rowena took a deep breath, her gloved hands folding one on top of the other over her handbag.

'You're quite right,' she said in an aside to Mrs Dillon-Brown. 'I have just come back from Korea and I must admit it was quite a shock to read the bevy of letters that were sent to me. I came here today to enquire as to what you intend to do with the building.'

The chairman cleared his throat, glancing around for some sign of backing from his colleagues. Confident he had that, he turned back to Rowena.

'Victoria House will be sold.'

She frowned. 'But it's not yours to sell. It belonged to…' She couldn't bear to speak aloud the name of a man who still haunted her. 'Someone else.'

'We already know that. Although foreign in pedigree, the gentleman you refer to has authorised the sale of the property. He has generously agreed to a fifty per cent split in whatever price we get for it. Quite a gentleman, I think.'

It felt as though all the colour and warmth had drained from her face. Kim had agreed to split the proceeds? He had always been a man with an eye on profit, not for sharing. What had changed to make him do this?

'I also understand a buyer has been found and contracts have been signed.'

Rowena's shoulders slumped. 'I see. And I suppose the buyer does not intend it to be used as a refugee centre.'

'No, which sadly means your post will be at an end, though I'm sure we can fit you in at the new centre. There's a junior post going under the supervision of Dr Grelane. I believe you've worked with him before.'

Rowena bristled. 'Yes. I've worked with him.'

'Then you have the offer of continuing your work with us. No need to rush. Get over your experiences in Korea and then pop along to see us, my dear, and mayhap we shall find you a little job.'

Leaving his cigar smouldering in the ashtray, the chairman got up from his chair, cupped her elbow in his meaty hand and gently but firmly guided her to the door.

Normally she would have reacted to his patronising tone, but he'd shocked her to the core. Without any input from her, the person who had facilitated Victoria House, they had brokered a business deal with the previous owner, a man she'd presumed dead but, it now seemed, very much alive.

The air was dry and tasted like glass on the tongue. She stood outside for a while thinking what she should do next, loathing the idea of working for Dr Grelane and still reeling from what was happening. Like a homing pigeon she set off for Victoria House, taking both her memories and her anger with her.

Before entering she stood outside looking up at its once luxurious façade, now stained and blackened by the years of war. Tilting her head back her eyes strayed to the very top where the great glass windows of her flat looked out over the dark blue waters of the Fragrant Harbour.

It seemed unreal that she'd only been home for such a very short time. As yet she had not caught up with what was going on at ground level, checking the workload, the surge of displaced and sick people. She hadn't even reacquainted herself with her old colleagues.

The windows looked dusty. Groups of displaced people were still cooking at their little stoves or fires fuelled by sticks and dung, though not so many as there used to be. The new refugee centre was only half built, but any new influx of refugees was being processed and treated there rather than here.

It saddened her but at the same time she knew there was little she could do about it. Victoria House had served its purpose but it belonged to the past. It seemed she would have to give up her glorious penthouse and that unequalled panorama she had come to love. Living with Connor – she knew he'd insist – wouldn't be the same. Besides, they'd argued. He'd stormed off leaving her and Kate with the dishes. That was when his sister had informed her of Barbara's visit and what had transpired. She still couldn't believe her betrayal and would have confronted her about her relationship with Colonel Warrington, the old man watching Connor's Bar from the house across the road, the glass doll meant to injure her daughter – things designed to have her fall for the colonel's powers of persuasion.

Barbara had fled for pastures new but still it had been difficult to wander around the ground floor even though old friends worked there.

Shaking away thoughts of the past she made her way towards the back of the first floor where mothers lay next to their sick children. Next to that was the small crèche where babies under one year old lay in snug metal cots lined with padding.

'Cressida,' she said softly, the name staff had given to this pretty child who was so unlike most babies born here. The child's hair was curly, her skin a warm coffee. The baby was older now, but she recognised her as the one left at the entrance at the time of the typhoon.

The baby stirred in her sleep as Rowena caressed the soft cheek. This was the baby born at the height of the storm and abandoned straight after, her mother disappearing into the darkness.

Never before had she studied the child so closely. The baby's hair had a reddish tinge and a trail of freckles over her nose.

'So your father was not Chinese,' she said softly and understood immediately why the baby's mother had run away. Judging by the complexion and the slightly woolly hair, it was reasonable to assume that Cressida's father had been an American serviceman of African descent. If her hair had been black and glossy, she might have been the offspring of a Lascar, Asian sailors who had served on merchant ships and for the Royal Navy for centuries. The fact that her hair was slightly woolly and reddish made her decide the father had been the descendant of African slaves taken to America to pick cotton or tobacco. Perhaps the mother, burdened with many children, had made a little on the side by selling her body. It wasn't uncommon, but sadly no family would accept such a child.

The rustle of a highly starched apron told her that she was no longer alone. A nurse was at her side.

'You're Dr Rossiter.'

'Yes. I am.' She nodded and continued to tickle the baby's face, mesmerised by the soft skin, the delicate eyelashes flickering with dreams.

'Cute, isn't she?'

The nurse was Chinese, somebody new that hadn't been here before she'd left for Korea.

'Very.' A thought suddenly came to her. 'Why is she still here?'

It was usual that once babies reached six months old they would either be offered up for adoption or placed with an orphanage. This child was slightly beyond that age.

'Nobody wanted to adopt her on account of her colour. Not Chinese. Not white either.'

'I see.'

Yes, she did see. She'd been right about the father being American and the descendent of slaves.

The nurse put her mental conclusion into words. 'Her father was black. A negro.'

She said it sadly. Rowena knew the Chinese were quite set in their ways when it came to pedigree.

'Would no orphanage take her?'

'They're overcrowded. We've been told St Anne's might be able to take her before the end of the year. She's been put on the waiting list.'

Rowena sighed. 'A waiting list.'

Her gaze travelled around the small crèche. Paint was peeling from the walls and newspaper had been stuffed around the window frames. The dark blue curtains were bleached pale by strong sunlight.

'Hopefully we will find somewhere for her before we move out of here. There's a larger crèche at the new centre, but only for newborns and sick babies. Cressida isn't sick and she's over six months old. She's been here too long already.'

'I know.'

She felt and sounded distracted. Another baby in need of a loving home unwanted by its own mother.

A wistful tightness settled like bindweed around her heart. The world was so unfair. Some women didn't want their babies and here she was, wanting a baby of her own with the man she loved and not getting one.

That night Luli took a night off and left the flat just after sundown saying she was going to meet friends and would not be back until late morning.

It was no great chore to have Dawn all to herself and hear her asking how long it would be before Summer was able to walk.

'I could take her out into the garden and we can see if there are any fish left in the pond.'

'I don't think there are,' said Rowena.

'We can pretend.'

'You could. I don't think Summer would notice if you made ripples in the water with your hand.'

'Are we going to live with Connor when we leave here?' The question came as something of a surprise.

'Who told you we were leaving here?'

'Luli said so.'

Rowena frowned. She hadn't said anything to Luli and didn't think anyone else had either.

'Who told Luli?'

Dawn shrugged. 'I don't know. It might have been her friends in Kowloon.'

Even more surprised, Rowena looked down into her daughter's face. 'In the old city? She has friends in the old city?'

'I know it's Kowloon and I know it's higgledy-piggledy – Luli told me so.'

The fact that Luli had friends in the old walled city wasn't that much of a surprise. Both she and Connor had suspected so for quite a while. What was more surprising was that Luli had given Dawn more details than she had anyone else. But then Luli had no children and had doted on Dawn from the time she first set eyes on her.

Summer's sudden loud wailing came from the bedroom.

'She's hungry,' declared Dawn.

'Then we'd better feed her. Would you like to do that before you go to bed?'

Dawn didn't need asking twice and once Summer had been fed, changed and put back down to sleep, it was time for Dawn to go to bed.

Rowena waited until she was sure her daughter was asleep before picking up the phone and dialling Connor's number.

There was a click. He answered quickly.

'I need to talk to you about Luli – and about Victoria House.'

There was a prolonged silence before he said, 'I don't know what you're going to tell me about Luli, but I may know a lot more than you do about what's happening to Victoria House.'

'Can you tell me over the phone?'

'No. I'll get the morning ferry tomorrow. Kate will be with me.'

Chapter 31

Earlier that day Kate had told him about the man introduced to her as Koos Maas and the fact that he'd given her a very good price for her businesses.

'Not just the lease, mark you, but extra for the goodwill.'

He'd looked at her, quite startled. 'And what will you be doing now without bustling around that old place? You're not getting married again to some wealthy mandarin, are you, Katie?'

'Men!' She threw him such a look that left him in no doubt that she considered him and his kind an inferior species.

'You'd better sit down and I'll fill you in.'

He did as ordered, sat and waited, his elbow resting on the breakfast table.

'Letting the rooms out across the road has whetted my appetite. I want more rooms and a bigger establishment. Hong Kong is going places and me and this family are going with it. A hotel, no less, and it so happens a business opportunity has come about and I've a mind to be buying it.'

He shook his head in disbelief and cocked a humorous grin. 'Kate, how come that fool Seamus never noticed what a fine business head you had on your shoulders?'

'Pah! That's why he was a blacksmith. His brains were never in his head until a horse kicked his ass and some bit of sense travelled upwards. Not much even then!'

Connor threw back his head, his great mane of hair brushing his broad shoulders. He couldn't help laughing. His sister certainly had a glib turn of phrase that was always straight to the point but never polite.

'The same man wants to buy this bar.'

His laughter lines became straighter, his expression more serious.

'Does he now. And what would I be doing if I wasn't here behind this bar?'

'Settling down with Rowena, and about time too. And helping me run the hotel. You can put the money from the bar and buy your share of it and take a share of the profits.'

He pulled in his stomach and set his chin downwards, as though his sister had punched him hard in the stomach.

'I wouldn't presume to tell you to settle down, so why suggest that I do?'

'It's different. I should never have married that big idiot back there in Ireland, but I didn't have much choice.'

'You didn't have to marry the man.'

'Of course I did. I was seventeen and wanted to be away from that farm and the family. As you well know, our grandfather never spared the bloody belt – boy or girl – he was too free with it.'

Connor rubbed his rear at the memory. 'You're right

there, but I didn't know. Somehow I thought he cared more for you than he did for me seeing as you were...'

'His natural daughter. Go on. You can say it. I went through his papers when he died. I know we didn't share the same father.'

'But our grandfather loved you.'

'Yes. Too much.' A strangely guarded look came to her face. 'So I got married to get away. If I'd run away he'd have come after me so I told him I was pregnant and that Seamus was the father.'

'And were you?'

She folded her arms and shook her head. 'No. I just wanted to get away without too much hassle.'

'I didn't know...'

'Never mind. Now you do.'

His face clouded as he thought over his last meeting with Rowena. They'd argued about nothing and he was missing her badly. Perhaps Kate was right and it was time they made their relationship official; after all, there might not be a position for her at the new refugee centre. He found himself hoping that there wasn't. Korea had parted them. He wasn't going to let Hong Kong do the same.

Resting his back against the bar, he folded his arms and frowned thoughtfully. He'd recognised the name of this man as being the one Brandon had mentioned as the new big wheel in the local crime scene. Strange, he thought, that nobody had seen this man – well, was he going to get a shock! Kate had seen him.

He leaned forward, keen to know more before Brandon ever did.

'So this man who's buying your place and wants to buy mine; what's he like?'

'Well. Let's see how I can best describe him,' said Kate, her index finger resting on her lips as she considered the question. 'It was dark in that car, but one thing above all others was certain. He was in a wheelchair.'

Connor frowned. This was not at all the description he'd been expecting. He had been convinced that this man Koos Maas was Kim Pheloung, but the description – at least so far – simply didn't match.

He thought of Kim's classic good looks, the aquiline nose, the expensive white suit and Panama hat, his confident stride.

'Did you see his face?'

Kate shuddered. 'I did. That was the worst bit. "Mangled" is the best way I can describe it, though it was too dark to see that clearly. But still, downright ugly.'

Connor was thoughtful. He'd suspected Koos Maas and Kim Pheloung to be one and the same man but if Kate's report was to be believed, then he'd jumped to the wrong conclusion. They certainly didn't sound to be the same man.

'You really should think about selling, Connor. You've a woman that loves you and you love her. Isn't it about time you set up shop together?'

'Shop?'

'Home, then, and with a ready-made family. Dawn's a right little poppet and that's for sure.'

He might normally have laughed off her suggestion, but the Korean War had made up his mind. He'd hated being apart from Rowena for so long. He was also regretful that they'd argued over something stupid and hadn't seen each other for a good few days.

He sighed, bowed his head and shoved his hands deep into his pockets. 'It'll be a hard wrench. This place holds a bucketful of memories. Me and my old buddy started this place and it was where I first met Rowena.' He smiled, his expression turning mellow with memories. 'She glided through that door like a swan and that's for sure. Like a swan…' His voice trailed off as he recalled telling her to leave. 'Unaccompanied women are not allowed in here.' She'd been defiant and, thanks to Kim, had stood her ground. Even when he'd told her that Kim was dangerous, she'd remained defiant; all through the war too. His heart seemed to skip a beat and he was aware that Kate was saying something that he wasn't quite hearing.

'I said that if the two of you are ever to start your own family, you need to be in a settled place.'

'You're not going to suggest I go back to England or Ireland, are you?'

'Don't be ridiculous! I came out to find a less dreary place than the one I left behind and it wouldn't be half the fun it is without you.' Her smile lit her face so that handsome became almost pretty. 'I'm never going to have a family, so it's down to you – if Rowena will take you.'

His gaze wandered around the bar. Kate watched and made comment.

'Memories belong to the past. It's the future you have to face. Sell the bar, Connor. Sell it and be the family man you were always meant to be.'

He nodded then jerked his chin decidedly as he came to a decision.

'You're right. There's me over here in Kowloon and Rowena over there in Hong Kong. Anyway, the fares are going up. Time to take the profit and run.'

Kate's beaming face was enough to brighten the gloomiest room.

'Leave it to me and Mr Gresham. He'll act for us. In the meantime we've plans to make for our new home.'

'So it's "we", is it?'

'You'll need me around. There's a new business in the offing. I've got it all planned and the place is mine – Rowena can stay there and so can you – unless we have a house built – a house big enough for the whole of the Connor clan...'

The words were ambiguous but rang an alarm bell. His eyes narrowed. 'What place are you talking about, Kate?'

'Why, Victoria House, of course. The refugee resettlement centre is moving to new premises so that lovely old building came up for grabs and I grabbed it!'

Kate's look of triumph diminished on seeing her brother's confusion.

'It's a big building – too big to live in.'

'Of course it is, though we might have to share it with the guests and diners at first. I'm going to turn it into a hotel and restaurant – like the one across the road but a bit more upmarket.'

He thought of Rowena when she'd first entered that place at the invitation of Kim Pheloung back in the time when she'd thought him charming, before she found out his true colours. The very act of changing it from a centre of organised avarice, the hub of the Hong Kong opium trade, into a place where the displaced and sick could get help had been incredibly ironic and had made him proud. Victoria House had been her life. How would she accept such a fundamental change?

He shook his head. 'I don't know what Rowena is going to think about this.'

Then the phone call came and he knew he had to get over there – but first things first. He needed to speak to Brandon McCloud. In the meantime he told his sister they were over to see Rowena first thing in the morning.

Kate didn't argue because she knew her brother's purposeful actions would lead to a rewarding conclusion and she was all for rewarding conclusions.

Chapter 32

The school bus clattered to a halt outside Victoria House and Dawn climbed happily aboard. Just as it disappeared around the corner, Connor and Kate arrived. There was Kate behind the wheel sporting large sunglasses. Her hair was covered with a white chiffon scarf, the long ends trailing out behind her.

If the purpose was to look businesslike, Kate O'Connor had failed the test. She looked like a movie star, her wide pink lips smiling as though she owned – or was about to own – the whole world.

'Good morning,' she said as she got out of the car, tilted her sunglasses onto her head, her eyes travelling the whole height of the building.

It didn't occur to Rowena to read anything into Kate's actions, and anyway it was Connor she wanted to see, Connor who she'd missed like hell.

He's unchanged, she thought to herself, but then why should he be anything else? A little time apart – that was all. A few days.

He kissed her cheek and his hand was warm upon her shoulder. Their eyes locked and she saw a look in his that she didn't quite recognise. Something had changed and although she tried to guess what it was, nothing seemed worthy of such a look.

'We need to talk,' he said at last, his expression more serious. 'Can you spare the time?'

'I've got coffee on.'

Kate dawdled, still studying the noble façade of the old building.

There were only a few people on the ground floor waiting to see the duty doctor.

Connor made the obvious observation. 'Not so many customers.' He said it with humour, purposely using the word 'customers' rather than refugees or patients.

'I know,' said Rowena, stabbing her finger at the lift button. When it came clanging down to the ground floor, she tugged impatiently at the rusting grille. It was the first time she'd really noticed how rusty it was, how stiff and old the mechanism. Tugging at the brass handle failed to open it.

'Damn it!'

'Frustration won't open it. Let me. I've got brute force on my side.'

Despite his boast, it took more than one tug to get it open.

Once in the lift she sighed and rubbed at her arms. 'This place is falling apart. I suppose it was only a matter of time before there was funding for a new centre. Still, I'll be sad to see the old place go. That's why I wanted to speak to you; I hear there's already a buyer.'

Connor frowned. There was something questioning about the way she'd said 'buyer'.

'I think we need to thrash out all that we know – all three of us. Are we likely to be disturbed?'

She shook her head. 'No. I've placed Summer down in the nursery. They'll make sure she's looked after.'

In her mind's eye she saw herself placing the baby in the cradle. Her smile had been for Summer but out of the corner of her eye she spotted the gappy smile of the baby in the next crib, the brightness of her eyes when Rowena smoothed her face and laughed at the baby's gurgle of delight when she tickled Cressida's tummy.

'At least you're smiling. That's the ticket. Keep smiling.'

'I have to say you're sounding very buoyant, Kate,' said Rowena.

Sunlight streamed through the picture windows.

'I feel I have every right to be buoyant. You will be too when I tell you the news.'

Rowena turned back from adjusting the Venetian blinds just in time to see Kate exchange a swift glance with her brother.

'I'd expected Connor to be as upbeat as me, but for some reason he's been a bit grouchy all the way here. It could be my driving, I suppose. Is it my driving?'

'No. Not your driving.'

Connor's mood was noticeably sombre.

Rowena stood very still, the blinds behind her throwing alternate strips of shade and sunlight across the room. A bulky rubber plant also threw its shadow amongst theirs, like a fourth presence, silent but noticeable all the same.

She clasped her hands in front of her lips as she regarded the man who had been part of her life for quite a few years.

'There's coffee if you want to help yourself.'

With slow deliberation, Connor poured for all three of them, his eyes rarely straying from her face. He had a lot to say but sensed she did too.

Rowena set her coffee to one side and remained standing.

'I've been told by the trust that the proceeds from the sale of Victoria House is to be divided between them and the original owner.'

Connor froze. 'Dear God.'

There was something in the tone of his exclamation that Kate couldn't fathom. She was perched on the arm of the settee clutching her coffee cup.

'Well it's not a bad thing, is it? Not under the circumstances.'

She looked from one to the other, comprehending that something was badly amiss but not at all certain what it was.

'The original owner. That means he *is* still alive.'

'He's signed the contracts as Koos Maas.'

'The original owner,' Rowena repeated. Her eyes locked with Connor's.

'Kate's met him.'

'Kim?'

Not understanding what was going on, Kate looked agitated.

'Will somebody tell me what's going on here?'

Rowena looked at her. 'The original owner of Victoria House was a man named Kim Pheloung. Now Connor says you've met him.'

'I have. He was most courteous but hardly the type you'd want to meet on a dark night.'

Rowena frowned. 'He was dangerous but handsome.'

Kate laughed. 'Then you must be mistaken. This man sounded as though he was on his last legs – though they weren't too much in evidence. I'm pretty certain the rear seat of the car had been altered to accommodate a wheelchair.'

'He was in a wheelchair?'

Rowena sounded flabbergasted.

Connor maintained a serious manner, a cover for the knowledge bubbling like a cauldron beneath the surface before he finally put it into words.

'It has to be him – but altered.'

For Rowena it was as if she was covered in an ice-cold veil. She thought about it, what might have happened to him in the intervening years. He lived life on a tightrope, bribery, extortion, prostitution and, most of all, opium.

'But why would he give half of the sale price to help refugees?'

'Perhaps he feels guilty – at long last – and yes, perhaps I am being fanciful.'

'Can somebody tell me what's going on here? We're going to be the owners of Victoria House.' She looked pointedly at Rowena. 'I thought you'd be pleased about that. You won't need to move out.'

'We're the new owners?'

'My sister did a deal. Sold the chop and flop house as long as she had first refusal for Victoria House.'

'I don't understand.' Rowena sank onto the settee. 'There

will be no more refugees, though I suppose we could open a private clinic or scrape around for funding to do some kind of charity work—'

'I didn't come out here to do charity work,' snapped Kate. 'I came out here to make more than a living for myself without having to depend on a man.' She took a deep breath, her chest heaving with the effort. 'I'm going to revamp this and make it into a hotel and restaurant. And my brother's going to sell the bar and come in with me.'

Rowena looked at Connor. 'When did you first know about this?'

'When she told me and not much before you; once my sister gets an idea in her head, there's no stopping her. Headstrong. Always has been.'

'So,' said Rowena, holding up her hand in an effort to gain time to take this all in. 'You've made a deal with Kim Pheloung.'

'Koos Maas. That's the name I was given.'

'I don't believe it. Why would he do that?' She shook her head in disbelief.

'I've asked myself the same question,' said Connor as he took a seat on the chair arm, crossing one strong leg over the other. 'So I had a word with Brandon. Word is that the man known as Koos Maas has only a short time to live.'

'Kim? I can hardly believe it.'

'We have to believe that it is or otherwise he'd have no right to sell Victoria House.'

Rowena's eyes narrowed. 'But that would mean he's been biding his time, allowing me to carry on with my little project over all these years. Why would he do that?'

'You knew him better than I ever did. Why would he?'

She shook her head. 'So it was him who had the old man watch your place? But that doesn't explain the doll. Why would he be so generous and then a short time later threaten my child? I ran away to Korea because of that.'

'He might have paid the old man to watch you, but he didn't kill him. Neither was he responsible for the glass doll. The killing of the old man and the doll were designed to frighten you so badly that you wanted to get as far away as possible.' He sighed. 'We were both fooled. We both thought it was Kim but it was not.'

Her eyelids fluttered in response to her wildly confusing thoughts. 'If it wasn't him, then who was it?'

'Warrington. I don't know how he did it, but he is in military intelligence which leads me to believe that he knows something of the Hong Kong underworld. Both incidents were meant to unnerve you and they did.'

Kate threw her hands up in the air. 'That Barbara person told me all this and it seemed clear enough at the time, but now I'm confused.'

'He wanted me to abort his daughter's unborn child because her father was Korean. He'd lived his life through his son. It severely grieved him when he was killed, and so his drive to preserve his blood line the way *he* envisaged was through his daughter. But Sheridan wasn't having that. She loved Jung. He was a good man. A nice man. So nice that she refused to leave him behind.'

'I would have preferred you to come home there and then. I was on the plane waiting for you. You cannot believe how I felt when you didn't board.'

Rowena shook her head. 'I couldn't just leave her, Connor. I couldn't. She was due her time and...'

'I was left waiting on a plane with your daughter and Luli. Can you imagine how I felt?'

'Yes, of course I do, but don't you see, Connor? Without me being in Hong Kong I felt that Dawn was safe. Kim wanted me, not her. That was the way it always was, but now...' She shook her head. 'It surprises me that he knew where I was and what I was doing but never approached me; let me carry on running a refugee centre in a property he owned. Are you sure of his identity?' She looked up at him, wide-eyed. In his turn, Connor looked at his sister.

'Go on, Kate. Tell her the rest of it.'

'Do you really mean that?' There was a look of amusement on Kate's intelligent face.

Connor made a sound of outright exasperation and strode to the window where he gazed out on an amazing vista he'd seen a hundred, if not a thousand times before.

'Well,' said Kate taking a deep breath. 'As I've just told you, he's buying my businesses and in return I get Victoria House. I'm not sure about calling it the Victoria Hotel, mind you, but no doubt the right name will come to me in time. But that can be left for later...'

'I don't think I want to stay here if it's turned into a hotel.'

'I don't think so either.'

Connor had turned round, his fingers interlinked behind his back, his brows fringing the blueness of his eyes.

'Rowena, me darling, I think it's time we were thinking about settling down. We've got Dawn and Summer to think of, and before you go protesting that getting children together doesn't seem to be happening, I knew the moment I saw you with Warrington's grandchild that she was here to stay. And I've nothing against that. If you can't get a family one way then get it another.'

'I need to think about it.'

'I know you do. You always do.' He sucked in his bottom lip and a pensive look came to his face.

'The man we suspect is Kim calls himself Koos Maas.'

The old familiar chillness swept over her. 'I refuse to believe it was him.'

Connor put an arm around her shoulder. 'Can you ever put him behind you?'

Rowena bit her lip. Her hair, loose around her shoulders, fell forward to hide her face.

'Connor, I don't think I can ever be at ease with you and living without fear unless I see him for myself.'

She felt him tense.

'I wish I could help,' said Kate, 'but I only saw him in that car. Everything was arranged by Mr Gresham at the bank.'

'I still tremble at the thought of that man.'

Connor massaged her shoulder and looked concerned. Kate just looked on and wished that she'd had a love like that in her life – unfortunately Seamus had been a convenience and not meant to be loved.

''Tis time you put the past behind you and made an honest man of my brother; and before you declare that you are one, Connor O'Connor, I know all there is to know about the gambling room and the bit of siphoning off you do – so much for the government of Hong Kong and a big fat wedge for yourself. If you call that honesty then the Pope isn't a Catholic.'

★

Connor didn't give Rowena the chance to protest but told her to get in the car.

'Where are we going?'

'To a nightclub.'

'At this time of day?'

'It has to be this time of day.'

A thick fog had fallen over the watery bridge between Hong Kong and Kowloon. The sound of the ferry's foghorn sounded a mournful note into the night.

On the voyage over they leaned against the ship's rail, looking ahead at the lights of Kowloon whilst Connor hummed and sang the words of the song he'd long ago devoted to her: 'Star of the County Down'.

Hawsers creaked and men shouted as the ferry ground her hull against the harbour wall.

Connor took the wheel and drove her into a place she'd never been before.

The Golden Flower was situated in a narrow alley close to the harbour. Blossoming cherry trees nodded in welcome over the high walls to both sides. Either this place had once been a house or whoever presently owned it enjoyed having a garden.

Rowena paused on the threshold. The main door opened onto an interior painted in dark greens and blues, lightened here and there by the swirling tails of dragons with bright yellow eyes and flowers that she instantly recognised. Chrysanthemums. Her heart skipped a beat and she couldn't help thinking of the first time she'd seen Kim, the most beautiful man she'd ever met. Connor's Bar had only recently been converted from an opium den, the customary couches becoming seating and tables. She recalled Kim's

414

golden skin and dark slanting eyes, his sensuous lips and the silky smoothness of his skin. At first those attributes had drawn her in, but that was only until she got to know him.

'We not open.'

'Tell Kim I'm willing to sell him Connor's Bar. He'll see us.'

The thug was built like a brick wall and all the charisma of a kitchen table. A vivid scar ran from the corner of his mouth into his jawline to give him a permanently sour expression. His tiny eyes flickered as he considered his decision.

'If he doesn't want me to change my mind, he'll see us. Kim. Koos Maas.'

The big oaf lumbered off into the smoky interior. Even at this time of day it was gloomy.

Connor took hold of Rowena's arm. 'Come on. Let's make ourselves known.'

With her hand in his, he headed off in the direction taken by the door manager.

Night was when the club was at its busiest, but there were still customers sitting at tables, dissolutely viewing an Indonesian girl swaying to the sound of the gamelang, discarding an item of clothing, alluring rather than provocative. Blue smoke drifted from long black pipes and lay trapped like clouds on the ceiling. The smoke was heavier in the shadows where figures lounged on couches totally unaware of the girl's performance, their movements listless, their minds lost in a fog.

Bulbous, though amazingly light on his feet, the doorman skirted tables and came back to them.

'This way.'

Through a veil of indigo gloom Connor saw Rowena's apprehensive expression, hugged her then reached for her hand and squeezed it.

Don't worry.

The words were unspoken. The squeeze of his hand was more than reassuring; he was there for her no matter what.

Dark figures lurked in the shadows, alive but featureless. Ahead of them a mound of black shapelessness was silhouetted against a red wall which was dimly lit by a hanging lantern.

Her heartbeat pounded in her ears and against her chest. If Connor hadn't been there her trembling legs might have given way. Gulping deep in her throat she swallowed the feeling of nausea. She had to be strong. She must not flee.

They came to a halt. There was nobody ahead of them except for the misshapen lump sitting in a wheelchair.

'Is it him?' she whispered.

'My beloved doctor.'

It little resembled the strident confidence she remembered.

She held her breath, surprised that his gasped words lacked the clearly remembered. Worse still was his appearance.

The man that didn't look or sound as she remembered was sitting in a wheelchair as ungainly and bulky as a sack of rice. The smoke from a dozen opium pipes swirled in front of her eyes blurring his features. The light was dim.

Through it all she thought she saw those narrowed eyes blink.

There was a rattling sound as he took a deep breath.

'You are still striking.'

She stared, not believing what she was seeing or hearing. She hardly recognised him. Gone was the sleek body, the perfect countenance as chiselled as that of a Hindu god. He was no longer a man that a woman could worship.

Like a king sitting on his throne, he was prominent amongst other smokers reclining on low couches, their pipes resting in front of them.

'I... we... thought you were dead.' Unless her ears deceived her, she sounded more brave than she felt.

That rasping again as he fought to swallow a breath he had struggled to inhale. 'So did the Chinese.' As he leaned forward the yellowish light from a hanging lantern fell over his face. 'They left their mark,' he wheezed. 'And left me for dead. Disease also found me, a disease that I could not fight.'

In that moment the fear that had sometimes merely smouldered and at other times had erupted into terror began to melt like ice in springtime. Her heart felt lighter, her shoulders less tense. The spectre that had haunted her dreams and her waking moments was no longer a tall handsome man but was hunched like a hideous dwarf broken in two and inelegantly put back together.

A red scar ran diagonally, making his features lopsided as though his face had been sliced in half, both halves then stuck back together by a pair of trembling hands.

'They used a Samurai sword... taken from a dead Japanese officer... It amused them to assail a man who had collaborated with the Japanese with a Japanese weapon... They left me for dead.'

He was fighting to pronounce every word, each halting breath like the sound of two sheets of sandpaper rubbing one against the other.

Despite everything she felt a twinge of pity but knew she

could not possibly say so. He would hate to be pitied – the final injury to a proud and cruel man.

'You're selling Victoria House to Kate O'Connor.'

'Yes.'

'And giving half of the proceeds to the new refugee facility.'

He paused, breathing taking precedence over speaking. 'Does it please you?'

'I'm surprised.'

'You and your kind, people of medicine, have the last laugh, Doctor. Disease is the final foe, the one to whom I have surrendered. The end is nigh, as you would say.' He smiled wanly. 'The end is nigh. This is surely true and I must act accordingly. I am beaten but I am Hindu; good deeds will be counted in my favour and weigh well on the scales of my next incarnation.'

His words surprised her because it sounded as though he really meant what he said. She vaguely recalled him once stating that he was a Buddhist. She hadn't believed him back then but this time his declaration of being Hindu sounded sincere, not least because he was close to dying.

The sleeve of his robe fell back, exposing a thin arm. Spidery fingers beckoned a servant to his side. His eyes downcast respectfully, the servant poured water from a blue jug into a champagne glass. He drank then raised his eyes. 'I pretend it is champagne… but it is only water.'

'No champagne.' She said it blithely with just a trace of humour, a substitute for the pity she could not mention. Both the man and his life were shadows of what once had been.

'You might only get halfway to heaven, seeing as your

portion of the money from Victoria House is being used to buy up most of Kowloon. My sister's leases and my bar.'

'Do you distrust my intentions, Mr O'Connor?'

'Yes. Does that surprise you?'

'No.'

It was a single word delivered abruptly before a bout of coughing took over.

Connor squeezed Rowena's hand. Always there, always reassuring, yet at this moment in time she didn't need reassurance. The ghosts of her past were finally being laid to rest. Now all she wanted was to try and digest Kim's reasons for dividing the proceeds of sale. He was telling the truth about being ill and maybe he was indeed thinking ahead to the afterlife. If Connor hadn't been holding onto her hand so tightly, she would have honoured her profession and gone to his side to give aid and reassure – though even at a distance she knew that his situation was hopeless.

His eyes fixed on her. 'My gift... the new hospital... recompense... truly. My one good deed in life.'

The sword that had so disfigured him had been wielded by anger as much as by a human being. And yet he'd lived – but not the man he had been. The Japanese might not have killed him, but the Chinese had certainly scarred him for ever.

He slumped in his chair with his head hanging forward, the gnarled chin that had once been so smooth-shaven almost resting on his chest. His breath dissipated.

Thickset figures attired in traditional black tunic and trousers of servants appeared like ghosts from the shadows. Their movements became agitated, their voices betraying their confusion and also their fear.

'He's dead,' whispered Rowena. She tensed, instinctively wanting to go to him.

'You don't have to do this.' Connor tightened his grip.

'It's my profession. I need to check.'

'No. Let's go.'

'No. I won't.'

Knowing he was beaten, he let go of her hand and watched as she checked for a pulse, gazing down on the man who had once sought to control her life and had ended up destroying his own. All she now saw before her was a pathetic heap of a man. She wasn't sure what had killed him but could hazard a guess that it was some kind of motor neurone disease.

She let his hand drop and turned away.

Connor was waiting for her. She touched his arm, feeling almost surprised that he was still there, that the two of them had been through those difficult years together and now, at long last, it was all over.

His smile said it all and his arm was like a cloak around her shoulders, warm and reassuring. 'Let's go home.'

Chapter 33

Victoria House was to be vacated in a matter of weeks. Already Kate was striding around ahead of Mr Clements, an architect who walked with a limp and had trouble keeping up with her. Everything was being redesigned and even though the patients had moved out, some of the beds were still in the ward awaiting removal.

The only place not yet embroiled in this great upheaval was the garden. In the absence of many feet trampling over it, plants had begun to grow, mostly weeds and shrubs, their verdant smell freshening the air.

Dawn was sitting on a stone seat in the shade of the dovecote with Luli, chattering away in a mixture of Chinese and English.

The two babies, Summer and Cressida, were lying on a blanket, their faces pink from the warm day.

Rowena looked down at them. Despite the circumstances of Dawn's conception, she had grown to love her. She would also grow to love these two babies, if she didn't love them already. All were of mixed race – not that it mattered to her.

Children of the world, she thought to herself. Victims of circumstance and war.

She was accepting of the fact that she would never have children of her own. Connor too was accepting, his arm around her waist as the two of them looked down on the babies who were orphans through no fault of their own, and Dawn who had never been abandoned.

'Three children.'

'All girls. Dawn, Summer and Cressida.'

'Cressida too. Are you sure about this?'

She nodded, her fingers tracing the strong fingers that lay so lightly on her shoulder. 'These children are the echoes of me and my life. I owe them a good world to grow up in.'

'Three children. Well I never expected to be father to three girls, but I'm sure I can rise to the occasion. It's a world we'll make for them together. Our world within our home and keep the rest of the world at bay – as much as we can.'